P9-CSC-584

HH

CHEAP TICKET TO HEAVEN

ALSO BY CHARLIE SMITH

FICTION

Canaan

Shine Hawk

The Lives of the Dead

Crystal River (novellas)

Chimney Rock

POETRY

Red Roads

Indistinguishable from the Darkness

The Palms

Before and After

CHEAP TICKET TO HEAVEN

CHARLIE SMITH

An Owl Book
Henry Holt
and Company
New York

Henry Holt and Company, Inc.
Publishers since 1866
115 West 18th Street
New York, New York 10011

Henry Holt® is a registered trademark
of Henry Holt and Company, Inc.

Published in Canada by Fitzhenry & Whiteside Ltd.,
195 Allstate Parkway, Markham, Ontario L3R 4T8.

Library of Congress Cataloging-in-Publication Data
Smith, Charlie.
Cheap ticket to heaven / Charlie Smith
p. cm.
I. Title.
PS3569.M5163C46 1996 95-26311
813'.54—dc20 CIP

ISBN 0-8050-5593-2

Henry Holt books are available for special promotions and premiums. For details contact: Director, Special Markets.

First published in hardcover in 1996 by
Henry Holt and Company, Inc.

First Owl Book Edition—1997

Designed by Paula R. Szafranski

Printed in the United States of America
All first editions are printed on acid-free paper.∞

1 3 5 7 9 10 8 6 4 2

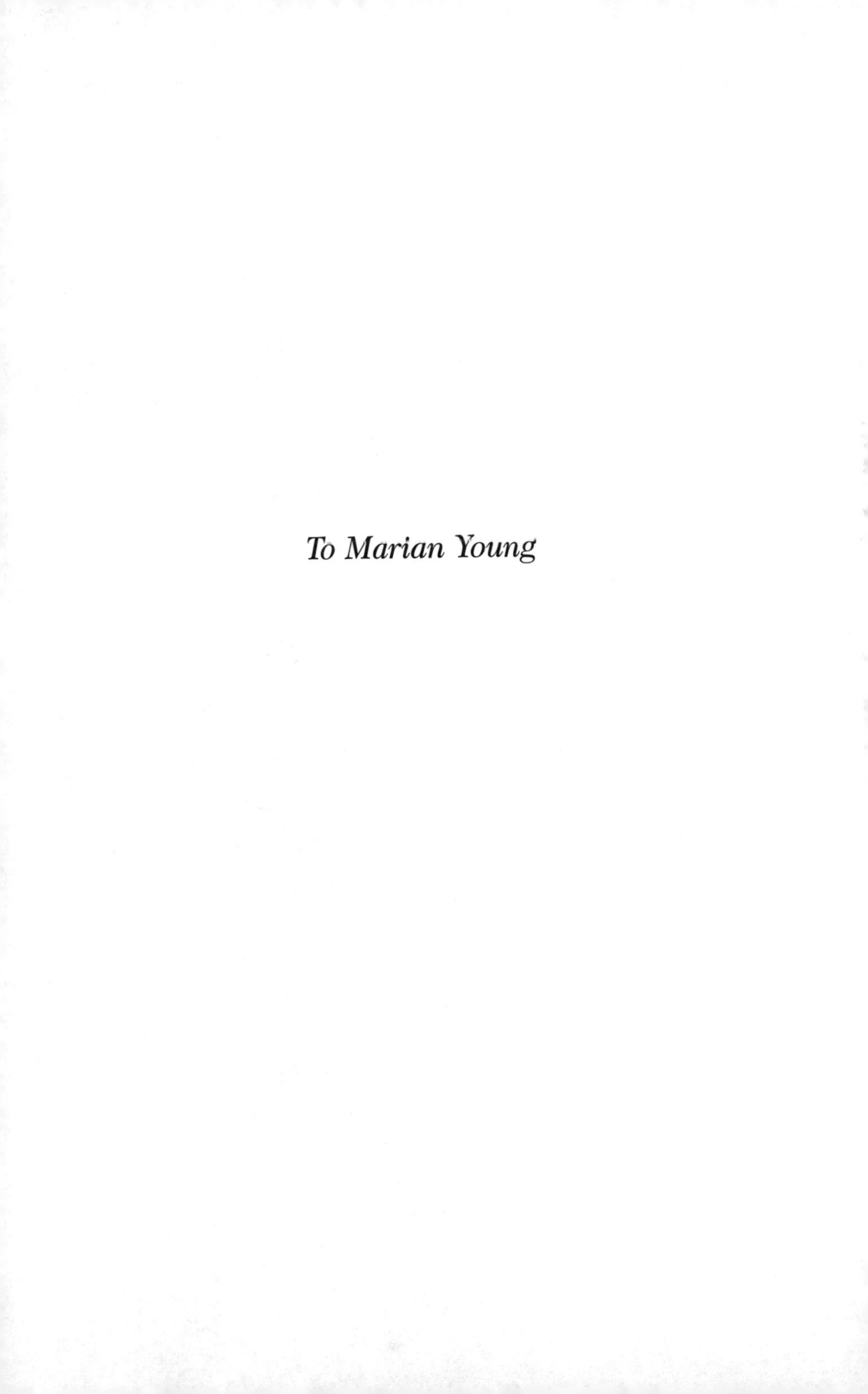

To Marian Young

CHEAP TICKET TO HEAVEN

Looking at it dispassionately, our life is but the application of the principles of the "quality of life" typical of our historic period. It is like a paranoid system. There is no incoherence in it. The authentic is always absent, because even if something approaching the authentic (however profound or unexpected) happens, it is no more than the attainment of what our "quality of life," conscious of its own violence, accepts as contradictory or anarchic.

—Pier Paolo Pasolini, "The Ideological Dreams"
(trans. Antonino Mazza)

But I want, I want—my ugliness, which I've earned hour after hour, is doing the talking, right?—I want you to stop looking behind you. I want you to lead me fearlessly down into the land of the shadow and the monster. I want you to sink into endless regret. I want—my ugliness, which I've earned minute by minute, is doing the talking—I want you to abandon all hope. I want you to choose evil, evil every time. I want you to feel hate, never love. I want—it's my ugliness earned second by second talking—I want you to refuse the brilliance of the night, the softness of flint and the honey of thistles. I know where we're going, Said, and why we're going there. It's not to get somewhere, it's just so that the people who sent us there can remain peacefully on a peaceful shore.

—Jean Genet, *The Screens*

In the destiny now forming
I may linger;
no other threat exists.

—Eugenio Montale, "Mediterranean"
(trans. William Arrowsmith)

1

He loved to watch her. She would—what? Take a deep breath, take another, press against the counter, then push herself off, an unnatural angel become manifest, she would raise the shotgun, bring it up bluntly from between the wings of her coat, she would point this mesmerizer at the guard, some derelict face in a formal jacket, she would press him against the back wall of his life, hold him there while he felt his heart beat against his spine, she would swing the gun in a talismanic arc clicking through the interiors of each customer's soul, registering for the celestial ledgers this one's child sick with the flu, that one's slide on the market, another's dream of the lover she would never have, some boy clutching his paycheck, dragged from the bed of his dreams—touch and pass on, pass into the money slots, into the drawers and enclosures, the vault where the collected metal and paper energy of a people was filed, fix this in perfect stillness of anticipation—of execution.

With her left hand she fished the whistle out of her side pocket, raised it to her lips, and blew a silvery trilling blast.

"Hey," she cried. "Hey! Wake up for glory."

Heads turned, lives began to buckle.

The guard, brought suddenly back from Valhalla in chains, gaped. She shrank him smaller than a boy. There was pandemonium. Strangers stared wildly at their neighbors. A ray of sunlight took on aspects of eternity. A spattering of coins was an artwork set on the marble floor.

She ordered everyone down, let them sink. A small woman picked at the hem of her farm dress, settled it over the backs of her sturdy legs. Old MacDonald whimpered, slapped at his son, and turned his face to heaven. A truant schoolgirl in the corner—maybe she was the banker's daughter, maybe she was a pregnant farm girl ridden into town on the back of a tractor, maybe she was a runaway one thousand miles from home—giggled helplessly. It was all right, he knew, with Clare.

Jack set his pistol on the counter and raised his hands.

"Don't shoot," he said to the teller. "I surrender."

He laughed and shoved a feed sack across. The teller was so dumbfounded she let the sack drop.

"You're supposed to catch it," he said. "Gather it up and don't press any buttons."

The teller was thin and wore wire glasses that pinched redness onto the bridge of her bony nose.

"Give me everything," Jack said. "Put everything you can think of—outside of exploding money—into the sack. Fill me to the brim. Make my back bend with the labor of transport. Convert me into the Sisyphus of bank robbers. Make my task an onerous one, make me a carrier of great loads, sister. Do it right now."

"We don't have much," the woman said. She wiped her nose with the edge of the sack.

"Don't wipe your nose with my property," Jack said.

The woman looked confused, but she began to pull money out of the slots. The small redheaded man down the way trembled. Jack winked at him. "I'll be down there in a shake."

The man jumped when he spoke to him. Jack wanted to make him do it again. There was someone behind the office door, a shape behind milky glass. Jack hoped it wasn't a hero. Heroes always forgot somebody might have to take one in the belly. *(It wasn't that I was getting old,* Jack said—to Rubens, to himself, to Jesus, to the unruly dead, to nothing—*that wasn't what was happening. I was flipping over; the other side of me was coming to light.)*

"I'm becoming less mysterious to myself," he said to the woman. "This troubles me."

"I'm sorry," she said.

She had the money stacked. He swept the packets into the sack, nodded thanks, moved down the counter, and repeated the operation with the red-haired teller, a man who quivered and stuttered as he poked money at the sack opening, missing with the bills until Jack had to help him like a man helping his heartbroken neighbor get the deceased family cat into the garbage bag. They both worked at it, finally successfully.

Jack thanked him effusively, as always, bowing, turning away—the shot came then, but it missed.

"Oh, wow," Jack said. "A killer is loose."

Everyone behind the counter suddenly was out of sight.

Clare pointed the shotgun at the guard. Seven or eight people lay on the floor holding their breath, pushing themselves with their mental transporters to the other side of the world. Jack was tired of handling the counter; he wanted to watch his wife work. The office door was closed. There was still time to get away, to flee like cunning entrepreneurs, like convicts on a spree, like escaped children running away from the world that had. . . . Like whatever he thought of, he thought. The shot had skidded off the counter, leaving a silvery gouged place.

"We're leaving now," Jack said loudly. "We've learned our lesson and we won't be back."

Clare called for quiet. He was glad she didn't shoot anyone. It surprised him that he was glad. He didn't think that way; he never had. She spoke to the assembled, told them to stay still, told them she was proud of them, told them she would remember each and every one of them, that she would remember—*that* pocked face, *those* runny blue eyes, *that* scar, *that* expression like a bad day at the welfare office—remember so well she could come back in the night, six years from now in the darkest drear and night, and find each one, asleep helpless in his bed, there in Bradley, Nebraska.

Then they were outside, larks, beings just created out of exhilaration and impossible chances pulled off, out in the sunshine and fresh air their schoolteachers had told them to get plenty of.

"That guard," she cried, laughing, "was making faces at me."

"We all do, honey, behind your back."

Then into the car, then out into the street where they were probably the first since pioneer days to flee carrying bank loot, then rolling past the mossy café they'd eaten breakfast in, past stores and cramped houses, past the crippled economy and itchy domestic arrangements, past uncut yards, VFW hall, cattle pens, and a ragged fence twirled up with blue morning glory flowers, past a little boy, another truant, bouncing a ball against red front steps. Up ahead, beyond houses and yards, were the hills, a distant patch of smoke like a wide gray wing hanging in the foreground.

"Go fast," she said.

"Not too."

"Somebody's coming."

He glanced in the rearview mirror. "Damn. Local cops."

"It was that man who shot at you. He called them."

"I should have spoken to him, explained the situation."

She ran her hand along his thigh, hard. He winced, thought, Ah—yes, I know: I want to press through to something, too. *(There he was again, he said, grinning at me: the boy in the woods. The day of Father's eleventh suicide.)*

He hawked and spit out the window.

They passed through the first range of hills. A cut between two blocks of uplifted terrain slanted and disappeared, winding through rough rock faces like a snake back. It was country you could invent, he thought, if you tried when you were tired enough. He looked for a side road, some surprise leaping off the highway, a getaway lane into another world. There was nothing yet. Last night, coming through in dark like the black of space, threading hills upreared like reproductions of shadows, there had been lights in the distance, far away, an outpost of lost souls, some farm back in the hills, where, so he imagined, as she spoke of drowning, touchy bachelors sat around a fireplace arguing about money. The lights had floated in the dark.

(There are paths, still, all over Minnesota: mountain to mountain, woods to meadow, from house through garden and woods to water, but there is no path across a lake.)

Now the road dipped, now it rose on solid haunches, and then they were at the top of a grassy ridge that opened into a sudden wide valley. In the distance he could see a fire line gnawing at the wheat.

"They're coming from the other direction," he said suddenly. "Cripes."

She glanced ahead, snapping fresh green shells into the shotgun's belly. Three cars, red top lights blazing, so far away the lights looked like sparks, hung in the distance, just entering the valley road.

"This is going to be interesting," she said.

"I wonder what we'll do."

The blue sky, touched here and there with thin smeared clouds, looked endless, like a painting where the background gave out into white, and then into bare canvas. The sun twinkled as if in anticipation, flashing its lights among the wheat tops. The land itself seemed to pull away as they passed, as if they were taking some of it with them, as if it was adhering, rolling up behind them.

"Straight on," he said. "That's it for now."

In the distance the fields burned. He thought: fire unravels yellow hemlines, fire denudes the bosomy wheatlands; fire pushes time back on itself. He thought of the Old West, as last night he'd thought of it as they drove through this country, one car following the other—both stolen—to the rendezvous beside Yellow Bear River, where in the beam of headlights they'd set up camp, fried steaks, and then lay beside the river listening to the water slip past, talking of life in old days they knew nothing about, enjoying, even so, and because of this, he thought, their rambling flights of ignorance, the tales they made up that were ridiculous and impossible, of trail drivers and fancy scoundrels and cons going haywire in pioneer days, of ruses and foolish boasts, of Indian sports and thieves, of characters they could travel with—if they lived then—get the best of and leave gasping in chagrin and bafflement by the side of some road; by this river road, she'd said, laughing.

The fire pushed back toward that time. The land replenishing itself, he thought, all that. He wanted to stop and watch, but they had to go.

Then he remembered waking in the middle of the night, looking at his face in the rearview mirror. Startled, as if he'd discovered a mark on his body he'd never noticed, he'd remembered the boy he once saw peering at him from behind a hemlock tree as he sat in his boat in Cauldron Cove. The boy had looked just like him. *(That day, he said, when Father walked naked out of the woods . . .)*

She swung the gun out the window, fired three shots. The intervals between them were evenly spaced. The police car was too far back; still, firepower wouldn't hold cops off forever.

She drew her head in. Her face was reddened across the bridge of the nose and on her cheeks. There were wind-tear streaks on her face and she had bitten her lip so there was blood on the lower one. He touched the place, caught a dab of red on his finger, and sucked it off.

"Salty dog," she said and grinned. She jammed new shells into the shotgun, then thrust it into the floorboards. "I don't like using this utensil," she said, drawing her pistol.

"It doesn't do any good, anyway. Even if you loaded with buckshot it wouldn't."

"What are those books in the other car?"

"Good and evil. I decided to study it."

"I would think you'd be able to teach it. When did you get them?"

"While you were off getting a massage."

"In KC?"

"That's right. They have a store that specializes in philosophical books. It's near the university."

"Why are you thinking of that?"

"This face I saw."

"The devil?"

"No—me."

"In the mirror?"

"In the lake."

"The man in the lake?"

"The boy. Not in the lake. In the woods, looking at me in the lake."

"Who?"

"Me."

"I think you need a rest cure."

"Probably a couple."

She glanced out. "Cross country," she said.

"Looks like it, doesn't it?"

"Can we make the ditch?"

"Not here."

She checked the other pistols, shoved the smaller into the belt of her jeans. "There's nothing else in here?"

"No. Everything's in the other car."

The police cars ahead, five miles away maybe, appeared to have stopped. The car behind followed at a steady distance. The way the wheat fields opened off the town square, the way the emptiness rushed right up to the civilized world, had intrigued him. They'd passed through a week ago, found the bank set like a golden egg on the edge of the square, but it had been the big yellow fields soaring off like runways from across the street that fascinated him: ornate smooth-topped grass you would probably run away into at least once if you were born in that town—fields children probably disappeared into, got lost in, and were never heard from again. Running for your life, you could vanish into wheat. As he had vanished time and again, it seemed to him now, onto Lake Superior, on the shore of which he was raised, and into the woods behind the house, and into the little lost lakes behind the Iron Range where islands cropped up out of the clear green water like castles. He had grown up in Duluth, and in Brandis, another smaller town he lived in sometimes with his mother after she and his father—the suicide king of northern Minnesota—divorced. After this, after that, he thought, as always.

"There," she said, "up there."

A track that bridged a culvert and dashed away in a wide curve into the field.

He said, "It looks like someplace we've been before."

"They all do."

He swung the car slightly right, then left in a wide turn, braking, tapping, holding the wheel in the turn, downshifting, popping the gas. The car bucked and skidded, but then the wheels grabbed hard; they swept over the culvert in a spray of grass and dust, slid off the track into the burnt field.

"Whoa, Jesus," he cried.

They bumped across the field, running the furrows toward the fire line. The fire gleamed like a long red tear in the dirt. The ground nearby was burned in patches, and there were places where the wheat was not even scorched: shimmering and glossy, even-topped, it stood up as if it had some power to resist fire, as if it were magic wheat you could lie down in, he thought, snuggle in there where the morning glory vines curled around the base of the stalks and the mice and the beetles ran—and hide. The furrows shone through the wheat like the shadows of old scars.

Behind them the trailing police, like obsessed lovers, followed into the field. "They're coming with us into the fire," Jack said. He watched the policemen bounce in their seats. "Shoot them again," he said.

She fired out the window, sighting along the barrel, popping a shot, raising the pistol, aiming again and firing. A piece of chrome flew off the top of the windshield. Then he could feel the pressure of the cops' desire behind them, pushing at them. It was often like this. Strangers yearned to be with them, to become part of their lives, they ached to place their hands upon their bodies. He caught a glimpse of the cop rider kneeling in his seat, pointing his carbine, jerking a shot, one, then another. A hole popped open on the dashboard. "Look at that," he said, indicating it. She ignored him, kept firing.

"The other fucks are coming," she said in a low voice.

The other cars, a bunched version of their future, had turned into the field; they streaked along the burn line, running side by side.

They were running along two sides of a triangle that would meet at the fire. Sun gleamed off the cars ahead, smears and streaks where it touched. Noticing this, pressing himself forward as if the car ran on his blood, it all began to seem strange to him, ridiculous even, and he wanted to address this, but there was no time—machines hurtling across a wild field, machines in the West in the valleys of grass—and then he saw himself again projected into the past, yesterday, or no, this morning, waking beside the river, swinging his legs out of the car, bending over them—remembering himself *looking at his double, he said, looking a twelve-year-old boy in the face on the day his father walked naked in the yard covered in dew*—staring dumbly into a patch of dusty willows, thinking then, suddenly, as if in revelation, as if in redress or correction, of how much he loved Clare, of how sometimes this love would come over him like a torment or a sweet disease, take him over and make him into its puppet government, and how he craved this, still craved it after eighteen years, and how when he mentioned it to her this morning she'd laughed and said, Sure, it's true, but then, shuddering with gaiety, had said, But the truth is, sweetie, I'd live with whoever I had to just to have somebody on my side. She'd said—gaily—that she was terribly lucky—and knew it: You are an extraordinary man, she'd said, good for the pluck and the fuck, and all the rest, but if you were a man with the soul of a cockroach, or you were the devil's plumber, and you cared for me, and you would come sit by me and take my part—I would love you, I would thank God in heaven for you.

He'd fallen back roaring with laughter.

Now the car leapt and churned, growling, skipping; the wheel vibrated under his hands. "Look how long the fire is," he said.

"Like a seam."

"What was that dance we did in Mexico?"

"When?"

"You know. Last year when that guy got fresh."

"Pup Wayne? Him? He wasn't getting fresh."

"What was he doing?"

"He was teaching me to dance."

"That's what I am asking."

"I can't remember what it was. The *guaracho.*"

"Yeah, that's it. All those women lined up in red dresses. Like a line of fire."

(. . . even so, he said, as if he could see right through her, as if the river was a lens, as if her words were a conjuring of the event, the boy appeared, fantastically, once more, and Father, stumbling down the rocks naked, dew shining on his body as if the night had licked him all over, appeared . . .)

They were coming on it now, out into it almost, like sportsmen into sunshine, speeding now, racing the representatives of civilization, the stiff men in suits who wanted them, careening across the rough furrows, veering left now, then swinging in toward the beckoning bright line. The smoke bent away to the east, it was ripped and sorted by breeze, black near the ground, going gray as it rose, fading to white and haze in the sunlight. The fire was deeper than it had looked.

"Let's cut through it," he said, brightly.

"It's hot."

"It can't be too wide. We'll run along the back of it to the hills over there. We can't be more than a couple of miles from the other car. We'll head for that bluff—that one: you see?—shaped like a bear's head."

"Monkey head."

"Okay—you see it?"

"Yes."

"If we get separated we'll meet on the other side of it."

"Separated? We're in a car."

"I know—but . . ."

The fire looked like red breakers. Thin Lake Superior breakers so clear that even after a storm you could see through them. The lake waves were glassy, the water clear as if everything had been vacuumed from it. In the old days the shore stank of fish. Of walleye, of sturgeon, of fat muskies split and hung on birch racks by the Cree come down from the reservation, the women quarreling, ordering the feckless, resentful men about, the sky always big in those days, the winter spruce logs jammed against the alder brakes; and then, walking to the cove where he kept his hidden tipsy boat, getting in and paddling out, heading somewhere

where the horizon gave way, fleeing crimes, looking back and seeing—what? Seeing the face, the boy's face, *his face,* peering at him from the hemlocks.

He shuddered. The fire roared. After that day there was no telling what might happen. After that, that time *(or some other, he said, some moment when life snapped, some point of contact, of horror, some night when the wind swung like monkeys in the trees, night when his mother didn't come, when his father once more took up the tools of suicide, some moment when a faction was refused the vote, some confidential aside turned into a lie, some place, some tendency, some era lasting too long, some day coming to in the bleak streets off to the side in Duluth, some exact moment his own house became unrecognizable and everyone in it became unrecognizable, some chain of crime dragged into the future, some blunt gleaming head)*—there was no telling.

Through a crack in the fire wall he could see the field beyond, golden and smooth, the wheat surging under the wind. Off there, too, the mountains they'd reach soon.

"Here we go, girl."

He swung directly in toward the fire.

The car crashed stiffly over the furrows. He heard the crack and tear of metal underneath. They rose, soared like an acquittal, for an instant the weight dropped away, they were going to heaven—and then they crashed down hard into the flames. The car slurred right, came up surging, bucking; he fought the wheel, alive now in his hands, but he couldn't hold it. The flames bunched around them, rustling, roaring, batting against the sides, closing behind as they cut through, the car laboring, grinding, a noise like cries from a world of misery shooting into their heads.

"We're not going to make it, Jackie."

She gripped the doorpost with both hands, bouncing in the seat. He saw her head strike, heard her soft cry.

He downshifted, but it was no use. The car slipped and slowed, trembling.

"We've got to get out," he cried.

The fire had closed behind them. He thought he could see cops in the field, but the smoke, the jellied air throbbing in waves, obscured them. He shut the ignition off.

"Come on, Clare."

They pulled themselves out onto the hood. "Take the coats off," he cried. He could hardly hear himself. "Jump down there and hold them up and run."

A rock hit him in the back, just under the shoulder, knocking him to his knees. The fire reared in his face. He could feel his skin tighten, go smooth, hard. "What do you want?" he cried.

"Jackie, they shot you."

"Come on, Clare."

Her coat swung in front of his face, flipped back; he could see the sky, a patch of it. It looked like the sky reflected in a lake, deeper blue than in life, glassy.

"Bastards," she cried. "Fuckheads."

He heard the shotgun, the grainy thump of the blast. And then her voice: "Let's go, Jack."

She knew where the light was, where the duty-free zone was. She pulled him upright.

"Jump," she cried.

He leapt with her; she caught him as he tripped, started to fall. The fire burned, leaping around their legs. The coat was over his head. She tugged him. The fire stabbed through his clothes, went up his nose like ammonia, quick; he twisted away from it, tumbling in the rows, thinking, *I will rise, shining.* His shoulder was numb, the fingers of his left hand tingled and jerked.

They ran, firewalkers, bouncing, leaping. He stumbled; the flames rushed him, he turned his body, falling, hit on his good shoulder. He felt his hair crimp and shrivel, his scalp clamp. She dragged him up, pulling at the sleeve of his coat. "Get up!" The fire rushed, bit hard.

"Go on," he said.

He couldn't breathe. You have to run without air. It was something he thought he could do when he was a kid, if he had to. In Minnesota he thought this. Before he saw the boy in the woods. Before he began to steal. He thought he could catch anything that fled from him, birds, deer, fish silvery in the stream, a bear loping across a hillside, flash of gold. He could live without air.

He saw his father falling through the tinny lake waves, sinking deep. Come up. *Come up.*

A spasm. His legs leaving the fire. Leaping out of it: like a horse plunging. The ground was soft under the flames. The earth stank. His coat was on fire. He lurched forward in blackness, counting steps to the open hillside, as if he had run this route every day of his life: *thirty more, twenty-eight, thirty more steps . . .*

He had turned from the rearview mirror to say, *Now I see faces I've never seen before. I see scared old men with unforgiving words in their mouths. Demented boys running. I see crazed women shouting at me.*

Women . . .

Yes.

He had made a single harsh gesture.

I'm upset that I've never seen these people before. Who are they? What are they doing looking back at me?

She had looked him in the eyes. *You're you to me.*

He'd agreed. But then her eyes had changed, something else had snagged in them, something feral and graceless, sharp, and though her voice didn't alter, though she began to speak of other, ordinary things, he felt a sensation of disengagement, of horrible loss, as if a common, indispensable weld had let go, as if some incidental necessity impossible to do without had given way, softly, obscurely, terribly.

I saw the boy again, just yesterday, he said, grinning at me from the woods. . . .

Now there were voices around him, strangers grabbing him. Now she was gone.

2

She was gone far, impossible to get to. They took him to jail, to court in chains, and then to prison, where men with faces like rusted knives met each day as if it were the day after Armageddon. A sign painted in red script above the white-columned main entrance said, THOSE WHO SEEK TO DESTROY JUSTICE WILL BE DESTROYED BY JUSTICE, and over the back entrance where they brought the prisoners, an area that stank of rotten cabbage and feces, a handwritten sign said HOPELESS. There were no messages from her waiting for him, no presents or telltale odors. He gashed his arm against a fence to taste his blood, which was the same taste as hers; he pressed his face to himself and breathed her that way only. They sank him deep into the prison, tied weights to his legs, and let him fall through the fathoms of anguish into remote chambers where incorrigible men whispered unbelievable tales about themselves and the world; in cement cul-de-sacs men with bodies stitched up from cuts that had reversed their humanity spoke of their lives as derailed jokes, episodes of renegade passion, and lies gouged into skin.

The wound in his shoulder ached, but it healed. At night he would reach back and touch it, press the waxy scar hard to make it hurt, to take him back to the burning field and the sight of her (a dream) skipping through the fire, of Clare not looking back but running hard through the fiery wheat. Sometimes the fire tore her apart; sometimes he did.

• • •

Now, in this time of sorrow and divination, a castaway, a figure from the basement, he argued in the harsh light of dreams tedious questions of discipline and instruction, losing meager advantage, haranguing a draped figure jailers had strapped into an iron lung and set in a bare room overlooking a steelworks. Prison dreams were often dreams of great color and wild occurrence, like the dreams of the blind; they were dreams in which men sped through cities where the buildings were painted scarlet and sunshine yellow, in which women turned on a lathe of pulchritude, in which young children swam in crystal blue pools. Shock bleached his own dreams, he knew this. In them, unable to gain reversal, he turned aside and wept, staring through chump tears at the figure in its pumping iron casket.

He was in for twenty-five; he thought he would be out in eight: he could do, he figured, maybe four.

The lights shone into his eyes and they revealed nothing to him. The noise in the cellblock was without rhythm or design. He placed his hands against the walls and pressed, like Samson, but the pillars of the temple did not fall. He shouted, blowing his breath as Joshua had blown into his trumpet, but the walls of Jericho did not come tumbling down. He pitied himself and shirked, he sank into a stupor of loss and recrimination, became an ugly character slinking down corridors, getting into fights. He was sent into the bean fields under guard to hoe and pull weeds, but he did not do this well. He capered foolishly, became bitter, fell to his knees before a counselor and begged for release, gained no privileges, fooled no one. To his cellmate, Morty Shaw, another bank robber, a man from California who lived in the suburbs, as to everyone else, he lied steadily.

When his father-in-law, the murderous unapprehended old man, visited him in the fall, he said, "There is a room just off death row where they let the prisoners stop just before they are taken to the gas chamber. The room is open on top to the sky. No ceiling. What does the condemned man think of, I wonder? Does he call to mind innocent pleasures gone forever? I doubt it. I figure he goes on thinking of the terrible immoral connivances he kept to, the rapes and the reprisals, the thefts, the assaults, the big scores he hoped for, the resentments like hot knives in his heart. Don't you think so?"

"I would," the old man said.

There was no such chamber. There was no death row in federal prison. But Jack wanted to discuss what it was like in the white roofless room he was taken to every night and left in. In the room there was no one to kill, there was nothing to take. An urgency pounded inside him. He could not subdue it, could not relieve it in any way. Always the dream ended with the urgency—wild desire—raging intact. How could he get out of this room? How did he get into it?

The old man, stumpy, strong, mustachioed, eyes dark as arc welder's glass, also lived in such a room.

He said, "She's in Michigan."

"Doing what?"

"Living there. Working. She's on the shore of one of those big lakes. Like the lake you come from. There're sand dunes, sea gulls. She takes walks. I don't know anything about it."

"How's her health?"

"Good."

"What was she wearing the last time you saw her?"

"A peach-colored dress with white ankle socks. Like the socks she wore when she was a little girl. She did it to torment me. She had on tennis shoes."

Each word was a hammer glancing off the head of a nail.

The old man, whose name was Francis Manigault, lay one hand flat on the table, smoothed it with the other. "A writer came to see me. He wants to do a book about you."

"I got a letter from him."

"You going to talk to him?"

"I haven't put him on the list yet."

"Don't."

"So I won't say anything about you?"

"I want to be the one speaks for me."

To keep some obscure crime hidden, Jack figured.

The big room had filled. Family groups—rousted, beaten wives on the edge of madness, balding children, lawyers in sport clothes—leaned toward men going through menopause in prison, men striking shivs into their arms, men who spent days talking themselves out of injecting laundry bleach into their testicles, men without backgrounds, men whose cells had been set on fire for racial reasons, saved at the last minute by big hoses turned on full blast breaking their arms, tough men, wisps, callow losers, spoolers, talkers, maniacal ramblers, bank robbers, child molesters, and even one man there at an orange table sitting in an orange chair talking to a man he despised, a man who blamed him for his wife's death, for more he didn't know about.

The old man tapped a short tattoo on his cheek, as if testing the ripeness.

"What is it?" Jack said.

He wanted to strip the old man, fondle his cock and papery testicles, kiss the last spot Clare had passed through before she exited into America.

"I want you to help me."

"From jail?"

"You'll get out."

"I don't make plans in here."

"It's a plan *I* got."

"They put me to work on the farm," Jack said. "I can help you with farming when I get out, but they don't plan to let me out soon. I am doing twenty-five. I'm straight down on it, I can't take my eyes off it. I'm into the day. We go to AA meetings so we stay in the day. *The time is now*—that's our motto. I can't help you, Francis."

"I got to tell you this plan. It's important to me."

The old man owned fields, he owned woods, he had once owned a canal company with which he planned to hook the Great Lakes to the Ohio River. He was from scoundrel blood, intemperance, Midwestern river trash, weaseling-and-conniving, taking-advantage blood. His daughter was a princess of this kingdom, a liar and a lover of crime, like Jack.

Manigault's big wet bottom lip trembled. "My son's been killed," he said.

Jack let the information pass by him. "Yes," he said.

"You know about it?"

Jack didn't like to be surprised. He said he knew. The wound under his shoulder began to ache. He wanted to go back to his cell and think about his wound, he wanted to push his dead brother-in-law into the hole, get him down inside where the bullet jammed, pull him apart down there, boil him down, press him like a duck, distill an elixir of dead relative, quaff it down to see what would happen: what crime would it fume into shape in his head?

"It was my other—bastard—son did it—Will."

"He shot James?"

"Kidnapped and tortured and shot him. I hate his pig eyes, sorry no-good—he got control of my son with a gun and took him out to the woods, in Florida, and hurt him before he killed him."

"James had his bad points."

"I had the funeral in the garden behind the house. I paid this fiddle player from Appleton one hundred dollars to write a song for it. He showed up in striped pants with the tune written on the back of a McDonald's sack. He played it standing in the strawberry bushes and it was beautiful. I made everybody who owed me money come. There were one hundred people, but there was nobody I was related to. My living son is a murderer and my daughter has turned her back on me because of it—she blames me and says I set the two of them in opposition. This has to change. You have to go kill this man who killed my real son and then you have to sweeten my daughter's heart and bring her back to me."

"I'm in prison."

"I will pay you."

"To do what exactly?"

"I want you to find Will Bodine and kill him."

Jack made a fist. He could drive it through the old man's skull. High windows let sunlight down like scatterings of yellow poppies. "I'll look around for him, but I don't think he's in this prison."

"You won't always be here."

Except for this, the old man would keep him here forever. He would have him burned alive if he could.

"I can't help you," Jack said.

"Yes you can. You will."

Jack could hear the prison, the undersong of the monster that lived at the bottom of it, growling, pushing its body noises through the hubbub. If he closed his eyes, he would see himself being torn apart.

"I'm sorry, Francis."

"You'll be sorry."

"No. I am already. Fuck you, Francis."

Jack motioned to the guard, stood up. *Shoot this fuck.* Guards carried no guns. The old man didn't budge. He stared at him out of greased eyes. "I know where she is," he said. "I'm the one who knows that."

Jack sat down. He would kill the old man sooner or later. "There's nothing I can do about this," he said softly.

"Oh, yes there is," the old man said. "As long as there's breath there's something can be done. And *you* can do something. I know about you. I know what you're capable of."

"I'm surprisingly still-minded right this minute."

"See? Right here at the crux, you won't be truthful with me. You won't open any door to me. I love that. I'm going to pay you two hundred and fifty thousand dollars. It's in the bank at home. You can take it out as soon as you do this. I love the way you are. You know the harm I could cause and you still won't let me in the door. There's never been anybody in there but you—and Clare—and even now you won't change. That's why I trust you."

"You can't trust me."

"Same thing," the old man said, grinning.

Clare could get him out, and the old man would turn her in if he didn't help, if he didn't go to Florida and drag the swamps or the East Coast bars for Will, so he said yes and stood up in unison with the old man and bent to him as the big shape smelling of the world began to turn, and called him back, and when his face swung to him suddenly kissed him full on the lips and spit a ball of phlegm into his mouth.

The old man recoiled, gagging.

"Don't spit it out," Jack said. "Don't if you want me to help."

The old man grinned. "It's our bond," he said. "I'll pass it on to Clare if I see her."

Jack could have killed Manigault then, he could have pulled a James Cagney and gone over the table and driven his fist through the old man's big skull, but he didn't. It wasn't because he was wise, it was because he thought of his wife, out there somewhere in the world. He wanted to know what she was doing. And because he wanted to be out where she was, wanted to be riding in a car or buying a plate of flapjacks in a restaurant in Oklahoma, doing laundry in Milwaukee, anything, waking up in a hotel in Corpus Christi, calling room service, rubbing mink oil into a pair of boots—or tracking a killer if that was it, coming on this bad man in stealth, surprising him with his death like an overnight package, *Hello, Will.*

His profession now was prisoner. Work, meals, walking place to place, talking, avoiding trouble, sleeping, taking dreams out of the cold noisy air, picking bits of skin off his palms—these were aspects of prison life; they weren't the life. They were only activities. The life was prisoner. Everyone knew this. Morty his cellmate knew this. Everyone on the row knew this, everyone in the cellblock, in the system knew this. You looked straight at it.

A man nearby went down, shanked in the side. Another died of a heart attack. Lucas Milton wasted with cancer of the bowels. In the AIDS dormitory young men turned to wraiths. There were fights over the TV. You could taste blood in the stew. Once, in the middle of the night, he was wakened to the sound of a woman singing. A high, quavering voice sang "Crazy." He lay in his bunk chilled, terror rippling along his skin. It wasn't a woman singing. It was only Cassius X, a black man from Texas.

Nothing diverted any of them from their professional duties. Not for long.

He didn't mention his father-in-law to anyone. Manigault he kept for himself like a madman hoarding the ripped-out heart. He wanted to gnaw this heart alone.

He waited for spring to come, looking out past the gray plastic curtain strung over the open door of the tool shop at the snowy yard, at the icicles six feet long hanging from the eaves of the metal shop. Late in March a small patch of snowdrops appeared; he noticed them, twinkling in a corner near the sheds, as he returned to the cellblock. A few days later new snow obscured them, but when he brushed the snow away they were still there, bent but alive, the petals crusted with ice crystals.

In April they went out to the fields, but the fields were too wet to plow. The black soil was gummy and it caught in the tractor wheels, bogging them down. They had to wait for fair weather. When it came and the fields dried, he rode out with the crew, bundled in his denim jacket against the early chill. Jays rose crying from the ditches and in the distant woods a pale green lucent haze hung.

In the spring his sister visited, bringing a letter from Clare. He read it lying on his back with Morty snoring in the bunk over his head and then he shredded the paper in water and flushed it. Clare loved him, she was hiding, there was a place in Michigan, maybe that was it, or maybe Michigan stood for Florida or for Labrador, some cabin by a lake where, so she said, she was writing a book defending their exploits, a bestseller-type book in which there were clear characterizations and good and evil were as elaborate and identifiable as movie stars. She described her body and told how she touched herself, and, in this letter, drew his hand onto her and placed it inside her, and then placed him there, in full bloom, and gave herself to him wildly. As he read he could picture her—it was excruciating, so powerful he bit tears back into his mouth—taste and touch, all but smell her. He sensed himself being drawn into her as if he were being drawn into sunlight, and then he remembered how as a schoolboy fever had melted, destroyed him this way, made him give in and become the undifferentiated shape fallen to its knees in the schoolyard one sunny afternoon; and he had known then, like a little Jesus, that the sunlight was what he was, light itself, and heat, a shape and presence of it, fever boy, who days later when he returned to the world could still recall this feeling, fiery and complete, so beautiful it was, as if nothing to come could be better. The letter brought this to him, like radium glowing on the end of a tongue.

Then she told him she was coming, that she had devised an escape. He had to find his way to it.

The writer appeared around this time, a man who had followed their exploits and wanted now to write of them. The man's name was Rubens.

I have a way with words, Rubens said. I can tell stories. Jack had once robbed a bank in Rubens's hometown. It's fascinated me since, Rubens said. It's become my quest, to discover you. I think you are a free man.

Pardon me, but I am entranced by you and your wife. I want to know everything.

I have lists, the writer said, I have short scenarios, scripts I can put into films, I have deep thoughts about all this, speculations and theories I have sat up nights in a small room above a hardware store putting together. Rubens said, I'm like some Pakistani student working in a shed behind his family's shop, drinking tea as he pores over his calculations. You and Ms. Manigault have become my text. I follow your adventures like the old explorers followed the rivers into the wilderness. I am like those French voyageurs where you come from, hauling their freight canoes overland toward some river in a country no white man has ever seen before. . . .

He showed two books he had written. One was about hunting dogs, the other was about a murder that took place down on the Mexican border. Two men, lovers, had formed a cult and drawn in hapless souls. They'd wound up murdering a man who exposed them. It was a problem of pride, Rubens said. Hubris.

In a letter Clare said: *When I die I want you to eat my body. Will you do that?*

Yes, he would. *I will eat all of it.*

In Bible class they had talked about the Crucifixion—cons loved to talk about the Crucifixion, about any violent act—Jesus hung up by his hands. The cons speculated about how the weight of the body pulled on the hands. August Young had once taken a spike through the meat of his thigh and he talked about that. They applauded the thieves who had been crucified along with the Savior. One of their own kind had made it to paradise.

By doing, Jack said, what came naturally.

What?

Working his con right there on the cross. He snatched paradise. The biggest theft of all. He conned Christ. He got there by being exactly who he was—what drove him to steal, to rush in and take, drove him to grab Jesus.

No way, they cried. No way, José.

A fight broke out.

It was all for points.

I go down to the lake, she wrote, *at night, and I swim out into it. The stars are shining on the water. I float on my back and I look up and I start to take Orion's buckle off and I undrape Cassiopeia, and it gets good for a minute, but then I start to think I am looking up into the lake where the stars shine, and there is no difference between the lake and the sky. I am terrified by this. We are already in outer space.*

Why do you do it? Rubens said.

I'm just trying to come in for a landing, Jack said.

She lifted him out. By means that would become legend. She flew in on a small plane, a yellow homebuilt Super Cub with bright blue patches on the wings, and lifted him up. He grabbed a sling under the fuselage as the Cub flew along the track of the farm truck he was riding on. Grabbing the sling was easy, though at the last moment he had to kick Pedro Manglona in the face, but it was difficult later when she had to drop him into a river. He hurt his shoulder in the fall, but they holed up for a few days in a motel four hundred miles away and then he went to a doctor and got some pills, found a doctor—lucky—who would treat him, and he rested with her at a river resort in Arkansas, up near the hot springs, until he got his breath back, and then they ran south to New Orleans.

Price Gutterson over there—so he told Rubens—had shanked Billy Poteet four years ago, and Billy, just before he died, had spit into Price's eye, giving him occipital herpes, which eventually rotted the eyeball, so Price had a red hole in his head that he was terrified some con would stick a finger into and punch through to his brain. When he talked to you he shielded his eye with the flat of his hand. And over *there* Rasheed X was reciting from the Koran, a passage about the duties of wives. His wife, a handsome woman with a scar like a blaze of lightning across her forehead, looked bored. And David Possable, a former bullfighter, so he said, in Mexico, cried like a baby into a red bandanna his lawyer held. The lawyer winked at something or someone. All around them were men whose lives had become so complicated prison was the only way left to get simplified.

What about you, Rubens said. Have you become simplified?

He said, Once my brother-in-law, the shunned one who has now killed his brother, in a rage at a woman he thought had betrayed him, dumped bloody articles he stole from a hospital waste bin on her front steps. He smeared her door with blood from bandages, he hung bloody towels, sponges, even used tampons he found, from her windowsills. It was the kind of business that would turn your stomach, set your teeth on edge. This woman, a few days before, had been the woman of his dreams. But she spoke wrong to him. He burned to humiliate her. And he burned to humiliate himself. He looked like a dog that just had the hair scorched off him. He wanted somebody to say something so he could pull a knife. All it was about was getting past reason. You have to get past reason. For good. For as long as you can, I mean. It doesn't matter how. You make the filling station attendant precede you like a prophet into the men's room and there you force him to kneel in a leftover pool of piss and you don't ask him anything important, you just press the pistol against the back of his head and you pull the trigger.

I don't understand, Rubens said. The man's eyes were hurt, baffled.

How do you put it to yourself, afterwards? Rubens wanted to know. What do you tell yourself—to get yourself to go along?

It was like explaining himself to a horse.

No, he said, it's not like that.

What, then?

Rubens looked as if no one had been kind to him, ever.

Jack had been there in St. Louis the night Wendell Price cut Jimmy Knight's fingers off. He had watched him do it. Wendell had sawed the fingers as if he was cutting celery with a dull knife, talking all the time about how he wanted to go fishing for sea bass off the coast of Mexico. It had been like this. In prison you learned to keep quiet. You watched your rowmate go down, beaten in the balls and kidneys until he would have to be catheterized for the rest of his life, and you didn't say a thing, you didn't show emotion, didn't cringe, didn't even, if it was your nature to, gloat. Men tried out terrible procedures they'd devised: they pushed filed spikes into their own eyeballs; they bit their wrists to the bone; they found enough metal for a shank and cut their own balls off, some in religious fervor, some to convince the parole board they were crazy; they tried to drown themselves in the laundry tubs; one scalded his face into pulp, another drank bleach and died foaming blood at the mouth; they sang hymns at the top of their lungs; they recited the warrants of their arrests, named their future children after the warden, sucked the lieutenant's dick, stabbed out with a plastic fork against the strongest man in the row, strangled their neighbors; they got down on their knees and cried to Jesus to come save somebody, not them but somebody—and then they turned around, as a man turned around in sleep, as a man remembering the time he caught his wife meeting another man at a bar turned around then into solitude and despair, and they watched the means of their deliverance appear upon the horizon, a craft built in the shape of a cross, wobbling toward them.

You didn't say anything.

(He could see the Indians standing on the rocky shore, he said, dejected even on their days off, jigging lines. The women were fat and the men were skinny. When John Two Hats broke his leg falling down the big rocks and Jimmy Bacon drowned when he slipped as he tried to go down to help him, his mother went with the families to help. His father was out of town with his brothers and he was left alone with his sister. His mother should have been back that night, but she wasn't. He was too young to fix food, so he and Rita ate crackers and drank water from the bucket on the back porch. He went out in the yard at night and called for his mother, but she didn't answer and she didn't come. His hunger bit inside his belly. He begged his mother to come for him, but Mother didn't come. When at last she appeared, worn in the face and exhausted, after three days, he hated her. She was kind to him, but he knew he would never forgive her.)

The yellow airplane wobbled under streaky clouds. It was late afternoon, the sun spilled orange out of a cloud bank slung in low over the Kiowa Range. The plane had appeared earlier, passed over the field, and flown away. A couple of cons had remarked on it, stabbing at it, one reeling in an imaginary line. Jack had kept to himself, afraid his excitement would show. He felt cold, charged with chilly emotion, as he did on the front steps of banks. He began to feel nauseous.

He pulled himself over the combine steering wheel, trying to see better. The cab smelled of the onions he had eaten for lunch. He threw the machine out of gear and leaned on his elbows, pressed his hand over his eyes. The world swam. He wanted to jump down and run.

With no more warning than this, only a yellow plane to highlight the moment, he began to be torn in half.

(After the plane ride we went to a motel, he said, outside of Patrice, Oklahoma, where the dust blew up into the air like a celebration of dust and your breakfast eggs tasted of dust and the cars were powdered white, and even the buildings, which must have been painted interesting colors once, were white, even the motel; even her face, as if she had lived those three years in a dusty place, or out of the light. . . .

We began to find out about each other again. . . .)

Clare's blue eyes were like inventions for a better way of life. He stared into her face without listening to what she was telling him. He missed the words, the explanations of filial infidelity, the hatred she conjured like a basket of snakes into the motel room, the two brothers coming at each other in jealousy and terror, in envy and recrimination, two thugs who went on jobs together, who burgled fur warehouses and industrial-parts shops and plant stores and boat sheds they towed cabin cruisers out of on trailers, who never got along for five minutes, but who taught Clare, the younger sister, how to go about the business of thievery and evasion, who spooked each other and assaulted each other and had been locked up half a dozen times for fighting each other, and who, this time, so Clare said as her eyes grew damp and began not to go out of focus but to sharpen, her gaze intensifying as if in this way she could bore deeper not into truth especially, not even into the facts of her brothers' struggle, but into the *presence* of it, this time, down in Florida among the palmettos and the beach trash and the big apartment buildings you rose in cool elevators high into, they had found each other again, each at the end of his rope, and one brother had stolen the other brother's common-law wife—not exactly, Clare said—a woman named Ethel whom Will had taken up with in a bawdy house in Jacksonville, and who had fallen in love with James without telling Will, without letting him know anything about it except for a few whiffs of perfume on his brother's clothes, and a tendency for his brother to mock him more openly, smirking as he asked him about his love life: James had taken Will's wife into his arms, fucked her on hot nights when Will wandered the streets trying to shake the drugs and the raw existential terror that had plagued him since he was a child, until Will, almost despite himself, stepping into the condo out of his deep distraction, had discovered James finally at this work, and dragged his brother naked from the apartment and driven him naked out into the jackpine scrub behind Daytona, back into the sandy rough country where alligators lived in blackwater ponds and you could go days without seeing anyone worth talking to, and he'd tied him to a pine tree and left him there for three days during which he'd gone back to the condo and beaten the woman Ethel to within an inch of her life, punched her so hard he put her eye out, battered her finally senseless and dumped her onto the concrete driveway of Daytona Butterworth General Hospital before returning to the woods, where his brother by now had gone insane and begged for his *mother* to cut him loose so he could go to the store for Tootsie Rolls, and sat on his haunches for two more days gnawing mouthfuls off a ham and washing the ham down with warm beer he dissolved amphetamine powder into, watching James disintegrate into something not at all human, not animal either, but a new life form entirely, one with a purpose that was smeared on its face and that could not be made to understand plain English, so that when Will attempted to explain why he was doing what he was doing, which at that moment was cutting off his brother's balls and showing them to him, he could not even get James's attention and so grew disgusted with this travesty of a brother, and with what he was doing, and with life in general, so he said—so Clare said—and took up his pistol and shot his brother six times straight in the face.

All this went by him. He did not hear it, but he would remember it later. It would seem like a dream he had. Like a dream that had come true.

He said, "I think about being good. No, not good. I never will be good. I think about making a break for the cross."

"Don't start," she said.

(He didn't say he was exhausted, as everyone in this prison was exhausted, worn out by what he loved, and how he didn't expect ever to get rest again, not real rest, and how all of them in here knew this, and hated life because of it, hated what had been taken from them; and

how each blamed the world and everyone in the world for his predicament, for the rejection and foolery of the world, the standing aside of friends and government, the drawing away of affection and acceptance from him, from each as exemplar of crime, crime he followed as a dog followed the trail of a beloved master, crime he loved and gave his life to—how each, how he, was an apostle of this Jesus of promise, this perfect master: crime, god that was thievery and murder, host of malfeasance, vizier of violence. He could have said: I love crime. But he had plenty else to say without mentioning this.)

When the plane snatched him—it didn't even land, caught him in a sling—they at first flew no higher than the prison, no higher than the white-sugar tower, and he was disappointed by this, but soon enough the plane gained altitude and he could see the land unroll before him as if the light were inventing it, see the fields and the big woods with their trees going to color, thickets in the low places like balled-up hair, the few scattered houses, bean fields and cornfields, the mountains turned blue in the distance, and then the river, glinting in late sunlight, snaking west, which they followed like the path to glory.

He said, "What are you going to do when you find Will?"

"I don't have to find him. I know where he is. He's in a little red apartment overlooking the Sun Fat Bakery on St. Simone Street. And at the Bee Club every night, where he is the club weasel and backstab artist."

"Your daddy wants me to kill him."

She sprang across the bed and slapped his mouth. He reeled back, clutching his jaw, furious. He raised his fist, but instead of hitting, he grabbed her, threw her away. She crawled at him, then dived for the bags on the floor, went for the pistol. He stepped on her wrist, slapped her across the back of the head. She rolled onto her back and looked up at him with angry, wounded eyes.

"It's Francis," he said, "not me."

"It's as good as you. You listened. What did he say?"

He told her. First he lifted her in his arms and lay her down on the sagging motel bed and looked in her face and then lay on top of her, half smothering her. He noticed the white plaster fountain out the window that greasy water poured out of, out of the mouth of a stained nymph, like a seeping rusty vomit, and for a second the sound of trucks passing out on the highway was like a nostalgia come to life, a sentiment that he'd carried now returned to him. He sensed tears rising in his eyes and looked down at her to see he had placed his forearm over her throat and though he was not choking her he was holding her down. Her eyes looked at him with the indifferent alertness of an animal, an animal poised for what held her to relax so she could bite and flee. He let her go.

"He came to the prison like some sentimental family mouthpiece. He almost fooled me. He had news of you, so I was listening to him in a daze because I was thinking of you and he told me he wanted me to kill brother Will because Will had murdered James. There were tears in his eyes, it was ludicrous, but he offered a quarter of a million dollars and he implied that he would turn you in if I didn't do it. I kissed him."

"You should have bit his lips off."

"I tongued him."

"Get off me," she said.

"Why?"

"Get off me!"

He rolled away, wary, watching her.

She sprang to her feet, pulled her clothes on. He retreated to a chair, squatted in the seat watching her. She threw on a coat, pulled on her slipper shoes, pixie shoes with pointed toes that she had worn the night before the fire robbery, and without speaking to him went out of the room. He watched her cross the parking lot, go past the fountain and up the hill. There was a road that ran up among some houses through a wood.

She didn't come back for two days. He stayed in the motel, ate in the Shoney's across the street, read the paper, took walks, dawdled partway up the hill, climbed it once and stared across a level subdivision where unsightly houses were set among brushy rained-on woods. This was in Oklahoma near the Bright Stone Reservation, where men drove around in Cadillacs, where there were banks they had once rifled, and rich neurotic sons, and terrible memories like bacon fat inside your clothes, he thought, and stones in the river, thrown there after someone had been bashed with them, and empty lots distraught boys stared into as if into the tent cities of hell. They'd come down through the greasy towns, past blue herons standing in canebrakes and frozen oil pumps.

He had plenty of money—from her bag—and he had the car, there were things he could do if he was really alone, maybe he could head to Cabo San Miguel or Carlsbad or to some little rotted corner of Venezuela, or even to New Orleans, but these were only thoughts, they were like onion grass come up in the motel yard in the Indian summer rain, fresh smelling but good for nothing. The ideas blinked out as he thought them, one after another, until he was left on the bed with only the dullness in his head, some torporous resentment lying underneath it, some gravel particulate washed out of the ancient losses, species and personal, nostalgia for the trees, etc., for the lost fathers and mothers, dead brothers, etc., for his sister Rita, who was dating the detective the FBI had sent to watch for him, for everyone's sister, for himself mostly—for the boy he'd seen *(who vanished finally . . .)*, suddenly remembered—half drowned with grief and anger.

On the morning of the third day he got out of bed early and cleaned the room. He scrubbed the bathroom with soap and a washcloth, picked up grit and lint from floor and furniture, made the bed, wiped his dried spittle from the television screen, picked up the pieces of the sheet he'd stabbed into ribbons. He was changing into clean clothes when she came in and flung fifty thousand dollars on the bed.

"There," she said, "there's a down payment. You don't have to kill my brother."

"No," he said. "I don't."

His mouth was dry. He was terribly glad to see her.

He said, "You look like you've lost weight."

"I'm on the run."

"Should we scoot?"

"I expect so."

She grinned at him.

He laughed outright. Starting on foot, one set of clothes, no gun, in pixie shoes, she'd gone off, grabbed thousands of dollars, and come back. Out in the parking lot was her fast new car. They loaded the bags into it. "I want to spend the money right off," she said. "I want to waste it, to prove to you that it doesn't matter. I want you to see how quickly it runs out compared with how long you will have to bear up under my hard looks and my assassin's breath if you take Daddy's money for killing Will."

• • •

Later he said, I would like Jesus to remember me. *As I am.*

They were moving fast by now, Oklahoma disappearing through a pecan orchard behind them.

"I'm not going to kill Will," he said.

"You can't kill my daddy either."

"Why not? I thought you would want me to kill your daddy."

"There is something strange going on. I don't believe this deal."

He had told her as much as he remembered about it. "Your pop was broken up. So it appeared to me."

"But about what really?" She scratched her arms meditatively, characteristically. "It's about you," she said. "Somehow it's about you."

"You mean about you."

"Because of you, yes. He wants me back. He thinks he can pull me back through the assholes of all the beasts I walked into the mouths of and got swallowed by; he thinks he can make me somehow give you up after twenty years and return to the farm where I will be his china doll."

"He's not that much of an idiot."

"Yes, he is."

The Bee Club was lit by blue lights like the lights of police cars and it smelled of degradation and body fluids fouled in mops. It had a dark wood floor that had been scuffed to fuzziness like wool, across which moved doomed men and women in various contorted and self-despising poses, tourists edging among them like egrets balancing on the backs of cattle in the slaughter pens, gunmen on alert, various bad actors given to dissipation and nostalgia, a few sacrificial victims, lambs with targets pinned to their backs, bleating forlornly. From among a clutch of women in black beaded dresses raising their pale powdered arms to the ceiling Donnie Bee emerged, skipping like a cat off a fence, his tiny lipless embouched mouth ripped open in a grin. . . .

• • •

In Arkansas Jack came into Clare's arms, crawling across the bed like a dog, and made love to her; and as the heat rose, and as he rose in himself to fight off the sudden desire to kill her, to harm her irrevocably, he began to think of Will, of the misshapen, fallible, ill-fated man, to think of him as an infant, a chubby bundle in his mother's arms, and from this begin to think of the pure holy desire that was the infant's life, and then he wondered where, for normal people, this went to, how it was possible to eradicate this desire, and then for the ten thousandth time he was amazed that any of it disappeared, that all of them, not only he and Clare and the other convicts, but every ordinary squarehead, was not ravenously and unappeasably grabbing every bright item he came across; he didn't know how anyone knuckled under for long, how anyone could stand not taking.

She looked up into his bony face, at his dark blue narrowed eyes. "Maybe you could paint me purple and call me Nancy," she said.

"Morty."

"Call me Morty," she said bitterly.

"I am thinking about my life on the cross."

"You're not Jesus."

"No. I'm the one next door to Jesus."

"Who is that—the Goldbergs?"

"The thief."

"You are a robber and a murderer."

"I have not been convicted of murder."

"In your heart you have."

"That's why I moved in next door to the Lord."

She cuffed his shoulder. "Please fuck me properly. Please fuck me properly right now."

He did as he could. Getting up off her onto his hand and knees, lifting with one arm her spare body, raising it against him, holding her as if they hung out over a precipice, slamming himself into her so hard they could hear the greasy slap of his cock going in, but it was all wrong, he lost his way—until she began to instruct him with her hands, to guide him with her voice, which came from her throat muted and pressurized as if she were deep down somewhere, straining underwater maybe, held him and guided him, showing him how, teaching him again, *softly, go slowly,* reaching him down to her, handing him down like a child handed down a cliff face, until even this rope broke, and they were both twirled haphazardly into a fucking out of nothing, the whole of it accelerating suddenly, become some fat dream gift they tore open greedily, so fast and madly they'd sunk their teeth into and ripped it crazily apart before they could tell what it was.

They rested later.

After that they wanted to rob something.

"I went into a nut warehouse once," she said outside the bank, "where they stored pecans and filberts and exotic nuts from other countries. Down in New Orleans. Some of the nuts had gone bad, shipment or something—that's what it smelled like, this river."

"In prison you like every little earthy smell."

"When I was in prison there were women who would never go outside. They didn't want anything to do with any other life. They were in a rage. They wanted everything artificial."

"It was like that in Turandot, too. Men like that. I wasn't one of them."

"Sometimes this river stinks so bad you can't get close to it. They say men get sick from breathing the air off it."

"The Mississippi."

"Yes."

"It rises in Minnesota. We went to see it. Where my mother used to go, when she was a girl."

"I remember."

"You and me and Donnie Bee went."

"Hateful man. That was so long ago."

"My mouth's dry."

"Suck a penny."

"Okay."

"Let's go," she said.

It was a snap. A snap until the man, a customer, a tall fellow in a blue cord suit, fell to the floor in a faint. *What is this?* Jack thought—Christ. He had backed away from the counter, backed away from the teller, who herself was so frightened she kept her hand over her mouth as she scooped packs of fresh bills out of the drawer, backed away and swung the pistol levelly, like a man opening a gate, at the assembled crew of

Monroe Mississippians arrived on a fall day for a little banking. The man looked like a prisoner, some monkey beaten to within an inch of his life, gone down under blows and the promise of horrors to come—*as all of us are going down,* he said—as he bent to pull the man up, for once doing something, but the man was out, heart attack or faint, some devilment playing fluidly around his lips: Jack had to leave him, rising to look around before he vanished, sheepishly he might have said if he were looking at himself from a distance, peeved too, angry even, but without recourse, able only to back away, aiming casually here and there, poking the chance of a bullet hole into that mind, and that one—victims always remembered the gun, not the face above it—until they were out again into the bright fall air, two satisfied customers running for their lives, who skipped through piles of yellow leaves—so witnesses would say—kicking up leaves like children on a spree, shouting to each other as they ran, careless love, wild delight, scarification, total terror the main features of the perfected economy they were ambassadors for, tossing broadsides as they moved, like riders on big horses fleeing: *out, out*—

They threw themselves into the car. "I am so scared," he cried—scared or happy, he couldn't tell which—"I have pissed my pants."

He swung the car out into the street. There were big naked oaks and oaks with all their green leaves. Each was familiar, like a story he just got the meaning of. *(Indians had stopped coming down to the lake to fish years ago, he said. The shore was crowded with cabin motels, denuded places where you could pull over and eat lunch with Lake Superior out there like a severed blue wing. His father, the suicide king, had been a tourist attraction. Locals pointed him out on the street in Duluth. Still, the northern lake was empty; even with all the tourists, you could go out on it alone.)* He knew this town as if he'd been born in it: gardens gone to seed, the little patched houses jammed together, cracked concrete streets, water tower painted with the word WILDCATS, the smell of fertilizer—they were all familiar. For a moment he had been raised here, he'd taken Communion here, loved his first girl here. They'd shot him down on the road outside this town, buried him under a beech tree in the town cemetery. You could visit his grave, linger mournfully there beside the blue stone cut with the epitaph HE MEANT EVERY WORD.

He jerked his pants down, kicked out of his Jockeys, jabbed at the accelerator and found it. The car roared.

"I like driving naked," he said.

"You have a hard-on."

"Don't tell anybody."

She pulled her leg back as his foot pressed the gas. The car spurted ahead. The town passed. There was no one in it they would see again. They wouldn't remember a name or a face—maybe the old man's face, lips slobbery and slack—but there would be many who remembered them. They'd never be identified, but their touch, the crisp sweep of a pistol, the timbre of their voices, the odors, the wavering gandered sunlight stuck like gold glue to the leaves of a philodendron—all of it would be remembered. It would be remembered and passed down. The survivors would make sure of that. In silent times after trouble, or after supper maybe when there was a period without telephone calls or family duties, in the bath maybe, or just before sleep when the witness lay on his side watching the moon drift behind clouds, this afternoon would return, bristling and rude, a stranger without grace, but alive nonetheless. In this Jack had always found his hope. It was a legacy, brought to him in a sack as he waited for the prison train. He knew it would all pass away. The survivors would die, their children would remember other aggressions. But for a while his story would be told. And then forgotten. He loved this. He loved to think of himself, of the last moment he was alive in another's consciousness, of the blinking out of memory finally, and especially of the space he left, of his vanishment, not into dust, but into nothing.

Clare said, "Donnie, you look like a cat wearing goggles."

Flying, hooked under the yellow plane, he wondered who might look up and see him; some boy driven half crazy by his rural life: look up and see a man, alive, just set free, dragged, like a disgraced god, backwards through the sky.

3

For a time, in his chair in the Royale Hotel garden, balanced it seemed to him on a minor precipice at the edge of the world, Jack sat very still. He sank into himself and did not pay attention to the yellow water flowers stuffed in buckets, or to the tourists practicing for a new life, or the mimosas, or the magnolia beyond the wall dropping leaves that fell with a soft crackling sound traffic erased from the blue tile courtyard floor. He shed the day like clothes dropped on the way to the bath. He could fall back far, all the way to Minnesota, to his brothers shooting sea gulls at the dump, to his mother screaming, to his father rigid in a folding chair down at the end of the dock as his best friend squatted beside him talking him out of suicide. His memories always led to his father, to some point of isolato performance, to the man collecting evidence against himself. His father had tried to kill himself a dozen times before he succeeded. It was a sad tune played at family gatherings, an old song no one wanted to dance to. He left notes, blaming himself, and blaming *the road,* which was always *playing out, closing in, running off the cliff, dividing*—some caricature of life that no one else could decipher, some despair in the form of metaphor, of futility described in notes left on pillows, on car seats, once pinned to the back door of their vacation house. The handwriting on the notes was always only barely legible, the lines seemed to tremble even as the reader held the piece of paper in his hands. *I have asked God one thousand times . . . to forgive . . . to allow . . . to remem-*

ber . . . to forget . . . to tell me . . . tell someone. . . . Why, he said, do I confuse the function of a meadowlark with that of a saint, or trees with a sense of opposition stronger than a legislature, why does the world deride and abrade itself WITHOUT MERCY. . . . Brought back, revived, from gas, from bloody cuts, from a gunshot wound that missed the heart, *from drowning,* his father wouldn't look at his notes or at his life. He was like a saint, his eyes clinging to his vision of eternity. In his face he wore the scars of failure, the expression of bafflement and outrage, of heckled determination. Jack remembered that he was always tired, exhausted. They had gone to movies together. Often *(sometimes, he said)*, after supper, they would walk downtown under the misty streetlights to sit by themselves at the nine o'clock show, in an almost empty theater. His father would take his hand. Jack would sit beside him, attempting to push himself onto the back of a cowboy horse, onto a battlefield laid out on the screen before him, as his father, erect beside him, wept.

He pulled himself back. Where was Clare? He ordered oysters, ate them with Tabasco and lemon. Always something tasty in this world. Some delight. How could you miss it? He knew how. He did not want to enter this family business with Clare. He did not especially want to explore the thread of mystery a brother represented. Will did odd jobs for Donnie Bee, and here was how the world worked: years ago, during a time of separation, Clare had had an affair with Donnie, had traveled with him in a red Cadillac to Illinois, where Jack was putting together a job on a string of small downstate banks, and with him had stepped in, overleaping, blown the jobs and got herself caught, jailed and sent to prison. When she got out he was waiting. He'd picked her up in a red truck at the prison gates, driven ten miles through the countryside where corn sprouted like fat green grass and the white farmhouses looked like summer sloops sailing the crests of hills, and stopped the car by a creek where big rocks had been painted white and lettered in black with the words BO'S COUNTRY STORE, and dragged her from the car, set her before him like a target and punched her once hard under the ear. She tumbled backwards down the bank, knocked out, sprawled in weeds among old lumber and soggy cardboard. Then she'd come to, gathered herself, washed the grit off her face and body, come back up the hill carrying a piece of board he hadn't noticed she'd picked up, and whacked him so hard across the side of the head he'd seen blue lights bursting along the horizon, gone stupid, and fallen to his knees. They'd fought like dogs. Then, when they were exhausted, they'd cursed and reviled each other. Then later, they'd staggered off separately into the woods. He remembered how the wind whistled in the trees. She'd come back first. When he returned he found her locked in handcuffs sitting in the backseat of a police car. He'd walked up to the cop, knocked him down and taken his pistol. After he unlocked her she took the pistol and shot the cop. They left him for dead on the side of the road. They were all right after that.

He'd done nothing to Donnie Bee, except make sure he was alive. He'd never touched him, never said a thing. He figured he was saving him for a rainy day.

(In Turandot Prison, in a fair fight, he said, he'd thrown Jimmy Sertoma against the red-hot side of a steel incinerator. The back of Jimmy's denims had caught fire and the fire had peeled his flesh and seared a tonsure into his hair. And then, one afternoon in spring, just after he'd noticed how the sun had climbed up and spitshined the tower windows gold, Davey Shrake, from Indiana, for reasons unclear to Jack, *had attacked him with a piece of shovel blade, catching him in the skin under his armpit before he could knock the blade from his hand and pin him against the tool shop wall. They'd pulled Jack off, but not before he'd yanked a fistful of genitalia so hard Davey fainted. Jack was going up under Davey's neck with his thumbs when they grabbed him.*

The attack shook him. He couldn't follow it. We're bad men, Morty had said, we get angry with each other and because we've got no governor, we act on the anger and somebody gets hurt. Fine, Jack said, but that doesn't help.)

They came around the corner carrying flowers in their hands, slipped through the pale blue doors of Donnie's place. It was a nightclub in full career. Jack, coming close to Donnie, coming this close, wanted to kill him, but he didn't do anything, he didn't even carry a weapon. He moved through the blue-lit room as on the balls of his feet, his hands out in front of him, the flowers stuck like a pistol in the waistband of his pants.

Donnie, his eyes seething, whirled up to them.

Jack pushed the flowers at him, Clare tossed her bouquet to him. Donnie made no attempt to catch the flowers; they bounced off his pale suit.

"Drinks," he said viciously. "We need drinks."

A spiral of bitter dust, he twirled them to a table set among Venus flytraps, jack-in-the-pulpits, and other flesh-eating plants. He bounced and slid, moving like a man walking on wax paper.

"It's good, yeah," he said, jabbering, "good; the lifeline's been thrown out, we got a method here, a way out of this place, as Hendrix said—we've cut another door—you know, Jack."

"I know, Donnie," Jack said.

Donnie slapped a waitress, slapped another, began a story, forgot it midsentence, quoted Tolstoy, quoted H. L. Mencken, quoted Fanny Brice, punched himself on the biceps, offered drugs that no one wanted.

"I have a pain in my side," he said. "I am in constant pain, like a saint."

"Not enough," Clare said.

"What?"

"Pain." She smiled. "You look like a cat wearing goggles," she said.

Donnie leapt into a chair, dropping lightly into it like a cat, arranging himself fastidiously, quickly, plucking at his loose dark clothes, lifting his chin as he touched himself, smiling. He glanced swiftly at Jack, his raisinette eyes darting. "The city's yours, Jack. You're like a great jazzman come back home. Buddy Bolden returned, from the grave."

"Where's my brother-in-law?"

"He's out with this guy. He'll be right back. I told Clare I was happy to help him. He's a strange man, so moony and agitated. He reminds me of an engine, a car, you know, that keeps running after you turn it off. Is that offensive? I don't mean to be offensive."

"Then you've changed, Donnie," Jack said.

"Don't be bitter, Jack. You're among your people now. Relax. Let me buy you things."

He jerked staggering to his feet, catching himself against the passing shoulder of a woman in a gold lamé dress. The woman spun on him, saw who he was and flinched, shrank under his touch, smiling meekly. "Mr. Bee," she said submissively. Donnie pushed her away from him, raised himself onto his toes. "I have to go order things," he said. "I have to make purchases, and tell the band what to play, and corner millions on various markets."

"You always were a sharp one, Donnie," Jack said.

"I'm so rich now, Jack. I have so much money. I own three blocks of houses in the old neighborhood. I had the house I was born in put on a trailer and hauled out to my estate on the bayou. I set it up there, like they do for the President's boyhood home. It's all complete and beautiful, down to the cracked green plastic curtains and the jelly glasses on the kitchen table and the smell of rotted meat in the drains. I can go in my bedroom and come exactly back to the ancient constipations of shame and degradation by just looking at the old iron bedstead I was tied down to many a night and at my dresser with the big knife gouge in it where Daddy tried to stab me through the heart. I feel so good about it. You ought to go back and purchase your boyhood home, Jack. It would do wonders for your sense of the rightness of life."

"I have no sense of the rightness of life," Jack said.

"That's what I mean," Donnie said, smiling gleefully. "That's exactly what I mean. You must get that sense. You must obtain it, as you would a precious animal, Jack, and foster and encourage it. The rightness of life, Jack. I was born to find it. You were, too. I am so glad you have been paroled. Clare told me. She said you paid your debt to society. I remember when we were paying our debts together, Jack. Those were terrible times, such times of dissension and pain. The country is a mess, it is a buzzard's pie, but you and I, Jack, we have paid our debt to society, we have swung the big freighter of our lives against the docks and off-loaded the cargo—time, Jack—by which we purchased our freedom. They thought this journey would be the end of us, Jack, but it wasn't. They thought we would simply wander off into the muddy useless future like thugs with nothing to sustain us, but for us such projections and idiotic prognostications didn't adhere. Look at us, Jack. I have my riches and my minions at my beck and call. And you have Clare."

His eyes gleamed like black olives plucked from a bucket of oil.

"Yes," Jack said, "I see the rightness."

Donnie's face seemed to collapse onto itself. An energy extinguished itself, like a torch plunged into water, disappeared. His hand jerked up, he caught himself by the throat in fork of thumb and forefinger. "Agh," he said, falsely strangulating, "I choke myself."

He bounded away on his small cat feet.

"We are hanging by a thread here," Jack said, watching Donnie's black silk back vanish.

"You mean he will turn us in if he finds out you are escaped, not paroled," Clare said.

"That is exactly what I mean."

"He believes me."

"Still, it's only a thread."

"We're like hawks—"

"Dropping on a rabbit? I wouldn't be too sure."

"No. Able to soar high."

"You are trying to make it so I can't possibly kill Will."

"I wouldn't use Donnie for that."

"Yes, you would. You'd use Donnie, or the garbageman, or that squarehead over there sucking his girlfriend's thumb."

She glanced around. "I wouldn't use him."

"Good."

A nostalgia, like an old enemy gone to chubbiness and despair, stumbled across his mind. He didn't hail it.

She said, "Where did Daddy say the money was?"

"The ransom for Will?"

"Where did he say it was?"

"In a safe-deposit box in Vandalia."

"In the bank at home?"

"He said it's in brand-new bills in a brand-new leather briefcase. A black cowhide case." *Rapping the table sharply as he spoke, baring his crooked teeth, making a fool of himself as a tough guy, sitting in an orange chair in Turandot Prison gym, where overcrowding had forced visitors to—*

She tapped her lips hard. "I know the truth now. He's trying to kill *you.* He wants to get you off where he can kill *you.*"

"Maybe right this minute you are being used as part of this enterprise, part of a trap?"

"Maybe I am."

"Maybe Will is out to kill me?"

"Maybe he is."

"Maybe Francis has gotten Donnie Bee to set this whole version up. Maybe all this goes back years—*as you said it did*—eighteen probably to your papa and twelve to Donnie Bee. Maybe I have stepped forth from prison like Lazarus from the tomb only to find before me—*as you said*—a set of circumstances arranged entirely for my annihilation. Maybe even the writer who came to talk to me was a part of this—*maybe the conspiracy, he said, is always deeper than we can imagine*—and the guards who looked at me funny, and the snaky little guy, Parkins, in the prison issue room, maybe Morty is in on this, too, and the warden, and my mother, who would rather see me dead than a criminal, and maybe even my sister has allowed herself to be used as a tool for the FBI, who are in on the caper, too, sweet, clumsy Rita, your friend—*that man over there, you said, looks funny*—used—*as we all are, you said*—for insidious, murderous purposes. Maybe there's nothing I can do to avoid my *fate.*"

"I wonder about that all the time."

"Whether I can avoid my fate?"

"Whether any of us can."

"What the fuck does that matter? Unless they are passing knowledge of it out with change at the gas station, who gives a shit? And who would give a shit even then? Only idiots think about their fucking fate."

"I'm not an idiot, Jack. Neither are you."

"Yeah, but you've made me think about my fate."

"Oh, darling, shut up, please."

A man near him, a man stalled at the edge of a stagger, a man weaving through some sort of gross internal punishment, began to make soft mewling noises into the drink he held to his mouth like a microphone. The man's hair was cut short like a Marine's, his neck was flushed and crepey, his hands were boiled red; he was close enough to touch. Jack pressed the heel of his hand against the man's hip bone and pushed him firmly away. The man looked down in wonderment. "It's okay, buster," Jack said. "Everything's going to be okay." The man slowly smacked his lips. "Thank you," he said.

"I mention it," Clare said, "because I think if there really is money, we should go get it."

"Okay."

"Okay?"

"Actually, I don't see why we ought to. Now I know I can just fire you like a missile at money."

"But there is someone in the world who wants to kill you."

"There was always that, honey. Let's dance."

They threaded among greasy tables that seemed to him to be occupied by the raving dead. The band played a jerky, resurrected Dixieland song, not dance music, but music that made you want to move. He took her in his arms, pressed her slender body tightly against him, and it seemed, for a second, that he was taking his life in his arms, that he was pulling it out of a dark place it had fallen into.

They danced hard, staring at each other, clutching each other. He flung her out, pulled her in. Sweat shone on their faces. He spun her to the ends of his fingertips, barely caught her, reeled her toward him. She banged against his chest. "Go harder," she said.

He pushed her away, let the weight of her body catch, surge toward him, then thrust into her, banging her shoulder, spinning off her, sliding off to the left. She twirled in front of him, her loose skirt snapping. She shook and swayed before him. "This is good," he said. "I like this a lot."

In his head he saw the old man in the bank in Monroe go down. There was a look of intense pain in the man's face.

"I wish we were strangers," she said. "I wish we didn't know each other's names."

"I know."

"I could be the woman on the run from a bad married life, come to New Orleans to forget."

"I could be the rough character she meets there, who fascinates her, who dances with her all night, then takes her back to his bleak room and tells her about Raskolnikov and the Posse Commitatus."

"He scares her, she knows she's made a mistake, but she is lost, she's drunk, she can't save herself."

"He ties her up on the bed, reads to her from the Psalms."

"She begs him to let her go, but he won't. She is sure he will kill her."

"He tells her of his childhood, of his father beating him, of his mother pouring turpentine into the strap cuts."

"She pities him—"

"No, not that."

"What?"

"No pity."

"Oh, sorry. Fling me out again."

He spun her away from him. She skidded across the floor, caught her balance, sank toward the floor, rose, drifted sideways, disappeared behind a crowd. He stopped. The music crunched the air, chewed smoke. At every table someone seemed to be confessing desperate acts. I've been out of the country, he thought, I have to catch up. He smelled the soybean fields. Some nights in his sleep he would drift out of the prison, fly up into the air, soar out over the fields; the dream would stop before he got to the treeline. It's time to straighten things out, he thought, get everything in line

Someone tapped his shoulder. He turned; she was there with Will.

"I found him," she said. "He was lurking and staring."

"I'm familiar with that approach myself. . . ."

Behind him, a shadow in a shadow, Will had the writer, Rubens.

It was out now, they had to go.

But as if life was only sweetness and fine days of plenty, Will lurched forward like a man leaping out of hiding and grasped Jack's hand. "Oh, you brother," he cried.

Jack squeezed hard, quickly, let the slight hand go. The dream, the story Clare told, some story, the death of James, began to come back to him. The writer looked at him, frankly delighted. "Jack," he said.

Jack pushed his brother-in-law aside, strode two steps to the writer, a portly man with a bulging chest, and shoved him hard.

Clare, alert behind him, stepped between her brother and Jack.

"Fuck, what are you doing here?"

The writer tried to smile. "Backgroun—"

Jack slapped him in the face.

The writer staggered back, cowering. He made an agile movement with his feet, attempted to spin away, raised his hand. Jack slapped him again. The writer backed to a chair, fell into it with a jolt that showed in his round, frightened face. "Ow," he said, "I hurt my tailbone."

"Lucky if I don't pull your tailbone out of you."

Rubens held his arms over his head, covering from rain. "Don't hit me, I'm on your team."

Will came up alongside. "I thought this guy was your buddy, Jack."

"Are you crazy, Will?"

He stared into his brother-in-law's faded gray eyes. Will had Clare's smooth skin, her square jaw, someone else's slippery disputatious mouth.

"I'm glad to see you, Jack," Will said. "Everybody's glad to see you, especially this little girl here. We're all glad you're out."

"Ah, damn. I'm caught in the headlights."

Will took Jack's arm, led him off to the side. Near the band three women in identical silver dresses leapt and squatted, like pistons. "You don't want to make a fuss in here, Jack," he said. "Not in Donnie's place. There's a delicate balance in here."

"What does Donnie know?"

"He don't know nothing. Not a thing. Clare told him you're out on parole. Why would he care what's up with you?"

"What's that writer said?"

"Said he was interviewing you for a book. Up in prison. Said he wanted to get background business for the book, color, that kind of thing. I'm impressed. He wanted to talk to me. I liked that. And he wanted to talk to Donnie, too."

Jack looked at him. "Are you keeping all right, Will?"

"I'm fine. Twisted, but fine."

"Your daddy offered me money to kill you. Did you know that?"

"No, not exactly."

"What exactly did you know?"

"Nothing, Jack. I been too busy."

"You sound like a cracker."

"I been down in Florida with the crackers. Southern Indiana's kind of cracker country, too, if you think about it. It's the north, but it's cracker country, too. We used to see the Klan and all that when I was a kid, grown men in white robes, cross burnings, all that. They burned a cross out in the middle of the river, on a raft. It swayed, I remember. It was beautiful."

"Okay, Will."

He could see his future becoming his past. *(Even the plants have memory, everything, the rocks warming in summer, seasons, birds, every creature, each molecule, every one remembers, we don't forget. . . .)* He saw it in his head like an old house come upon in the country, an abandoned place where the owners had left in a hurry years before, and now the rats and the nesting birds and the foxes had gotten at it, and eaten all the fine goods, and you could stand in the living room *(remembering)* and not know what happened there, not be able to figure why the suitcases were open on the sagging bed or why someone had pulled all the dresses into a heap in the closet, or why, when you were still a moment, there was the low sound of weeping. *Do unto the least of these,* Jesus had said, *and you do unto me. (The least memory,* he said—*do you understand?)*

He said, putting his hand on Will's shoulder, "In the Bible, imagination and intelligence got you to the top. Just like it does out here sometimes, but it couldn't give you a life you could be sure of. Look at Moses, and Solomon, and Jesus."

"I don't follow you, Jack."

"You got a plan to kill me, Will?"

"No, I don't, Jack."

"Ah, Will. The trouble with the criminal element is you can't be sure we're telling the truth. Even inside the family, eh?"

"I don't want to think about the family, Jack."

They returned to the others. Clare and Rubens sat at a table beside the flowers that looked carnivorous and famished. Rubens was begging. He was trying to save his life. As she listened Clare broke bits off her cuticles and flicked them at the open jaws of Venus flytraps.

Jack suggested they go somewhere else. "In case Donnie gets giddy," he said.

"I'll go anywhere you go, Jack," Rubens said. He jumped right up.

He watched Clare sink into the black river. The water was black, but he could see her, he could watch the slow fall as she sank on her back, looking up through tons of water, the gun coming up steady in her hand, rising, aimed at him like the whole of Minnesota was aimed at him, like his whole life in prison, the long nights of insomnia, outlasting sleep, outlasting the night, all aimed at him, and the day, too, deep in the fields driving the combine, watching the beans flourish, waiting for her to appear over the horizon as his sister told him she would, rise in an airplane like some goddess come for him, a woman now flying backwards through the water descending into the night under the night, the pistol raised, aimed at his heart, both of them defiantly grinning.

They sailed through the night. In cabs they passed from the streets of the Quarter into the Garden District, and then, backtracking, headed along the river past the docks, crossed the bridge and roved through the Chattermaine District and Tangiers, out to Fresco, where Dooley and Cortez had been killed, where Jack had shot a man in a fight over disposition of holdup spoils and had to flee downriver on a shrimp boat. They got drunk on mescal, blustering out ahead of the sorrow in their faces, eating chicken and oysters. Somewhere between two ashen moments Rubens confessed he had left his wife and lost his house because of his drinking.

"But I am on the way back now," he said, sloe gin dripping down his bare raised arm. He had rolled up his sleeves. "I am on my way back up the slope. By way of Jack Baker and Clare Manigault. I've found my purpose, my meaning. I will tell the story. I have studied, Jack," he said, licking his wrist, "I have gone among the files and searched out the truth. I am awash with facts. Ah, Jack, I take parts of you out at night and set them on the table before me like fragments of ancient human bone. You are my missing link, Jack. I knew it, years ago I knew it."

When Jack shifted his head he could see where the street ended at the river, the lights held back like supplicants at the dark gate.

"I am way down, but I will be back up," Rubens said, dramatizing his life as if he had the ruling hand in it, as if he could take it and make something out of it. "I know, they had their foot on me," he said. "The truth is I have been in prison, too. It was alcohol related—I hit a guy in my car. I killed him in a hit-and-run. I didn't mean to kill him, and I didn't mean to run—but I was miles away when I remembered myself—and they put me in jail. I did twenty-six months in Laurens."

"In Carolina?" He was barely listening. Now, on this side of the dark, he could see Clare out on the deck talking to her brother. Will was as thin as a stalk, wasted from nervousness and disconsolation turned into murder; a point man for the dark, Jack thought, watching the two of them, watching Will lean toward Clare, bending at the waist as if bowing to her, and to her power, gesturing with his bony hands, picking at the air as if there were gnats in it he could catch.

"Laurens is in South Carolina," Rubens said.

"When did you get out?"

"Last year. August twenty-third. It was a hot cloudy day. Cotton was blossoming in the field across the road. Yellow and pink flowers. I caught a bus home."

Jack smiled at him.

"I want you to do something for me," he said.

"You bet." He noticed the liquor on his arm, dabbed at it with a paper napkin. "I'm a mess," he said. "I haven't got enough will power to live. That's what my wife said I needed. Drive and talent, too—that's what she said. You got to have that. Where they keep it I don't know. You can't seem to earn it."

"I want you to go back to the hotel and pick up some money. Our stuff's there, but you won't be able to get that. Just get the money. It's in a green canvas suitcase in the closet."

"Where, Jack?"

"At the Royale Hotel, on St. Eustace Street. Room 679. I'll write it down."

"You don't have to do that. I'll remember it."

"I'll write it down. There's a restaurant in Tangiers called Stomine's. Bring it there."

He gave him the key.

"Okay, Jack. I got it."

"Good. Take a cab."

Rubens lurched to his feet. He stood in the smoky amber light of LouLee's swaying, gathering himself. Jack could picture him talking to his wife, trying to explain, outargued. The man was short and fat and he had a small puckish face. His bald head gleamed. "I am coming through the corn," he said. "Like a bride, I am coming through thc corn."

He was gone shortly, and then Jack and Clare, with Will in tow, were gone. They were still registered at the Royale, but they no longer lived there; they were transient now, migrants. Jack was explaining this as they rode in the cab taking them to Lafay's on Bayou Teshmarine, saying to Will, who leaned forward as if he wanted to catch the words in his hands and wash his face in them, that he had sent this man off on a fake errand, and now they were free of him for a few minutes before the wheel turned and some other snarling configuration reared its monstrous head, and Will was laughing his laugh, which was like a smirked-up cough, something you did to cover bad pain at your arraignment, and he was staring at Clare with a mournful look, just as the cab headed down the Aylene Fork south along the bayou, leaving this part of the fuckup behind, when they passed Rubens in his cab. The writer lay back against the middle of the seat. His arms were spread like wings and he stared straight ahead. He had a foolish look of misery on his face. There was exaltation in it, too, as there sometimes is, and hope mingled, and a dumb gathered-up stubbornness that must have been there right after he killed the man in the hit-and-run. Jack didn't say anything. He didn't have to duck out of sight; he knew Rubens wouldn't turn his head. They could be on fire and the man wouldn't turn his head. That's how you did it. When it got bad that's what you had to do: keep looking straight into it, as if the dedication of your eyes, like the touch of a lover, could change everything.

His father's twelfth, and last, suicide attempt had been a shot in the mouth with a .45 pistol. In his office. He'd told Rubens this, described the afternoon, his wedding afternoon, told him of how he'd sat in the Morris chair in his father's office one last time, waiting for him to speak; hoping, as always, for the rough dust of silence to dissolve. It hadn't.

He left no note.

You could go right on to the end making the mistake that would kill you, he said. Even after you knew it would, even after you could see it sitting in front of you like a fatal guest, and everyone else could see it, and those closest commented on it, and shook you, and shook their fingers at you, and abandoned you finally and moved away and even forgot you, even then, you could go on making your ruinous mistake.

What was it could make you stop?

As the light came down like snow through the high prison windows, to Rubens, perched on his orange chair, leaning forward, writing without looking at his pad, he said he robbed because it was erotic, because he was good at it, because he loved crime, because he'd learned early that common life wouldn't work, because he hated his mother, because he wanted to live fast, because he feared boredom, because he couldn't resist a bargain, because he was an addict, because he had no relation to a God, because he loved Clare and wanted to please her. He said, Do you know the story of the thief on the cross? Yes, Rubens said. It's the thief *of* the cross, Jack said. He stole heaven.

(The light falling from the high windows was like a yellow plane descending, he said.)

At Lafay's nightclub and motel they got rooms eventually, but they did not go to the rooms. They drank on into the night and into the gray motley dawn. Jack removed himself, went out onto the screened porch and sat thinking about his life. It came up to him like the cottony mist rising on the bayou. He thought of his brothers, of Sam, who in a rage took a pistol to his Army induction, threatened the sergeant with it, and was taken off the bus by MPs and put in jail. They inducted him from jail and put him in the stockade and then sent him to basic training, where he proved to be a deadly, resolute soldier, a force, who was shipped out to Compton in California and then to Vietnam, where he distinguished himself quickly. He led a recon team that worked along the Cambodian border and he was one of the Americans who tore pieces from the bodies of dead Vietnamese soldiers and wore them as trophies. He took scalps and teeth and ears and fingernails (and odd bits of flesh that curled up like fried pork rinds, he said). He was killed by a rock ape. Jack had met a man who said he knew about this. His squad had bivouacked near some stone outcroppings where the apes lived, and the apes had set up a racket during the night that infuriated several of the soldiers, especially his brother *(Mother screaming at one more suicide attempt, one more bloody passage scrawled on the bedroom floor . . .)*, who had taken it on himself to put a stop to the noise and ruckus. He'd climbed up into the rocks with his rifle and a night scope to kill as many of the primates as he could, but he'd gotten lost up there, so the man said *(as a man could anywhere)*, and gotten caught in some kind of cul-de-sac with apes in it, no way out, maybe like a cave, some black hellish place—the man swore this was true—and the apes had somehow, they figured, tumbled out panicked past Sam, rushing onto him despite the weapons, despite even the grenades, he apparently got free, but was unable to get unpinned, and they killed him. The apes ripped his body apart. Afterward, the men went into a frenzy of killing, went after the apes, but they were gone, vanished. It spooked everyone, the man said.

They shipped the body back zipped up in plastic, shipped it to Duluth. Jack's father had gone to the funeral parlor *(where he window-shopped)* and he and the director, who was his good friend from high school *(former suitor of his own wife, he said, who when they were boys he'd fought to near death at the edge of the lake one summer afternoon when the clouds were white pictures in the sky and you could smell the iron ore that stank like dried blood—thinking of his own death)*, had picked pieces of the body out of the big stainless steel sink where they set the parts, and tried to match Sam with himself on the embalming table, but all the parts weren't there. They had given up when they realized this, and saw, too, how battered he was. His father had showered at the funeral parlor before he came home, but Jack remembered how when he hugged him at breakfast he smelled of rot and Jack knew this was the terrible odor of his brother's body.

And then Gurney Baker, his next and last older brother, a brown-eyed taciturn man, a sailor on the USS *Hornet*, had stepped out of a pedicab on Chartres Street in Saigon into the path of a truck delivering Thanksgiving turkeys to the hospital in Fu Chow and been smashed dead to the pavement. It was ignominious and even silly, but the Army said it was the death of a hero; his commanding officer said this in a letter his mother read aloud, laughing sarcastically as she read it, making exaggerated, wet lip motions. His father had sat without speaking in his big orange chair in the living room and stared at his wife as if she was some madwoman he'd never seen before. His mother began kissing the letter and screaming that it was all his father's fault. "There are no men," she cried. "Now there are no men."

His father had sat in the chair as if he was tied to it. As if he was tied to it, Jack thought, and dropped over the side of a boat into the deep sea, where he rested on the bottom looking out across the vast salt wastes at nothing in particular, slather on his lips.

He could bring tears to his eyes sometimes about all this, and sometimes his brothers came to him, like sad tourists in loud shirts, and now he let them come again, softly, meekly, as whipped men in prison came up to him bearing gifts of tinfoil and cigarettes; it was the first time in years. *(There was no place in prison far enough away for crying, he said. The whip stroke reached you no matter how deeply you dug. Sometimes a dream might take you around a corner, down through some blasted orchard of pain into a cave where no man had set foot for ten thousand years, cover you with a blanket and leave you, but, even there, there were spiders that might sting an unwary man.)* He sat with his chin in his hands, thin sparks of license going off inside him, looking out through the screen at the weedy bayou, where on the far side a mist had come up like a banal conclusion and above it the last stars faded into the graying sky, and he let himself cry. The tears were small, acidic, and squeezed out. Even his pain felt forced. The brothers were catalysts only, as was anything from family *(he remembered the boy now, he said, saw him suddenly, remembered the path he would have had to come down . . . forgot him immediately)*, the past years useless, he thought, and the present, too, not a substance, but only a medium like air, no configuration, no marshaling of time in blocks of memory or reconstituted occurrence of any importance—he felt as if he were dying, what he called dying, something in him that whirred and gathered, seizing up. Now he recalled watching

Morty turn out a guy in the tool shop, watching him beat the guy with a wrench until the guy's resistance collapsed and he crouched under heavy blows whimpering and begging. He'd seen this a hundred times, a thousand times, and after the first few you let the emotion *(the deep, penetrating sorrow)*, the exhilaration *(and delight)*, slide into corners behind an impassive face, but this time, as he watched the fat muscles in Morty's back go taut as he bent over the con, he thought for one instant that his pal was hitting the guy with a red tulip, banging him with the bright red crown of a spring flower. It was only the punk's blood staining the head of the wrench. In a second it was over and life rolled on anonymously, there was a beaten unconscious man somehow left in a heap in the corner, but in his sleep that night, or at the slippery edge of it *(near the spider cave, he said)*, Jack saw the red tulip waving above the man's head, and the flower seemed to him to be the flower of some kind of revelation, an offering of some kind, like the embraided bleeding heart of Jesus in the Catholic pictures. He was astounded and grateful. Delighted. But what amazed him, and broke his heart—if there was such in him—was not that he had seen this, but that afterward, after the look and the thought and the dream disclosure and the momentary delight, the anticipation, nothing happened. Nothing at all. The picture, the thought, the visitation, faded. He was remembering it for the first time in a year. He hadn't said anything about it, even to Morty, and now it came back to him in secret, as if out of another life (*as if out of someone else's life*), one he'd forgotten about, the red flower descending in violent benediction on the man's head.

Then Clare came out, followed by Will, and then Will went back inside, where he made night arrangements with the sleepy bar hooker and took her to his room.

"What happened to Will's wife?" Jack said.

"He hurt her too bad for her to want to follow him."

"What about James?"

She looked at him funny. "James is dead."

"And you don't feel like revenging yourself on Will?"

"Sometimes, but love stays my hand."

"For how long?"

"Long enough for us to get out of here."

There was the rattle of a boat chain down at the dock—fishermen setting out. He got up and they walked outside and stood on the damp steps looking at the bayou. The air was still, moist, and smelled of fish. He said, "Is Will one of the reasons for moving on?"

"I can't tell for sure. He says he's grateful you're not going to kill him. He'd hiding something, but I'm not sure what it is. And we have to get the money. I'm compelled."

"You had it right the first time. He's planning to kill me."

"Is that what I said?"

"Yes."

It seemed to him he had come to the truth of it. He felt calm, relieved. It did not bother him.

"It makes me sad," she said.

"Because your brother is so twisted?"

"No. Because I won't get to see him. We'll have to quarantine him from now on, at least for a while. If he's going to kill you, he can't come around."

"I want to go to Mamiel's grave."

"I haven't thought of Mamiel in a long time."

"Me neither, but he's buried out here. I remembered. His family has a plot outside Corliss."

Mamiel had been with them early on, three or four jobs at the beginning. They were young, excitable. He'd gotten shot as he hung out the back window taunting cops on a getaway in Iowa. Jack had dragged his body back into the car. There was a small oozing hole in his temple; he was limp, as if he'd passed out. They'd gone without a partner then, until Robert Joleen, and after Robert, no one.

Out on the river north of Anacondia, near the town of Poolerville, as they sat on a bench watching men scrape the bristles off half a dozen slaughtered hogs, an old man said: It was so rough in this country in the beginning that the only crime they hung you for was stealing a horse. You could commit murder, you could burn barns or even rape a woman, but if you stole a man's horse, you stole his life. He couldn't make it without a horse. But even before that, before there were roads at all, and before anybody put in the first crop, every law applied. The Indians built towns. They farmed, they had cities even, streets, councils, members who took care of sanitation and distribution of produce. Everyone had a place. There were very strict laws. We were the ones who put an end to all that. We came in and struck the Indians down and we struck down their laws. We had to start from scratch. I think that's what we loved. There were people who loved standing in the middle of a wilderness where you had to make up everything. And I suppose, he said, looking at Jack, there were men who could survive only if they kept the law back behind them a ways. They lived in that space between the crime and the punishment. Out here once it must have seemed like that space was as big as the continent.

They were out early, riding in the hooker's car. Will went to sleep again in the backseat. They parked under a large live oak from which rain dripped from mops of Spanish moss, crossed the small cemetery to the grave. It was under a lime tree in a little alcovelike place among large rose bushes. There were buds like red knots in the bushes. Clare said it touched her that the roses probably had been there since before any of them were born, and Jack said there were many things around in that category, including most of the graves and all the trees and the road, more items older than younger. Clare got angry and they began to argue in frustration and then she walked off by herself to the other side of the graveyard and sat on a large loaf-shaped stone in the misty rain.

In her dark clothes, humped up inside herself on the stone, she looked like a funerary monument, Jack thought, like a monument they'd seen in Illinois the night they tumbled off the train with Mamiel and walked in the rain through a large cemetery. There'd been a woman, a stone angel, crouched over a grave, a child's grave. The figure's face was hooded, but as they passed it had seemed to Jack that the dark eyes looked out at them with a lively interest. Clare was tougher, though, than any angel; she didn't look.

Then Will eased up behind Jack, saying nothing, and Jack had the hollow sensation of a suddenly opening space between himself and what was behind him, of a space that was about to be violently filled, but when he turned around Will was looking up at the sky.

"They can't bury me in consecrated ground," he said, rubbing his wrists. The hooker, whose name was Betsy, waited in the car.

"That only applies to Catholics," Jack said.

"No. It's an understanding I have now. It doesn't have anything to do with religion. It's deeper than religion, deeper than fucking churches. I'm a brother killer. There's nobody like me but me, and I know it. I'm separated. Forever I will be separated."

"Fratricide Anonymous—that's what you need."

"Don't joke."

"I'm sorry."

"Thing is, I'd do it again. I know that about myself. I know a lot about myself. I've had time to think. I took a train to New Orleans. Caught it in Jacksonville. I thought on the train. James and me always hated each other. It started with James, not with me. I used to come out to the farm, go through the damn woods and spy on him, but that was out of love, not hate. When I was a little boy I did that. Hid in the sassafras bushes. I'd come home smelling like an herb. James hated that I was his half brother. He was greedy, he didn't want to share. He was a one-note wonder: anything you had he wanted. With me it was life: he wanted my life. You ever want something bad?"

"All the time."

"I guess so. Out of prison, for one thing, huh? Clare. Yeah. I wanted to be next to my brother. My mother hated me, too. She blamed me for my daddy not having anything to do with her. She was probably right. This where your friend got buried?"

"Guy we ran with a few years ago."

"Back at the beginning. When everything looked like a promise. Sure. I know. I'm the optimistic type. You ran with Donnie, too, didn't you?"

"I knew Donnie up in Joliet. And later down here for a while. It was a long time ago."

"Yeah—Donnie. He's an evil one. He likes to come up under the belly. He's smart, though. He knows how to make the business work. Clare broke you out, didn't she?"

"If I say yes, then you're an accomplice."

"You don't have to. I understand. Look at this place. I hate cemeteries. It's where the ghouls are. Creepy with all that wet moss and the way the ground just turns into water. You ever see those quicksand movies?"

"Sure."

"They used to be the scariest movies to me. Somebody walking along and then *oh no:* quicksand. Sinking, nobody around, the guy stretching his arms out trying to grab a branch or something, but the sand shifting and pulling on him like a mouth drawing him in until he was down in there and you couldn't see nothing but a head, and then one last cry and nothing but a hand stuck up. *God.* That terrified me. All these swampy places are like that to me. Can we go soon?"

"Yes."

"James—the whole situation: it was like that. Quicksand, pulling me down. Ethel. She was part of it, too. She liked convertible sofas. And sweet corn. And restaurants up on the top of tall buildings. And about one thousand other things."

"Don't," Jack said.

"Don't what?"

"Give me the explanation."

"About James? About down in Florida?"

"That's right. I don't want to hear it."

"Why not?"

"It's the same explanation every time. It's the one we all make about everything being inevitable. I don't want to hear it."

Clare had left her stone, a contrary angel come to life, swinging a sprig of some fall flower against her leg, looking up into the trees as she walked toward them, dreaming, he figured, of impossible possibilities.

"That doesn't leave much."

"No," Jack said. A flight of pelicans made a brief necklace above the distant trees and broke apart, the beads scattering toward the surface of the narrow bay. Everything now: the row of gravestones, the waxy leaves of a camphor tree, grass stalks, the taste of brine in the air, a sparkle on the water where a mullet jumped—everything swelled with power, with immanence. It was this way after prison, objects stood out, paint glistened, each face was fully formed, bold, packed with life, life surged in sweat and touch, in a glance. There were moments now—always like this after prison—when a look might knock him down. Walking in the subdivision after she'd gone to rob, he'd realized this, tucked himself under a tree out of the way, shielded his eyes; had to stick to the dark.

He turned. Will had put a pistol on him.

"We could work on explaining *this,*" his brother-in-law said.

"Why not?"

"This is my plan to straighten my life out. This will set things right between me and the family, Indiana part at least."

"Are you sure?"

Jack felt a sudden intense sensation of loneliness. It flickered along his skin like a sunbeam and went out. The tops of the cypress trees were orange. The bayou shone like a glossy black pelt. There was nothing out there that had anything to do with him.

"It won't work," he said.

"It'll work better than what I got now," Will said.

"That's the mistake we all make."

"Money and love aren't mistakes."

"Neither of those are here."

"This is the means for them."

"Ah, fuck."

"Yeah, it's bad, isn't it?"

"I promised not to kill you."

Will laughed soundlessly. "I'm glad of that."

Will's face was red and his eyes had a blistery, bulging look, as if they were swollen with fluid, and his small mouth was wet from his tongue, which darted out like a tiny agitated animal, touching the lips. Jack wanted to pick him up and throw him in the bayou, but there was no way to do that at this moment. He wished he hadn't spent time thinking about his brothers. Memory now was like a boat prop churning through weeds: things came up. The past made him angry *(not all of it, he said: there was the other, this* boy *among the trees—he couldn't remember now)* and, beyond the anger, he could see *(it was the same for everyone)*, there was only forgiveness and release *(everyone knew this)*, a version of peace, and death—

"Will," he said, "this is another unredeemable act you are perpetrating, and I hate to see it."

"You won't have to look at it long, Jack."

"I never liked James much, but he was right about you. You are a freak of nature and an ugly one. You never had a minute's love for anybody and we all know it."

"You shut up."

"It's the truth, you snake. You're a skinny side-slipper, a fool."

"Jack!" It was Clare's voice. She stepped from behind the largest rose bush. She had a pistol in her hand and it was pointed at Will. "Don't berate him," she said.

Will snatched a look at her. "I got to shoot him," he said.

"No, Will, you don't," Clare said. Her voice was very firm. "You might think you have to shoot Jack, but you don't. If you do I will shoot you and nothing will come out good with Daddy. Do you see?"

"No."

"Well, *think* about it."

Off in the car, in the crybaby blue car that belonged to another world entirely, the woman Betsy was paying no attention at all. No, Jack thought, not to another world, but to this world, which was going about its business. Will's gun was the color of aluminum *(the color of shark backs, he said, of train sheds, lathes, coiled fence wire dumped from the back of pickup trucks on early-morning runs out to the edge of prison lands, of the interior walls of Turandot prison itself, of certain thoughts, sweat-beaded, of muddy puddles on a trail in Minnesota, of somebody's eyes of rain, of shivs and spikes, of dead promises, of dreams going bad like meat in buckets, of the skin of a corpse come upon in the woods after three days of rain—)* and Will was coldly livid, tensed, reduced for one second to purity, a clean fit in the socket of destruction *(a hero, he said)*, capable, redeemed.

"Just put the pistol down," Clare said.

"All right."

Her brother lowered the gun, raised it again, and then let it fall from his hand. Jack sprang at him, punched him hard in the face. Will went down cringing and grabbed for the gun, which had bounced against the side of Mamiel's gravestone. The stone had the words JESUS WEPT engraved on it above the dates. Jack kicked the gun out of reach, took Will by the collar and spun him around. Will cowered and pulled to the side, scrambling against the edge of the stone, pushing with his legs in the slick grass. Jack backhanded him across the eyes.

"Oh, Christ," Will said.

Jack dragged the man by the collar away from the grave. He pulled him to his feet and jig-walked him down the road. Clare called his name as she came along behind, running to keep up. "You can't do anything to him," she cried, but Jack paid no attention to her. The sky was thick and dense with overcast, a soupy, pudding sky congealed out of some awful set of circumstances they were all having to pay for. His brother-in-law was crying, whimpering. "Keep it up," Jack said.

He came to an open grave. The grave had a little fringe of plastic turf around it. Jack flung Will into the hole. "Stay down there," he cried when Will immediately began to crawl out. "Put the pistol on him," he said to Clare.

"There's water down here," Will said.

"Fuck, I want a shovel," Jack cried.

"Don't kill him," Clare said.

Jack screamed.

Will raised his wet face, raised his hands, which were streaked with white bayou clay. "Please, Jack," he said. "Please."

Jack kicked him in the head. Will fell against the side of the grave, slumped down into it, into the silvery water at the bottom. Jack turned away and did not say anything to Clare when she jumped into the grave after her brother. He stepped away looking for a spade, a board, some tool he could use to bury this. But there was none. He pulled his wife out a few minutes later when she asked him to.

"He's knocked out," she said. "I got his head out of the water."

"I didn't kill him."

"No, you didn't."

"Come over here," he said. "Follow after me."

She followed him to a spigot next to a small oleander bush. There were soft pink messy flowers on the bush. He twirled the handle and washed her face, washed her arms and hands, knelt in front of her and washed the milky clay off her feet and legs. As he bent to cleanse her ankle, sliding his hand down the long arch of her delicate foot, she leaned against him, pressing down with her hand on his shoulder. The weight of her body lightly centered in her hand, poised on his shoulder, felt like the goodly, firm connective weight of life itself. He rode, for an instant, the seam between heaven and earth. For once, in a moment like this, in this moment, the world meant something. As it did in a bank, or in a car fleeing the cops. For once, there was meaning and purpose and you could follow the line of things like a seam in a floor right to the treasure. She was pushing him along that seam. She pushed him into it and pushed him along and he was moving and getting somewhere and there was a reason for all this.

He bent down and kissed her feet.

• • •

In Anacondia she brought a cup of tea to him as he lay in the garden. While the teenage girl next door watched through the fence, they made love, washing themselves first with fingers dipped in the warm tea. (There were times when the house of their lives fell in on them, when the disaster, the blank wall, the rigid oppressed empire of it, gave way and fell. They couldn't get enough of each other then.) She brought a cup of tea and they made love in the dirt. They let the girl see everything, contorted themselves so she could. On the radio beside them in the row, under the potato plants, a troupe of players acted scenes from Richard III. *As he drove his cock into her, they could hear Richard seducing his dead brother's wife, showing her the murderous truth even as he placed his gleaming ambition into her, as he shoved his power along her flesh, lifting her on the spike of his plan until she screamed with pleasure. Like Richard wooing, they let the girl see everything.*

Back at the motel where Betsy dropped them off, they found Rubens waiting for them. He was wearing the false face of happiness, an anxious delight. He capered in front of them oddly.

"You pulled one on me there, Jack," he wheezed. "It doesn't bother me because I know it was part of the procedure, part of the method of Jack Baker. It was a strong ruse. I fell for it. They told me at Carmine's you were out here. Or I found you by looking. Whichever. I've been wandering all night. I couldn't get into your room."

"What are you talking about?" Jack said.

They were getting gas out at the pump in front of the motel. The drizzly day had begun to turn fair. A fresh breeze snuffled moss in the live oaks at the edge of the bayou.

"I mean there were cops in the hall. And they were in your room, too, Jack. Somebody set them on you."

"Donnie," Jack said to Clare.

"I like your car," Clare said to Rubens.

"Thank you, Clare. I decided to bring it back in case you two wanted to go somewhere else. I was afraid you might be stranded out here. I'll take you wherever you want to go."

"You are a nice man."

"I've been trying to tell both of you—I can hardly say it—you don't know what it means—you and Jack—I've been waiting for this—I was bereft when you escaped—I've followed *everything,* I know the crimes—I can't say what it does—it's like a light—what it does to me to see you in the flesh."

"We're enjoying it, too."

"I know I'm being an idiot. I get carried away, I start thinking about how I look, what I've got to say, I'm worried—but I'll calm down. I haven't had any sleep. I thought I'd lost you. What do you think, Jack? What is it with the cops?"

"It could have been anybody," Jack said, looking at Clare. "By now. Some guy at the Royale. A stranger, or someone we robbed. Some child maybe I looked suspicious to."

"You look suspicious to every child." She smiled. "I'm sure it was Donnie."

"Don't humor me."

"Who else could it be?"

"It could be the idiot in the grave hole for one, if you mean who among those we know. That's just a start. This guy maybe. Or Delia over at Lafay's, or maybe Mamiel's come out of the grave and made a call. Shit, how can we know?"

There was an eerie soft feeling in his chest, a hollow something just pushed into. He wanted to lie down.

"Are you tired?" Clare said.

"Yes."

"You look as if you might collapse."

"Do you remember in Nebraska on the way to the fire how I was talking about seeing faces?"

"No, darling."

"I was talking about it."

"I was too busy holding off the cops."

"You mostly did that well."

"Not entirely."

"It was then—I saw this other face. I had seen it before, but it came back."

"That happens sometimes."

"To you?"

"Sure. To everybody."

"I thought I was the only one."

"No. You shouldn't worry about it. I used to see my mother all the time. Sometimes I still do. She even jumps out at me."

"Like out of a closet?"

"Out of the bathtub."

"This was *me* I saw. The one I saw looking at me from the woods."

"I like that. You shouldn't be troubled at all."

"It wouldn't trouble you to see yourself looking around a tree at you?"

"No. I'm at home with me."

"*Two* yous?"

"Why not? I like company."

"We have too much *company* already."

"Don't be bitter about it. We only have it until we show them the door."

"Hey, Rubens," he said, "you got money?"

"Sure."

"Then go in and pay."

When the man went inside they got in the car and drove off. In the rearview mirror Jack watched him run out of the station. Rubens ran a little ways, stumbling on his heels, and stopped. He stepped out onto the road and looked after them. He didn't do anything, didn't shake his fist, or wave. He wrapped his arms around himself, that was all. And he looked after them. As long as Jack could see the man, he was gazing up the road at them vanishing.

4

They drifted north, following the river, a halt and infirm progress, delaying in this way and that, obscuring their trail, dallying, stepping often from the car to stretch, to consult the trees and certain aspects of prophecy they believed in; they joked with each other and slept late, coming down for lunch in river hotels where the managers were glad for the business. This was an old pattern, a way of life persisted in, reveled in, but passing now, like life in the small towns, speed obscuring all things, revolution in thought, stupor, careless dispositions crept into the pantries and the beds of family members, phantasmagorems biting children and giving them disease, changing their minds, causing forgetfulness and a feeling of futility like an odd wasting fever to take over—a pattern become almost instinct, sustaining; depleted now. Everything had changed.

There was a destination tacked onto consciousness, but they didn't consult maps.

They robbed, sticking a crooked hand out of the dark into rural stores, into shops on bleak main streets, even into booths where apples and the root vegetables of autumn were sold to travelers. There was a sourness often about them now, and a dinginess in their thoughts. They tried to eliminate this, finally, by action, by movement, by talking out loud to each other, by reciting difficult moments in their pasts, but it wouldn't go away. They often slept in separate beds and sometimes they waked up as strangers. *I don't enjoy your face being foreign to me,* she told him; he said it was the same for him. But they began to accept the strangeness of it after eighteen years together, accept that this might come upon them now, like a disease of some kind, and they began to wonder about it, to construct figments and scenarios in which amnesia, sudden mental absence, blanks and unexplained disappearances played a part, but they did not speak of the real reason for their journey. They did not want a reason. Each felt somehow disfigured, misunderstood, because there was one, because there was a purpose beyond the aimless necessity of excitement and desire played out in the form of crime. They irritated each other; often it was difficult to talk; memories stung like bites of bitter fruit; jobs became difficult.

The days were warm. There were white butterflies in the cornfields. In the rich autumnal dusk, plain farmhouses took on aspects of beauty, and the yellow cornfields shone in the recumbent sunlight like the triumphant spoils of kings. The river was so wide it was blue sometimes, like the Great Lakes, and it kicked up waves on windy days like the lake of his childhood. There were fields, ruddy and stripped by combines, and bluffs the rocks in sheaves thrust from that made him think of Minnesota, but he was not entranced by these parallels, thought this was the reason it was so easy to mistake the natural world for a reflection or emblem of human life, some correspondence between the buildup of clouds this afternoon and the fall of cities, a river like God's army moving into desolate country, just the kind of fantasies losers and convicts were suckers for, nuts going around the bend of their sorry lives. He was from some other place; not here, not dreamland.

He spoke to her of this, but it was difficult for her to come to an understanding about it with him, because, as she said, everything was already like everything else. There were no real mysteries about that, she said. I've always known it. But there were some things she was unfamiliar with. They were things that hadn't happened yet.

In Eulalia, Tennessee, she shot a man. The man had talked back to her from behind a baitshop counter. He was a slender man with a fuzz of red chin beard, and when she shot him he ejected a wad of tobacco onto the floor. There was no one else in the store. Clare knelt over the man and looked at him. He was dead, the shot had hit him high in the chest and taken him straight out.

"No more sass from him," she said. She was crying.

"Come on, honey," Jack said from the door. He held the screen door open. Three glossy blue flies wobbled in.

"I want to look at this a minute."

"They don't do anything after you kill them."

"Do you think he thought I was paying him back?"

"No. I think he was just surprised."

"I wonder if something slides in at the last second—God or something."

"I've wondered about that myself. No one I've seen has mentioned it."

"I wonder if James did?"

"He could have."

"Did Will say anything to you about it?"

"No."

"He did to me. We sat on the edge of that barroom in Bayou Teche and he told me again about what he did to James. He's told me four times now, like it's his favorite thing. I hated him the first time. But I let him tell me. He explained the procedure, the particulars. I still do not get it. I would have to have been there. Even if I was, though, I would have had to have been James to get it. Maybe even then it would have escaped me. We recognize things, but does that make us connected? Do you get what I mean?"

"Maybe."

"I mean just because I see I'm like you, does that mean I am connected to you?"

"Let's go."

"With you I'm not afraid to think my worst thoughts."

"I understand you."

"That's become unusual."

"Hasn't it?"

They left.

She was close to the edge of something, a fit or a fight, maybe even something worse than shooting a clerk, something that would bring an age of suffering, some explosion that would bring a ridiculous and awful mayhem, a town burned up, a water works poisoned, confusion overtaking half the downstate population, but he didn't think there was anything he could do about it. She bounced and agitated, snapping, popping her fist against the sides of things. This continued until she began telephoning her father. Jack would listen from the car as from some country phone booth she berated the old man, calling him names, swearing to him that she was going to make him pay.

"This craziness is your sick cat come home," she screamed. "You've ruined everything, you pathetic weasel, you glass-eyed trembly fuck. You're responsible, you are the one, Mr. Gospel singer and big-time contributor. I will make you pay, Papa. What do you mean setting brother against brother? What were you thinking? How could you dare interfere—*now*—in my marriage? Did you set Will up to shoot Jack? My husband? I am going to kill you in your sleep. You *better* not sleep. I will be the one come in the night, Papa. It breaks my heart. How could you do this? Did you think I would come back? Do you think Jack *took* me away? That's so insulting. I couldn't go on my own, I needed Jack? Well, Papa. We left Will in a hole in Louisiana. It was only because of me Jack didn't kill him. But if he does get killed, it will be one more death at your door. Just like James's death is your fault. . . ."

On and on it went. For days she kept it up, stopping at way stations like a pony express rider to deliver her bitter mail. At first Manigault tried to talk to her. He tried to soothe her, she said, offered her gifts. Then he threatened. He said Will was after them. And others. Posses. Packs of men. Dogfighters, killers, farmers with shotguns. The law. Donnie Bee maybe. Even now, he said—he's so cold, Clare said—they were closing in. Watch for them, he said, rolling around the corner—

But she was not diverted. She lacerated him, scalded him with words. The phone booths rocked on their concrete platforms. Beside fields dusty from harvesting, under blue skies, by the big river that spread away like a lake, she shouted her liturgy of revenge. After a while the old man left the phone off the hook. She would return to the car with a stunned, outraged look in her eyes. She'd sit with her feet out on the ground, bent over her knees, staring.

"I don't want to look at myself as a psychopath," she said to him finally. "Do you think I am one?"

"Maybe not, but you do push up close against it."

"You and my family were always what prevented me from being one, I thought."

"Because you cared about us."

"Yes. And because I respond to your feelings. It *does* break my heart. What did you tell Rubens? Did you tell Rubens about this? Is that his name? Did you say it is a life where mismatched pieces get shoved one against another and made to fit? A *gun* goes into a *face*—did you mention that? Strangers come in and take your most precious possession. We criminals get terrified if we can't take some stolen item into our hands. We yearn for things we have never heard of. Doesn't Papa know that he is just like us? That we are like him? What did you say to Rubens?"

"I said that."

"What?"

"I said we know the beauty of juxtaposition. We experience high contrast. One object that seems totally unlike another set beside its seeming opposite—and suddenly you realize they are the same."

"Yeah."

"I told him. I said one minute the man is alive and the next he is dead. I said your best friend goes around the corner and comes back your enemy. A thief can go into Marshall Fields in Chicago and buy a ten-thousand-dollar suit. I wash blood off my hands before I take into my arms the most beautiful woman I have ever seen. A fugitive stands on the edge of a lake looking out at a pure selection of beauty, at blue skies, clear water—all of it—and he is part of it, too, he comes all the way to it—it's impossible, but it's so. I told him."

"My love is like the deep blue sea."

"Yes."

She dropped then onto her knees in the dirt. The dusty ground was fragrant; it smelled of fresh hay, of grapes, he thought. There was a swag of fox grapes in the sycamore above their heads. They were at a roadside park. There were white concrete picnic tables under big mottled sycamores and oaks.

He got out, went around the car and bent over her. He didn't try to lift her up.

"Would you please stop me from going crazy?" she said.

"I will do my best."

"I can feel it, Jack. It's like a dream and like a pressure, like gas, both at once. It's like a memory taking me over, like I am coming to believe something I despise believing, like: children are bad—something, some voice talking to me that won't shut up until I give in, except it's not a voice at all, it's a sickness seeping into me like bitter memories come back, some experience that reappears like the time I slapped an innocent little boy, and it turns you."

"It's all right."

"It's not. It's frightening. Can you stop it?"

"Of course I can."

"Good. Please do it, then."

He knelt and took her in his arms, feeling all through him his inadequacy and his confusion. There was nothing he could do. Faithless, bedeviled posturers, betrayers, jackrabbits, terrified, bold, fascinated, confidential souls, they held each other tightly as he patted her and let her moan and weep. After a while she calmed down.

She rubbed her face against his, sighed. "There's no excuse for us, is there?"

He laughed. "No."

"And there's no way to fix this, either?"

"No, there isn't."

"Shoot."

"Maybe I could *entrance* you in some way."

"We've had a little of this trouble before."

"Once or twice."

"We live through it, don't we," she said, almost hopefully.

"We keep going."

"Are you tired?"

"Yes I am."

"Then let's go."

"All right."

(It brings things together, he said, you never thought would be together. A spring morning and bloody death. The sadness in the eyes of some punk just like the sadness in your mother's eyes. In prison, I knew, nights I knew, I could tear her apart. And I knew I would leap through a fire to save her. On my worst day as a child a boy appeared to me and smiled at me. He came along the forest path and looked out at me swinging in a boat in Lake Superior. My sister said she saw a rainbow arched opposite the moon. I watched a man kill another man with a flower. . . .)

In Osco, Arkansas, she bought a hat, a white straw Panama with a blue batik band, and then they drove out of town, north, into a swampy country near the river where there was a farm that had cockfights. The farm was on the chicken circuit, one of the stops for gamblers and loose characters traveling the southern tier. There were farms all over the southeast and as far west as San Antonio where you could put money on a rooster, and there were men who spent their whole lives climbing up and down the ladder of a chicken wager. In some places the cops were rough and you had to get someone to tell you each week where *she memorized songs from the radio, the names of all the flowers in the garden, the streets, the companies represented by various businesses around town, makes and models of automobiles, the names printed on the sides of boxcars passing in long clacking trains, children's names, the names of towns they had passed through, the instructions for assembling a pool table, two hundred Spanish phrases, recipes, gemstones (precious and semiprecious), the names of the families on their side of town, the names of all the river towns between Anacondia and Vandalia, the high-school fight song, and forty-three secrets told to her in confidence (in grocery stores, riding in cars, after work in cautious asides, over the telephone, down on knees in the garden spading in tomato plants, once in the bathroom as she wiped tears from her face) by neighbors and "friends," by Anacondia citizens enthralled by her vivacity, her enthusiasm, the ability to become suddenly gentle and* the fights were being held, but in others the cops were bought off, and in a few they ran the action. The Osco game, run by an old tobacco farmer named Willis, was one of the quieter fights; if the cops knew, they didn't bother with it. Part of it was that Willis was a mean man, and the other was the county was one of those empty places where it was too much trouble to roust folks who might shoot you as you were doing it. Nobody out that way wanted to get shot over a chicken. And the federals were busy with river traffic and white liquor.

The farm backed up on a wide, swampy creek that let out a couple of miles down onto the river itself; the run into it was along a dirt road that cut through a hickory and oak wood. The hickory leaves had turned a speckled yellow that made them look as if they had disease, but the oaks were still green mostly, only a few of the red oaks having turned the deep maroon that would go quickly to brown. The entrance to the farm, where a busted metal gate was pulled loose and laid on its side, was manned by an old fellow who sat at a picnic table under a beach umbrella. On the table in front of him he had a double-barreled shotgun and a telephone.

"Hey there, Ozee," Jack said.

The old man squinted at him. "Jack Baker. You been a long time gone. When'd you get out?"

"Few weeks ago. You still running the fights?"

"Sure am. This is the last one of the season. That Clare? How you doing, Clare?"

She leaned across Jack. "I'm fine, Ozee. You sure look handsome."

"Thank you, Missy. I keep myself up."

"Tell Willis we're looking forward to seeing him."

"I sure will, Jack."

The house was a mile on, a ramshackle gabled place weather had worn the white paint off of. Willis met them in the yard.

"Jack, Jack," he said, striding up to the car with both hands held out as if he was carrying something, "I'm so glad to see you."

"He isn't glad at all," Clare said.

Jack smiled at her. "You'd think criminals would be better at pretending, wouldn't you?"

They got out, shook hands, and Willis conducted them around back and down a path through a small stand of pines to the barn where the fights were held. "It's awfully good to see you, Jack," he said. "How long you staying?"

"Just the afternoon."

"Well, you stay as long as you want to," Willis said, grimacing. He had a high domed forehead that wrinkles ran up into in little shutter waves. "We don't see you out this way enough anymore."

"I've been tied up."

"I heard about that."

"You hear about my release?"

"Maybe something. I don't know—what was it?"

"They put me on a plane and I was gone."

"You're a scamp, Jack."

There were thirty or forty people in the barn, standing around a waist-high board ring. Inside the ring, on the dirt, as a couple of Dominicans hovered, two roosters thrashed violently. There were shouts, a rich yodel off to the left, and someone was barking commands as if these were troops fighting, but mostly the men hung back in silence. Some kept their backs turned as if they were affronted by such as this; the distance was professional.

"What do you do with the dead roosters?" Jack said.

"We bury the champions," Willis said. "The rest of them the boys eat."

As they spoke one of the roosters went down under the heel blade of the other. The down rooster was a glossy green with a fat red head; the other, a yellow maverick with a bloody breast, trampled him, scuffing as a man might before angrily entering a house. There were cries off to the left. "Damn Henry," Willis said. Jack couldn't tell whether he was referring to the rooster or to someone else. The green couldn't get up, but it kept fighting from its back, striking with its taped yellow feet. The cry came again from off to the side and then a man in a black suit leapt into the ring. He had a pistol in his hand. He grabbed the yellow by a wing and snatched him off the green rooster. There were cries all around. The man swung the yellow around his head and then threw it on the ground. The rooster bounced and lay twitching, one wing slowly patting the earth. The man stepped on the rooster's head and then, as others leapt into the ring, he put the pistol hard into the bird's back and pulled the trigger. Blood spattered his sleeve. The men who'd jumped in fell back.

The man raised his head and looked around. "Fucking cheats," he said.

Then he wiped his pistol on his pants leg, took two quick strides and placed a foot on the rail to jump out. As he did so, another sport, a smaller man in jeans and a cowboy hat held by a chin string on the back of his head, struck him with his fist. The man in the black suit tumbled back into the ring. The cowboy jumped in after him and began beating him with his fists. The suited man either went out quick or he didn't want to fight back because he did nothing but lie there. He was out maybe, Jack thought, but he didn't look it. But then it seemed he was because when others stepped in and pulled the cowboy off he didn't move. Maybe there was a tiny new hole in him somewhere. A couple of men frisked him, one pocketed his pistol, and then they picked him up by the heels and shoulders and threw him over the ring wall. He fell in a heap against a tractor tire. No one came to get him.

"Well, that's fine," Willis said. "That's just fine."

He stepped into the ring and began to address the crowd, trying to calm everyone. He offered free drinks and money back on the fight. This didn't satisfy, in fact it raised the volume on the irritation, so Willis backed off and proposed the payoffs be made both ways. That suited everyone.

"It's a fucking disaster," he said as he returned to Jack.

"Always is, isn't it?"

"Make yourself at home, Jack—man, I don't know—it'll get better."

Clare slipped off, looking for a soft drink.

Someone called his name, a man in a dirty white shirt and a gold-and-black-speckled vest. It was Jimmy Acajou, a colleague from the old days when they ran cars out of Florida for the South American trade. Jimmy was a gambler now; he'd made his living on the circuit for years. Jack nodded and made his way over to him. Up among the rafters blue pigeons fluttered.

"Coodge," he said, "what are you doing this far north in October?"

"What are you doing anywhere in October?"

"Breathing deep."

"I heard about Clare cutting you loose. It's a good story."

"She did it all by herself."

"Clare's a remarkable woman."

"Where's Buster?" Buster was Jimmy's partner. They'd been together since before Florida. You didn't see one without the other.

"Buster got killed." Jimmy's mouth twisted as he said it and he turned away slightly.

"Damnation. I'm sorry. When was it?"

"Nineteen months next Thursday. A woman shot him in the back."

"The world's gone crazy."

"It wasn't the world's fault. It was his, and mine."

Jimmy sipped vodka from a water glass, his usual drink. He didn't really drink, but he sipped on it a little from time to time. When one of his cocks—he owned a share of several—began to falter, the Dominican handling the bird would bring it over to the rail and Jimmy would ruffle its feathers, thump it lightly on the breast, and spray a mouthful of vodka into its face. It was mainly ritual and didn't do much one way or the other, Jimmy said, toward straightening out the rooster. The fights were quick, sometimes only a matter of seconds as the cocks kicked at each other with razor knives taped to their heels. But you could win—and lose—a lot of money. Jimmy was good at wagering; he did it without passion, with the cold nerves that Jack had seen him unable to shake even when he touched a woman he loved, and he made a good living.

Now, with Buster gone, there was a fresh look in his eyes, a desperate, loitering look, some place showing where metal had snapped and he'd worn himself out licking the spot; he'd lost more than he could get back.

Usually *(this was a world, he said, in which no one was interested in anyone else. Not in a normal way, not in the way of communion and friendship, no harmony or hope. Everyone was separate. A competitor, at best a subcontractor. You might have breakfast with a man every day for ten years, he said, and then shoot him the next time you saw him, or he might shoot you. There was no relationship above betrayal, and everyone knew this.*

—A little like the monks.

—How so?

—So dedicated to God they exclude the human.

—It's something like that. It's because what you are after is so important—you can't let anyone stand in the way.

—Crime is love.

—I'm part of this world—

—Hemmed in now: in Tennessee, below Memphis there at the cockfights. Cops, family, ex-partners after you—

—Yes.

He'd come off the road bloody, he said. He longed to talk, longed for companionship. He would pay, that didn't matter, usually) he would have despised this, but now he did not.

"Let's talk about Buster," he said.

"You staying around?"

"If I do, Willis'll have the cops out here dancing with me. He's probably on the phone to them right now."

"You probably shouldn't have come, bro."

"We needed—" He stopped.

Jimmy wiped his forehead, licked his fingers. "All I do is talk to Buster inside my head." He laughed a soupy little laugh and glanced off into the world of sorrow. "He's no better a conversationalist now than he was alive."

"I'm sorry you got cheated out of him."

"I wish it was a cheat. I really do. But it wasn't; it was fair. It would be easier to take if it was a goddamn cheat."

"We'll talk about it."

The fight was over; the bookie had come around. He had bills stuck between the leaves of a notebook. He creased the book, counted out six hundreds, and handed them to Jimmy. Jimmy gave one of them back to him. "Thank you, Mr. Coodge," the bookie, a short, narrow man, said.

"I've got a boat down on the river," Jimmy said. "Why don't we all go down there after a little bit."

Jack said that would be fine. He looked around for Clare; didn't see her. There were others in the room he knew, men he had chanced on here and there, malfeasants and hoods, lowlifes with the muck of their failures in their faces, lost mama's boys and narcissists, gamblers with bad backs, screamers, drunks about to fall, whiners, a couple of wrung-out party girls teetering on the last step before oblivion. Over there was Shobeen McCay, the mother of Curt Blackshear, who had been cut in half by a shotgun by a bank guard in Memphis. The man tipping a beer into his fat mouth was A. J. Bullock, a gambler who had had one of his eyes poked out by a woman he beat up. Sassy Mink, a driver and mechanic who once worked with Jake Tillman out of Quad Cities, a hijacker and transporter of various contraband, argued a point of rooster performance with Acey Mock, one of the cutthroat ruffians who used to hang around Casio Molina, the bolita mogul in Terre Haute. Jess Bragg scratched his balls. Fortunato Berrien looked as if he was remembering his childhood in Constance, California, where, so he told Jack one drunken night, he had been tied by his best friend naked to a tree and shown off to high-school girls. Orlando Merced, known as the Cuban Gent, one of the circuit gamblers, traded bills with the bookie.

No one was going anywhere, no one was getting out. There were too many byroads, there was too much backed up in the mind and heart, nobody could find the door. They stood, these cons, in the torn-up rooms of their desolation, stinking of a hooker's cheap perfume, lighting cigars they stubbed out nervously into ashtrays filled with olive pits. They were nosy and frail, craving fame, clever but stupid men, unable to keep the orderly ways of world commerce in mind, fanatical, vengeful but often without means, serial explainers, rage-aholics, scorched liars, men who called their mothers bragging about adventures as if they were six-year-olds *(they squatted by riverbanks, he said, himself among them, distributing the meager spoils of a robbery in which men of five different ethnic origins, men whose roots went back three thousand years, had been left for dead, bodies scattered like abandoned soldiers along the road, and no one could think of anything to say, except for one clumsy joke no one laughed at that made Jack sick to his stomach and was a means by which he later began to teach himself that criminals, so he said, loved the absolute, loved what couldn't be turned by con or whisper. He craved this, he said, this negative dependability. I, too, he said, would give it all for a sure thing),* men who imitated life.

He wandered around for a while, speaking to this man and that. Each acknowledged him, most with respect, some jocularly, some with hatred in their eyes. *(The boy looked at me:* my *eyes, except completely innocent, without judgment or reproach.)* In a corner another fight broke out, but this time, Estelle Mims, Willis's big man, broke it up quickly. Estelle, who was called Buddy, broke the hand of the man who started it by cracking the hand against the side of a horse stall. "Now go home, Peanut," he said and the man, clutching his hand, staggered out.

Suck Jackson, a grifter and flimflam artist from Houston, came up to him. "I'm working on trade for Mexican bathtubs," he said, sucking in air between words. "I'm going to make a killing."

"One day you will."

"How've you been?"

"Run ragged lately, but right now just fine."

"Where's Clare?"

"I don't know. I was looking for her."

"You want me to go find her?"

"She'll turn up. Let's go outside and get some air."

Suck was a small man, almost a midget, but he carried himself with a big man's flair. He rolled when he walked, and he twitched his shoulders as if his muscles were agitated from throwing punches. He was not a shooter or a cutter, but he would take from you anything he could trick you out of. The little man strode out the door ahead of Jack turning a silver medallion between his thin fingers.

"That inside atmosphere'll give you a sick headache," he said out in the yard. He patted his domed chest, looking around. "There's Clare over there."

She was sitting in an Adirondack chair by the barn lot fence looking off through the pasture toward the road.

"She looks beautiful sitting in that chair," Suck said. "You've always been lucky, Jack."

"Extraordinarily so."

"Clare's something. She's not like the rest of us."

"So far she's been a lot tougher."

"You're right. I wouldn't want to get on her bad side."

The air smelled of walnuts and of the tawny, sun-baked field grass. Nothing ever changes, Jack thought—or what changes is too small to register against what stays the same. "Those men in there," Jack said. "You think any of them will ever do differently from how they are doing now?"

"Most of them'll be locked up sooner or later."

"That won't change them."

Berry bushes—raspberry bushes—grew in a tangle along the fence row. Unpicked dusty purple fruit hung among the leaves. Out in the field mullein and some bunched weedy bush were still flowering. Suck breathed deep. "I think those boys in there just got screwed up too high inside themselves," he said. "I've been thinking about it. Somebody asked me, I don't know who it was—yes, I do know, it was that writer, that one who wanted to know about you. . . ."

"Rubens?"

"Is that his name? Yeah, I think that was his name—he was down in New Orleans. . . ."

"When were you in New Orleans?"

"I been there. I was there until last week when I came up the river to Memphis. I was working on my Mexican deal. The guy said you stole his car from him. That's what he said. He was looking for you, but I don't believe it was to press charges. He'd been hanging around over at Donnie Bee's. Donnie's got a spell on him, I think."

"What kind of spell?"

"The kind where if Donnie barks he shits."

"Did you see this or are you relating gossip?"

"I don't gossip, Jack. A man like me can't afford to gossip. What if what I said wasn't true? I'm too little to defend myself."

"Only if they don't turn their backs on you."

"Don't defame me, Jack. It gives me a headache."

"Did you talk to this guy?"

"Only on the angle, Jack. He wasn't interested in Mexico."

"Did you see my brother-in-law?"

"Jack, I need to ease my pain here. It hurts me to talk this much."

"How much does it hurt you, Suck?"

"You know doctors, Jack. They charge extravagantly."

Clare was watching them. The white Panama made her look like a carefree woman. She called to them to come visit. He took Suck's arm and walked him toward her.

"You're going to be good, aren't you, Suck, and not say anything you shouldn't?"

"I can't be good, Jack, but I won't talk about you."

Clare leaned back in her chair stroking her fine white neck. Suck bowed to her, his eyes gleaming with appreciation. "Such a vision you are, Clare."

"Thank you, Suck. I have been taking care of myself."

"Any more care and they'll found a church in your name."

Clare smiled without showing her teeth. She stroked Jack's hand. "There are two policemen in a powder-blue car down there just past the driveway," she said. "I've been watching them. They look very dedicated."

"You know," Jack said, "I don't feel alienated from this culture or from this place or time. I love all of it. Don't they know that?"

"They have never really understood you, honey."

"Suck, aren't we the ones who love life so much we want to use up every part of it?"

"I like to make these deals, Jack."

"And you are a master, my friend. The next time we hook up I want you to tell me again about that truck exchange you worked out in California."

"The one with the Army?"

"Yes. That one. He traded one hundred trucks, Clare, for one hundred thousand dollars, and there were never any trucks."

"You're a wizard, Suck."

"Thank you."

Jack patted his shoulder. The bone under the cloth was sharp. This was all lying convict business. Specters addressed as if they lived. Crook deals that came to sorrow and gunplay in the dry beds of Western rivers.

"Suck has seen Rubens. And he saw Will."

Clare swung her legs around so she faced the little man. "Tell me," she said.

"He's at Donnie Bee's. Both of them are."

"Both who?"

"Your brother and that writer."

"I've forgotten the writer," she said to Jack. "Isn't that funny."

"Hilarious."

"My windpipe hurts," Suck said.

Jack scratched his palm. From her purse, more a sack on a string than a purse, Clare took a hundred-dollar bill, straightened it with her long fingers, and handed it to Suck Jackson. "Oh my, that is pretty," Suck said.

"What is up with Clare's brother?"

"The usual."

"What is that?"

"Agh—"

Clare's eyes blazed. "Don't you dare forget on me, Mumford Jackson."

"That's right," Jack said. "She'll rat you right back to rat land." He smiled. "Mumford?"

Suck grimaced. "He's talking about money, Clare. He said yall humiliated him, drove him crazy down on the bayou. Took his dignity from him."

"He tried to kill my husband."

"That's what he said you tried to do to him."

"What about the money?" Jack said. The car down at the bottom of the drive hadn't moved. No one had gotten out.

"He said his father would pay to have you killed. It's complicated."

"This kind of murder always is."

"Your father-in-law hates you, Jack?"

"I stole his daughter away from him, his wife supposedly died of it, he's getting old, and now his bastard son has murdered his legal son. He's wrecked. He's firing into the dark." *(As if the devil was a crook, he said, who'd cheated him; like my brother running into the dark in Vietnam, racing after ghost apes; any of us, he said, come to desperation, nothing left but to lay down a wall of fire. . . .)*

"He might have a bead on you."

Jack patted the small shoulder. "Would you go back in the barn and ask Coodge to step out here a minute?"

Suck said he would be glad to. He jogged off toward the barn.

Jack squatted beside Clare. He rubbed the side of his head where the fire had touched him. "I get these prickles and flares in the skin around my ear."

"Let me rub it."

She took his ear between her fingers and twisted it.

"Shit—ow."

He fell back on his heels, glared at her. Her face was stony.

"Don't say anymore that my mother died of my marrying you."

"We both know that's the story."

"She died of spit in her eyes, for all we know. She was too lonely to live, she was stupid and frail and a self-pitying woman who got beat in the game she played with my daddy. For all we know. She slipped on a patch of ice on the way to drown herself in the Ohio River, one winter's day, and had to go to bed, and started thinking—*for all we know*—and she thought about loss until she couldn't find one area without loss, and this frightened her first, and then it changed her into a little bird of passage without passage, *for all we know,* and she wasted and wept and died, going down cranked out on drugs with tubes stuck in her body. *For all we know.*"

"Whew," he said. "Whew—that's too much."

"It drives me crazy sometimes that I have to make up lives for these people, but I do and that's that and I can't change it. Now is as close as I can come to changing it, and all I can do is let myself be drawn—in a rage—into what is probably some stupid trap we will have to cut our way out of. What do you want Jimmy for?"

"He's got a boat."

"Ah." She gripped his hand. She was silent, then she said, "We agreed on this, didn't we?"

"Yes."

"Good."

One thing as well as another.

In places such as this, at the edge of a woodland, or standing over some ditch exhausted, coughing out the terror of some botched job, having fled through nighttime and hostile country where the police knew their faces and their crimes, they would come to this. Their lives were jumbled in a bag and had to be taken out from time to time and reassembled. It was harder and harder to do this, he thought. It had become impossible nearly. He thought this as he looked at her, at her face, which had become worn now, which was aging into gauntness and a fixed, bitter expression. What was once tenacity was becoming stubbornness, in both of them. Ingenuity had become hostility. Their fear had become anger.

Jimmy Acajou came up rubbing his stomach. He was a man who liked to touch himself. "What we got?" he said.

"You think you could take us upriver a few miles?"

"Sure. You want to go now?"

"Yeah. There's a couple of bad boys down there."

"Po-lice?"

"Yep. Or their outraged kin."

"Let me go cash out."

"We haven't got time, Coodge."

The gambler sighed. "Okay."

"Go ahead, Jimmy," Clare said. "We'll wait for you."

"Good." He swung his arm, pointing. "Go down there past the sheds into the woods. There's a road. Follow it to the river. The boat's there."

"We're going now," Clare said.

"I'll be right with you."

Jack followed Jimmy into the barn, crossed the lively space where men yelled at roosters, and went out a door on the other side. He made his way through the barnyard, behind the sheds into the woods. Clare was waiting. They walked through the woods toward the river. The hickory trees, gone yellow, were filled with nuts. Clare said the color of the leaves and the wind running through them made her think of young women in new yellow dresses. To her, she said, the life they had lived once had range, capacity, a lovely long arc between action and rest, between money taken at terrific risk and ocean sunsets observed from a chair in a bonny village on the Caribbean coast. She had grown up and learned her life, she said, she had gone among the animals, she had moved about the country, had hooked on with Jack believing she would never have to be just one person or just one set of choices, each day she would wake up someone different.

But I have been waking up the same person for a long time now, she said. Was this how it happened? she said.

He said he didn't know.

Where are we going now?

Upriver, he said. Just upriver.

Toward home, she said. But I don't want to go there. Not yet.

We talked of the money. Of your father.

I don't remember.

Yes, you do.

She was silent a moment, then she said, They'll kill us if we go there.

Energy and concentration had always saved them—if they could call themselves saved—and he did not live with a sense of opposition exactly.

We are criminals, he said. That means there are things we will cross all lines to get. The things aren't as important as the fact we can't prevent ourselves. This separates us.

Now it will get us killed, she said.

He looked around at the painted woods. The colors were fresh, just come upon. Even the leaves fallen to the ground had not faded yet. The road sank toward the river. "That's a hermit thrush," he said, lifting his head to the three silvery notes.

"You can walk out here and hear all kinds of business," she said. "It used to fascinate me, but I got over it."

"I know what you mean. There's a limit. Animals are more habit-bound than we are."

"Yeah. Some people like that. What I like is how straightforward animals are. I like the killer business they go in for. It's terrifying, better than a fright movie. You look at what animals do and it will scare you to death. Make you come alive."

"Don't talk so bloodthirsty. You sound like you're bragging."

"Okay. I'm sorry."

The road jagged through bushes and opened on the river. The wide water fell out in front of them. "It's beautiful," she said.

"Yes."

In another second they would shatter. Each would break into a thousand pieces and fall to the ground. Each piece would begin to scream, each would writhe and scream and burn on the ground, cracking into more pieces, shattering along invisible fault lines again and again, until there were millions of pieces, until the pieces broke to gravel, to crumbs, to dust, and the dust blew away screaming like a wind in the trees. . . .

He looked away, gasping.

The river was more than a mile wide. The surface varied, black and glossy near shore, and farther out a dark gray, nappy looking, like an old felt coat. Streaks of current rippled in the late-afternoon light. The boat was tied up among some alders. It was a wooden cabin cruiser, blue-hulled with a white deck and housing, a Gulf boat.

"Coodge must have come up from New Orleans," he said.

"Shobeen said Buster was killed."

"That's what Coodge told me. He's taking it hard."

"He ought to. He ought to tear his breast and wail and go down into dark depression and anguish and blame and horror and all the rest, and then he ought to get up out of his bed of grief and go forth and kill whoever did the death to his friend."

"Coodge said he deserved it."

"It happens so quick sometimes it looks like that."

You could look down inside me, he thought, and see for a mile.

He drew the boat along its bowline. The cabin cruiser came heavily, then lightly, smoothly into the grass at his feet.

He said, "Did you hear the owl this morning?"

"No."

"I did. It was early, just at first light. I got up and went out. There was fog in the fields, a mist. The world felt like it does when it's new, when you're new—as if anywhere you touch it you're going to leave an impression of yourself. I think this is an amazing feature of the world, that it comes up new again and again. It was like that even in prison . . . especially when we went out into the fields. I liked being a soybean farmer."

"Well, we'll put in a crop."

"But now we have to go."

"Yes, sweetie."

The bow was high, but he was able to pull himself up. He pulled her up after him. They had been watching the woods all the time, but there was no movement by the police. "I used to love the chase," he said.

"Me, too."

Jimmy came trotting down the road. He had their tote sacks under his arm.

"I was going to pull the car around into the woods," he said as he scrambled aboard, "but then I thought they might see it moving and come on, so I just grabbed these bags. You want them, don't you?"

"Sure. Thanks," Jack said. They always left everything behind, discarded it all, but he didn't need to explain that to Jimmy.

They stowed their bags in the cabin, a narrow space with four bunks, lockers in the walls, a table and stove, and a head in the bow. The place was neatly kept, like Jimmy, who was a fastidious man. The gambler poked his head in the door. "Which way?" he said.

"Upriver," Jack said.

He followed Jimmy up, went forward and retrieved the bowline. Jimmy started the engine and backed into the current. There was no human habitation, no human sign along the bank, just patches of willow and hardwood, a rough field fenced at the waterline, and more woods. No one was about, up or downstream. For a second Jack had a picture of the river as it had been before white men showed up, this quiet embankment rubbed by the passing of water, the ragged trees ganged together like weeds in a garden, over it all the blue-painted lid of the sky. You couldn't be lonely in such a world, he thought, because there was not another world to be lonely for.

He went aft, pulled out a folding chair near the rail, and sat down. Clare came up and sat beside him. She started to speak, but he raised his hand. "I want to watch this a minute," he said. The river looked like a long open tunnel behind them, a tunnel cracked open and laid out in the light. To the west was Arkansas, or maybe it was Missouri, he didn't know. The land over there rose from the banks in low grassy terraces, the beginning of the slow, steady uplift that carried all the way to the Rockies.

He had grown up on wide water, empty wide water backed by empty woods. Even at the dirtiest places on the lake, even off the docks in downtown Duluth, the water was clear. You could look down into it and see the yellow and brown rocks. They were rounded and massed like the roe of some gigantic fish. In northern Minnesota the towns, the few along the lake and the towns back from the water and the towns up in the Iron Range, were just settlements, they had the quality still of invention and impermanence about them, outposts surrounded by the heavy woods, ganged around by birches and spruce.

Clare leaned her head against his shoulder. He kissed her hair. It smelled citrusy and clean.

"It's interesting," he said, "how there are things you can't come to the end of."

"I think all the time how everything comes to an end."

"You've got a mind that tends toward the galactic."

"What are you thinking about?"

The bank receded, the trees began to become anonymous, a secret, an indivisibility, figments in a place they'd never been. The boat headed slowly upstream. "Don't get too far out into the open," Jack said to Jimmy. The gambler waved. He'd put on a blue captain's hat.

"I was thinking about this river," Jack said, "how there are still places on it where you can look back into the centuries. And that made me think about Minnesota, the lake and the big woods. And then I was about to start thinking about my father."

"You always think about him."

"He's one of the things I can't come to the end of."

(The twelve suicides, he said, like twelve pulls on a starter cord.)

"I'm harder than you."

"No. You're the woman who was devoured by a lion. Like the guy in the Bible. Except in the Bible the lions wouldn't touch him."

"Who?"

"Daniel."

"I've never heard of him."

"He was a prophet."

"Don't start with the Bible. And I don't weigh my life in my father's scales, either. If there was a phone on this boat, I'd call him again. I want to threaten somebody. Then I want to wait a while and then carry out the threat."

"Yes," he said, laughing, "we both love carrying out threats."

(But we had failed so many times, he said.)

(You look up one day, he said, and there is a bright yellow airplane coming for you. You are riding with twelve convicts in the back of a stake truck and the plane swoops suddenly down and you see it is dragging a sling on a rope and you realize this sling is meant for you and so you gather yourself, a terrified man, and when the plane comes even with the truck, you leap, from among your flightless fellows, and you thrust yourself into the sling, and so are carried from hell into hell. . . .)

Jimmy called him. The gambler wanted to know how far upriver he wanted to go.

"The fork of the Ohio at least."

"Cairo?"

"That'll help."

"I was on the way to Mexico," Jimmy said.

"Fine. You can drop us off wherever you need to turn around."

"No. It's all right. I'll take you. Since Buster died I need the company."

(It was curious, he said, how far away after a robbery you could get, especially after a busted robbery. You could do crime often enough that it

became a kind of grief. Leaden in your body. You didn't want to eat. You didn't want to talk. You sat places, beside the road maybe in a car during a rainstorm, and you looked without seeing much. You didn't see much inside, either. You sat there on some rainy coast, and the rain beat on the car and it filled the road with ponds, and the one beside you ate her sandwich and fiddled with the radio, and you sat there knowing you were beyond human touch, that nothing could reach you; you were entirely still, a monument to grief. It was a kind of heaven.)

To Clare he said, "Coodge says he can take us as far as we need to go."

"Maybe he only *thinks* he can. Look at that."

A large dog, rangy, black and tan, had come out onto the bank and was running along it. The dog had something in its mouth. The object was bloody, raw-looking.

"They used to call those German *police* dogs," he said, "but now they've upgraded them to *shepherds.*"

"It's torn something loose."

"I see."

The dog ran in a steady lope, dodging trees, disappearing where the shore dipped, rising again with it. The land folded back in low ridges, tree-lined and thickened with bushes that looked like patches of fur. The object the dog carried was heavy, the size of a baby, but the dog never let go of it.

"That dog's serious," Clare said.

"On serious business . . ."

There was an ache in his side. Abruptly he remembered the face from the woods looking at him as he rocked in his childhood boat. A mirror image staring back where there was no mirror. The ache burned around a hollowness. As if a piece of me has been torn away, he thought. Piece of someone passing for me. They'd autopsied the lion that attacked Clare, years ago, winched it onto a steel table and split it open: they'd found a piece of her flesh in its belly. There were blond hairs on the skin of the piece, she said, from my armpit. They'd given the morsel to her—to hold a moment, in reverence, to shock her, to humiliate her, to show her how powerful they were—she'd rubbed it hard between her fingers and, as the veterinarians looked on dumbfounded, eaten it.

The boat gradually pulled past the dog and left it behind. They watched until it was out of sight. The dog never broke stride.

He sat down beside her, stroked her arm. The skin was hot.

"Our luck's giving out," she said.

"I know," he said, "but maybe we don't have to mention it."

"I'm just a mouthy girl." Her eyes flashed. "I don't want to hear it, you're right."

"Good. Let's stay off that."

"I'm naturally bloody-minded."

"Yes."

"It always looks scary when we're between things."

"You're right."

She grabbed him around the neck, held on tightly.

"What is it?" he said.

"Just then, just that minute, I felt flushed down inside me. I'm wet. I touched you and got wet."

"I do that?"

"Not usually." She turned her head. "Look at Jimmy there. He's lost Buster and now he's a wandering soul, he doesn't know which way to turn. It's in his face like someone's painted it on him. Like a whore's face of sorrow."

"He's crying right now."

"I believe in that. I got hollowness in me about other things, but I believe in grief. I don't want to miss you again like I missed you these last three years. For more than a year of it every day was like the first terrible day."

"Like prison. I can't take any more prison."

"I hate when we talk this way."

"We come to conclusions and then there's nowhere to turn. It's the mistake of the criminal: the fixed position."

"It's impossible to tell the truth, even to each other."

"Like your family."

"Yeah. Them. I do wish there was a phone on this boat so I could talk to them about it."

"You weren't actually talking before, sweetheart."

"What was I doing?"

"Ranting and raving was more like it."

"Oh." She grasped him by the shoulders and pulled his face to her. She kissed his lips, licked him. "I want to make love to you now, please. I can't wait any longer for it."

"I thought that was what we were headed to."

"Don't joke."

They excused themselves like houseguests, descended into the cabin and closed the door behind them. They undressed each other quickly, staring into one another's face, pulled a mattress off one of the lower bunks and lay down on it on the floor. The engine throbbed underneath them. At first they were quick, in a hurry, rushed, as if the momentum that had carried them this far *(their whole lives)* wouldn't let up. They gripped and jostled each other. She bit his shoulder, hit him lightly along the ribs, popping him with her fingertips. He bent her backwards, pressed the heel of his hand against her jaw, stretching her long neck. Rage flared, he started to choke her, but even as he did, the rage blurred, gathered in a knot, spun—then he forgot it. "I want to unroll myself like a rug," he said.

"Do it," she said. "Do it to me, too. Do us both."

"I have to get inside you."

"Yes. Jump in with both feet."

"I can't go fast enough."

"Me, either."

He tried to catch her, but he couldn't. He never could. "Go faster," she said.

"I am—it's killing me."

She laughed. "Slow down, then."

"I'm possessed. The rip-and-snort's got me."

He shoved into her. She rose to meet him.

Then they lay together entangled and it was as if death had retracted itself from them for a moment because a sweet languor came upon them. They swung inside its haven rosily, nerveless, and without suffering pain. The feeling was not fertile, it contained no promise of a better life, but they accepted this and did not expect anything different. It was a drug's glow, and passing, and they knew it. He breathed into her mouth. She pressed her face against his. Her skin smelled like fox grapes. She said, "You're sweet to the taste." He nuzzled her, sank his head along her breasts, licked the tallowy scars that dipped under her ribs. In these moments he could look at her straight on, as he could not other times, and he could look at the world, maybe—sometimes he thought this, realizing it—as he could not other times. He had never been able to look straight at things, had needed distance, variance of sight lines, a blur, gaps; he knew this about himself. He had loved the hollow places in his knowledge. Now it seemed, as he lay in the boat's wood cradle, that somewhere in the last few years, in the fire maybe, or in sleep, or bent over a railing calling some con, a new clear sight had appeared, and taken over his eyes, a clearing of vision that showed him the world, wrung and convinced of its accuracy. He hated this. He had spoken of it to Morty and Morty had told him he was foolish to think it. "Nobody sees right—ever," Morty had said. But this was not so. Life blared its facts. You could see. I shouldn't have let Will out of that hole, he thought. The thought struck him as funny. She asked him what it was and he told her. "That's the way, isn't it," she said. "One more thing you should have got right, but didn't. What amazes me is how life goes on fine even with all its parts stuck in crossways."

"Not forever," he said.

"Don't get gloomy."

"I've been getting presumptuous in my mind."

"Just now—I can tell."

They got up and showered, taking turns in the small closet. The water was cold and as it poured over his strong back the chill of it met a chill rising from inside him. The walls of the shower were a cage collapsing. He shoved against the flimsy aluminum, but it didn't give. He closed his eyes and he could see the walls crumpling as they crushed in on him. He cried out, but when she answered in a clear voice, he was unable to say what it was. For a second, he said, I thought— No. He thought he was being smashed inside something, collapsed up into it. My coffin, he said, laughing, but that wasn't what he meant. The action was the power of it. Not the thing. It was being rolled up, he said. Crumpled up inside. I know, she said, but he wasn't sure she did. They were like elephants nudging around in the elephant graveyard, she said. Yes. Something like that. Stupid and grieving, dumbfounded by what they'd come on.

Topside he discovered the sun had set. In the west the land was bunched against itself, slathered with darkness. A swirl of orange, dissolving like powder into clear water, lay across the top of the farthest western ridge. Out in the channel a tug pushed a long string of barges upriver. The barges had bright blue plastic tarps covering them.

"Sporting life, eh, Coodge?" Jack said.

Jimmy sat in a high padded chair behind the wheel. "I'm about to forget myself," he said. He had turned the running lights on, but not the cabin lights.

"How far have we gone?"

"Thirty miles, I guess."

Jack scanned their wake. "Anyone following?"

"Nobody after *us*."

Jimmy let Jack take the wheel—"Stay this far out," he said, "but don't get out into the channel"—and went below to fix dinner. Clare went forward and lay down in the bow. She spread her arms and hung her head over the point of the bow, staring at the water. She called back to ask how fast they were going.

"Twelve knots," he said.

He opened the motor up, briefly took it up to full speed—twenty-three knots—and brought it back down. The speed in the dark scared him.

Jimmy came up bringing sandwiches, beer, and a bottle of vodka on a tray. He unfastened a small folding table from the bulkhead, set it up, and placed the tray on it. "Let's eat," he said.

"You're a good provider," Jack said.

"Buster always said I was."

They anchored a hundred yards offshore and ate the dinner of sandwiches. The bank in both directions looked abandoned, the land a dark thought the night was keeping to itself. What life there was passed on the river, out in the channel, creeping along in lighted parade, barges and flatboats, tugs with their tall lit-up pilothouses, maybe, he thought, a few runners and wanderers like themselves. *(Or, he said, who knew what other shamed characters and cutthroats might be out there, what ghosts winding their dead lives up between thumb and elbow like fishing line, what lost children, or crazed losers talking back to dead forefathers, what American drifters pushed on by promises made in high school, what touts, what smoke jumpers stinking of ash, what bar girls, or ex–lion tamers maybe—the population of a prison, he said, like the whole remedial class in a depressed country high school—what long-haul obsessives, or the swept-up trash in truck-stop booths—ex–Cub Scouts, failed hoodlums and drifters fired from straight jobs—just off crumbling federal highways, what Jansenists and politicians passing out flyers, what dancers or trum-*

pet players, what small-time preachers down on their knees in some cabin belowdecks imploring God to give them another chance—or maybe children eating supper as they pushed their minds far away, or bankers, or policemen still trembling from shootouts; or maybe the boats were manned only by the howling dead, he said.)

They ate like wolves and busted the beer down, smacking their lips with pleasure, and when they begged for more Jimmy came back with a big cake with pink coconut icing, and they tore this up, grabbed off chunks of it that they shoved into their mouths, licking their fingers after each bite. When they were done they leaned over the side and washed themselves with river water. Then Jimmy opened the vodka and he and Clare began to drink. Jack lay back, not thirsty now, sated, lounging against sacks of pecans Jimmy had bought to send to his relatives for Christmas, thinking about Jesus on the cross and about the river and their time on it, about his mother straddling the Mississippi once, up in Minnesota.

(The quiet around the house after the suicides, he said, was different—after his father was brought back one more time from the rim of the afterworld, like an explorer hauled in blankets out of the terrible wilderness, carried in and set in the place of honor, and the family, the friends, the curious onlookers, all those who had waited for news, collapsed themselves on sofas, on loungers out on the back porch, where, if it was winter, the aurora borealis smeared the sky with vaporous color, or, if it was summer, the night clouds looked soft enough to ride on. . . .)

If they ran the Crucifixion in the prison yard, he thought, you would have to punch your way to the head of the line. To see it and to get in it. There would be many who'd want to go up on the cross, too, and many who'd want to pull the Savior down, to take his place, or kill him with bare hands. The thief made it to paradise by doing what he had always done. He stuck his face into somebody's business, grabbed. What ruined him saved him. But what if you couldn't keep going with what ruined you? He did not believe there were other portals. Everyone lied about this. About heaven and about sin and about the end of things. The truth was: nobody held up. Everybody went to pieces in the end. But sometimes the pieces sat up at the right moment and asked Jesus for a ride. It was all timing. It was fate or luck or special privilege, something that made you ask the right question at the right time. Is there room on this train? There *was* a grace that supplied you with the right question. He had seen it again and again. James didn't ask the right question. He should have asked how do I get loose instead of how do I get my brother's wife. And his own brothers, trampled by the present, circa Vietnam. They should have asked where is the exit. And his mother, who asked about saving the world. Who sat alone now in her house in Brandis writing her memoirs, telling the story of a radical's life, of salvage attempted and failed at, of succor offered and refused, of the small righteousnesses of hope and faith—busted out. She was a derelict, his mother, a derelict of the spirit, a lost soul on the roads of charity, failed marchesa of the homeless. In the end, after a lifetime of offering service, of working the soup kitchens, of resisting, of writing petitions, of demonstrating, of laying her body down in front of the tanks, of jails—letters between them sent prison to prison—of lawsuits, she had come to nothing. It is another kind of robbery, he'd told her, another lie. You are protecting treasure just like the others, he said, hoarding, sticking the truth about yourself into an interior vault, locking it up so neither you nor anyone else can find it. You exploit the bereft just as the bereft exploit themselves; you are a robber like me. She had looked at him with sad eyes pitying him, offering him, even then, her solace, her willingness to forgive everything. No, he had said, No! like a child refused.

His father hadn't asked for anything. That was his mistake. You had to ask for something.

But here, now, was Clare, the woman he loved, who asked for everything.

She begged for his life—she got down on her knees under the big tree among the acorns, which were like brown marbles—anyone could see how the acorns hurt her knees—and she begged for his life, pressed her face against the murderer's shoes, kissed the black shoes, kissed the ground around them, offered herself abjectly, promised anything, so that the men were appalled, frightened by the power of her abnegation, and stepped back from her, gasping nearly, reaching for her even as they lurched from her, almost turning in their tracks, their pistols held slackly, the shotgun aimed at nothing, as his blood dripped off the knife and down the wrinkled stiff gray bark and collected in a pool at the base of the tree. . . .

Each breath then was like a bird released from a cage. . . .

• • •

The vodka burned in her eyes. She looked at him, growling.

"What is it?" he said.

"Jimmy said Buster raped a woman."

"I'm sorry to hear that."

There was no hardness in Jimmy at all; he looked as if he were melting. "It's the truth," Jimmy said, nodding his head slackly. "I hate that it is, but it is. It's what got him killed."

"Say on."

Jimmy took a heavy swallow of vodka and wiped his mouth. He stared out across the river. A long line of barges moved upstream. The running lights looked like a wobbling lighted fence. The moon had come up.

"It was a year and a half ago—I told you—down in Alabama. We were coming up from Florida after the winter season, following the cockfights." His dark eyes were murky. "You know how sometimes you do something, something simple that shouldn't mean anything, and you don't know why you do it, but it winds up meaning everything?"

"Sure."

"Well, that's what happened. We were riding on the interstate, headed for Mobile, when Buster suggested we get off at one of the little towns, go into it and have a drink. He might have had something on his mind, but he didn't say, it was just an idea. I always got pleasure out of giving Buster pleasure, so I said okay."

"Sure."

"We went into this town, a crummy little farm town, and found a bar. It was a tiny square brick place across the street from some warehouses right at the edge of the downtown. I never liked those trashy places, but Buster did, so we went in. We drank, Buster played penny shake with the bartender, and amazed him, and we met some girls, a couple of women. The women were local, they were out celebrating something, two big girls with country faces. We hooked up with them."

"What was the name of the town?"

"Ribideaux. Ribideaux, Alabama."

Clare held a full glass of vodka to her lips and sipped levelly from it, eyes up. Like some animal drinking at a stream. Light from a ceiling fixture shone directly into her face, but it did not penetrate her eyes; they seemed to be looking at Jimmy out of the dark.

"These women were from Ribideaux," Jimmy said, "out having a time, you bet, and we hooked up with them. They took us home." He scratched his wrist hard. "We went out to the house of one of them, way out in the country, this big empty house in a little pecan grove surrounded by fields. The night was warm, I remember that, and it had been raining, but the rain had let up."

He rubbed his forehead and his mouth opened, went slack for a moment, as if he was suddenly exhausted. He shook his head. "I think about this every day of my life. It's as much a part of me now as eating and sleeping, it's there all the time like a disease that night diagnosed for me."

"I know."

Jimmy smiled sadly. "I hate the country, I never liked it at all, and there we were, in the middle of the night out in these fields where something, some bushy something, tomatoes or cotton or some stupid crop, was planted, and we were inside this house that smelled of rat poison and perfume with these two women, and Buster was charming them in that way he had, telling stories, making jokes, getting up to rummage in the refrigerator like he was as welcome as the favorite son come home. Those girls just loved him. You could see it. They were both big women, big boned, with sharp farm faces and dyed hair, solid women really. We were in the kitchen, they'd brought out homemade pickles and cake and apple brandy, it was a party, all set up, you bet, to ease the way into the bedroom, which was fine with me, I didn't care—you know me, I don't think about that business much one way or the other. . . ."

"You were always like that. . . ."

"Yeah. But Buster wasn't. He was always a little strange about that stuff—he was liable to force it."

"That's what he did?"

"That's what he did. We were sitting there in this big rural kitchen, linoleum everywhere, eating pickles and drinking brandy. Buster had just told a joke and the women were laughing, one of them, Susie, the biggest one, cackling with her head thrown back, slapping the table with the flat of her hand. She had an Adam's apple just like a man's and big bony hands bigger than Buster's. Those girls had been lacking for entertainment, and Buster was providing it."

"What happened?"

"Buster. He happened. A crazy man. Right in the middle of the laughing he pulls out his big Bowie knife and sets it on the table. I've never known a gambler who liked ugly weapons, but Buster did, and that knife was an ugly weapon. He pulled the knife, laid it down, and everything in his face changed. The women were drunk, but they saw it. They looked at Buster and then they looked at that knife. It was as if he had pulled out a death sentence, which he did. It was strange. The women didn't say anything, they just stared at the knife. And then the big one, Susie, sighed. It was like she had been believing in a dream and now she saw it wasn't true. I was reading this article about how girls are enthusiastic and curious and full of happiness like boys are up until the age of twelve, until puberty I guess, and then something happens, they falter, something turns in them and they start to doubt themselves and they begin to get depressed. You could see something like that happening right there in that room. They went from glee to despair like snapping out a light."

Clare's breath came harshly. She looked at Jimmy with pure hatred in her eyes.

"I feel bad about it," Jimmy said. He didn't notice Clare. "It's men do that to women, it's boys do that to girls—that's a big part of it at least—and that's what Buster did to those women. He knocked the joy right out of them."

"Did they fight back?"

"Not at all. The big one, Susie—the other one's name was Margaret—had this terrible look of disappointment on her face. She looked at the knife, and then she sighed again. Everything she had reached for and hadn't gotten was in that sigh. Margaret hadn't caught on completely, but then she went quiet, too. We all just looked at the knife. And then Buster stood up. He didn't have to say anything. He looked at Susie and she got up, too. Maybe this had happened before. Maybe these girls had brought men home before and maybe the men had turned on them and hurt them. Maybe this was just business as usual, or maybe they thought it was. Buster took Susie's hand and he led her into the bedroom. He didn't bother to close the door."

"What did you do?"

"I just sat there. Margaret and I did. We didn't say a word. I sipped brandy—it tasted like fire—and waited, like I was waiting in a bus station. Margaret started to cry, but she kept it quiet, sniffling a little bit, but not even bothering to wipe the tears away. I patted her hand, but I didn't do any more than that."

Clare got up, went to the stern rail, and sat down on it. She looked out at the river, which was black and in the dark wide like an inland sea. In the light of the half moon the far bank was darker than the water. It looked as if west of them, beyond the few barge lights, the land hadn't been discovered yet, that it was empty, unexplored terrain, enormous. She looked at Jack, a slow perception moving in her gaze, and it seemed to him that the vast spaces beyond her shone in her eyes, as if she was looking at him not out of them but as them. Nothing he had done, he thought, nothing either of them had done, had made the next day safe or commonplace; each day, no matter what they did, they stepped farther out onto unexplored ground. And it was this way for Jimmy, too; Jack could see it in his face, see the shock under the surface corrosion of sadness and grief, could see the silly bafflement like the dumbfoundedness of a man coming out of sleep, and it seemed to him they were all entangled in this, this baffled pioneer wandering, he and his wife and his friend, and everyone he knew, all the time.

Clare stepped from the rail, poured more vodka into her glass. "Why did he have to force her?" she said. Her voice was low, weak as if she had been crying.

"Buster was like that," Jimmy said. "And you're right, those girls would have taken us to bed fifteen minutes later, but Buster wouldn't have that. If he had waited he would be alive right now, but he didn't." He rattled his knuckle softly against the table. "But that was Buster. He was willing to bet his life on that fifteen minutes."

Jack said, "What happened after they went in?"

"He had his way with her. He hurt her, too. We could hear it, hear her groan and cry out. Maybe he hit her—I don't know—but he hurt her. It didn't take long. After a while he came out of the room and then we went outside into the yard. Everything was wet from the rain. We stood under a tree smoking cigarettes, and then we moved because the tree was dripping on us. Buster didn't say anything about what went on in the bedroom. He talked about the season, about Mobile, and then he asked me about a time we went flying out in Odessa, Texas. We'd gone up in a biplane out there. We saw this plane out at an airport, it was a reconstruction, a model, something, one of the old World War One planes, a Spad I think, and there was a pilot who would take you up for rides. Buster wanted to go, so we went, for twenty-five dollars apiece, up in the air in that little rattly plane. Buster said how he had really enjoyed that. . . ."

"Clare came and got me in a plane. But you know that."

"I heard it was a plane."

"She swooped down and plucked me out."

"Buster would have liked that. He would have liked to have been there to see it. He liked that combo of old-fashioned and absolutely bizarre."

Jimmy looked at Clare and it seemed then that he was explaining things to her. There was an earnestness in his voice, a twitchy sincerity that was probably the best a gambler could do in terms of coming clean. "We were out at the edge of the fields," he said, "out there with these stupid plants that all smelled as if they had been poisoned, and Buster was talking about flying. He said it was one of the best times he ever had. 'It made me cockeyed,' he said, and he laughed."

Jimmy clutched himself in his arms and began to rock. He looked around. "I won this boat in Memphis," he said. "Took it off a guy who'd brought it up from the Gulf. He put it up in a poker game, and I took it. I could have told him he was going to lose it, that it was the wrong thing to do, but I didn't. I've never been able to do that. I always let the play go the way it goes. Now I regret myself. Because I should have told Buster."

"How could you?"

"No. I don't mean I should have stopped him from raping that woman, there was no way to do that. Buster—if you wanted to be around him, you were going to let him have his head, you couldn't stop him, but I mean I should have told him it was the wrong thing to do."

"To rape her?"

"Yeah, all of it. I loved Buster. It didn't make any sense, nobody liked him much but me, but I loved him." He tapped his lips with the tip of his first finger. Clare had backed to the rail again. She held her arms close to her chest, sipped the drink by bending her head down to it. Her eyes blazed. Jimmy spoke to her. "I think I was going to say something to him," he said. "We were standing out in that smelly field, Buster was stripping the leaves off a bush, talking about going flying in Texas, and I was about to speak, when the woman, Susie, came out on the porch and started firing a pistol at us. It was so shocking neither one of us moved. I looked at Buster and he was wide-eyed, just about I think to start laughing. He turned his head to look back at the house and a bullet caught him in the forehead. He went down like he was pole-axed. I knew he was dead. I could feel it in my own body; I felt him vanish. I jumped back and started to run; I wrenched myself into it, but I didn't get three feet before a bullet hit me."

"She got you, too?"

"Yes. Right between my shoulder blade and my spine, the shot knocked me flat on my face. The last thing I remember was my face smashing into the ground, how the ground was like a taste that was sweet, then bitter, and how it was soft, then hard, like I was smashing onto rock.

"When I came to the women were standing over me. They had turned me onto my back. I could feel something, but what it was was heat in my back and wetness under me. For the rest, in my body, there was nothing going on. Susie was looking down at me, holding the gun in both hands. The other woman, Margaret, was standing beside her crying. Susie told her to shut up. She said it over and over, 'Shut up shut up shut up,' real softly, but Margaret went on crying.

"I looked straight up past them, past them both, and I could see the stars shining up among the clouds. The clouds were puffy and white and the stars were very bright. Everything looked perfect. I asked her if Buster was dead. She said he was.

" 'He's going to be dead from now on,' she said.

"I told her I couldn't move.

" 'You don't have any place to go,' she said.

"She told the other woman, Margaret, to go call the police. And an ambulance.

"I thought that was good of her, calling an ambulance, and I thanked her. She told me not to. She said it didn't have anything to do with me. I told her I appreciated it nonetheless. She kicked me in the head. 'Shut up,' she said as I was going out."

"That's a startling tale, Coodge," Jack said.

"There's more to it," he said, getting up.

"Where you going?"

"I want to show you something." He started down the steps into the cabin. Jack followed him. "What happened next?" he said.

"I was paralyzed for two months. They chained me to a hospital bed, tried me and gave me three years for being an accessory to rape. They would have given me more, but those women got me off. They said it was Buster's idea, that I had nothing to do with it."

He opened a locker by the stove and took out the vest he had worn at the cockfight. It had a gold-speckled front with a black leather backing. "Here," he said, "try this on."

Jack took the vest. It dropped through his hands, hit the floor with a dull thud. "Jesus Christ, you got a lead vest?"

"Not lead."

Jack lifted it. The vest sagged in his hands. "It must weigh twenty pounds."

"Twenty-five."

"What's in it?"

"Gold. Seven two-pound rolled sheets in the back, five one-pound sheets in each of the front panels."

"How much is that?" Jack said. "How much is it worth?"

"It fluctuates. But two hundred and fifty-six thousand according to this morning's market report."

"Where did you get it?"

"From Buster. It's what he left to me."

"He gave it to you?"

"I was his sole heir. He'd made a will I didn't even know about. It all got worked through while I was in jail. He didn't have much up front, but there was a key to a safe-deposit box at a bank in New Orleans. When I got paroled—not really paroled, that woman Susie got me out early—I got the key and the other stuff, went down to New Orleans, and found this vest in the box. It was Buster's life savings. He'd been putting it together without me knowing a thing about it. Every time he went through N.O. he'd add to it: go off and buy some gold and have it made up into a sheet and put into this vest. . . ."

"A gold vest. It's like something out of mythology."

Jack put the vest on. It was heavy, dragged on his shoulders, but it felt snug, comfortable. "I like this. It's the kind of secret you want to stand in the middle of a room and have."

"I wear it sometimes at the fights, or sometimes lately when I'm by myself running this boat." He brushed his fingers against the front of the vest. "Buster was a mean man. He didn't care a thing about either of those women. If Susie hadn't shot him, like as not he would have gone back in there in a little while and raped the other one. He was not really a killer, but he liked to see people suffer. Or at least he didn't care if they did. But he was a good time to be with, mostly, and I never knew anybody else to stick so close to you, to keep on being with you no matter what happened."

There were tears in his eyes. He dashed them away with his fingers.

"Let's go show this to Clare," Jack said. "She'll love it."

"She can't take it, though."

Jack ignored the remark, bounded up the stairs. Clare leaned against the stern rail. She had her pistol out. Jack noticed the gun, and noticed the heavy menace in her eyes, but his momentum carried him. "I have something you'll love," he said.

Clare looked at him without speaking. What was in her eyes he had seen before. The cold radiance. He stopped.

"Put the gun away, honey," he said.

"Not until I'm finished with it."

Jimmy came up behind him. "What is it?"

"Be quiet," Jack said. He stepped toward Clare. She raised the pistol. He smiled. "Are you going to shoot me, darling?"

"I'm going to shoot *that* son of a bitch. That brother to a rapist. I'm going to shoot him dead."

"It's not necessary. He's dead already."

"He's not dead enough."

"Clare."

"Don't interpose yourself, Jack. I'm about to start firing wildly, to say the least. You'd better run for cover."

"No, honey, I won't."

He edged toward her.

She shook the gun, not exactly at him, but in his direction. "Don't try to sneak up on me, Jackie."

"I won't. I just want to get myself a drink."

"It's too late for a drink. The crime has arrived. I am about to shoot this bastard."

"Don't move," Jack said to Jimmy.

Jimmy looked as if he was dead and propped up. His hands were clasped on his chest and he held himself very rigidly with his chin pulled in, leaning back. Jack smiled at him. "Pay attention, Coodge," he said.

He slopped a jolt of vodka into a glass. He was closer to her, almost within arm's reach. There was a tunneling sensation burrowing up through the incident. It would open out in just a moment, he knew, into action. Sometimes she got outraged, sometimes the bitterness of life, the sad humiliation of having to live on earth, became too much for her. She took it out on her fellow inmates. He said, "Have you ever noticed how birds are the only creatures that can detach from their own shadows?"

"And you, Jimmy," Clare said, "running around the country ruining women. What is the matter with you? I don't believe you about Buster. I think you're the one who set up that rape. I think it was your idea. You've always been slippery like that, turning things around so other people take the blame. If I touched you, grease would come off on my hands."

"It's true, Clare," Jimmy said. "I was lying. I'm sorry."

Jack snapped a glance at him. Jimmy's face was white and sweat stood out on his forehead in round beads, like rain on a leaf. "Shut up, Jimmy," he said. He licked the rim of his glass. "Everyone else," he said, "people, woodchucks, lizards, we all have our shadows attached to us, right there hooked to our feet . . . but not birds . . . they launch off and disconnect from them."

"What shadows, Jack?"

"The ones that follow around with us. The ones the sun makes."

"I'm not interested in shadows."

"What do you guess birds think, when they see that dark patch down on the ground running along with them? Do you think they want to shake it?"

"Birds don't think, Jack."

"But we think about them, and we see how there's a gap there, a space between the bird and its shadow, and if we think about it, things become eerie."

He tossed the glass at her, ducked and sprang at her. She shrieked, as if he had jumped out of a closet. The gun went off as he caught her at the waist, as he hit her with his shoulder hard, and she went over backwards into the water. He clambered behind her onto the rail, almost caught her, but the vest slowed him. She sank like a puppy. He could see her in the water, which was black when you looked across it, but was clear enough, like tea, when you looked down into it, falling backwards. She sank without resistance, as if there was no hurry about this, drifting, and as she sank she fired the pistol. He saw the spin of froth from the muzzle in the same moment the bullet snapped through the surface with a sound like a slap and hit him in the chest. He felt the sting as the blow kicked him off his feet. His head hit the deck.

When he came to she was kneeling over him. Water dripped from her hair onto his face. She rubbed his chest with the flat of her hand. "Jack," she whispered. "Jack, Jack. Don't go away."

He couldn't feel anything where she was rubbing. "Am I shot?" he said.

"Yes. But the bullet bounced off you."

"The river," he said as a mist settled on him, "the river slowed it down."

He drifted out with the mist. In it was a dream. Across the top of the dream was a banner with the word TEMPORARY written on it in gold letters. He had longed for crime. This thought came as he looked at the banner, as he came to himself walking naked down a sandy road in northern Minnesota. All around him the birch woods had turned yellow. He was accompanied by the boy who'd looked at him from the hemlock woods, that is, by himself. This is intriguing, he thought, but in the dream he was shy and unable to say anything to his double, who was also naked. Then he was the double looking at him. Then he couldn't tell who he was. *I longed for crime,* he said, and a voice, his voice, answered him: *No, you didn't.* Then there was a bright sunlit splashing, and a voice calling in his head, and the boy was slipping away. . . .

He looked up into her face. His chest had begun to ache. Her mouth moved, but he couldn't quite hear her. "What?" he said.

"I don't think you're hurt," she said, kissing him.

"Yes, I am," he said.

She drew back and looked at him. There was a mix of emotion in her face—anger, fear, drunken romantic grief, longing, glee, misery, defiance, joyless stony posturing, a willful unstartled acceptance of all things, impatience, boredom, excitement, shame—but mostly there was dumb animal delight, as if she was the one risen from the dead, upright once more telling jokes at the party. He stroked her cheek. "There aren't many who could make a shot like that," he said and smiled. "Where's Jimmy?"

There were tears in her eyes. "Jackie, Jackie," she said, kissing him again. "We're so lucky."

"This is not luck," he said. "Don't get confused about it." It was painful to talk. He was weak, but not so weak he couldn't grab her. He pulled her by the collar down to him. "I could kill you," he said. "I could kill you even like this. I could backhand you with a club, or drive a nail into your forehead, or I could shoot you, or I could cut you up in your sleep. There is not a minute of your life with me in which I couldn't kill you. But I don't. Do you understand that, Clare? I don't."

"I've ruined myself," she said.

"It's not about you, Clare."

"Oh, Jack."

"Let it go. Help me up. Help me sit."

Jimmy lay on his back. His head was under the table, in shadow. "Did you shoot him?"

"No. I can't find a wound, but he's out."

Jack pushed the vest off his shoulders, stood up. "There's two hundred and fifty thousand dollars inside that vest. That's what I wanted to show you."

"This?" She lifted it. "It's heavy."

"Buster had gold made into sheets, and sewn inside it."

He bent over Jimmy. The gambler was breathing, but there was a peculiar directedness in his face. His breath was mucosal and slow. His eyes were tightly shut as if against some sight he hated, and his face was locked in a bitter grimace as if inside him an ugliness struggled to get out. Jack touched the stuttery pulse in his neck. "I don't know what this is," he said. "Probably a stroke."

Clare sat down at the table, leaned her elbows on her knees. There was a blankness and exhaustion in her face, but also, from the river maybe, or from the drunk action, a radiance in her skin, a flush. Her life continued to pulse through the seams of her fatigue. "My head hurts," she said.

"It ought to."

"Don't scorn me, Jackie."

"I can't for this moment help it, Clare."

"I didn't mean to kill you."

"But you did, didn't you?"

She looked out over the river. Red and white moving lights, blinking and disappearing lights, bobbed in the channel. "We used to fish on the river at night," she said. "On the Ohio—bottom-set trotlines—for catfish. Once we caught a fish that was bigger than a man. It was thicker than a man and heavier. It was strange and black and smooth-skinned and had gigantic whiskers and a mouth big enough to swallow a little girl. I screamed at it and begged my father to throw it back in the river. I was terrified to be living in a world where such creatures came up out of familiar water. For years I was afraid to go into the river. I will ride on it, but I won't swim in it. Falling in just now"—she shuddered—"just now I felt myself being swallowed up by that huge black mouth. I think the shot was a way to grab someone. As if I could haul myself back up on the trajectory of a bullet."

"What do you think," he said, "Jimmy's probably going to die if we don't get him some help."

She stretched her arms down and out, clasping her hands, and looked at him. "I'll tell you this story another time," she said. "When you can listen to it. I am a disorderly and fractious woman. I have an uncontrollable temper and I was furious over what Jimmy said about his foul buddy. I can't stand that kind of business, Jack, and you know it. The truth is, I shot at some big shape above my head, in panic and in rage I shot. I'm terribly sorry it was you. You are my husband. I love you. I don't want you to die ever."

"Okay."

He got up and took her in his arms. She came readily, but there was a new elaboration, a formal quality to it, as if, for a moment, an embrace had become a kind of decoration. She smelled of the river, like something that lived in its heavy mortal waters.

"It's okay," he said. "It's okay."

The bank smelled like his grandmother's house. He could sense Little Mikey and Joe Cane behind him. Where would she come from this time, from what corner, from behind which tree would she step out and shoot? Maybe she would kill Donnie. Maybe she would kill Rubens, maybe kill her brother, too. He had watched her disappear into the garden, duck behind the corn. They had set chairs in the garden and sat there on summer nights. Potato bugs came from somewhere, but where—how did they find potatoes when there had never been potatoes in the garden before? Mikey shoved him. Stop, *Jack said.* Be calm. *His grandmother's house smelled stale and airy at the same time. Large rooms with air that never changed. She never opened her windows, she thought it was bad for you. Her father had come from Norway. She talked of Norway, talked of the island in the north her father had come from. Winter all year basically, he'd concluded. The sun on the shortest days of sun dipped behind an island. Even then, they were cut off. The smell entered him, it made him tremble. Joe Cane saw and smirked.* Brave boy, huh, Jack, *he said.*

Be still, *Jack said.*

• • •

He brought the boat in to a small town upriver. The town was hardly more than a village, called Anacondia according to a sign above gas pumps at the dock. A man sitting in a folding chair beside a shack at the foot of the dock directed them to the hospital. This is the part I like, Jack thought as he called the local taxi, this part where we might be recognized, where regular people begin to notice something strange has showed up among them. He had an urge, which seeped over him like a penetrating fog, to go straight into the heart of life in this place, to try to pass.

The taxi driver came in an old Buick and they loaded Jimmy's limp body into it. The driver was a small man who had been waked from sleep to come get them. His hair was knotted above his ears. "I never get calls this time of night unless it's an emergency," he said. This is emergency enough, Jack told him. The man asked what happened. Heart attack, Jack said. Clare looked a question at him: Is this the way you want to do it? Jack smiled. He wore the vest under an old sport coat.

They got Jimmy into the hospital, which was a large two-story house converted to a hospital, and after a while the constable came. Jack told him they were traveling upriver to visit their folks when their friend, Mr. Donald Bernardnick, had what the doctor said was a stroke, and collapsed. They'd been eating dinner, Donnie had been telling one of his tales, when he choked and fell to the floor. *(You come on corpses sometimes, he said.)* The constable seemed unsure what to think, but Clare's obvious grief and Jack's earnestness convinced him. *(This is our loved one sprawled on the floor.)* "It was like a bolt from the sky," he said. "Donnie was telling a story about the time some high-school boys molested him—"

"What?"

"It was a long time ago—when he coughed, made this squeezy little choking noise, and slumped over. It scared us silly. We thought he was dead."

"These are terrible trials," the constable said. He was a middle-aged florid man who also had been waked from sleep, by his deputy, to come in the middle of the night to the hospital. "Mr. Bernardnick is a very dear friend of ours," Jack said. "We feel it's our duty to take care of him now, to pay his expenses and watch over him until he is better. Is there a place in town we could stay?"

The constable directed them to the hotel. "The big yellow building next to the courthouse," he said. "It's mostly empty now, but it used to be one of the two or three finest river hotels between Memphis and St. Louis."

Jack thanked him and almost gave the man a friendly pat on the back, but the look of annoyance on Clare's face stopped him. The doctor said the first twenty-four hours would be the touchiest, they'd just have to wait for the outcome, Jimmy might die, it was possible, he said, and would they like to bunk in the hospital with him? Jack said no and smiled comfortably at the doctor, who was a little taken aback by this. "We have faith things will turn out all right," he said. He was spooked and troubled now by being in this place. The gesture was turning into a direction and he didn't like that. "We'll go to the hotel," he said.

"You can call us there," Clare said. She held herself stiffly and Jack thought she must still be slightly drunk. There was a pain in his chest from the bullet, but it didn't seem dangerous.

As they went down the front steps, he thought about this, about the wall that separated them from regulation life—they often speculated about life on the other side—so high he had to be careful around doctors; they were lucky to find one who'd work on them. He felt suddenly lonely, like a schoolboy without a pass, and then Clare took his arm and leaned against him and he felt better, but still the disengagement of it all, river, shooting, their journey, which had become a journey, all the rest, flight, prison like a cave he'd been forged in, made this little burg with its two stoplights and its levee and its constable wearing an old varsity letter sweater over his pajama top, and its doctor, who was so thin he must have a disease of some sort himself (and now Coodge blowing bubbles out of his hairy nostrils), into some kind of fantastical, indescribably shoddy, beaten-to-shit overworked figment put together in bitterness and outrage by a crackpot disgusted with everything human: and here they were, some kind of reverse royalty, he had always figured, slinking down the street toward a hotel, a couple of whipped individuals actually, hardly worth noticing unless you were working on your criminal identification merit badge, unless, maybe, you yourself were about to go out the window of your own life, take to the roads. Here they were, he thought, punched-in and nearly obliterated by years of this carnage—it came to him like that as they walked down the chilly October street where leaves were pasted to the sidewalk like stamps, and the big oaks stood up like half-naked and abused creations—carnage; and then, in stride with her, he saw them heading as they had headed for years, straight at some terrible disaster, and then he realized she was talking about this, telling him about her brothers and about her father, saying it all over as if he hadn't heard a thing, ever, and he understood that she was still beside herself with all this misfortune, kicked right through herself by it, and he knew any second she would start yelling, would begin to call out the townspeople so she could put them out of their stupid misery—and why not, he might as well join her—and then he thought, No, we have arrived somewhere, someplace, and we have to endure what is here with it for this moment, and he thought, *How gallant,* and then he saw the yellow, roughed-up face of the hotel, its painted brick entablatures and turrets, and he remembered, six years ago, they had robbed the bank in this town and ridden out past this monstrosity as he craned his head out the window like a little kid to take in the splendid sight of it.

"It's fate," she said, recognizing it, too.

"No," he said, "just a joke."

They were still nearly laughing when the clerk brought his sleepy face up to the desk and checked them in.

In bed later as he lay beside her under the torn quilt, the chill came back on him. I am troubled for my soul, he said out loud, but she was asleep and didn't hear. I am an obscure functionary in the cavalcade of crime, he said. He thought of Rubens. He was not sorry he had stolen the writer's car, and abandoned him, but he was sorry he had, for the moment, lost his access to the media. To the telling of his story. A whispering at the window caught his attention. It had begun to rain. He watched the rustling quick drops splash lightly against the glass. Maybe they should stay here. How about a sign, Lord. The sound of the rain became steady. It was the first sound of winter. Now the hard winds from Canada, from the Great Lakes of his homeland, would come, bringing cold rain and then snow. Winter, in flocks of white, would descend on the river, on the woods, and on the little towns. Sometimes, in the big winters of his childhood, when the snow had been heavy on the roof, he had gone up into the attic to listen to it. The beams and joists creaked under the load, and in the dark, sitting on the floor with his back propped against his mother's old college trunk, he had imagined himself lying under the weight of space itself, under the weight of heaven. It was a weight that could crush him, and he had used all his power, all his will, to hold it off. Doing this, he had felt deeply alive. He began to grow sleepy. The rain continued. Poor Jimmy. Poor Buster, poor country girl, poor . . . It was best not to start. No wonder the idiots looked for space invaders to come fix things. Or Jesus. Or booze. Or crime. The boy had looked at him across a patch of lake water like a bed of black flint upon which a million sparks had just been struck. *(For years, he said, I could call him up in my mind, as precisely, as alive, as if he had just looked at me. He took my complete attention.)* The rain, just as he was falling asleep, seemed to be returning him on its rivers to his home. Where this was he could not say.

5

This is what it came to then, for a while: Jimmy Acajou alive but immobile, a pair of blue eyes flickering in a pasty slack face; three weeks in the hotel, then a move to a shabby white house off Main Street; a job for Clare, as a substitute teacher at the local grammar school; occasional work for Jack in the apple orchards outside town bedding trees, setting and pinning saplings, some work stacking hay; a gray pickup truck bought from an unpaved lot across the street from the Gulf station, which also served as bus depot; dinner at the neighbors' on either side and across the street; long walks; fishing trips up the backwaters of creeks draining into the river; long periods of agitated quiet between them; winter, cold and rainy, cut by storms blown in from the north and west; spring brushing its yellow hair; summer and the smell of corn in the town streets, evenings on the porch under a sweet jasmine vine, sipping tea, telling each other stories; fall in a rustle of dry sticks and fields of blond grass.

He drove to Nashville, converted some of Jimmy's gold to cash, brought the rest home. Jimmy stayed in the hospital two months, did not get better, and was moved to a nursing home at the edge of town. One of them visited him every day. They massaged his arms and his legs, bathed his face, told him of their life in the village, told him stories of the places they had been. They placed bets for him, though he never asked them to, with the bookie at the Lingerlong Billiard parlor on Main Street, betting football and basketball games and the heavyweight championship fight in February. Jimmy could not speak—there was a meandrous emptiness, like a path through an overgrown lot, behind his eyes, in the look fixed inside them—but sometimes, with blinks, with a change in the tone of a look, he could indicate pleasure or sadness, yes or no. To them, to Clare especially, as she sat beside his narrow bed, he seemed angelic—she said—as if he had died and come back from death partway so that now there was an angelic, embryonic quality about him, a pale fuzziness of wings, and a faint radiance on his skin; she told Jack she wanted to believe he watched over *them* in some way, but they both knew this was only sentiment, maybe grief. When she began to touch Jimmy intimately, she told Jack about it. But she did not tell him how far she went. He discovered this for himself one night when he came in and found her sucking the gambler's dead cock. He watched her, and then he touched her face, let his finger slip along the joining, trace the scrawl of vein on Jimmy's cock, stroke lightly. They couldn't tell if this pleased him. It was vaguely horrifying to do this, to touch someone so helpless, in this way, but they did not stop. They liked to feel the sad impotency of it.

"We are becoming helpmates," he said. "Demented, but maybe helpful. Maybe this is how you find out about helping—trying this stuff."

"Is this how ordinary people do it?"

"How would I know? It seems all right, doesn't it?"

"Maybe," she said later, "we should get introduced to some straights. Maybe they would invite us to their homes and show us how to act."

"We could watch TV. One of the family shows."

They tried this. They bought a television from Mr. Drummond—she wrote his name in a notebook—at the Western Auto store, hooked it up and watched a program called *Bennie the Butler*, in which a young black man taught a family of white people how to love one another. This was done through sarcasm and threats and a kind of facetious cajolery that turned their stomachs. They did not find it funny at all. Clare cried when she watched the program because she was unable to understand why these people did what they did and because she could see from the beginning that nothing in their lives, hers and Jack's, was translatable into such a world. "We don't even have driver's licenses," she said.

"And think of the political life, the fashion trends, the technological breakthroughs that pass us by."

"It makes me nauseous."

"I'm overwhelmed—let's don't watch this."

They put the television set out with the garbage, which produced a minor scandal when Archie Conrow, one of their garbagemen—she wrote his name down—came to the door to ask if they really meant to throw it out. Clare offered to pay him to take it away and Archie told this to his partner and to his wife, both of whom passed this information on, so that the next time Jack was in the supermarket he overheard a Mrs. Sanibeau whisper to a Mrs. Cullen that she understood this man's wife, Mrs. Dawson, as Clare was calling herself, had sold all the furniture in her house in preparation for major renovations that would go against standards and zoning laws, most surely destroy the harmony of the neighborhood. Clare had to invite the neighbors in for coffee—she had written their names in her book—to sanctify the situation, but it was only after she memorized a couple of recipes from a book in the library and passed them on as family heirlooms to Mrs. Johnson Bivens, the major town gossip, that things calmed down.

"I never want to go through such shit again," Clare told Jack.

"It would drive anyone to a life of crime," Jack said.

But they improved, adjusted. They cooked, cleaned, took long walks, participated, shopped, gave money to small boys who came to the door bearing canisters. There was a thrill in it, not only of learning what they didn't know, but the thrill they felt as they scrutinized the faces of people they had robbed. Everyone had money in the bank and everyone had lost money when the Bakers came to town. No one recognized them. They were careful not to speak of this, and this not speaking—of this and of many other things—maintained in them the sense of separateness, the diffident and often raging sensation both carried inside of being *refused* by the world, and though many of the activities were designed, in their own nature, to mitigate this feeling—church, PTA, school itself, labor—they did not feel as if they were becoming a part of things. In the evening Jack would come in from the orchard to find her sitting at the kitchen table in the dark doing nothing, staring into the gathering black without even a glass of water in front of her. If he asked what she was doing, she often was unable to say. When she did say, she told him she was trying to keep certain monsters out of her head, and he knew what she was talking about because these monsters of demand and gangling oppressive desire gnawed at him, too. He was afraid there was nothing they could do. This was not how he'd felt in years past, but it was the way he felt now. They were both afraid.

"We used to simply go on to the next thing, wildly," she said.

"I wish we could backtrack."

"I don't want to go back at all," she said.

They were out on the front porch this time in the orange-flavored dusk, sitting on the steps sipping iced tea from jelly glasses. Across the street their neighbor Bill Morris—she had his name—watered his lawn in wide sweeps of a hose. Jack imitated him, swinging his arm. "I don't really, either," he said.

"Why don't they just let us live our lives?"

"It ought to be like cowboy heaven," he said. "You know, how in cowboy heaven they're roping and rustling and riding the range. Everything going on upstairs just like it does down here. If anybody thought that way, if they just would, then they would see what we do is what we are meant to do."

"What about what *they* do?"

"What about it?"

"Will, all that?"

"You don't want to start on that business."

None of the upset or the rage had gone away, but they occasionally were able to replace it now with activity. She had stopped calling her father, but sometimes in her sleep she talked to him or talked to her dead brother James. It was one of the things she said she thought about when she sat in the dark. Now, on the steps in front of their faded wood house, she began to talk about her dead brother.

"He was so pretty," she said. "Sleek looking. Like an otter."

"More a weasel."

"No. Not at first. He was weirdly nice. He would go get things and give them to me, like gifts. They were always things he had pulled out of somewhere, awful bits and pieces really, bird wings and hanks of cloth and half a cherry Popsicle with the syrup running off it like blood—ha-ha. He was terrible, but I am enchanted with how much I loved him. Do you know what I mean, honey, about how you could love someone so demented and awful? It makes me think there is a God. I was one who loved this man who used to crush living chicks in his fist and eat bugs out of the ground, and pushed little boys into swimming pools and off street curbings into traffic, etcetera, etcetera, etcetera, goddamn, who did every evil thing you could think of, including betray me, and betray everybody, and who was meaner than Will Bodine himself, if that were possible, but whom I still loved."

She gave him a dopey look. "We barely knew Will until we were teenagers. He came around some, sneaking, you know, but he was never invited. James was mean to him, everybody was; me, too. James and he caught up with each other in high school. Everybody knew them as brothers. They looked alike, they could have been twins really, except for different eye color and Will's terrible eating-itself mouth, you know. But everybody could see it and everybody talked about it."

"Like with us."

"Even more. Or different more. James got teased about it. People knew too much. He was humiliated. It contributed to his meanness, it turned him, like in prison when you get the big whipping. Will was already mean, so James just built himself up to meet him where he lived."

"We were turned, too, sweetie."

"Not like that. James was turned like a dog. He was an unattractive man—you know those people, the ones who smell or are obnoxious, or crooked in some way—"

"Like us."

"Yes—who can't go along, who get into stupid devilment, stuff that doesn't even work, and get caught and embarrass people, shame even bystanders, people like that—"

"Like us."

"Yes—and then everybody makes it worse by turning on the man, kicking him when he's down in the pit of his own degradation, you know—that was James and that was Will; they took turns being in a pit for each other, took turns getting kicked and spit on."

She washed a swallow of tea around in her mouth, spit it into her hand, and touched her face with wet fingers. "I've been stacking bricks toward the house of my hatred all my life," she said. "I take my losses out on everybody, but it's only lately that the evil spirit of my family has come for me."

"What does *that* mean?"

"Daddy and all his craziness. He's like a gunman in a speeding car and you're standing there going about your own wicked business, robbing, etcetera, but you're really only waiting until the gunman gets to you, until bullets start to strike you—"

The air was fragrant with the smell of jasmine. Anacondia. They could be anywhere. They could be in South America. Or India. Or out in the desert behind an air base. Someplace no one had ever heard of. The jasmine flowers gleamed like tiny stars. They were white, Jack thought, no, they were yellow, slightly yellow. He got up to look at his truck. He liked to look at it. It was the first he had owned since the beginning, since Florida when they took a bank in Boca Raton and left their car with the keys in it over in Little Havana for whoever might take it. There were a couple of apple spriglings in the back wrapped in burlap. He intended to plant them in the front yard. "Maybe they were only each other's device," he said.

She grimaced, but she didn't snap at him. "Maybe. I don't know. Maybe they were doors or something, means or something. They were the people everybody else can draw all kinds of conclusions from."

She had insomnia. Sometimes she got up and walked through the house. Once or twice he'd waked and followed her. She would go through the rooms, all furnished roughly by their landlord, and walk around touching objects, running her fingers over the hairy chair back, picking at the worn fabric on the living room sofa. She would stand at the front window in the dark staring out, making tiny semaphoric signs at the dark. Occasionally she would go into the kitchen and cook something. He could hear metal banging. He found her once studying a recipe in one of the books she got from the library, muttering to herself as she ran her hands lightly over assembled utensils. When he asked what she was doing, she said she was "going to bake a fucking cake," and for him to leave her alone. The cake didn't work out—a brickish dilapidated chocolate—after which she snatched up her equipment, shoved it in a sack, and hurled the sack into the garden. He found it in the spring, rat-gnawed and rusty, when he spaded up the area to put in red potatoes.

"They went on a trip once," she said now, "on the Fox River"—speaking of her brothers—"one of the Ohio tributaries, a canoe trip their senior year in high school. Neither of them knew a thing about the woods and I heard from my boyfriend Billy Butler, who was on the trip, that they broke everything they came close to. They knocked holes in things, tore tents, spilled gasoline into the stew. Trying to build a campfire, Will set fire to the woods—at least James accused him of it—and later, after they were airlifted out, and after the fire got on the television and houses burned and fields and crops were destroyed and the whole natural disaster of it had become a scandal, James accused Will of trying to drown him, which probably was true, and everyone turned on Will, and even though he got off for the fire, still he was shunned, and hated, and known in that area as a manslaughterer, since people died in the fire, including a little girl who had been a champion baton twirler—it was awful, burned to a crisp—and there was nothing to do, he was a loser, an outcast, so he went with it, you know, just rode it like a bad pony and began to do devilment on purpose, chase the meanness that had bit him so hard. He caught James and tried to kill him, tried to saw his head off with a knife. They fought. But they couldn't escape each other. That was the strange and terrible part. Do you know how that works?"

"I've seen it," Jack said.

"Yes. Surely, honey. They couldn't take their eyes off each other. They followed each other around. They fled each other, from town to town, from state to state. What one had the other wanted. And it was like—curiously—like all the devilment, the criminal behavior, had nothing to do with it at all. It was that pit each had fallen into. Each had to kill something that was down in the pit. And the only thing down there was himself or the other. It gets confusing. They would stand on either side of the pond out at Daddy's shouting at each other. Cursing each other. Swearing to kill each other."

"One did."

"Yes. It's odd how a promise kept can sometimes be so surprising."

Sometimes they stole. Intimately, lightly, confidentially, she lifted produce, scissors and ribbons from the millinery store, various items from strip-mall shops, a KEEP OFF THE GRASS sign from the hardware store after they reseeded the front lawn. He took fan belts, cans of soda from the supermarket out on the highway, peanut butter logs, newspapers. It was dangerous but incidental. They went to church, visited all the churches one Sunday after another; they liked the Catholic church best because the services were short and predictable. He talked to the priest about converting and the priest was interested; but one afternoon, the man, a short fellow in his early thirties, a man with the prim and distracted air of a secret masturbator, looked at him sharply as if he suddenly recognized him and Jack was spooked and did not come back. He went to the

Baptist minister, who lived in a pink brick house next door to the grammar school, and talked to him, but the man only wanted to gossip about other members of his profession, so Jack didn't stay long. He wanted to ask a few questions about provenance, about the originating points of crime, about the thief Eve and the murderer Cain, and about—who was it?—Jacob, the grifter who weaseled his brother Esau's birthright out of him, about Joseph, the Pharaoh's procurer, the first corporate crime figure, and about David, who had a man killed so he could screw his wife, and about Saul, a great figure, Jack thought, who—disheveled and busted out in his kinghood, an old man going down—had tried to murder David, the conniving prick, with a spear, and about Solomon, who even with all his so-called wisdom—mainly pop-psychology fluff he'd picked up from the lonely hearts column, including his trick with the two mothers and the baby—go ahead and cut him—couldn't keep himself from going sour in the end *(as we all do, he said)* from winding up a solitary, depleted, antagonistic, carping, ruined old man nobody wanted in his house. He saw that Jesus was clearly the smartest man in the Bible; he was really the only man, with the exception of Moses, who had any real range at all, had any idea, at all, of what reality was *(the real one, he said)*. But he was a nut. Jack wanted to speak to someone of this, about what Jesus must have been thinking when Judas planted the kiss on his cheek, of what it was like to hold the end of things in your hand like a kitten and not throw the cat against the wall. If Jezu and the thief were going to meet in paradise this afternoon, then they were both somehow the same—birds of a fucking feather—wasn't this true? And what do you think, Preacher—is there a distinction between the saint who's scraped for sixty years to get holy and the crook who makes a dash for sanctuary in the last second? Purloined paradise? He stopped going to the Methodist church when a little girl after one service asked him why he squinted so meanly at the minister and he was embarrassed and felt exposed—guilt-ridden criminal snared in the light—and he began to stutter and sweat like a burglar.

And then in the Presbyterian church, where the minister beat on the podium with a big onyx ring he wore on the middle finger of his right hand, Jack, sitting alone next to a family in which there was a small boy afflicted with some terrible disease that made his body twist horribly around itself like a vine and whose eyes rolled up into his head until only the marbleized whites showed, but who, so oddly, seemed completely happy, one spring morning when he could smell freshly mown grass through the open blue-stained windows, suddenly as the stout soloist rose for the offertory hymn, felt in his guts, deep inside in a place he didn't know existed, the clutch of death.

He did not expect this. To Clare he said as they lay in the bathtub facing each other, "I did not expect in church to feel death grab me."

"Maybe that's not what it was."

Her breasts gleamed.

"No," he said, "it's not that I didn't expect it, it's that living here has lulled me to the point where I'd forgotten to expect it."

"That's different."

"Don't tell me it means something's about to happen."

"I won't. But something *is* about to happen."

She touched his cock lightly with her foot.

"Agh," he said. "*That* death."

In the nursing home, where Jimmy Acajou lay like an effigy, were all the demented and busted-up and outworn folk from the county and surrounding hamlets. Relatives brought these ruined characters there to get rid of them. They didn't want psycho Grandma hanging around the house anymore. Jack appreciated this. He understood. There were limits to what people could take. In the rest home, he got to see what became of good intentions, and of bad intentions since there were people aboard who hadn't much wrong with them beyond being members of a selfish family. Some had been unloaded into the home at the first sign of weakness, dumped. Others, however, were the remains of struggle. You could see, Jack thought, what was left of some terrible fight to stay the course of agreed-upon righteousness: some grandfather with a blood and bowel problem, a screamer maybe, who was up by three, breaking things and yelling, but who had been held on to by his daughter for months, maybe years, as she attempted to love with a kind of love she thought she had to keep firing, but finally couldn't, and so had brought old punched-in Gramps here, dumped him and returned home guilt-gnawed and sobbing to face the empty room that, even as she looked into it for the first time, she felt herself rising lightly from to freedom, a freedom she was forced to hate because it represented the betrayal she couldn't avoid. Terror in the heart, then, Jack thought.

But even that you get over, he thought. Life chooses life. Is that what was going on with the thief?

Once, as he picked up a plate of orange slices from the floor where a nurse had placed it so she could wipe a patch of yellow vomit off an end table, he saw his father in Duluth, standing in his office, which looked out across the docks and beyond them to the blue glossy lake, and it came to him with a jolt that his father had "loved" him but was so afraid of himself and his own loneliness that he could not bear living even, because life was only a mockery of death, a mean joke in the face of itself, like Nazis spitting into the rabbi's mouth, that he (his father) had to labor furiously every day of his life to find some way to get successfully off the planet *(It was his life's work, he said, his job and vocation; and he was not even good at that, he couldn't come up with the formula; he was like a backyard scientist straining and laboring, tabulating, building rockets out of cans, keeping notes, pondering, in some quest that was ridiculous on the face of it—or maybe not: maybe the failure, the rocket exploding on the launchpad, was what he was after—some idiotic destiny only a crazy man would choose, but one that gets you so engrossed, nonetheless, you forget that and just go after it, work hard . . .)* because *simply being here* was so unbearable.

As always now on such occasions, when for a second something in the past cleared up, the present skipped and he experienced a sense of his own death. This experience was not painful, as the experience in church had been, it was only a tiny jolt in his brain, a clear glass bead dropping off the necklace of thought (which, when all the beads were gone, would *be* his death—he was sure of it), but even so, he had to sit down and take his bearings.

He sought accommodation. A con. He was a man who loved crime. He had loved it since he was a child. He stole by the age of four, by six he took cleverly, got caught at seven and was punished by force, strapped, and felt the bite of the lash deeply and angrily, vowed to give back what he received, continued to steal, to take with guile, stealth, confidentially, and sometimes with wit, sometimes purely with force, force if necessary, continued in this way of life uninterruptedly through childhood *(I was alive in crime)* into puberty and young manhood even as his so-called normal life accompanied him like a puppy through school and sports and early love right into the University of Chicago, where he was busted for beating a boy who stole from *him,* and did not *(as he claimed)* go on from there to law school except for a year of night courses at the John Marshall School of Jurisprudence in Philadelphia, which was, as far as he was concerned, no school at all but only a training ground for criminals and cops.

It was urgent business. He could not resist his desire to take what he wanted. He did not want to resist. Not often. He loved the business. There was remorse, but he learned to live with that. His belief was conservative: that there was a huge vat of goodness wickedness polluted only little by little.

In prison the first time he had been beaten until he begged. They did not give him mercy and he became for two months the punk boy of a tough con from Cleveland, Brady Gunnison, until he was able through what agency he did not know or understand to gather himself as a man would gather up a bag of spilled groceries and attack this man Gunnison with a blade he'd fashioned from three pieces of stiff bound wire, and stab him to death through the right temple. This set him free *(not free, no: set him loose, he said)*, he was not charged with the crime; the other cons came forward then and celebrated his existence with cigarettes and chuck beer, and Donnie Bee, who had watched developments with the eye of a pimp, enlisted him in a scheme for the distribution of mail, essential goods, and television time, which they were able for nearly a year to keep going before he discovered Donnie skimming profits and turning them into dope for distribution through an entirely different network. When he confronted Donnie, the man denied everything, but later he'd tried to have him killed, and for a period of time the cellblock was divided into warring camps, a situation that easily could have escalated into armed conflict but for the administration's intervention, the warden's, in fact, outright release of Donnie Bee on some new program a naive governor had put into effect. He didn't see Donnie for three years, until he and Clare came to New Orleans and discovered him working a river scheme ferrying aliens up through the bayous.

(But the heart's reasons aren't Reason, he said—and you see quickly that the church, the temple, the ashram, and the mosque are all constructed to support the practical philosophy of the moment, the bourgeois philosophy at this *moment, capitalism; and so you find yourself one day after a bank job in which two people were killed—cleanly, as it were: shot once each—find yourself leaning over a bridge rail in some rural county vomiting your guts into a stream that is already stained bright red from effluents and some biological discharge that kills everything it touches, and you begin to wonder why God hasn't reached you yet, hasn't called you back; and then*

you pull yourself together slightly and you go on down through the woods to the clearing where your cohorts, your sullen partners, are dividing the money, and you accept your share, you jam it into the sack and you walk up the hill and maybe then you stop a second and look up into the trees that are going yellow with autumn and you realize you missed summer, didn't even notice the heat, and then it's as if you've been grabbed by the neck and carried by some big lion mother to another planet entirely because you have no idea where you are, what country this is, what they do here, or who that woman is staring into your face, grinning, and you suddenly get it how gunfire has become religious. . . .)

In the afternoons, between his occasional orchard jobs, he took long walks on the levee. Grassy, fifty feet high, as wide as a ship, the levee separated the town from the river. On the river side were the floating docks, a couple of warehouses, and a small loading facility. In the late afternoons the shadow from the high wall reached into the town, muting colors, flooding the streets and the houses. Two worlds were cut off from each other by the long line of dirt and grass, and though no passport was needed to cross from one side to the other, the years of separation—so it seemed to him—had changed both parties. The river was no longer the infiltrating presence, destroyer or abettor, but now only an untrustworthy stranger who had to be kept in its place; and the town, once humble enough to accept whatever came its way, whether flood or heavy, slow passing of time rolling downstream, imagined itself as indestructible, as exemplar of a shape and style that would endure forever.

Sometimes, from the levee's south extension, up above the trees and the cornfields that began abruptly at the edge of town, he could see Clare outside the small brick grammar school she occasionally taught in. The job had been easy to come by. Only a sober articulateness and a willingness to be waked early on short notice were necessary. After school, sometimes, she would sit with the children on a bench talking. He could see, even from a distance, the ease in her, the delight. Actual children had always been strange to her, she disliked them and had never wanted her own, not real children (there were children she imagined, brought to life in the mind, to play with, walk about with), but now, maybe because there was no rough business around them, she drew pleasure from their company. She said it was because they were like her. They, too, believed in the perfection of their desires. They, too, felt the world tumble like a monkey through their bodies. "I watch you talking to them," he said as they sat after dinner on the porch. A dry breeze blew through the trees.

"From where?"

"From the levee. It comforts me."

"I don't really care about the regular kids. It's the others I'm waiting for."

"Which others?"

"The retarded children."

"Oh, yes."

"They come out later. I love them. I know all their names."

"I remember a retarded boy in Minnesota, from Winona, whom everyone tormented."

"Yes. It's easy to do."

She pushed back in her rocker. The restlessness in her was calmer tonight. "At first you think they're just gross and clumsy, like bad imitators of the rest of us, and then you realize they're a different, what—species, not like us at all. It's not just their brains and their bodies that're different, it's everything—their feelings, their spirits, everything."

"How do you know?"

"You can look at them and tell. They'll say something ten times because they want to hear you answer it ten times. They like to rub small private places, shiny places or stones, the knob of your wrist. Their hands are smooth. Some of them don't even have fingerprints."

"Are you sure of that?"

"Yes."

"We ought to get them to work for us."

"They like to do the little jobs, the difficult, humble, forgotten jobs."

"You're getting sentimental, sweetie."

"Am I? I hope not. I don't think of protecting them, anything like that. They remind me of dolphins. Land dolphins. Wallowing and basking around and grinning."

He laughed. "Another species we've destroyed. Another nation disassembled. Sweet idiots drowned in the nets of our greed."

"That's sentimental. And pompous."

"No, honey, it's delight."

"It delights me to look at them. And excites and frightens me. I'm glad they like me. I want their blessing."

"I don't think any one of them would deny it to you."

She gazed at him fondly, from a dream. "I don't think so, either."

"All the afflicted love you."

"They're not afflicted—that's certainly not so."

"Coodge is like them. And he loves you."

"Yes," she said. "He's in another world."

"Could I talk to them?"

"Who?"

"The retarded children."

She said he could, so he went to school one afternoon and addressed them. He had intended to interview them, but when he entered the classroom and discovered the children with their disfocused eyes and their clumsy hands clapping and their dopey smiles like makeup smeared across their faces, discovered their delight and their willingness, he saw he could make them do anything he wanted them to do, and suddenly he was afraid he might, like some bedeviled piper, entice them to their feet and march them right into the river, something. He instead took a place in front of them and began to speak as if that was what he had been ordered to do, reciting first a couple of nursery rhymes and then singing a song about Wayward Willie and his little red truck, and then launching into a speech about God and his minions, which seemed more a long question than a speech.

"I don't have an answer for it myself," he said finally, "but I've been haunted since I was a child by this apparition or ghost or whatever it was I saw once when I was out on a boat on Lake Superior. I was looking in to shore, I heard a noise I guess, and suddenly I saw this buckeroo peering out at me from behind a tree. He was an exact copy of me. Have any of you ever seen anything like that?"

Several children raised their hands.

"That's good," he said. "Maybe I'm not alone."

He thought he was doing something terribly wrong, but he could not stop himself.

"Who do you think this was looking at me? Was it me, or was it some better self—or was it a devil? Maybe Jesus? Maybe some trick of light? And why then? The night before, my sister saw a rainbow opposite the moon. She came in from the fields where she'd been walking and told us. My father scolded her. He was between suicides at the time. Just barely. He had reached the end of his rope again. We were in the kitchen, all of us, and no one said anything when he rebuked my sister, but we all looked at him. With such scorn. He saw it and turned red with shame.

"It seems to me we are all a race of idiots. I don't mean you. I mean everyone. We're nuts and we're stupid and even when we mean well we ruin everything we touch. Look at this town, look at the levee, which is like a battlement to keep the bestial river out. What it means is that when there's a flood the water's going to be that much higher downstream for the next town. The next town is going to be put under like a sack of puppies. But up here everyone feels safe and righteous. Actually they're killers. We're all like this. In our attempt to reach the exit we trample our neighbors. If somebody ever acts slightly different, through some slipup, or even some temporary goodness, lets some crone get ahead, it is so unusual and so unbelievable that reporters come to see him: he gets written up in the paper and the President gives him a medal. Jesus H. Fucking Christ. Wait. Do you see what I mean? Jesus H. Fucking Christ. Can you say that?"

Halt and lame, the class repeated the words.

"Good. Here's the deal: If there is a God, how is it possible not to acknowledge him? I have been in prison. In prison you see men who are beyond hope. Do you understand me? Take God out of the church, put him instead inside a wet potato some bum picks out of a garbage can on a South Side street in Chicago, some bitter night. Make God the spike poised over our vampire hearts. Say he's the third birch tree on the right at the end of the empty field you walk out into the evening you realize you are not going to make it in this world. Or reduce him even further. Make him a memory, a tendency that slips by on a sad night in a motel room in Tulsa. Make him the spin on a breadfruit chip dropping down a gutter drain yesterday in Bangkok. Grit. A molecule. The last atom in a raddled row of atoms about to be busted in a particle accelerator. Or smaller. A quark, a heavy speck spun off the lonely rim of the universe. A burp on a baby's lips ten thousand years ago. What then? Even this, no matter how you shake and muster this being, he can still be denied. Do you get it? Do you? What is going on?"

The children beamed at him.

He stopped. Around the walls muddled lovely pictures painted by the dumb hands of the retarded were set under tacks. They were beautiful, he thought, ridiculous and hilariously stupid and perfect.

He said, "Did the thief repent? That's what I would like to know. Did he repent? Did his question constitute repentance? Or was it his rebuke to his partner? I don't think so. Jesus asked nothing of him. He didn't ask the guy to change. I don't believe he did—change. Jesus wanted acknowledgment. Go on being a thief, Buster, but believe I am God. That's where the connection is, don't you think? Speak to me so I'll know I am real. Jesus was into it. So are we. All of us. Look around you—all these buildings and this action, these guys running after women, love, fresh delights on the TV—they're all about getting over. We want to be apprehended by love. Even robbing banks."

He began to get a sick feeling in his stomach. It was time for someone to reach in and stop him. Where were the boys he had grown up with, the boys who *hadn't* become criminals? Billy Braddocks and Louis Gold and Jake Noonucks and little Davey Gusset—what had become of them? They had all once sat in classrooms like this, fidgeting, dreaming about life to come. Who was giving it to them now? *God bless them,* he said silently.

This thought, this moment, passed in a flash.

"Now," he said, "there's something I want you to do."

He stopped. He had been lying on his back in the boat when he saw his double. The boy, the sweet face looking at him, the Jesus of his nature beckoning. *But what of the rest of it?*

He said, "I'm going to teach you to say a prayer. Do you know what a prayer is?"

Several children waved gaily at him.

"Good. Everybody: say 'My name is Willie.' "

Their sweet rainy voices came back to him: "My name is Willie."

"Good. Now I want everybody to repeat after me—"

Several children said, "Repeat after me."

"Good. Dear Lord—"

Their voices followed him.

"Please help us all, and especially David and Sue"—their Anacondia names—"to reach our goals."

The children droned along behind.

"Help us to live long and free."

". . . live long and free."

"Give us happiness and money and good getaways."

"Good . . ."

"And may we all meet—but not today—"

". . . not today . . ."

"In paradise."

"In paradise."

"Amen."

The children looked at him. Several had folded their hands. "God bless this food," one, a skinny boy in the corner, said solemnly.

"Yes," Jack said, "God bless this food."

"Hooray," a little girl said.

"Yes," Jack said, "hooray. Hooray," he said loudly.

"Hooray, hooray!" the children shouted.

(It wasn't that I was rattled, he said, though I was rattled—it wasn't, because I was always rattled—we all were—so that didn't matter; it was that I could no longer see ahead, upriver, you might say, and this scared me. I didn't mind getting glimpses of death, or whatever, I knew they weren't going to have to chain me to a bed—or I thought they weren't—but I felt left out, that was the problem, excluded from my own variation, *the crib sheet I had come up with years ago to deal with my sense of exclusion. Do you understand? I had become excluded from my own answer to exclusion. That old man I told you about, the one by the river that day when I went down to watch the hogs being slaughtered—that old man, who was a nobody, as everyone in that town was, told me he had to work his whole life without letup. He meant at a job, and at his family, at staying alive in that little town, and I thought about this, deeply thought about it, because* what was so hard *if you were born to it? I mean so hard about doing the job in a town like that? But the old man meant something else, he meant staying alive on the planet, meant it was terribly hard to put two breaths together, to get up and go into the day, to keep alive; and one night it came to me about how we each seek rest, and we think rest means* lying down, *but how could this be, since when people* lie down *they simply get sick, unhappy, and die, so you can discard that: it must mean work, or at least involvement; so, if this is true, what kind of involvement? And that's the problem we face, and maybe that's what we're doing: working our asses off every day of our lives as we go on and on inside our heads wondering about what kind of involvement we're supposed to have here on the planet. But what do you do when you have come to the end of involvement? Like when they close the factory? Then what? Do you go back to the*

woods? I asked the old man this. They were scraping bristles off the hogs. There were fires burning, it was fall, just before the debacle occurred, cold, frost on the pumpkin, you might say, a whole community out cutting off hams and sides of bacon. These hogs hung up by their heels, they looked almost human, pink and helpless. How far back do you go? I asked him. Is there a point—back there—where you can find perfection? Find a way to go, be? What about my mythic moment, what about that? A boy in a T-shirt looking at me from among hemlocks across an expanse of open water. If I had looked down that afternoon, I could have seen the bottom, the water was so clear. There were gray and blue and purple rocks on the bottom, round as cannonballs. The boat was painted dark green. There were yellow-button flowers at the base of the hemlocks, piled gray soft-looking rocks heaped on the shore, a low shore that rose easily to the woods. Behind the boy there was nothing but woods, nothing but wilderness all the way to the Arctic. I didn't say this to the old man, but what kills me is that every time I think of this, and I think of it a lot, I realize I am not that boy, not the boy looking at himself. He is not me anymore. Do you understand? There is no way possible that boy who rocked in that boat staring into the face of himself could have become the man you see before you. But I must *believe he is. Do you understand? There is the act of faith. I must make that leap. I must somehow come to believe that this man here and that boy are the same.* That, *I think, is what the Crucifixion is about, the thief part, I mean. The two, the Christ, this perfect character who never did a bad thing, and this unruly thief, this ruffian hanging there: they were, for one moment, the same. How did this happen? What occurred? I believe it was this: there was an act of faith. For a long time I thought it was the thief's. But it wasn't. The thief did what he always did. It was Christ's. For the first time in his thirty-three years of life, Jesus believed what he was saying. But more important:* he admitted that someone else was like him. *The thief grabbed for the flash. Do you understand?* But how does that apply? *I became unhinged, in a manner of speaking. Actually, I think that's what happens to people out there in the cities and towns. Everything's a paradox. Too tough to mix, ingredients that just can't be made to adhere. They are all crazy, I figure, all these straights. The arrangement drives them crazy. That's why they work so hard. I told the old man this, the snappy version:* it's so fucking complicated, *I said,* they work themselves to death so they won't have to think about it. *[What I meant to add was that was not all that happened out on the lake. There was more than one recognition took place. There was not only the pretty boy peeking. But I didn't.]*

This is what I got into, he said, *when I lived among the straights.)*

In the fall they became agitated. They were like berry bushes picked at by birds. They argued, but they understood what this was about, how the argument was a kind of housecleaning, a preparation. She told him she felt a huge pull in her, toward home again, toward her father, toward some kind of resolution of the business with her brothers and with him. "If I think closely about it, about him being set to kill you," she said, "then the rage comes back."

"For me, too," he said.

Jimmy's money was paying their way. Jack converted the gold to cash in Nashville, at crooks' prices, and spent it on Jimmy's expenses and their own. The supply dwindled.

The harsh, brilliantly lit dreams of prison came back, returned for them both. They felt the dreariness upon awakening, the sadness, the foulness in the mind that was for them a kind of death, a shame and despair that sat inside them like a muddy shadow-being brooding over their crimes. Each found the other alone in the house in the dark or walking around in the dark outside, in the garden or along the sidewalk that ran into town, found each other staring into the hardware store window, into the fish market, where the empty cases held troughs filled with ice stained pink with fish blood. He walked the railroad tracks behind the house, sometimes thinking about walking away to another town, another city, some other country. She painted the rooms, or started to, but gave up when she didn't have enough yellow to finish, found herself unable to complete the job. They stopped making love.

Once in the checkout line at the supermarket she burst into tears and had to leave the store. He began, on their walks, to make small involuntary moaning noises that annoyed her, but which even after she begged him to he was unable to stop. Looking out at the river, which in fall was the color of tar, and sprinkled near the banks with red and yellow leaves, he felt a violent urge to throw himself in. He began to take trips on Coodge's boat, excursions upriver, ostensibly fishing trips, but more often tethered journeys in which he imagined them heading upstream past St. Louis, past Quad Cities and Minneapolis–St. Paul, on up into the wild lands. But always, as he leaned against the wheel looking out at the open stretch of water ahead, he felt the pull to the right, right at Cairo, cross country and upriver, up the Ohio to Indiana, to the ugly green farm buildings and the big ramshackle house Clare was born in, where as far as he knew the old man sat up nights watching for them to appear on his big weedy lawn like phantoms risen out of the river, come to get him.

Why don't we just forget this? he asked her, but she could not and she told him she could not.

He himself, growing stout on country food, grown irritable and oppressed, knew clearly that this family business was in itself only a ruse, a diversion. In prison he had discovered that he was tired. These days of what he called rest did not rejuvenate him. He did not long for banks in the same old way. If he did, the desire was fleeting. But he did not want to become a townsman, a citizen. She bared her teeth at him when he asked if such a life would be acceptable to her.

The miseries of interiority did not subside. He found her leaning over the bathroom sink staring at herself in the mirror. She told him she was thinking of killing herself. He understood this, had in dreams begun to see himself being crushed by large objects, by falling houses, by ships keeling over, by landslides and avalanches. Webs of paranoia began to appear, strung up between here and there, which they walked face first into. They thought the townspeople were staring at them. The retarded children had not turned them in, but only, she said, because they were unable to. He thought the clerk in the hardware store recognized him, and he was sure the bookie at the Lingerlong, a frail, ugly man who worked the line to Nashville, knew him from some former episode and was only biding his time before turning them in. A rustle in the pecan trees behind the house became sinister, there were unexplained dark patches at the bottom of the garden, beds of trampled ferns by the railroad tracks looked as if they contained spring-traps, and when the weedy growth by the road out to the nursing home died all in the same week—sprayed by the county to kill poison ivy—he thought this somehow had to do with them, that it was a sign by angry councilmen that they were to watch out. He became afraid that local crimes would be pinned on them, that a burglary at the Holiness Church would be sniffed to their doorstep, and when the Caprice Lounge out on the highway to Coralton burned, she had to grab his arm to stop him from getting up in church to explain to the congregation that they had nothing to do with it, that he, in fact, since he was burned—with scars to prove it—had a horror of fire.

He missed Rubens and wanted him to appear, wanted him to tell their story so he could put a copy of it in the dairy case at the supermarket, tack it to the school door, hang it like wallpaper in the nursing home, roll it up like a newspaper and toss it onto his neighbors' front lawns. He wanted everyone to know about them, but he was terrified he might suddenly begin talking, spouting the facts of their crimes, jabbering of banks and getaways and death.

And then one night as they crossed the street in front of the Lingerlong a small man stepped out of the door and hailed them.

"That's Suck Jackson," Clare said.

"Jesus dammit Christ."

Suck scampered up to them. "Jack and Clare," he cried, holding out his small hands. "We were about to come looking for you."

"Hello, Suck," Jack said. "Who's we?"

"Guys come up the river with me."

"Who?"

"Little Mikey Breen, Joe Cane. Donnie Bee's here, too. And that writer—Rubens—you know him. And your brother, Clare."

"What's Donnie doing here?"

"Just traveling through, Jack. Guy told us you were living up here. We thought we'd come by." He looked around. "This is a real small town, Jack."

"Now it's bigger."

Suck reached to stroke Clare's sleeve. She drew her arm away. "Don't be mad, Jack. We're just visiting. Donnie really wants to see you."

Jack looked at Clare. Clare looked back at him. Here, not at home, the look said.

It was a gauntlet. First Will at the door, bobbing and weaving, his skinny face crimped with a grimace that his eyes looked coldly through. He did not shake Jack's hand. Clare took him in her arms, but she let him go quickly and stepped back, wary. Will said, "I've forgiven everything. I'm not worried about any of the past." The skin of Will's face was very smooth; it looked as if he had no need to shave. He scowled and hooted a hollow laugh. "I've given up getting back at people," he said. "It's the worst thing in the world for your peace of mind. I'm all for going on as if nothing happened."

"I didn't miss you, Will," Clare said.

"I wish you had."

"I'm not going to miss you anymore."

"Maybe you will. Maybe you'll remember me and come around to thinking good thoughts about me."

"Donnie still got his thumb on you, Will?" Jack said.

"I think it's about to slide off in your direction, Jack. I sense it."

Rubens lurked at the bar halfway down the room. Jack could see Donnie, not at first, but then he could, sitting at a back table out of the light. There seemed to be a shadow of pain around him, an area of desolation and mendacity. Behind him on the wall a blue neon beer sign hung like a molten quivering emblem of suffering.

Rubens waved, a slight, weak hand movement. Jack had thought he wanted to see this man, but he realized now that he had no interest in him. Rubens slid their way, grasped Jack's sleeve as he passed. Jack stopped. Rubens dropped his hand.

"I've been writing everything down," he said. "I have some fascinating material. I'm doing the story now. The only way I can get it properly told is to put it in a book. A biography, true crime, love saga thing. It's really beautiful. But I need to talk to you. I'm scared—"

"Shut up, fuckhead," Jack said.

Donnie rose to meet him. The Cheetah, Clare sometimes called him. Cat face. But not a cheetah's face, Jack thought. He had the round fat face of a house cat. Fat cheeks, lipless prim mouth. *Hey, Jack. Hey, Jack, how are you, beautiful boy, how is everything?* It was like a voice from the creepy dark, from around the bend, from out of the stuporous river on a still night of pain. *Jack, Jack. What are you doing, Jack, off here in this little lost burg? How come you got yourself hid out here where they don't have any tamales or flashing lights, Jack? Where you got the action, Jackie, you got it in your pocket, you got it out front, you open up a restaurant and retire, Jack?* There were thugs on either side of him, pistol-whippers, loose boys from New Orleans, from one of the country parishes across the river actually. He knew them, Little Mikey and Joe Cane. Jack reached in front of Little Mikey and slapped Donnie lightly across the nose.

Donnie's head snapped back. "Ow."

Little Mikey, in one fat quick move, threw Jack to the floor. The thug's gun was on him like a snake's head.

"That's okay," Donnie said. "That's quite all right."

Jack got up. There were bursts of dust on his pants as if he had shattered small globes of it. "There's always going to be that lag time, Donnie. Between when I hit you and he hits me."

"Always was, Jack," Donnie said. He rubbed his nose. "Hello, Ms. Clare Manigault."

Clare didn't answer him. "I'll be over here if you need me," she said to Jack. She moved toward the bar, drifting into the space between the door and the hoodlums, claiming the territory they would have to travel through to get out.

"Fine, fine," Donnie said as if she had spoken to him. He had a bushel of yellow apples in front of him. He ran his hand over the fruit as he spoke, rubbing his thumb into the curve of each piece. He smiled thinly. "You're not going to let Clare shoot us, are you, Jack?"

"Clare does what she wants, Donnie."

"Righteously yes she does. Damn."

Jack pulled up a chair, shoved it between Little Mikey and his boss.

"I'm tired," Donnie said. "We've come all this long way up from New Orleans. These are good apples. Don't you want one?"

"I work in the orchards. I get plenty."

"You got a job, Jack?"

"Sometimes."

"I never would have thought that. I never would have pictured you working at a job."

"It passes the time."

"You must be getting old, Jack, to think like that."

Donnie selected an apple, fat, with a pink blush along one side, and bit into it. Juice spurted between his lips. He chewed noisily, looking around the room. "There's not much going on in this town," he said. "Or am I wrong?"

"You're right."

Will was playing pool by himself. Clare stood next to Rubens at the bar.

"What are you doing here, Jack?" Donnie said without looking at him.

"Looking after Jimmy Ack."

"Coodge's here now?"

"Coodge?" Joe Cane said. His eyes opened wide when he spoke, as if words pressurized him.

"Jimmy Acajou," Donnie said. "You know him. He's a gambler."

"Oh, yeah. I heard he hadn't been good for anything since his partner got killed."

"I heard that, too. What's Coodge doing here, Jack?"

"He had a stroke out on the river. We brought him here."

"And you've been living in this metropolis taking care of him ever since?"

"Yep."

"Jesus, you're a sweet boy."

"What are you doing here, Donnie?"

"Go over there, you two," Donnie said to the thugs. He leaned over the table, looked at Jack directly for the first time. Jack thought of the river, of the flights of ducks that had begun to appear above it, headed south. Last week Clare said she saw swans. He turned to look at her. She was talking to Suck Jackson. Suck waved his arms, capered before her grinning, as if he was trying to mesmerize her. He felt a tense sadness begin to press at him. *(We could imagine each other, he said, that was the key. Any feeling, any action, we could come up with it in times of silence and separation. I dreamed my way out of prison into the narrow bed she slept in on the shore of Lake Michigan. I dived into her body and rested there, looking up at the crossbeams and the pale yellow boards of her ceiling. I thought her thoughts, and she came into the prison and thought mine. Sometimes this was terrible. Sometimes it was like being trapped inside a nightmare, and maybe this was the terrible draw each of us had for the other, the fascination, this reduction into dream that we shared, the horror of seeing the other, of experiencing the cramps and blusters of each, of stepping into a cold river and sliding your feet along the slick bottom, feeling the quick fish bite, and going on, going down into the dark water where the monsters lived. . . .)*

Donnie said, "I heard about the trouble in New Orleans—the cops, Jack, and about Clare's brother. He set you up, turned you in, I know. He's a mean boy. I was sorry about all that, but we've got him calmed down now."

"What do you know about it?"

"About your father-in-law?"

"About the money."

"That was just a chimera, Jack. There was never no money. It was a dream reckoning the old man came up with after his other boy got killed. You sit poorly in his lights, Jack."

"Why are you here, then, Donnie?"

"Actually, Acajou drew me. You know me, Jack. I can't stay away from a sure thing. Word's out about the gold. Did you know about it before?"

"No."

"I knew Buster down in the Quarter. He was an evil character. I'm the one put him on the gold man, Stimey Franks. I got them together a few years ago. Took me a while, until just recently, to find out what the write-up was, but I came on it. Suck was a help, little smirking bastard. It's a hundred pounds of gold, isn't it?"

"Not hardly."

Donnie's eyes blazed. "It's got to be. I kept a count. It's got to be at least a fucking hundred. I made a trip up here. I want a hundred."

"Gold's not yours, Donnie."

"It's sure as fuck not yours, Jack."

"Most of it's used up. We've been paying Coodge's expenses at the nursing home; we paid his medical bills, all that."

"And spent the rest on yourself?"

"The rest of it's in the bank here."

"You put the money in the fucking bank?"

"I like banks."

"I know the fuck you do. But what the hell you putting gold in a bank for? Man, shit." He turned his face away, shook himself. "I knew this," he said, turning back. His cat face was screwed in a grimace. "I knew you had crumpled. I saw it coming. You never learned how to get on the good ride. You never learned it. You always either went too far or you didn't go far enough. That was always you. You tried to use your fucking imagination, you tried to discover things. Fucking, Jack. Man, I got you in the palm of my hand. I'm a goddamn magician. I can change you into a rabbit, into a fucking piece of cheese I feed to my rats."

"How long you felt this way, Donnie?"

"Shit. Since Joliet at least."

Jack grinned at him.

"Fuck you, Jack," Donnie said.

Jack grinned.

Donnie leaned back in his chair. He slowly scanned the room. "I hate these places," he said. "These grubby little pool halls in these grubby little towns. They make you feel ashamed of yourself. But these idiots," he said, indicating his partners, "they like it here. They're always on the lookout for somebody lower on the shelf than they are." He licked beads of juice off his apple. "That's the difference between people: there're the ones who want to better themselves, and there're the ones who just want to pound anybody worse off than they are. It's like politics. You been following the election?"

"Not really."

"You ought to. Politics is very instructive. The Republicans—these guys. You know what the secret slogan of the Republican Party is?"

"No."

"Keep the nigger down."

"—"

"Yeah, that's it. *Keep the nigger down.* Don't let anybody lower than you get a leg up. Jesus. It's all about fear. That's all it's about. Republican—*I'm scared to death.* That's all that word means. More laws. More police. More intrusion into a free man's heart."

"I'm sorry they're such a torment to you."

Donnie smiled his feline smile. "Ah, Jack. You never let anybody get close to you, do you?"

"I guess not."

"Jack. You know why I really came all the way up here?"

"You smelled dead meat?"

"No. Ha-ha. I came up here because I'm lonely. I need somebody to talk to. You don't like anybody much, but you're the best talker I know, Jack. I used to love to listen to you talk. Up there in Joliet you taught that class, the one on the great books. I remember that class. I loved to hear you talk about those books. You made the whole other side of life come alive."

"You've been pining all these years?"

"I didn't know it, but I was. Will, he was the one made me realize it. He likes to talk about you."

"I don't know him that well."

"He worships you, Jack. Down deep he does. He talks about you all the time. He thinks you've gotten away with everything. It frustrates him a little, you can tell that. But mostly he worships you for it. He thinks you are a blue-ribbon character. And I promise you—all that shit about his father, the old man with a gun, is just bullshit. It's simply not true."

It would go on this way, he knew. Donnie liked to poke into private life. He liked to nozzle around in the sheets of your privacy, to lather up your soap, get into your clothes. He wanted to know secrets, the dirtier the better. Like many who could see to the heart, he preferred gossip to facts. Jack knew what he had got Will to tell him. And Rubens, who looked now, leaning over the bar as if he was about to leap over it and flee, Rubens was caught by Donnie, too, and had revealed everything.

Now, by plan, Jack's life, too, would become a suit Donnie wore—this must be true, like the gold vest Jimmy put on in memory of his partner, put on with avarice and love in his heart—and Jack would be asked to pay for this suit—that was the project—to compliment Donnie on the cut of it, on himself hung on to the frame of a killer, his own life draped across his back, and made to learn to live like this, would be asked to do this, too, instructed carefully in the means of it—how to comply—and, like the thugs, would be given the hope of a pat on the head, a kiss maybe, if he got lucky, given a postponement on his death scene, which would be waiting for him at the checkout counter, along with the torture scene and the scene in which he watched his wife go down on this devil—Jack knew this. But he did not flee. He could not, not yet, not now.

Time passed not in increments, not in flashes, not in thoughts, but in pictures. He lay under the bunk seeing things. There was the path through the woods that he and his sister Rita walked each day, back to the barns where in the old days cattle had spent the winters. Now the barns were empty; they smelled of old hay and of broken, useless implements. There were cribs—he saw them—where corn was stored, and a harness room, and even old plows stacked on top of one another like big insect skeletons. He saw the plows and saw the discarded cans of his grandfather's Prince Albert tobacco, the flat red cans, each with a tiny pinch of tobacco left inside; and his sister, he could see her blond hair pulled back and tied with a blue strip of dishrag, and then beyond her slender body, through the open door, he could see the summer day, which from the dark seemed like a great promise come true, shining; and suddenly, as he looked at the light, he felt, for all of them, a terrible pity.

Donnie mashed the remains of his apple onto the table. It broke open crisply. He said, "In prison there are two main categories of convicts: the bad men and the drunks. The bad men don't care, what they've done doesn't bother them; they fix on something and tough shit for you if you're in the way. The drunks, on the other hand, are filled with guilt and remorse. What they've done eats at them, and they are ashamed of themselves. Both categories show up for AA, NA, and all the As, for therapy and school, but only the drunks take it seriously; the bad men hope compliance will set them free. They just want to get out. That's how it is. But there's another category that nobody looks at much. I'm a bad man myself, I always have been, but you're in this other category, Jack. You guys, you like all this robbing and thieving and carrying on, and you don't have remorse about it like the drunks do, but you still believe in redemption. I know about you, Jack. You think there's another side to things. That's why you're up here taking care of Coodge. What'd you say he had—a stroke? I'll bet he doesn't even know you're here. But you do it anyway because you've got some idea about the sweetness and nobility of life. At the same time, you are a sneak and a killer, a man of rage who will shove his buddy off a cliff any day. I hate your type. You're never straight, you use your scruples and your *wondering* about life to make you believe you care about things you don't care about. You live the worst kind of masquerade. I know you plan to get this money, no matter that you have probably already spent four ninety-five on Coodge. I know you. And you are going to open the door for me. Hello, Clare."

She had come up behind Jack. Her hand nested lightly on his shoulder. "I'm tired, sweetie," she said.

"I am, too," Donnie said. "I am worn out. You know how far it is up here from New Orleans?"

"Yes," Clare said.

The men got up. "You always know that kind of thing, Clare," Donnie said. "Mileage. You want an apple? They're local. We got them from a stand outside of town. That the outfit you work for, Jack?"

Jack didn't answer him.

"You look fit, Donnie," Clare said.

"Thank you. I feel fit. I took up jogging for a while, but it was so hard on Joe and Mikey—them wanting to accompany me and all—that I had to give it up. Now I swim—an hour every day. I like that better. You exercise, Jack?"

"Only incidentally."

"You ought to do it regular. I never felt better since I started. Of course, you never went in for any of that iron pumping—in prison, I mean."

"No."

"I never did, either. In prison I just thought about getting out, didn't you?"

"That's right."

"We're staying at the hotel." He knuckled his knobby chin. "You got power of attorney over Coodge's money, Jack?"

"It's in safe deposit."

"Good. We can go down in the morning and slide it out. Does that suit you?"

"Anything you say, Donnie."

"Jack and I have worked this out, Clare. We've got it evened out. I don't think there's any reason for anybody to get upset about it. Good things are coming for you."

"I'm not upset, Donnie," she said and smiled. There was a hard, low, confident menace in the smile. Donnie smiled back, not so confidently. "Joe, Mikey," he said to the men who hovered nearby, "take Jack and Clare home."

"We'll walk," Clare said.

"Fare thee well, then," Donnie said. "Until we meet again."

They went out into the night, which was calm and smelled of the river. The sky was filled with stars. There was a thin thief's moon, a sliver with no radiance. The wind had died. Suck had told Clare about Donnie's desire for gold. "It's a ruse," Jack said. "There's something else going on."

"This makes me think the daddy business is what's real."

"I suppose that's it."

"When are they going to kill us?"

"Tomorrow, after I take them to the bank."

He told her the story he'd passed to Donnie.

"That's pretty flimsy," she said.

"It's worse than that. It's got no purchase, and it's harmful to Jimmy."

"Jimmy won't mind."

As they passed the overgrown VFW park, beyond which was a creek that each spring crept to the back steps of low-lying houses, near a clump of young tulip poplars, Jack saw a man lurking. "It's Will," he said. "He's following."

"This whole thing is following."

"Yes."

"I still would rather you didn't kill him."

"We're being baited into the trap."

"Yes. It troubles me how much this means to me. I am so drawn to it."

"I understand, but for me it isn't the same."

"How is it?"

"It's as if I have been here before."

(The whole day before he saw the boy was a dream. They argued, his mother and father, he could hear them, and later he saw his father standing in the yard looking toward the hills, clutching his own bereaved, slumped shoulders. . . . Rita said she saw a rainbow opposite the moon. . . .)

"But last time you were only passing through."

"In expensive clothes, on my way to the Ritz."

"Yes."

"I'm going to slip around this way and catch up with the future, for a minute," he said.

"Don't try to change it."

"Okay."

At the corner *(where, to get to the house, he said, they turned up Fontaine Street for a block and then turned down Main and walked by the Billingses' house, and by old lady Adams's house, and by the preacher Revel's, and the house that was nailed up in shutters, where someone's father had died and the son hadn't been able to go back in the place, and by the old town spring, which was filled in now but still kept as a monument by the council under a square board box and pretty round blue-shingle roof, which children were brought to from first grade to see where water was drawn for the settlers and trades were made with indigenous Indians, past this and the green bench and the flock of daylilies rampant right to the edge of the street, past the tear in every room, and the shouts of outrage from the Porterfields' back porch, past the desperate pleadings he heard one night from the Galliards', by the grassy depression he lay down in and sobbed, where they'd made love twice, once on purpose, once blind with lust, and by the patch of nameless bushes, and the trickle of creek, the peonies, the gladiolus, the hollyhocks, and the burned, failing floribunda roses, and so finally to their gabled white house slashed with streaks of boarded-over rot, home at last)* he ducked away, doubled back behind the blackberry bushes Margorie Willis made a thin wine from in summer. He caught Will coming up the other side, caught him sneaking, half bent low, dark's commando. Like a kid in school, Jack stuck his foot out and tripped him. Will did a somersault and landed sprawled on his butt with his long legs stuck straight out. His head must have clipped his kneecap because his nose was bloody. Jack stepped from the bushes and took away the gun he'd dropped. Will raised his hand for it like a child grabbing for a toy, but Jack had it in his side pocket quick. Will stared at him and didn't say anything.

"Sorry," Jack said, "but neither Donnie or me want you to kill me just yet."

"I wasn't trying to kill you, Jack. I was just tagging along."

"With your pistol out?"

"I think you broke my damn nose."

"Probably."

Jack squatted in front of him. His brother-in-law smelled of grime and sweat. His coarse, corn-colored hair was spiky, thorny around his narrow head. Will touched his nose. "Agh—agh." He lay back on the grass. Jack waited for him to say something, but his brother-in-law didn't speak.

After a while Jack said, "So?"

"I always do that," Will said.

"What?"

"Wait 'em out. They expect me to talk, to explain, but I don't say nothing. It spooks 'em every time."

"Very crafty."

"I'm just looking up into the stars. That's the secret of waiting 'em out. You keep doing the thing you're doing like they don't exist. Smoke your cigarette, eat a peach, whatever, go right on with what you're doing and it drives 'em crazy. I learned it from the movies. Not exactly from the movies, but from movie actors, how they do a scene. One of 'em, I don't know which one it was, that one with the big blond hair—"

"Like you."

"No! Another one—he said when he's in a scene with some cunt where he's supposed to be talking to her, he'll just go on doing what he's already doing, tying his shoelaces or whatever it is, and the cunt'll have to wait and he'll get the points in the scene. It's acting. And it drives people crazy."

"That's what you want to do, all right."

Will blinked. "Agh. The stars are pretty. I don't think you broke my nose."

"Good."

"For a family member, Jack, you sure are rough."

"I'm the violent type, all right."

Will raised one hand, ran a tracery in front of his eyes. "You ever think how maybe the stars might not just be dots? How maybe what we are seeing isn't points but the bottoms of the stars? Maybe the stars are these huge columns and we're looking at the bottom of them. Maybe they are columns holding up the roof of heaven, and maybe we are looking up at the floor, this glass floor, like the glass bottom of one of those tour boats down in Florida. Maybe we're like the fishes looking up at the glass bottom of heaven."

Jack shivered. Will's voice had become toneless and grainy, the pitch was lower, it was as if he were dragging his fingers through the soft sand of it. This was what he must have sounded like during the two days he sat in the woods watching his brother die.

"Maybe that's all we mean to God, Jack. You ever think like that? Maybe we're just fishes and snapping turtles and crawfish and such to God. Maybe he and his cohorts are up there dancing in this big ballroom like kings and queens and we're just this dumb sideshow down here under the glass floor. Maybe they're tourists looking down at us—"

"Shut up, Will."

"I can't shut up, Jack. You got me scared shitless."

"Shut up anyway."

"Okay."

Jack waited a while longer, but nothing was going to happen. There were no human sounds in the night, none but their breathing. A dog barked on a distant street, stopped abruptly.

Jack stood up. "Shit," he said, "this is a fool's errand."

"Not if I survive it," Will said.

"What's Donnie after?"

"Everything he can get. You know him, Jack. He's greedy. He'll just keep adding to the pile. He doesn't even bother to hit the total button."

"You told him Francis put money on my head."

"He got it out of me."

"Man, your sister is the only thing that stands between you and your glass-bottom heaven."

"I praise her every day."

"Don't joke."

"Clare is not a joke to me."

He made the man get up then and he walked him over to the bottom of the park, where heavy oaks hung big branches out over the creek. After he stood there a minute thinking it was hopeless, unable to come up with anything else to do, he pushed Will into the water. The water wasn't deep, but the bottom was slick. Will slipped and fell, went under. He came up cursing. Jack felt the sudden meanness that had brought him to this act subside. He did not pity his brother-in-law, but for a second he felt as if he should, as if he should extend his hand to him in some way. A chilly sensation flicked through him. If his brother-in-law were the thief, he would have made it to paradise. Will would have jumped on the con—*I believe in you, Lord.* He would have—believed. For *that* moment, which was all it took. There was always a second, an instant inside the con, when you believed it. It was the spark, like the seed of uranium in a reactor, that made the con work.

He pushed Will back into the creek and walked away.

On the corner Little Mikey loitered. "You kill him?" he said.

"No, you cross-eyed fuck," Jack said and continued toward home.

Alert, perched across from each other at the kitchen table, for this evening as fond as ever, they ate a supper of sardines and saltine crackers, washed down with cups of hot tea. The house was large and poorly lit and she had told him it made her feel as if she was a mother whose children had left home. She made up stories about these children, she said, and she would sit in the fat ripped chair in the living room with a candle beside her thinking about them. I have two daughters and three sons, she told him, and they are robust, vigorous children who want their own way in the world. I wish very good things for them. Sometimes, she said, I wake in the night terrified of what might happen to them—the world is dangerous, Jack.

He would look at her then and think to himself that she was a remarkable woman and that he was lucky to have found her that day in Philadelphia. What are our children's names? he asked her. She told him readily. They were not names he had heard used for children before. From time to time as they lay in bed, sometimes on the difficult nights when the pull toward disaster, toward violent, unrepealable action became overpowering, he would ask her to tell him stories about these children, to calm her down. Sometimes this worked. Sometimes she raged at him as if he were a stranger cruelly taunting her. But not once did she say she wanted real children. These others were only conjureys, sops.

"I feel like we are about to give something we have stolen back," she said.

"I do, too."

"Let's go out to the garden and pick all the vegetables."

"There's not much left. Just a few tomatoes and maybe some of the hard-shell beans."

"Let's do it anyway."

"All right. I have to make one phone call first."

While she packed a bag, he anonymously called Chaney, the constable. The man was guarded, but he thanked him for the information. "Who is this?" he said. "Your voice sounds familiar. You sound like a neighbor."

"How sweet of you to say," Jack said and hung up.

"You have a plan," Clare said when he came out onto the porch where she waited for him. "I really enjoy it when you have a plan."

He told her what it was.

"That's risky," she said. "I'll have to come up with something good and fanciful, too."

"Will you tell me?"

"No. But you'll get a kick out of it."

She gave him a basket, one of the round white ones she had bought at a farm stand on the highway. "I love all the paraphernalia," she said. "It's like normal people think they are really getting away with something. It's like they believe things will last."

"Maybe it's their way of loving life."

"Don't get sentimental now that we are leaving. You used not to do that."

"I'm not now. It's not sentiment."

"Good."

He could see she was excited. The risk was bringing life to her face; it was calling up blood and verve and a fine tension that made her fingers tremble. In himself, too, he felt the augury of action, the good hard feeling of difficult maneuvers taking shape. At the same time there seemed to be a branching in him, a veer in his spirit. But even as he sensed it—if he did—the veer faded.

In the garden she ran along the rows snatching at the last ripe fruit. There had been no frost yet; the tomatoes were ripe to bursting, bending the vines to the ground. The bean pods had yellowed and stiffened, but he picked them anyway. The harvesting gave him a sensation of wealth, as if he were a rich man who would continue to own, if only in his heart, the fields that were being taken from him. That's how it works, he thought as he stepped over a ragged bean bush. On the other side of it Rubens crouched.

The reporter shrank from him. "Don't hit me," he said.

"Fuck I won't," Jack said, startled.

"Please. I've already been hit enough."

"Not enough for me."

"I've never meant you any harm. I am here to be your chronicler."

"You're with Donnie now, aren't you, stud?"

"I'll admit it, I am. Donald Bernardnick is a strange and powerful man. In some ways he is mesmerizing. He has theories about everything. He wants—I think he does—some of every piece of life. I wanted him to tell me about you. He was in prison with you—I know that. There was a time you fought each other. And there was all that business with your wife. I'm sorry."

"Clare's right over there."

"I see. Yeah." He raised himself on his knees. "Can I get up?"

"I'll sit down."

Clare stepped into the row. She was eating a tomato, wolfing down chunks of it like a starved person. "It's Rubens," Jack said.

"You want a tomato?" she asked.

The reporter said he would, and thanked her.

Clare gave him a large one. "I'm going in to put these vegetables up," she said.

When she'd crossed the garden, stepping from row to row holding the basket against her hip like a farm woman, like a woman with no cares beyond the steady, daily cares of a life in the country, Jack asked Rubens what it was he wanted with them now, in this place where they were about to be killed.

"He can't kill you," Rubens said. "He told me he wouldn't kill you."

"He would have killed me before now if it wasn't for Clare. He knows she would kill *him.* It is one of his major mistakes, one of the few he probably still broods about—that he didn't kill me ten years ago when he had the chance. Or he thinks of it that way. The truth is, Clare would have killed him then, too. She would have risen up in his bed like what's her name, the woman who slew Holifernes—"

"Judith."

"That's right."

"He said he wanted to take treasure. He knows about the gambler's gold. That's all he wanted, he said."

"There's a bounty on me, apparently."

"You mean your brother-in-law. Will. He frightens me. I'm afraid he'll kill me."

"I expect he will."

"Oh, Jesus, I know you are right. I don't see him often. I go in and out of New Orleans, I travel, looking for information, talking to people about you and Clare—I've been everywhere, actually—and I don't see Will Bodine much, but every time I do he tries to get me off somewhere; he asks me to go for a drink or something and I get this feeling he wants to get me out of sight of people so he can hurt me. Do you know what I mean?"

"Yes."

"He took one man out fishing for Donnie, out on Bayou Techmarine, and the man didn't come back. Nobody ever saw the man again."

"There's no telling what happened."

Jack felt an urgency, a desire to speak. He leaned back in the raw dust and looked up at the stars, at his brother-in-law's glass-bottomed heaven. He had never learned the constellations, not even the North Star; there was nothing up there he recognized. It was beautiful anyway. He thought about this as Rubens began to give his scrambled itinerary of travels, thought of the beauty of unexplainable things, of stars, and mist, of patches of woods where blue moss grew on the stones and the sheets of Precambrian rock had long gouges in them, as if some ancient god had dragged his claws. And he thought of the love of his wife, and of their loyalty to each other, and of their phantom children Gospel and Lucky Strike and Pudding and the others, and of Clare's stories of them building igloos in the Aleutian Islands, of the family walking across the ancient land bridge, returning up the continent through the icy valleys, over the steaming peaks into the lost lands of Siberia, where the forests were black in the sunlight and rivers shone like streaks of diamond in the snow.

And he thought of Jimmy, and wondered again, as he had not often, what the gambler thought of in the prison of his stroke, wondered if he thought of the old days when he followed the cockfight circuits with Buster. You could not tell what Coodge was thinking. His face was blank. Sometimes bits of emotion showed in his eyes, like rags flicked in a window, but when they did Jack found himself turning away, now ashamed. He did not want to see, and for some reason he feared reproach. Clare, too, moved lightly around the gambler. There must be a world behind his eyes, Jack thought, but what does he do with it and where does he go in it? Maybe thought became as they said hearing did for blind people, an enlarged sense, maybe thought grew more acute, refined, honed to sharpness, so the mind cut through the tangles of misery and stupidity each life was snarled in and stabbed to the heart of things. Maybe, maybe.

He stopped himself. This was the kind of sentimental thinking his wife hated. He looked at Rubens. The man sat with his arms around his knees. He was talking about—what? About a trip he took to Minnesota to look at the sites of Jack's childhood.

"What did you see?" Jack said.

"The houses you lived in, your father's house. Your school. The camp. The lake house. I took a hike along the lake shore. It's grown up now. There're all these little cottage motels, fishing camps and such. There's really no open shoreline left."

"Until you get into Canada."

"I didn't go into Canada. You didn't spend time up there, did you?"

"A little in the Quetico—the Boundary Waters. There are lakes where you can lose yourself."

"That's what I want to know about—hiding. Is that what you were doing?"

"Did you go to the headwaters of the Mississippi?"

"No."

"My mother took me there. There was an old guy, he said he was a Cree-Fox Indian, he told me stories about the ancient days. He took me out to the stream and showed me how you could straddle it, and he told me that in olden times young men stood with their legs on either side of the river and scooped fish out with their bare hands. Trout, he said, as big as your thigh. As *his* thigh." Jack laughed. "It turned out he was just some old idiot hanging around the place, not really a guide, not even an Indian. He didn't know anything about anything. He just made up stories. But the truth was I liked it. I had dreams about men scooping fish up from a running stream."

"Your father and the car in the snow."

"How do you know about that?"

"Your mother told me. She was happy that I'm doing a book about you."

"It's a book now?"

"I've got an outline and a couple of chapters done."

"What did my mother say?"

"About—?"

"My father and the car."

"She said you and your father were trapped in his car one winter in a snowbank for four days. He said you walked out and got help. Is that what happened?"

"Yes. We were coming back from Tilton over the Hogan Sax Range, around the back way. We got caught in a blizzard. I don't know why my father wanted to go that way, or why he set out in such bad weather. In those days we were used to waiting for the right time. But he wanted to get home. I had gone to Tilton with him on a land sale. He was brokering some property over there, some busted-out farm some busted-out farmer was trying to sell. That was my father's specialty, those ruined farms up north that nobody wanted anymore. Sometimes a farmer would just walk off one of those places like a man would walk off a job, leave everything, house and outbuildings and equipment, just give up. Those were the places my father handled. He was in it too early for the yuppie vacation trade come up from Twin Cities. Back then nobody wanted a rock farm in Minnesota."

"What happened?"

"We hit ice. The car went off the road into a snowbank. We hit a tree in the snowbank, a big birch that still had all its leaves. They fell on the car, a lot of them, from the impact. All these brown crumbly leaves. We weren't hurt, but we were shaken up. It was terribly cold, too cold. The cold that jumps directly into your bones, as if you are naked. We decided to stay with the car. My father was sure someone would come along."

"How far from town were you?"

"I remember it as ten miles. Too far to walk in a blizzard."

They had eaten from a bag of apples and sandwich crusts. There were candles in the glove compartment and they lit these one at a time and set them on the dashboard to keep from freezing. From time to time they tried getting out of the car—they couldn't help it—but the blizzard was too fierce, a whiteout. By the second day his father had become afraid they weren't getting out. The wind kept the snow from piling up on the car.

He said, "My father became very frightened. He began to come apart. He started talking in strange ways, telling me awful stories about my mother, about their life together, letting me in on secrets, speaking of their sex life, of how she berated him for his fear of her body and of sex. He jabbered. He wailed. He sang songs that made no sense. He grabbed me and held me to him and then he began to beat me, or try to. We were locked in this Chevrolet together. There was nowhere to go. We didn't have much food. My father—"

He stopped. His father had accused him of stealing food. He had called him a liar when he tried to protest. "Little shit thief," he had called him and attempted to beat him. Jack had fought back. He was twelve, not yet a man, but he fought his father in the car, desperately, fought for his life. This was on the fourth day. He had got the door open and tumbled out into the snow. The snowfall had subsided, but the wind, tearing out of the north, blew the snow up in a ground blizzard. Jack could hardly see, but he could make out the gap up the hill where the road would be. He had called back to his father that he was going for help. He climbed up the slope and made his way down the road, running at first as best he could through the deep snow, forcing his way like a man forcing a way through big waves, crying as he ran, disgusted, hating his father, terrified. A mile on, maybe it was that far, he came on the snowplow, one of the big plows come up from the valley. The road was already clear all the way back down.

Jack scooped up a handful of dirt and rubbed it away between his palms. Rubens had his notebook out; he was writing the story down. Jack didn't stop him. In the house Clare had turned on all the lights. There were small floodlights above the back porch. The naked illumination made the yard, which they had worked on, clearing away brush and weeds and the dead pyracantha bushes, look as if it was already abandoned, as if, still, a year after they moved in, no one was living there.

Rubens raised his bland, wide face. His small eyes gleamed. "Can I ask you," he said, "can I ask you, if you don't mind—I'm sorry—how your father came back from that? Did he come back?"

"He was shamed, and he carried the shame. He packed it like provisions on the portage between suicide attempts. He wasn't a talker; we never spoke about it. Everything—like with Coodge—you had to get from his eyes. He wouldn't speak. He even, I believe this, tried to keep his body from giving anything away. He probably read a book about it. He'd hold himself like happiness. You'd have to study him like a lover to catch the slightest sign. You could go through years of watching and still miss it."

"Until he tried to kill himself."

"Yeah, until then."

Rubens put his notebook down and lay back. "I'm trying not to drink," he said. "But when I don't drink, the world scares me to death. It feels like life is coming at me in a jet plane."

"I don't want to hear it."

"But—"

"Don't get confused, buddy. I'm not your pal. I'm not going to be your pal."

Rubens sat up. "Let me ask you—how many times have you told that story? About your dad?"

"A few."

"What does it mean to you?"

"I don't ask about that."

"Maybe you're his son."

Jack got up. "I'm going inside."

"I'm sorry," Rubens said, scrambling to his feet. "I didn't mean to cross the lines."

"You got to cross lines in your business. Don't con me. If it bothers me, I'll tell you."

"Can I stay with you? Can I go with you?"

"No, buddy, you can't."

"Can I stay out here in the yard? Maybe over there, in the toolshed—is that what that—"

"Go back to the hotel. Donnie isn't going to kill you. I'm sure you've got him believing you're going to tell his story, too. Donnie loves to gather information. He might not want you passing it out to the world, but I'm sure he's happy to know you are out there collecting it for him. To him you're like a truck farmer, harvesting your tomatoes and peas and potatoes and hauling them fresh to the city for Mr. Donnie Bee. You're a supplier. Donnie would never shoot a supplier."

"What about Will—would he?"

"Who knows?"

Abruptly, Jack turned away and walked up the row toward the house. He didn't like to hear himself talk, not like this, not to such a man.

"I'll see you tomorrow," Rubens called.

Jack did not turn on the steps to look back. And he did not look around before he turned off the porch light. His father's panic in the car had humiliated him, and then it had enraged him. He wasn't afraid of his father. He had wanted to be, he had tried to be, but he wasn't. He knew—and the thought had come to him then—that he could kill him. It was like a bad joke. He could kill the man who was dedicated to killing himself. He shivered. What made his father's hand slip, all those times? The dosage too small, the noose improperly configured? Had he only been waiting for a betrayal so huge it would propel him out? *You fuck, you killed yourself on my wedding day.* What maniacal dedication was this? How could a man go so long looking into one corner?

On a bench against the porch wall, Clare had set the baskets of vegetables, her basket of tomatoes and his basket of beans. It didn't really have anything to do with him, he thought. Maybe it had to do with his father's father, or that man's father, or someone on back, something, maybe a horse shying on a Scandinavian road, a robbery in Norway, some incident in a cave long ago—there was no telling, no bringing of the truth of it to light.

Remember me, Lord, today in paradise.

It was clear to him that a year of silence and quiet living had not moved them an inch.

Death all around, whispering into the beaten, gouged, eyeless face, death reared up like weeds, like some animal jumping in the weeds, all around us come now: the brother, the friends, the bystanders shot down, the old lady gone, nothing to interpose between us and death but some old poems we came on, some kind of written talk that we read to each other, some words—do you understand?—nothing out here in the world that can stop what's happening, each day the same, compelled by this action, death all around, on the back stairs, on the streets, out in the fields near the woods where some child comes on corpses laid out as if to be counted, the graves already dug, piles of crumbly gray earth, not used for corn anymore, but for this, flies buzzing, everywhere else an emptiness, empty woods, the fields cut over and barren, nothing in the world but this. . . .

When he came out onto the porch at eight, Donnie Bee was sitting on the front steps peeling an apple. There was a ground mist in low places near the street, in the neighbors' yards, but the sky was clear. "Come in for breakfast," Jack said.

Donnie said no, he didn't want to. "I don't like to eat in people's houses," he said. "I like to go out."

"Fine. We'll go to the café."

"Where's Clare?"

"She's not coming."

"That's not the way I want it, Jack. Go get her."

"She's not here, Donnie."

The cat man's eyes narrowed. He turned his head and pursed his lips as if about to spit. "You're fucking me up, Jack. I can't have that."

"I'm not Clare's boss. She's already gone."

"Joe, Mikey," the thin man called. "Go in there and check for the woman."

The two men went into the house.

"This is exactly how you do, Jack," Donnie said. "This is why nobody can trust you. This is why nobody will work with you. Something gets going and you immediately start into this wily shit. I ought to shoot you right here."

"You wouldn't be able to get the money then."

"Shit, I don't know if I can get it now. You got Clare waiting out there somewhere to bushwack us."

"Your boys were here all night."

"Yeah." He shook his head. "My whole life's a damn one-man operation, I swear." He stood up. "She in there?" he bellowed into the house.

"Nobody here, Chief," came the reply.

"Come on out, then."

The two men came out, looking sheepish. "She must have run out the back," little Mikey Breen said. He was a short man with spiky rat-colored hair. He was known to have eczema, which he scratched as if it were poison ivy. His buddy, Joe Cane, thicker around the middle, and with dull gray eyes and fat hands that looked boiled, said, "It's like nobody lives here."

"You already checked out, Jack?" Donnie said.

"We never keep much stuff."

Suck sat in the car behind the wheel leaning forward.

"She's probably standing in the bushes with a gun on us—right, Jack?"

"Could be, Donnie."

"But then you don't want to make a mess here in this town where you still got Coodge to take care of, right?"

"He's your ace."

Donnie smiled. "That's right." He stepped off the porch, walked into the yard, and looked back at the house. "This place is a wreck, Jack. Don't you keep it up?"

"We like it this way."

"Doesn't make any sense to me. Life's too difficult not to make it nice as you can."

Across the street the one-armed ex-captain had come out onto his porch. He wore a blue bathrobe and sipped from a cup. He waved at Jack. Jack waved back.

"Who's that?" Donnie said.

"My neighbor."

"He didn't run off, too?"

"He's just a neighbor, Donnie."

"You want me to go talk to him, Chief?" Little Mikey said.

"No, you idiot. Get in the car. Let's go to the café, Jack. You got everything you need?"

"Yes."

"That's a nice vest—where'd you buy it?"

"New Orleans."

"You're so middle class, Jack."

"How so?"

"Dress up to go downtown."

"You're right, Donnie." He didn't know about the vest.

They ate breakfast in the café among farmers and local businessmen. A couple of men at the counter looked at them, but there had been no sign of extra police as they came through town. The night wind had blown the streets clean. The buildings, even the trees, half-stripped of leaves, looked cleaner, freshened. From the river, as they got out of the car, had come the long blast of a tugboat horn. There were gulls in the sky, circling and diving; a few walked on the lawns.

Donnie watched Jack eat. He'd had nothing but coffee. "I forgot how much you can pack away, Jack."

"I like to eat."

"I remember it now. And you never put on any weight. If I ate like that, I'd bloat up overnight."

"You're a slow mover, Donnie."

"I get there, though."

Suck Jackson said, "I once traded a restaurant for a box of silver spoons." It was the first time he'd spoken.

"Spoons for a whole restaurant, Suck?" Donnie said.

"Well," Suck said, "it was one of those moving restaurants, a mobile unit."

"A pushcart?"

"No—you know, like those ice cream trucks. Sell hamburgers out the back. I like that business best," he said, fluttering his thin hands. "Trading things, shifting weights, things coming out one door and going in the next. This business makes my heart palpitate."

"If it doesn't work out, it's going to stop entirely, Suck," Donnie said.

Suck jerked back as if he had been slapped. His face turned red. "I'm a trader," he said. "I don't like violence."

"Then pray for success, darling," Donnie said. He looked at Jack. "How come Coodge had a stroke?"

"Clare shot at him."

"Shit. Now she's going to be shooting at us."

"Maybe not."

Donnie looked narrowly at the door. "You've got some plan, haven't you, Jack? Some wily plan that Clare is out there putting into action." He drummed his fingers on the table. His nails made a tinny sound. "You say you got up here on a boat? How come you came up the river on a boat?"

"Didn't Suck tell you?"

"Yeah, he did. I wasn't going to turn you in, but now maybe I will, no matter what happens."

"I hope you don't, Donnie."

"I'm restless. I'd turn you in even if I didn't hate you, just to see what would happen. I'd love to follow your trial in the papers. Rubens could write it up. You've got a real creature there, Jack. He's your fool."

"Where is he?"

"He's back at the hotel. I left him handcuffed to a fucking bed. Mikey," he called to the thug who sat with his buddy at a table by the window. The man came over and Donnie told him to go let Rubens out.

"Where's Will?"

"That I don't know. Mikey said he had a little accident—fell in the creek. It's late in the year to go swimming, don't you think?"

Jack didn't answer.

"I'm glad he's not around," Donnie said. "He scares me. Murderous lurking bastard. He told me he had a theory about all this. He said we are all controlled by our shadow selves, which live in another dimension. Some kind of opposite universe where the beings we really are, big god-like creatures, mirror our business down here. Something like that. He said these other beings, Shadows, are a couple of steps ahead of us. In fact, so he says, the life we have here is a kind of instant replay of life there. Is that right? Maybe I have it backwards. That man can talk more than me. He gets going and if you try to interrupt him his eyes start to burn. He'll pull a knife on you as soon as say hello. He thinks we are controlled by the shadow beings and that everything we do is preordained. It's already been done, off in this other dimension. If we realized this, we would be completely free. Why should we worry about what we are doing when we have already done it?"

Donnie shuddered. "His eyes, you know? Runny. Like they been *spit* into. That's some family, those Manigaults. Clare worries me. She's thin. Is she sick?"

"No."

He had dreamed of high snows banked against the house. And then he had dreamed of spring, of the pale green growth in the spruce trees, of the first violets, of the day in April when the lake showed up blue again, soft, delicate blue, ice free. He had seen the first fishermen, young boys scrambling over rocks carrying long poles baited with crayfish. From somewhere up in the trees he had seen a line of boys, a hundred of them maybe, standing on rocks along the shore, casting into the blue waters. And then he was standing close to a boy who bent down and grabbed a big trout from the stream beneath him and held it up high by the gills, and the boy was his father and his face was red and frost-burned and he was saying terrible things to him, accusing him of terrible deeds.

He smiled at Donnie. "You should be enjoying this, DB."

"I am. But I'm wondering about where Clare is. And her fucking brother, too. Both of them. I should have shot you immediately. I am going to shoot you as soon as this is over. Then I'm going to shoot Suck."

"Why me, Donnie?" Suck said.

"Because you are such a weaselly little fuck. You can't be trusted at all. You sit there eating your eggs, but if I ask you what you are doing, you'll say you are talking on the telephone. I am outraged and depressed by such stupid lying. You need to be back in prison, Suck. You need to be sent back to prison for training."

"I've been in prison, Donnie. It was torture."

"That's because you are such a rank weasel. He ought to be up in Joliet, Jack. Those boys would crack his case. They'd teach him right from wrong. That's your problem, Suck: you don't know right from wrong."

Jack leaned back in his chair. The breakfast crowd had mostly gone. The gossip table, the same table in all small-town cafés, a large table in back, was still full, its constituency shifting as characters arrived and left. Jack knew a few of the men by sight, a few by name. He had argued briefly with Stanley Mack, the white-haired man eating a doughnut, when Mack, a farmer in town with a load of corn, had proposed, as he fingered wrenches at the hardware store, that the country be cleared of all adults who earned less than eight thousand dollars a year. Jack had disagreed, but the man wouldn't come off it. I'm one of them, too, he'd said. I should be sent away, too. And he knew the school principal and the Baptist church custodian and the woman who visited houses to take in sewing and washing, and he knew Frank Douglas, the wandering yardman, who had helped him pull chickweed out of the garden so he could plant vegetables this spring. The town itself had become a bank, a place he studied as he had studied banks, walking around inside it, looking into corners, counting exits and guards, cameras, taking in the rhythms and the customs, the quirks, getting a feel for the habits of Miss Sutherland, the chief cashier, who took her coffee cold, without sugar, who wore a rubber thumb for money counting and stopped off on her way home to flirt with Sam Custer, the manager of Goldberg's department store, coming to know Stacey and Harry, the other cashiers, watching Mr. Billings and Mrs. Considine, coming to understand the sudden irritations that assaulted Mrs. Hurrell like a nausea and held her gripped in contrariness for hours. The truth was he knew something about every street now, some fact of residence or occurrence. He had no love for any of this, none he could discover. These people were witnesses, that was all. Their stiff small stories were the facts that passed time as they waited, as *Jack*—the thought coming to him now as he watched Little Mikey Breen slide into his chair opposite Joe Cane—waited to be recognized—even as the thought terrified him—as he waited for the old man on the river to raise his eyes from the coil of hog intestines he stripped, to say, *I know you,* waited for a child running his hand along the top of a boxwood hedge to spot him, to discover his own future in Jack's bony face, for a housewife to remember some lover from years ago, a man she almost married, approaching now in the form of an anonymous bank robber come to borrow the lawn mower, for anyone, for Mrs. Sanibeau, or Mrs. Barnacle, or Mr. Green—anyone—to say, Here, you—stop: *I know you.*

Instead there was Donnie, come like a summons in the night. Mr. Cat on Silent Feet. Who looked around him now with an amazed expression, as if he had just entered some stupendous hall where inconceivable pageantry was taking place. Donnie could grab quicker, pull out more than anyone he knew. Jack smiled at him.

"What's so funny to you?" Donnie said.

"You."

"That's not news. You always laughed at me. *Almost* always." He snickered. "Look at those fucks, that Mikey, that Joe. Those idiots. They couldn't keep a rabbit in a box if they nailed the lid shut. Let's have some more coffee."

"Fine."

Suck patted Jack's wrist. "He's always like this beforehand. Sometimes he has to go into the bathroom and throw up."

"There's nothing to worry about, Donnie. We aren't actually going to get the money right now. I only have certificates in the box."

"Yeah, I figured. I was thinking about that. I think maybe you ought to just go in and rob the place. Damn, I can't stay on track."

"I still wouldn't get the money. They don't have it on hand."

"Jesus. I never should have come up here. This was a terrible mistake. Fucking Jimmy Eldorado." He dragged at his chin. "Man, I don't like to be out in the country when the leaves are off the trees. All this nakedness gives me the willies. Where's that coffee?"

The waitress appeared with a glass pot, poured coffee around the table. Donnie handed her a five-dollar bill. "What's this for?" she said.

"Because you look so good. Is there a jukebox in this place?"

"No, there's not."

"Well, save it for when you get one. Then play all of Otis Redding."

The waitress looked a question at him—a question for herself—and walked off.

"Don't stir things up too much, Donnie," Jack said. "This is where I live."

"Don't worry about that, Jack. After I get this money you're not going to be living anywhere. Jesus," he said, "I hate these small towns. You can't do anything without somebody seeing you. Right now I have my pistol out under this table and I would like to shoot this fucking midget across from me in the stomach, but I can't because everybody would see. It's like school, man, or jail. I tell you, this country is going crazy. There is no respect at all for privacy anymore. It's something else the Republicans have screwed up. The police. They love the police. They want to let the police go wherever they like, any time they like." He straightened up. Suck had turned pale. "You know what I always said?"

"What?" Jack said. He patted Suck's wrist.

"There is no system, there is no way of doing things that doesn't tend to devilment. We carp and snarl about forms of government, but I'll tell you, sweetie, even this old capitalism is no better than the worst we can imagine. It's not going to hold. It doesn't hold. You know why I want that fucking gold? Because I want to have inside my house every pretty thing I can get my hands on. I want paintings and fine rugs from Persia and I want clothes and cars and glass figurines with imperial markings. You know what drives me to this? Do you have any idea?"

"Boundless greed?"

"Ho. Of course. But it's worse than that. *Special treatment.* That's what it is—that's what I want. It's what everybody wants. From the crib on we pine for it. Hell, man, nations die for lack of it. From international summits to the corner grocery store, where I want the fucking artificial American clerk not to charge me that extra penny for my goddamn cup of coffee. Take it back! Don't break my nickel. *Treat me special.*"

He looked around the room, where farmers and shopkeepers, where young men going nowhere, sat over coffee. "Everything we do," he said in a soft voice, "is because of our longing for it. Money. Love. Power. All of it. Sex. That's what it is. We want someone to take us aside and treat us special. Be nice to me! That's the cry. Even the weasels are into it. These minor operators like Suck here and old Mikey and Joe over there picking at nits. Think about it. You ever wonder what it's like for such as them in their lonely beds at night? What do you think Mikey gets into when he's alone? You think he dresses up in a Zorro suit? Does he have a stash of magazines? Does he sneak out of the house and go to the girlie shows on Bourbon Street? I know for a fact that Mikey does attend these shows. He sits in the back with a drink that he never takes a sip from. The girls know him well. They know he is cordial and gutless, but if one of them goes home with him, Mikey will make her put on an old skirt and sweater combination his mother wore when she took him to the doctor for his eczema treatments, and parade around the room in this outfit. Get him by himself and he becomes this person who lays a trail of dollar bills to his little room, where such business takes place. Is it about Mom? Strange sex? Of course not. He just wants somebody to be sweet to him like his mama once was. And Joe, he's the same. And Suck. And you. I'm not talking about quirks. I'm talking about standards and practices. About need. About drive. All this, all this business, this swell little town with its cockeyed hotel and its windy, smelly, fucking streets and its river like another dimension busting along beside it, is just one more hotbed of longing for special treatment. And the reason these yokels live in this shoddy burg is because they couldn't *get* any special treatment. The only people can stand them are the fools they grew up with. They're the muddy glass of water nobody drinks unless he is very, very thirsty—"

Suck tugged at Jack's sleeve. His face was white, collapsed. "Is he going to shoot me?" he said.

"No, he isn't. Did you put the gun up, Donnie?"

"Yeah. Yeah, it's in my pocket."

He gave Suck a small, feline smile. "I wouldn't shoot you here, darling. I never shoot anybody while I'm eating."

"He killed Coodge," Suck said.

Jack felt a tiny, brittle snap inside him. "He did what?"

"He killed Coodge. He went over to that nursing home this morning and he went in and smothered him with a pillow."

"Did you do that, Donnie?"

Donnie glared at Suck. "You bet your money on the wrong horse, little man."

"So did you, Donnie," Jack said.

"Don't get upset, Jack. Coodge was going out, anyway. I couldn't resist."

"If he's dead, maybe I can't get his money."

"I thought about that. It's too much trouble to get that money. I want you to rob the bank. Mikey and Joe'll help you. If it's a big enough bank to accept that much cash, then they're bound to have plenty on hand. I shouldn't have come up here, I know it—this is fucked. I had a plan, but now I've got a better one. I've got you, and if I've got you, Clare'll come in. We'll take this bank, and hell, maybe we'll take a few more. Ha-ha. I'm going to put you to work for me. Get some good out of you before I turn you in."

He pulled bills from his pocket, slapped them on the table. "Let's go."

"I need to sit here a minute."

"What are you upset about? You've been in *prison*. You haven't seen Coodge in years."

"I've seen him every day since last October."

"He was already a damn corpse. There wasn't enough breath in him to stir a feather. I just issued him a pass out of trouble."

For one second he thought he would burst into tears. The speckled gray plastic tabletop looked as if it had the glistening black backs of hundreds of insects embedded in it. Someone might now hand him a package containing proof of a terrible crime. He thought of a morning in Mexico, years ago, when he'd sat at a café table at dawn longing for something he couldn't put a name to. There was a fish he'd caught once that had a piece of cloudy green glass in its belly. Where was that piece of glass now? His head ached. For an instant he thought, *Good, good,* but the thought disappeared and in another instant he saw Jimmy's raw blue eyes looking at him, saw the strain in the eyes as he attempted to pull the world in through them.

"Let's go, Jack," Donnie said.

He got slowly up. The little man Suck got up, too, staring at him. Everything was in Suck's eyes, too. All the despair and the disgust and the horror. That's where we'll be keeping the craziness, Jack thought. That's what this man is for. "You are the creature he keeps around to fill up with the devil," he said.

Suck blanched. He backed up a step and turned. Jack clapped him on the shoulder. "Don't run off, son. This is what you came for. There's always one such as you on a job. The one who carries the demon. It's a hot potato, isn't it? You've got it."

Suck looked as if he was about to faint.

"You better let him be, Jack," Donnie said. "We don't want a fuck like him coming apart." *Not till we can get him off to the woods, anyway,* he said to himself.

"Shut up, Donnie. I'll be transferring his load to you in a second."

"Might be more difficult than you think," Donnie said as he turned swiftly and headed for the door.

They walked down the sidewalk to the station wagon, which was parked around the corner from the bank. Donnie wanted everyone to get in, so they did. There wasn't room for Rubens, who had come up, shambling like a man in chains, so Donnie made him sit on the hood. The writer looked forlorn, as if he hadn't slept. Donnie told everyone there had been a change in plans.

"Jack's going to rob the bank. It's fat and he can't resist."

Suck said he wanted no part of it. "I'm not a robber," he said. "I can't do this."

"Good for you," Donnie said. He punched Suck in the face. Suck kicked back, surged forward, and his head hit the seat in front of him. He slumped against Joe Cane. Joe folded him over his knees. He rapped the back of Suck's head with his big knuckles. "How do we go about this?" he said.

"Jack's going to do it," Donnie said. "You two have to go in with him as backup. Follow along, make sure he doesn't fuck up, make sure nothing gets out of hand."

Mikey scratched himself, squirming in his seat. "You got a plan, Jack?" he said. "You got a routine you want us to follow—something special?"

"Stay close to me and don't take your guns out."

Mikey blinked rapidly. "Okay," he said. "I think that's okay."

He got out of the car. "What do you want to do with Suck—and the Rube?"

"Throw a coat over Suck." He looked at Rubens. "Fuck the Rube," he said. "We'll come back and get that bastard Will—wherever the fuck he is—to take care of him." He got back into the car.

"You not coming, Donnie?" Mikey said.

"No, you idiot. I have to stay here to watch the car. So we can get out in a hurry."

"This is a fuckup," Joe Cane muttered.

Donnie took his hand, shook it. "There's hundreds of thousands of dollars in there. Wads and buckets of money. This stiff little bank will crack like a pecan. I already see us—I see you, Joey boy, sitting out on the dock at Lafay's with your feet up, sipping toddies and telling lies to the waitresses. I see that."

"Okay, Donnie," Joe said.

It was a simple setup. There were three extra cops in the bank and there was Constable Chaney in a dark blue suit. Maybe there was someone around from the state, but Jack didn't think so. Who did Chaney think was coming? He was probably afraid he'd been taken in by a prankster. They weren't looking for him; Jack knew that. He felt some of the old daredevil exhilaration, but now it was tainted, encroached upon by a hundred other feelings. These feelings, these halts and hesitations, seemed to be scattered on the floor. He crunched them as he walked, like dead roaches. There was nothing he wanted here but his own survival. Clare was outside somewhere, whirling through the October sunlight toward him. The tellers looked alert.

He took a withdrawal slip from the counter, scribbled on it, and got into line. Joe and Mikey got into line behind him. The teller was a slender woman with dark red hair. Her face was freckled. He had seen her shopping at the A&P. She had two young children who were difficult to control. When he reached the window, he pushed the slip to her. She tried to take it, smiling as she did so, but he held it down with his fingers. She looked at it. Across the front in black ink he had written, *The two men behind me have guns.*

The woman flushed. Her hand didn't move. There must be a toe button, Jack thought. The woman excused herself. "I'll be right back," she said. She walked down the row, entered an office beyond a bank of desks.

Jack turned around, leaned back against the counter. He smiled at Joe and Mikey, shrugged his shoulders.

Beyond them he watched the cops move in. They came up behind the thugs, their guns drawn. Joe and Mikey didn't notice. The constable moved down the row of windows. When he reached them, he looked Joe and Mikey in the face. "Game's up, friends," he said. "You're under arrest."

Joe Cane's shoulders slumped. "Goddamn," he said. "I knew this was fucked up." Mikey slipped a hand inside his coat, jerked a pistol out of his belt. Jack leapt backwards, going down onto his ass. A woman screamed. There were shots—two, four. The constable and one of the cops went down. Mikey went down, falling sideways, two blood spots as big as roses on his chest. Jack crawled for the front door. People rushed past him. One man was sobbing. A woman made a high wheezing sound, as if she had been shot in the lungs. Someone stepped on Jack's hand.

He got to his feet and walked through the door without looking back.

The town had planted oak trees along the street. They had age on them, they were large trees. The sky above them was a pale, cold blue. The car, which had been parked beside one of the largest trees, was gone. Clare sat on the curb. He crossed the street to her. She was crying, the way she cried, without touching her face.

"I feel so bad," she said.

"Where's Donnie?"

"He ran before I could get here. Jack, they killed Jimmy."

"I know. Donnie suffocated him. Rubens was with him."

"Rubens is right here."

"Where?"

She turned around. "He was right—oh, there he is."

Rubens stood just behind a large yellow children's ride pony in front of the shoe store. He had his hands on the pony's back as if he was about to climb aboard.

"Come over here," Jack said.

Rubens came, half turning away as he walked. "Are you crazy?" Jack said. "Have you lost your mind? What were you thinking of, going with Donnie to the nursing home? Did you help him kill Jimmy Ack?"

"There was nothing I could do," Rubens said, cringing. His drawn-in narrow shoulders made him look like a scolded child.

Jack sat down beside Clare. Customers were still pouring out of the bank. Deputies with shotguns ran in the front door. One of them slipped and fell as he pulled the door open toward him, hitting his head against the edge. His partner knelt beside him. People swept around the deputies, ignoring them.

"Where's the truck?" Jack said.

"Around the corner." She kissed him on the cheek. Her lips were wet.

"I'm sorry I missed Donnie," she said, "but he took off the minute you were inside the bank."

"You sure?" he said sharply.

"Don't start that. If I'd gotten a pistol on him, he'd be lying dead on this sidewalk right now."

"Maybe—I don't know, Clare. Jesus. Look at what this fucking year has come to. You," he said to Rubens, "you are a word-muscled fuck who has brought pain and trouble into our lives. I ought to kill you right now. Fucking A. Jimmy. God*damn* it."

Clare said, "These police are going to notice us in a minute."

"I don't want redemption," Jack said, "I just want to get it right. One goddamn time I would like to get it right without you or me, or the two of us, or some interloping fuck like this one here, or Donnie Bernardnick, stepping in and shooting somebody, or strangling them. And where is old Will? He ought to be here now, now there're bodies to gape at. Did you see him on your morning goddamn ramble? You two share a cup of coffee? Get the family fucking mystery straightened out? What *is* going on, Clare? Is there really a plot I am somehow the object of? Are you in on it?"

"We have to go, sweetheart."

"I have to go, too," Rubens said. "Can I come this time?"

Jack glared at them. For a second he didn't know either of them. He had it wrong. Redemption was *all* that was possible—if anything was possible along those lines. There was *no* way to get it right. "Come the fuck on," he said.

The truck was around the corner, parked on the street.

"I don't think we came close to normal life at all," she said as they got in. "I think we invented some space version of it, some convicts' idea of what normal life looked like, and this is what it comes to."

"Probably," Jack said. "Did you bring the vegetables?"

"They're in the back."

Two men in Boy Scout uniforms, wearing sashes speckled with merit badges, passed. The men acknowledged them with short military salutes. "Looking good, boys," Jack said.

Rubens got in between them. Jack started the truck, wheeled a U-turn, and headed back up the street, then took a left down Main Street past the bank, where townspeople milled about. His neighbors they were, already outside his life, men who had almost been compatriots.

maybe, aficionados who helped spade the garden, a fellow from the feed store who'd given him advice about fertilizer, a woman, Mrs. Dupree, whose window he had inadvertently looked into as she changed clothes—come upon as he cut through her yard from the railroad tracks—others of no interest or impact, but fellow citizens nonetheless—maybe they were not even real themselves, Jack thought, but only apparitions, figments put aside from his life—passing soon-to-be strangers who chattered and gasped, who gaped at this imperfect example of his life's work. How do you like it, folks? he thought, pressing his hands hard against the steering wheel. Does it have a necessary and indisputable beauty? Is it clever? Is it worthy of a man's best efforts? And what comes after this? he thought. Paradise? He almost hung his head out the window to call to them.

"I'm going to get Coodge," he said.

"He's at the funeral home," Clare said.

It was just north of town, on the river road in a big gray house set among beech trees. Tall Victorian windows were shut off from the day's light. The beech leaves were bright yellow, glossy, as if they had been painted, but the trunks were gray and battered. The trees reminded him of old men in sporty hairdos trying to look young.

It cost two thousand dollars to get the body. The funeral director knew them, knew they had taken care of Jimmy Acajou. Over the months Jimmy had shrunk, and his body had cramped and curled, but the undertaker had straightened him out. Jack asked the man how he did it. "Small cuts," he said. "A touch of the knife and the tendons snap like guitar strings." He was a thick, pale man with soft brown eyes.

Jack counted out the bills.

"A man with friends is a man who has had a good life," the undertaker said.

"Thank you, you shyster son of a bitch," Jack said.

The undertaker offered them a casket, a flat aluminum traveling case, but Jack said no. The attendant zipped the body into a thick green plastic bag. They put the bag in the back of the truck. "We're taking him home," Jack said.

"Once they're out of here, they all go to the same place," the attendant said. He was a tall, narrow boy, so thin he looked as if he had been cut in half.

"You ought to be more reverent than that," Jack told him.

"You wouldn't be reverent either if you saw as many as I do. And saw what we do with them."

"You like working with corpses?"

"Yeah, I do. They're quiet. They don't cause any trouble at all."

(There was the rotted stink of his brother, he said, it was there, immaculate, carried through time, to that place.)

He knocked the attendant down, left him in the parking lot kneeling over the puddle of bright blood dripping from his nose.

North of town the land rose in a series of low ridges. Pines grew on the slopes and there were outcroppings of slate near the crests. Sycamores and willows were thick in the ravines. The road dipped to the river, through a narrow valley that opened onto a meadow that was cut by a small stream. There was a farm loading dock among reeds. Clare had left the boat there after she moved it before dawn. The taxi had come up to bring her back. "I told the cabbie we were going to keep it here from now on," she said. "I told him it was cheaper."

"Did he believe you?"

"No, but he likes me. It was all right."

Jack and the writer carried Jimmy Acajou aboard, laid him in the stern. Jack returned to shore, drove the truck up a track road into the woods, and left it with the key in it. He heard the boat start as he got out. The woods were quiet, all the trees had gone yellow and brown, there were no birds. He stepped in among the trees and stood there. The leaves on the ground were wet. He could feel the elastic, hollowed-out presence of the woods. It was a presence that was like an absence. A silence that was its own form of speech. He began to feel as he had as a boy, standing at the edge of a tamarack bog in the north woods. There was something very large around him, something that had never been born and would never die. It closed on him, like a weather, and then it entered him. He felt his body go light, felt as if he could rise, be lifted up. He sensed the balance and weights of his body shift, begin to change and dissolve. Then a terror like a knife.

He started, jerked back into himself. It was the same as when he was a child, the same as it had been standing in the Minnesota woods, or, on nights of bewilderment, lying in his bed listening to the wind pick its way through the big cedars at the bottom of the yard. There was too much to see, too much to find out. It was so huge, the mystery and confusion were so great, you were forced to give a con's explanation, some circuitous, vocable lie that you could tell in all weathers, that no one could unravel and everyone hated to hear. What had it meant, the boy come forth from the woods to look at him? The second selection of himself? Why had he not spoken to him, did he have no *power*, why had nothing happened? Could there be visions that meant nothing? Visions whose only purpose was to haunt and trouble the receiver?

(His father had scolded Rita, he said, that night, had reprimanded her for lying about the rainbow. His mother, quickly, had rebuked him, and then, that night, which they all knew, he said, was a night before one more ridiculous suicide attempt—it was always like this, he said, the tension building, tempers flaring, your guts twisting tighter and tighter—even so, they had turned away from him, as his father had gone red in the face. Then they all had looked into his father's shame, into his shame at being alive on earth, at being a man, at having to live this life of degradation and failure; all of them could see. His father had turned away from them, gone out.)

He turned. Rubens had appeared behind him silently.

"You had better watch that," Jack said.

"I'm brokenhearted," Rubens said. "I am so damn sad."

"It goes like that," Jack said. "It comes for you on days like this, and then it takes you and you have to live with it."

"I don't think it's possible."

"For certain people it is."

"I'm not one of them. Of course, I already knew it. I knew it in prison, those months. They hurt me in prison, just like they hurt everybody. They broke me, as a matter of fact. But you know, when I got out I began to get over it. I began to start fresh, like a kid. My drinking got bad, but I thought it didn't have anything to do with anything, it was just drinking, life was tough but I was adjusting—pour me another. Now I can see I was fooling myself. You scare me. All of you scare me."

"Do your work."

"What?"

"Do your work. Or run for your life, or go get saved or renovated or relocated. I don't know the answer to what you are asking me."

"What am I asking you?"

"You want to know if there is heaven on earth. You still believe there might be. And you're scared to death you've got no power to bring it into your house. You've pulled the curtain back an inch and outside you see it's one bleak day. But you want to believe in paradise."

"Don't you?"

"I already believe in it."

"Is that right?"

"I don't know," Jack said.

"What?"

"Let something come to you."

"What do you mean?"

"Let something come. See what happens. Sit there. Take it, whatever it is. Eat the demon, if it's that. Sup with the angel, if it's that. Don't resist."

"Is that what you do?"

"Not if I don't have to."

"I hated watching that man die. Donnie didn't care. He held the pillow with one hand and screwed it into his face, like he was screwing on a top. Agh. That picture will haunt me from now on. The man didn't move. *He* took it."

"There are times when you like it."

"Not me."

"You never believed you could, but you do. People want to think it's only the deranged, the outlaws, who get pleasure from crime. But that's not so. It will draw you in. Everyone's available to it. It has a huge, tottering beauty."

"The thought of it makes me lonely."

"That's the start."

"Of what?"

"The bad music."

"I don't want to hear it."

"You're already a member of the band."

Rubens turned white in the face.

"Let's go to the boat," Jack said, suddenly tired, tired and angry. "We don't need to be out here, and I don't need you trailing around after me."

They returned quickly to the boat. Clare backed the cabin cruiser out into the river. The shoreline fell back into itself, into its indivisible trees and terrain. Jack locked Rubens in the head. He didn't want to see the man's face. Then he went topside and sat in a folding chair with his feet propped on the green bag, propped on Coodge's stiff shoulder, looking out at the river, which seemed to be taking light into itself. The day was fair and cold and the air was so clear that everything on the shore was distinct. The highway they had come down on ran beside the river and after a while Jack saw a car following. It was going slow, keeping pace with them. There was a lone man in it. The man was hunched over the wheel and he seemed to be watching them. Maybe it was Will. Jack didn't say anything to Clare about the driver. He asked her to swing the boat farther out into the channel and she did.

They buried Jimmy that afternoon on an island miles up the line. A channel cleaved the island from the mainland, set a hundred yards of black, mud-streaked water between them and pine woods. There was a cabin on the island and Jack broke into it, twisting the lock off with a crowbar he found under the porch. He and Rubens carried the body up to the house and past it, into the woods to a clearing in the middle of the island. They could hear the horns of the tugboats from the river on the other side. Jack made Rubens dig the hole with a shovel from the house. Then they lowered Jimmy in and covered him up. Clare cried and then Jack began to cry, too. They knelt in the sandy soil and patted the top of the grave.

"Why don't you say something?" Jack said.

"Is there any point?" Clare said.

She was angry. She had not spoken to him all afternoon. When he brought her a beer from the galley, she tossed it overboard without drinking from it. Now she looked at Rubens, who stood aside leaning on the shovel.

"Who are you?" she said.

Rubens opened his hand. There were arrowheads and little bits of broken pottery in it. "These were in the soil," he said.

"This was my baby," she said. "I'm burying my baby. He was my crimped-up, back-broken, stupefied baby. I loved him. Hey," she cried, "hey, you," looking straight at Rubens. "Do you write this down or do you memorize it as it's said to you? How close do you think you will come to getting anything we do here right? And why should you be interested in us? Why doesn't everyone have his own reporter trailing around behind him to take notes and write it all down? I want to be recorded, and I want everybody to be recorded. Every word. I want every coo and fart, every lazy aside and drooling declaration, every vomit scene and scream recorded, written down and played back to me. Are you getting all this? I sure hope so."

She thrust her hands into the soft dirt. They went in up to the wrists. She twisted them out, clutching handfuls of dirt, and flung the dirt at Rubens. He flinched, but he didn't turn away.

"I'll use everything," he said. "I won't leave anything out."

She patted the grave. "Ah, Jimmy," she said, "you were such a fine pet. You were better than any goldfish or puppy I ever had. So big and expensive and so obedient. Not obedient exactly, because there was nothing you would do. But you never ran off and got into trouble, that's for sure. I hope you do get to heaven, even though you were friends with that rapist bastard Buster Bradley. If you were his friend, you were of him, too, a part of him, too, and he was part of you, so there probably won't be any forgiveness. That's what we call guilt by association, and it is cause for legal action, as you well know. You were, I'm afraid, hung on his chain, too. Well, too bad. I came to love you nonetheless. You were in some ways better than an imaginary child, and far better than an actual child."

She looked at Jack. "I forgot to kiss him."

"We've got the sexton right here. He'll dig him up for you."

"Okay."

Jack made Rubens dig the gambler up, made him drag him out of the grave, unzip the bag, and fold the green plastic back from the face. Jimmy looked as if he was holding his breath. As if any second all this would be over and he could go on with his life.

"He's so pitiful," Clare said.

"He's not anything anymore," Jack said.

His tears had dried up.

"Do you want to kiss him?"

"No."

"How about you?" she asked Rubens.

The writer didn't want to kiss him, either.

"Fine."

She bent low over the body. "He smells of rubber and disinfectant. He smells like something left in a basement." She kissed the gambler on the lips and then, before she raised her head, Jack saw her tongue dart out; she licked the gambler's mouth.

"Bye, Jimmy," she said.

Then she told the reporter he could cover the man up.

She returned to the cabin while Jack watched Rubens work. He had no inclination to help him. It was getting dark. In the east the new moon hung like a thorn in the pale sky.

6

Jack sat inside the pilothouse shadow watching the man swim toward him. The moon had gone down by two, but the cottony stars were bright enough to see clearly by. The river was streaked with wide ribbons of a pale stain the current pushed into eddies and stretched into long lines. The man had been swimming for half an hour, pushing a float ahead of him, being pushed by the current toward the narrow tip of the island, working his way upstream toward the boat. Clare had gone to bed shortly after midnight and Jack had sat up with the writer talking about his past. Then Rubens, too, had gone—been allowed to go—to sleep, up in the cabin Jack had broken into that afternoon.

The man swam strongly, steadily, but he did not swim now directly toward the island. The current had dragged him downstream, so he swam nearly parallel to the shore, aimed at the boat, which was pulled up among alder bushes inside a shallow cove. It could only be Will. Jack leaned forward, to the edge of the shadow, watching. The man shoved the float, a child's raft, some kind of beach toy, ahead of him. He kicked underwater, so that his body seemed to move as part of the river. Starlight gleamed in his hair.

Clare had told Rubens her lion story, the story of how she had gotten her scars. She had been attacked at a safari park in Pennsylvania, caught in a buck lion's jaws when she went to rescue a Thompson's gazelle. The lion had trotted across what she said was a former cow pasture to get to her. It had chased her and caught her just as she reached her truck. She had, after what she said were "six desperate minutes," been able to tear herself loose, get into the truck, and drive away. Then, in a rage, she had turned the truck around, returned to the pasture, and run the lion down. She had chased the lion along a fence line, cornered it under a large maple tree. The lion had tried to go over the fence, but was unable to. She had caught it with the truck and run it down, snagged it like a snake under her front wheels. Then she got out and beat the lion with a branch she picked up. She beat the lion even after it was dead. Then she had passed out beside the torn carcass from loss of blood.

She'd taken her shirt off and showed Rubens the scars. There was a puckered, hooked scar on her left breast, a long straight waxy scar under it, and three short scars along her ribs on her side. Along her jawline, faint, like a razor cut, was another scar where the lion's tooth had grazed her.

"For six years," she said, "I had no feeling in my breast, no feeling in my nipple except for a slight ache. And then the feeling began to come back. It came back first in cold weather, when my breast would feel chilly, like it wasn't covered. That was a good sign I found out. Then it came back, slowly, all the way."

She let Rubens touch the scars. He was shy to, reluctant. He said, "I don't trust anything here, anything about this, and I am afraid."

You get over that, Jack told him, but Clare said, No, it wasn't that you got over it, it was that you got so the signals of alarm became a nuisance you hated but could live with, like a paper mill down the road, and went on despite them.

Rubens said it wasn't like that for him yet, even after a year around Donnie Bee. "I think prison wore me out," he said. "It made me so nervous my hair fell out. That's why I shave my head now," he said, "because when my hair grew back it came in patchy. I've never been the same since prison."

"Me neither," Jack said.

Clare burst into tears then, and cried unashamedly, naked to the waist, standing in the chilly October twilight before the writer, who stared at her with a fever in his eyes, stood openly displayed, crying, bending into the tears as if they were a spring she washed her face in. Jack tried to take her into his arms, but she shooed him away angrily. "I am in mourning," she said, and then she walked down to the end of the island and sat on the bank looking downstream for a couple of hours before she returned to the boat and went to bed.

He watched the man swim toward them. The man continued to swim parallel to the shore, twenty yards out maybe. He drew steadily closer.

Rubens said he had visited the Manigault farm in Indiana. He had talked to Francis, had sat beside him on the red velvet sofa in the dim living room and listened to him tell his story of outrage and despair. He said he had asked questions in the town of Vandalia, that he had asked certain citizens about Will Bodine, and about his brother, James Manigault, and about the old man, who was hated there, he said, and without honor or respect even in such a town, a place that had once been a receiving station on the Underground Railroad, but whose town council, when an Afro-American historical organization had offered to erect a statue to the slave struggle on land they were willing to purchase inside the city limits, said no without a single dissenting vote. Even there, he told him, in this town that could only be claimed as happy ground by the worst elements of the Ku Klux Klan, which was still active out of certain roadhouses, even there the old man was hated and despised as a beast who would lure you into false dealings and even robbery, even murder, everyone supposed, so that when he traveled around town in his old Cadillac collecting his rents in the mill section and down in Ragtown, where the blacks lived, no one would speak to him or even acknowledge him if he happened to tip his hat, which he rarely did.

"The woman," Rubens said, "Will's mother, is still alive, but she is destitute and dying of sugar diabetes, as they call it, wasting away, now without a left leg, which the doctors cut off, gone numb, too, she said, in her hands—I went to visit her—and mostly from the waist down, but oddly without anger or even resentment or even any blame for old Manigault. He pays her no attention at all. He won't help her, and when I asked him about her, he screwed up his face as if I had emitted a terrible odor suddenly there in his house. He owns five thousand acres of land, a lot of it river land, and very valuable, and grows corn on some of it and has developed some of it, and some of it he's sold off for a cement factory that pollutes the Ohio River."

"What of the brothers?" Jack had asked him.

"It's funny," Rubens said, "the town thinks of the brothers' story as sad and selfish, even stupid, but they, at least now, with James dead and Will gone, are forgiving. It's the father who sees all these Greek tragedy implications in the thing. He says he's part of a terrible story, of grief and tragedy that goes back generations. 'The black misery,' he calls it, as if it is a taint or curse the family carries. He said the Manigaults had always been successful, brighter and more energetic than anyone around them; they had dominated the trade and economy in whatever towns they lived in—always river towns along the Ohio, all the way back, so the old man said, to Daniel Boone, even beating Boone in business, which I guess wasn't that hard to do—but there was always this black misery on them, this sordid stupefaction that descended on them like a plague and caused whatever they'd built up to fall apart. 'Somehow the world turns around on us,' he said. 'It coils around and begins to choke what it fostered.'

"That was the way he put it," Rubens said, "as if he was some modern-day Laocoön being strangled with his sons. There was a story around town that Will had tried to kill the old man, that he had attacked him in his own house, and Manigault had to run him off at gunpoint. The old man favored James, that was clear, but he had no sense of it himself. His philosophy was that quickness and grit and determination work great unless you have a curse on you. It was said in that town that he drove his wife insane, that he beat her mentally and emotionally until she died of the suffering, but he thinks it was you, or at least your action as part of the terrible curse, who killed his wife, as he thinks it was you who turned his daughter away from him. Clare is not remembered kindly in that town."

"We were both crooks early on," Jack said.

"Yes. Something like that. People noticed deviation. They talk about how she exaggerated things."

Rubens had stopped then. "I am reluctant to say these things," he said. "They're not attractive."

Jack had said he was reluctant to hear them. They were sad facts and each opened another small hole inside him. But then he began to feel as he listened a small tenderness, a measure of it, seep into the holes Rubens excavated.

"Make sure you tell her the bad things about me," he said.

"She was overeager," Rubens said, "she was considered unreliable and petulant, and she told lies. In a small town everyone notices that kind of thing, and it's always true because everyone knows everything about everyone else."

"Not always."

"Sorry. She was foul-tempered and she had strange enthusiasms; she loved violence and speed and as a girl accepted whatever dare anyone put to her. She was not like the other girls. She was confrontational and willing to fight. She was aggressive and cheated at games. She got in fistfights, with other girls, with boys, and once, in the middle of a Harvestland parade, with her own mother as the two of them rode a float that was dedicated to the Corn Queen of Indiana. She ran away from home at fourteen and went to San Francisco, where she was arrested attempting to push a scam in which she offered tickets for hoochie-coochie shows where she claimed underage boys took off their Jockey shorts. There was no such show, even in San Francisco, just tickets she'd had printed up. She was given probation and sent back to Indiana. Two weeks after she got home, she set fire to a warehouse in Vandalia and was sent off for a year to a juvenile hall. That's where she got involved with animals. The place had a zoo, made up of local animals, deer and skunks and such as that, and they put her to work in it, cleaning up cages and sweeping out. She loved it, as you know."

Then Jack could picture her *(prison brought her to me, he said; prison taught me to make her out of nothing)*, a girl in a blue uniform, her thin legs speckled with dust, sweeping the walkways around animal cages, speaking in a low voice to the animals as she worked. This was at the very center of delight for him. This fact that he could imagine her. Everyone else's life was a mystery to him. He could picture her in Indiana, a raw girl, hating everything around her. He could picture her in bed turning under the twisted sheets, raging even in her sleep against every restriction. He could hear the sound of her girlish voice. He could smell her, smell the vinegary stink of her unwashed armpits, of the small of her back, of her sex. He could feel the ache in her joints as her bones grew. He watched her bend over the sink to dip her face into cool water, watched her squat on the chamber pot she had used as a child, felt the cold rim press against her buttocks, felt the pressure of her bowels gather. *(I have touched it all, he said, seen it all, tasted it all; I have licked her urine, eaten her bitter shit, smeared her sweat on my body, bent down between her legs and lapped at her blood. . . .)* He saw her standing at the window of her bedroom on the winter afternoon, when as the early flakes of that day's snowfall ticked against the glass, she felt the internal emptying of her first menstruation begin and felt the mixed delight and sadness of it, the pitiful lostness that for a moment overwhelmed her as she sensed her body turning away to itself and its own means.

He stopped listening to Rubens. A vague sense of betrayal, of shame, entered him. The sky above the writer's head was vast and without meaning, contained nothing human, nothing that could be of any use to them. The moon looked like a cockspur, he thought. It was poised to dig into the stars. But this was only a figment in his mind. It was not real, it was only some imagining of a spur that could rip a hole in the night. The moon as a spur. His sister had seen a rainbow opposite the moon. And his father had been shamed, they had watched him turn red in the face and walk out of the room. *(I hated that delicacy, he said, that fucking sensitivity. I wanted someone like Clare, someone who could take it. I wasn't going to let myself love someone who could fold up on me like that.)* His hands had touched her, his hands had drawn forth cries of passion from her, doubling them both. Was that it?

"She forgave everyone in her family," Rubens had said.

"No," Jack had said, "it wasn't forgiveness. She was simply used to them. Their craziness didn't bother her."

"She's an American phenomenon," Rubens said. "She and her family are. We know all about these great pioneer families and their terrible anointed struggles to survive. They're emblems of courage and faith to us. We celebrate them now in all ethnic groups—blacks now, even among the Indians—these souls who were steadfast and creative, who exemplify the values that are important to us. But there were also these other families, these twisted, devious, criminal groups, not gypsies, not isolated bad men, and not just some white-trash underclass that throws up a Dillinger or a Dahmer, and not the Mafia, with their rituals from some antecedent culture, but these others, original Americans, killers and thieves, these families who have thrived along with the country, who have endured and prospered, who are living right now in towns all across the U.S., the Manigaults and I don't know who else, outfits who generation after generation conceive one or two dynamic individuals whose dream is not to become president of the local bar association but to steal and con, to relieve the law-abiding citizenry of their goods and chattels. Clare's one of these. She's as purebred as any aristocrat. I am amazed at her. Her bloodlines are as unblemished as George Washington's, or Sitting Bull's. You look back into her family, which I did, at the library in Vandalia, and you find her relatives figuring in outlaw episodes going back two hundred years. I believe what her father said about some ancestor getting the best of Daniel Boone. I'm sure in those days pioneers out on the frontier knew of the Manigaults and feared and despised them.

"Your family, too," he said. "They're one of the other sides of the coin."

"Other *sides?*"

"Yeah, sorry—you know. They're from the activist, populist, radical group. American free thinkers. Resisters. Your mother's politics. Her refusal to accept the government's word about anything. They're a kind of righteous equivalent of Clare's family. All this excites me so much. You are both American types. There are scores of types, I am sure. By now, all this time after the founding, there must be schools of types that are identifiable. Probably there always were, but now they're beginning to show up, like snow on the road when it begins to accumulate. There are the ministerial types and the sports types and the addicts and the bankers and the convicts. Probably by now you can isolate certain groups that have for two hundred years been playing minor league baseball. The military families. I am overwhelmed by it all. And so grateful. I'm in awe, as a matter of fact," he said, reeling in his chair as if he might get up and throw himself overboard. "I fall back in admiration and respect. I know I sensed this from the beginning, back years ago when I began to read about you in the newspaper. I came across a couple of stories in a little downstate paper in Illinois. There was something about the stories, about the crimes—about you—that intrigued me. The reporter described you as *perennial.* Like a flower that returns every year. Like a flood season or a kind of weather. I began to wonder how far back it all went. Was it just you and your devilment? Or did it go farther back? The country is full of families like yours and Clare's. There are clans down south that have been stealing land for generations. California wine growers who have been putting it to Latinos since the time of the Revolution. There are political dynasties in New Jersey and New York State. It's marvelous. It makes me feel so secure. We have continuity in this country—we *are* something."

"What about Donnie?" Jack said.

"Mr. Bernardnick? He's a kind of spontaneous combustion. Another American phenomenon, actually. He's not related to anyone. You probably couldn't even find out who Donnie's parents were. He was probably left as a baby beside the road in some country parish outside New Orleans. I think in fact that was what happened. Nobody knows who his parents were, or what ethnic group they originated in, or anything else.

He just *sprang up*, as they say. It's almost more American than you and Clare. These guys who come out of nowhere like a bunched-up energy field and just knock down everything around them. There are certain American characters like that. George Washington, actually, was one of them. He came from somewhere but no one came after him. He didn't have any children. None of these flamboyant big Nietzsche types ever have offspring. There are a lot of great actors and artists who were like that. Marilyn Monroe. Clark Gable. Madonna. They jump out of the woods or off the street and light up everything around them, but they lead nowhere and leave no legacy except their brightness. They almost never have children, and if they do, by some miracle of in vitro fertilization or something, the children are stunted and ridiculous. Unless Donnie gets written about, in fifty years there will be no one on earth who remembers that he ever existed."

"Aren't we like that—Clare and me?"

"In a way, maybe. You don't have children, but you could. Maybe you will. And there are two of you, not just one. I picture you disappearing from the scene. Drifting away maybe, slipping off after some last robbery to your farm in Michigan or to some beach town on the Florida Panhandle, where you live out the rest of your lives as quiet citizens. That business back in Anacondia, the year living incognito, was probably a trial run, don't you think?"

"I don't know."

"I think it was. You're the kind who pass their genes on. Fear that you won't, or of what they'll be, is probably why old man Manigault is so crazy. He's got some kind of feral terror on him that his seed won't be carried on. These types, these generational malefactors, they have to pass on what they've built. The whole thing comes down to continuity. With his son dead and his daughter run off—and for years now without progeny—he probably figures the game is up for him. He was a sick man when I saw him, and I doubt he'll get better."

"But you figure Clare and I will, in a way, save him."

"I think so. Don't you? You and Clare might even break the chain entirely. I'm not saying this would be a good idea. Don't get me wrong. I carry no brief for the wholesome way. I was attracted to crime, just like you. I was attracted to the beauty of it, to looking at the beauty. But I found out in prison that I don't want any part of the criminal life, not in terms of my commission of a crime. I know I am in trouble now and this has me beside myself. I wish I could call someone to come get me. It's why I'm sticking so close to you. You're my only hope. I know it's ridiculous. You are a criminal. You are not a good guy with just a few criminal tendencies, a quirk or something. I know I am in real trouble. But anyone could see if he looked that I myself am not a criminal. I'm a writer. This is my story. This is the story I am working on, I mean. I haven't been able to look away from it for the last four years. It's only now, only since you got out of prison, I guess, that it's become . . ."

"Unendurable?"

"Yes. I had no idea really what you have to put up with in this life. The law is bad enough, prison is bad enough, but you've got Donnie Bernardnick on your trail, and your brother Will, and there's all the volatility you and Clare carry around normally, and then you have to eat and find a place to rest and money runs out—"

"Sometimes we get sick," Jack said, laughing. "That's the worst."

"God. I didn't even think of that."

"I'll bet. Six years ago Clare got bronchitis right before we were supposed to do some work up in Ohio. I thought she was dying. We were in this little town and I couldn't find a doctor to write her a script. Sometimes in cities where you know things these episodes are not much of a problem, but out in the country you can get into trouble. I had to threaten a doctor to make him give her a prescription, and then we had to run, and on the run find a pharmacy, and then find someplace to hole up so she could recover. It was ludicrous. We wound up in a lake camp outside Beauregard, Ohio, living in cabins that looked like something out of the 1950s. The proprietor didn't like us, but we had to get Clare to bed, so I took the chance, anyway. I wound up—it was a mistake—trying to pay the fucker off. Never pay anybody off if you don't have to. They've got you then. I knew better, but I was desperate. Clare looked like a dead woman."

"What happened?"

"The guy took my money and turned us in anyway. The law came around. In those little towns they can get away with rousting people. Donnie thinks things are bad with the Republicans. He ought to go into the little towns. It's medieval. The cops flushed us out of the cabin as if we were rats. They beat me and they beat Clare and they took all our money and then they tossed us on a freight train and ran us out. They could have had us in prison, but they didn't want that. They wanted to hurt us. The world is full of assholes like that. Clare and I are sometimes among them. But there was nothing we could do. That scar on Clare's nose—the nonlion scar—that's from Beauregard, Ohio, home of the scumlike cops. Clare nearly died. She was sick to the death and beaten up and riding in a grain car on the Baltimore and Ohio Railroad. We weren't even going in the right *direction.* We were headed east, where Clare and I never go anymore. Then the bulls came around and threw us off the train."

Rubens said, "I'm sorry, but this is great. I need to write it down."

"Remember it. We wound up in the Pennsylvania farm country. Mountains and farms, western PA. The only thing we had going for us was it was almost summer and not very cold. I took Clare into the woods. I built a hut for us beside a creek back in the woods and I nursed her for two weeks. I thought I could get along in the woods, but I couldn't, not well. I stole a calf from some farmer's lot, carried it into the woods and butchered it. The fucking cow mother tried to follow me, but I hit her in the head with a piece of wood. It was terrible. It seemed as if everything I did turned into craziness. I remember the cow going down on her knees like a horse in the circus. The stupid expression on her face, and the calf mooing in my arms. It was a newborn calf, born late. Veal. I cut the calf's throat with a piece of glass. I used the glass to skin the cow, or skin it enough to cut off a haunch. We had no matches, so we had to eat the meat raw. I had to force Clare. I found some wild turnips and dug them up to go with it. We were by a stream, so there was plenty of water, and the hut was sheltered under some oak trees, so we knew we would survive. But then these kids, farm boys, found us. They'd tracked the cow, tracked the blood or something, and they came into the woods after us. They were some kind of rural gang. They liked to go into the woods weekends I guess and fight each other. They found us, surprised us as we were eating dinner, and attacked. They had chains and sticks and baseball bats. They got in licks, but we were able to get away by running down the creek. We went into the creek, that is. A couple of the boys followed us, but I was able to convince them to go back. The rest didn't want to get wet. We tumbled downstream, running, then swimming, floating, carried away by the current, Clare nearly recovered but battered, both of us slightly battered. We stayed in the stream all night. There was a period when it opened out and became a river—later it narrowed again—and we floated holding on to this wooden pallet we'd found. The stars were out like they are tonight and at one point we passed what must have been a flower garden because the air smelled as sweet as perfume. The stars glittered on the water like mica and the air was sweet and warm and for a moment it seemed we were floating on the river of heaven, a couple of beat-to-shit crooks who'd been surviving in the woods on raw meat and tubers, and even now when I think of it all these years later, it still seems like that—heavenly, sweet all the way through."

"This is what I mean," Rubens said softly. "Historic. I think you can only feel like that—dreamy, whatever—if you come from a history, from a line of people like you. That's a kind of breeding, breeding of thieves, maybe of anything, any kind of folk, but real I am sure. . . ."

He'd trailed off then, lost in his thoughts.

Jack had looked around to see Clare watching them. The woods came in close to the water and she sat under a young beech tree looking at them, listening. Her face was the face of a girl, wrung clean by river water or tears, he didn't know. He had seen her before, somewhere else, some other time. She had looked like this—he remembered now—and it was nothing like the way she looked in his imagining of her. She had fought against the gang of boys with a fury that amazed him. She had leapt up screaming, she'd whirled, and struck repeatedly. It was her blow that burst a boy's skull. The boy could not have been more than fourteen. The blow had sent him tumbling down the bank to hit his head on a rock. The other boys had stopped then, gaping in amazement. The boy was clearly dead. They had all stared at one another, for a second the lunacy giving way to shock, to the solidity of complicity and kinship. For a second everyone in that small clearing was appalled. Everyone except Clare. She mourned later, later she cried on her knees for the boy's soul and for her own, but in that instant as she stood on the crumbling embankment looking down at the sprawled rag body, she had not flinched from her duty to save herself and save him. He would have let himself be taken then, he did not have the heart or the will to continue, but it had been Clare who had forced their way into the stream, who had shouted for him to come on as the boys crowded toward them.

He felt sorry for her. He had discovered on that afternoon that there were limits to what he could endure. He could come to the end of his road—it was the first uncomplicated indication of this, the opening strains of the music he had learned to sing well in prison—but she had learned none of it, not then or, he thought, later. Not yet. Maybe there was no end for her. Looking into her face as she listened to him tell the story again, he had seen the fierce vehemence fill her eyes. He had seen her come alive in the clearing once more, soon the weight and the timed swing of the blow that caught the boy flush in the forehead. He had been a small, round-faced, wide-eyed boy. Some foolish child trying to prove himself worthy to older boys. Jack had done the same thing. He, too, had capered for the amusement of elders. But Clare saw none of this. She knew none of this. Maybe it was as Rubens theorized: she was born for a certain fierce way of life, maybe there was a twist in her blood that directed her in ways others could not comprehend. Sorry, yes. He felt for her, felt in his heart a sadness and love for her, a tenderness.

Her eyes had snagged him then. The ferocity, the savageness penetrated him. It roved through his body. It rang inside him like a gong beaten in an empty hall. He was being called. He was being pursued, tracked by something that would not give up. He felt puny and small in his thinking, a man without any honor at all.

"You're white in the face," Rubens had said.

"It's better than invisible," he'd answered, and Clare, hearing, had laughed. He'd joined her, and anyone listening on that part of the river could have heard their hard cackling voices carry over the water.

(That night, afterward, he said, after Father walked out, none of them slept. If you had come around then, he said, and walked in the yard, which the moon had turned white, you could have seen us, seen my mother and my sister and me, each sitting at our bedroom window looking out; and you could have seen Father standing in the yard, looking out toward the lake at something, some construction, some terrible armament being pulled into place, batteries of cannon, rifles, bayonets fixed, whole armies massing in the dark, bearing down on him, the lone figure, a man too delicate to live, *who had somehow to resist them, to convince them to lay down arms, to convert their ravenous greed into love and harmony, but could not. . . .)*

Jack pulled his revolver from his belt, got up and went to the stern. He met Will just tapping the edge of his float against the hull. Will clutched a pistol against the raft, held it down as if it were a small animal he had trapped there. Jack pointed his gun into his brother-in-law's face. Will looked at him, almost raised his pistol, but let the gun drop back. "I am too tired to fight," he said.

"I expect so."

"Would you haul me aboard?"

"Not just yet."

"I am about to drown."

"That would be all right with me."

"It wouldn't be all right with Clare."

Jack cuffed Will in the face. The man tried to kick away, but Jack grabbed him by the collar and banged his face against the side of the boat. "When your hand comes up, bro, I don't want to see that gun in it, okay?"

Will raised his hand, empty.

"I have to have protection," he said.

"You've got enough."

"Please let me get out of the water, Jack."

"I don't think so."

"You got to, Jack. You got to show me some kindness. Somebody's got to show me some kindness. I can't go on."

"Nobody can go on, Will. That's the point."

"I'm going to drown if you don't pull me out."

"Yeah."

Will began to call for Clare, but his voice was feeble and did not carry.

"Where'd you get the float, Will?" Jack asked.

It was striped red and white and had a clown face in one corner.

"I got it at a store. Come on, Jack, please have mercy on me."

There was no point in reminding Will—or himself, either—of the times he'd shown no mercy, but Jack couldn't resist. "The ones who never give it are always the first to ask for it," he said.

"They need it."

"You need quite a bit. That is right."

Will cursed and pushed away from the boat. "I'm near to drowning," he gasped. He kicked the float toward shore. The water was deep on that side of the boat, near the bank.

"Don't," Jack said.

"Fuck, go ahead and shoot me. I got to get out."

Will crawled out of the water and dropped onto his face on the bank. Jack jumped off the boat and approached him. The man wheezed, gasping; the fingers of his left hand beat against the sandy soil, pushed at the dirt. Jack squatted beside him.

"Are you just going to keep trying to kill me, Will, until I kill you?"

"You could have been nice to me, Jack," Will said into the dirt. He didn't try to look at him.

"How is that?"

"Let me breathe here a second."

Jack waited. The sky was beginning to come gray in the east. An owl called from the woods across the river. Then another answered. As he looked at the woods, at the pines, which were black and strung together by webs of darkness, he saw a patch of white between trees. Someone else was over there, watching. Jack thumped his brother-in-law on the back. "Who you got with you, Will?"

"Nobody, Jack."

"That fellow over there just showed up on his own?"

"I don't know, Jack."

Jack stood up, and with his foot rolled Will over. The man drew his hands up over his face, looked through fingers. "Don't shoot me, Jack," he said.

"Who's your partner, Will?"

"I swear, Jack, there's nobody with me. Who would work with me?"

"Get up."

"Aw, Jack."

Jack made the man get up and shove-walked him up to the cabin, where he waked Rubens and made the writer tie Will up with clothesline. He put Will in the writer's bed and covered him up. "Save him from hypothermia," Jack said. His brother-in-law whined at him, begged him to let him go. "I got to have protection," he said. "You don't understand. Donnie will kill me. He's on my tail. That's who you saw, Jack," he said, squirming in the bed. "That's one of his men over there on the other side, watching me. He wants me as much as he wants you. I swear it."

Rubens brought Will some soup he'd warmed in a can.

"Maybe he's telling the truth," he said.

"But there's no way to know," Jack said. "Did Donnie send you over here, Will?"

"Yeah, that's right. He made me come. I had to do it. You know Donnie, Jack. He will *kill* you. He thinks we're all snakes. He just wants to chop us all."

"What about your plan, Will?"

"I don't have a plan anymore, Jack. No plan but to get out of here and disappear."

Rubens offered Will a spoonful of soup.

"I can't take it sideways," Will said.

Jack let the writer prop Will up. He grinned at them. "I'm going to be all right now," he said. "I can tell it." He winked at Rubens.

Jack popped him hard across the nose. Will flinched.

"You got to quit that, Jack. I can't take any more of that."

"Who's the guy, Will?"

"He's Donnie's boy. There was another of them. They had a car waiting outside town. Another group. They came up after. Came up to Memphis and rented a car. He's one of them. They made me follow you. Made me come after you along the river road. I'm sorry, Jack. I'd already given up on my plan. I didn't want to kill you no more, I swear. I was humming and fretting about something else entirely. My daddy's real sick. I just found out. I called home and they told me Daddy is sick. I was on my way there, I swear."

Jack made Rubens get more cord and he had the writer wrap it around the bed and Will, truss him up in the bed.

"At least you're not going to kill me, huh?" Will said. "At least it's not going that far."

"It might slip over," Jack said.

"We're related," Will said to Rubens. "Jack's my brother-in-law. We're family. I don't have any real family much, since I am a bastard, but Jack is part of what I got and I am grateful for it. We'll get something going together, Jack. I think me and you ought to get something going, a duck ranch or a bank-robbing operation, something like that. I got ideas. Nobody ever asks me about my ideas, but I got plenty of them. I would have liked to share my ideas with James, but James hated me. I didn't mean to kill him, Jack, but he pushed me. When he stole Ethel I thought I would lose my mind. Maybe I *did* lose my mind. I couldn't take it. He got everything. He got the name and the love and the money and the honor and the respect, and then he got the goddamn woman, too. I couldn't take it."

He snapped his jaws at Rubens.

"You have to understand the serious strain I was under," he said, pleading with his wet gray eyes. "Anybody else would have been driven mad. I was a little mad, I guess, but it was the kind of mad that's good for you. I got that fucker out of my system. That's what I did. It was preordained. It was in the stars for old Jamie. Anybody could have seen it coming."

"I guess James didn't, huh?" Jack said.

"Don't sport with me, Jack, please. I can't take any more. I am a broken man. All I ever wanted all my life was a little kindness. Just a few goddamn seconds of it. You ever walk around thinking of the last time anybody stroked your hand, Jack? You know what that's like? Clare loves you. She loves you like you're the one who makes the fucking sun rise. But nobody ever loved me like that. My mama should have, but she didn't. She hated me. She blamed me for my daddy cutting her off. She said it was my fault. She used to stick my hands in hot water to hurt me. She wanted me to feel the pain she felt, she said. She'd do that every day. She'd be doing it right now if I didn't rise up and made her stop. *Feel the fucking pain!* I busted my own mama in the face. I beat her to the floor to make her stop torturing me. What kind of business is that? *Feel the fucking pain!* What kind of world is it where such shit goes on? Where a young boy has to take arms against his own mama, has to bust her in the face to make her stop hurting him? I can't stand it. I used to walk around the streets remembering how some whore touched me. The way she ran her fingers down my back, like I was special to her. I wasn't special to no whore, I know that, but I had to have some belief of it in my mind. I had to hold on to it. You got to have that, don't you know? You have to believe you are special to somebody. I know I am special to Clare. I have come to know it lately. You know how I know, Jack?"

Jack looked at him. Will's pale straw hair was wild around his narrow face. "How?"

"'Cause you hadn't killed me. If it wasn't for Clare, I'd be dead right now. I know that. She's the one made you hold off. She's still making you, even when she isn't around. That's strong love, and I got it. I want to hold it to me like a puppy. I want to hold it against me so I don't fear nothing."

He nudged Rubens with his knee. The writer jumped.

"You ever been bad scared, Rube?" he said.

"Yes, of course. I'm scared now."

"Nah. You haven't ever been bad scared. Whatever you scared of being in, you still think you going to get out of. Bad scared is when it's horrible and you know you won't get out. That's the kind of scared I am. I been that way all my life. I think I was born that way. Terror's on me like a birthmark. I got no one to be sweet to me. I never had no one. That marks you. It sets you up in a horrible way. Whatever I did, whatever trouble I got into, and I admit I got into a lot, it was all because of the terror. I been trying to do something about that terror since I was a child."

"I don't know what to tell you."

Rubens looked at Jack, who sat at the window watching the dawn come up through the trees. Jack thought of Jimmy lying in his grave in the grove of poplars, of the gambler resting in his plastic sack. He'd gone from being nearly dead to dead. A long way. In the trees above the grave long swags of fox grapes hung. The purple grapes were unpicked. They hung like withered rosaries in the vines. As if it were a lost place, Jack thought. Where no one ever came.

He looked at his brother-in-law, who even tied up and thrust under a yellow blanket looked as if he was jackaling in some way, sliding, slipping the noose. He had no feeling for the man, or for Rubens, or for whoever might be coming after him. The boy Clare killed, the farm boy who had come at them swinging a bicycle chain—Jack had no feeling for him, either. The boy was an idiot, he had been capable of killing them and he deserved what he got. What broke in him that evening broke not because of a death.

"Let's go," Jack said to Rubens.

"Good idea," Will said. "I've told you everything. Let me up and let's go."

"What about him?" Rubens said. "Has he got a place?"

"Not with us."

Will cried out. "You got to take me," he said. "You can't leave me here. They're killers, Jack. Please, I'll do anything."

"He's probably right," Rubens said.

"You're not in on the decision, sport."

For Jack, in the far distance of his mind, a lone man swam toward the bright white sun.

"Brother," Will said, squirming, kicking his tied-together legs at the blanket. "Let me suggest something. I can help you. I know the ropes of this situation. I been with Donnie for over a year. I know his habits. I can help you. Don't leave me. I swear—don't leave me, it will be a bad thing."

He kicked and thrust with his body, writhing, swinging himself in his sack of restraints. He porpoised up, crying out his sister's name. "Clare, oh, Clare," he screamed. "Darling, come save me. Come save old Will, oh please."

Rubens bolted from the room.

"Oh God and Jesus," Will cried. "Oh Jack, don't leave me here. If Donnie doesn't get me, the animals will break in and eat me. I've heard about that. Pumas. Wolverines. Raccoons or something—they'll come get me. I'm scared of animals, Jack. I hate them. I can't even stand dogs. I don't want a goldfish around me. *Don't let the rats at me.*"

"What's the plan, Will?"

"There isn't any plan. There's just Donnie. He wants money. He hates you, Jack. Ever since Clare went back to you. Something, I think it goes back farther than that. I'm sure you know all about it—all that prison business years ago, that stuff. Donnie wants that gambler's money and he wants the money Papa set aside—"

"Your father put money on my head?"

"Yes, he did, Jack. He put a quarter of a million dollars on you. He's the one you are after, not me. I'm weak. I can't restrain myself. How could somebody like me, somebody in my situation of destitution and abandonment, ignore so much money? I want my father's gratitude. Can you blame me?"

"Sure, Will, I can blame you."

"Oh God, help me, please."

"Nobody here but us, Will."

"Oh God, I wish there was somebody else. Somebody I could talk to. Will you please go and get my sister? I want to say good-bye to her. I love her and now I know she loves me. Let me speak to her, Jack. You can give me that, can't you? I'm going to die here, I know it. Donnie is going to come and shoot me, or the animals will come get me. And oh Jesus—that corpse. Don't leave me in this place with that corpse. Will you go get Clare, Jack? Will you do that?"

Jack ignored him. He took the can of soup from the table where Rubens had placed it and drank from it. It was Campbell's vegetable. He remembered it from his childhood. His mother had fed it to him, with saltine crackers and banana-and-mayonnaise sandwiches. The mind returned always to the points of betrayal, but it also returned to the sweetness. What had Jesus thought about on the cross? Had he thought about Judas's kiss, or about the time he and the disciples walked through the field picking ears of wheat and eating them? That moment in the field, walking in the sunshine with his buddies, everything going great, the miracles grabbing, all the women swooning over him, must have been almost perfect for Christ. He must have thought it was all going to work out. He must have felt all the strands of it, the lines of love and offering and intention, coming together in his hand. Did this come back to him on the cross? Did he taste the wheat in the blood that was in his mouth? It was great that he forgave everybody. The preachers always told that part as if it was the big deal, but it wasn't so great if you had to spend your last moments on earth thinking about all the rascals and what they'd done, and how now, oh Lordy, you were letting them all off the hook. That was real overtime, Jack thought. What about the sweet parts? What about thinking of them? What about Mary Magdalene and the girls washing your feet? And the perfume? And the feast of Canaan, all that? When he turned the water into wine, that must have been a swell feeling. To raise the jug and say, Here boys, we got plenty to drink now—

Jack patted his brother-in-law's shoulder. Will flinched from the touch. "I thought you wanted to get rubbed against," Jack said.

"Looked like a blow to me," Will said.

"You'll have to let me know how this turns out."

"I'll tell you right now," Will said, his voice cold and thin.

"You got the script?"

"Yeah, I got it. You going down with this one, Jackie boy. You going to a cold lonely death. There're too many people got a bead on you now, boy. If it ain't Donnie, it'll be the law, and if it ain't the law, it'll be me. I'm going to get free of this predicament, you can bet. I know you won't kill me. You can't. Not with my sister there. And if you don't kill me, I'm going to get you. I've had enough of this. Enough. People been mistreating me all my life and I have reached my limit. If James rose up from the grave, I'd kill him again. I don't care anything about my daddy, either. That selfish bastard. I'm going to kill him, too. Right after I get his money."

"Fine," Jack said.

He turned to go.

Will began to shout at him, to beg him to set him free. "I'll confiscate it all for you," he cried.

Jack could hear his shouts as he came down through the trees, but by the time he reached the boat, he could not differentiate them from the sound of the faint morning breeze lifting through the pines.

(That night, he said, the night before the boy appeared, he had heard his mother praying, he had heard his sister crying. Then the house was still. He thought they slept, but they didn't; after a while he could hear them, hear sighs, shiftings of their bodies, hear his sister singing softly to herself. He had taken down a volume of the encyclopedia and read the entry on Egypt. An owl called, driving its anxious questions into the dark.)

They turned right at Cairo, swung by under the wooded bluffs and headed up the oily, streaked Ohio. They were inside the force field now, there was a pull on them they both recognized, but they did nothing to resist it. An odd, fumbling passivity overtook them, like an illness, a strange lassitude descended and held them rocking in its arms.

Rubens asked questions, probed, but they told him to cease. They did not want to talk, they did not want to hear talk. They let Rubens pilot the boat and they sat together staring out at the passing shore, occasionally pointing out to each other interesting features of terrain or development. There was a tower north of Cairo that Jack said he would like to climb, but he did not want to stop the boat to do it. Clare saw a flock of geese in a cutover cornfield, but she turned away without counting them, without doing anything more that pointing at them. There were scraps of cloth in the trees and soapsuds pushed against the bank. Effluents from fertilizer factories stained the water white.

He told her about Will, but she did not ask for details. "There's nothing I can do for him," she said when Rubens asked if she would have tried to save her brother. "He ruined himself a long time before I could get to him," she said.

They began to return to bed early in the day, to pull covers up and sleep long hours. They rose in the late afternoon and sat on the aft deck sipping tea and staring out at the passing river. Rubens cooked their meals, interviewing them while he worked. They were not generally hungry. Clare took an occasional piece of toast smeared with butter and Jack ate stale cereal from the food locker under the sink, but not much else. At night one or both would get up and walk around the deck, sit topside alone, and stare out at the shoreline. At night there were the lights of towns, of farmhouses, of the big factories lit up like carnivals. Sometimes one or the other would stretch a hand out toward the lights as if they could be touched from there.

There was a haze in Jack's mind, webs of undistinguished thought; obscure ideas rose like ash-colored fish and sank. He thought of his mother scraping rust from a metal pan, of his father sitting in the living room reading the newspaper. Sparks of anguish flickered among the thoughts like lights in fog. Strings of reproach pulled through coupled in long trains. He began to smell himself, to smell the gross and foul odors of his body. He could hear noises at night, small voices whispering the words to songs. The fact that the words were from songs and that the voices would not sing the songs infuriated Jack. He cried out at his mind. Rubens and Clare stared at him, but Jack was unable to explain what was happening. He could not say, and then he could not remember.

"I smell bad," he said and the look he gave them frightened the writer. Jack heard him speak to Clare about his condition, but he grew confused as he listened because he thought Rubens was speaking of someone else, of another man who had come onto the boat and was riding with them. Who could this man be? Had Will returned? Was Donnie there? Jack searched the boat, opening every door, peering into cupboards, looking under the sink, into the bilges, and behind the engine, but he could find no one. The man was always one step ahead of him.

Finally he went to Clare and begged her to tell him who it was.

She tried to reassure him, but she became quickly exasperated. "It's no one," she screamed.

Jack shrank from her, terrified.

"Why is she treating me this way?" he asked Rubens. Then he began to apologize. To both of them he offered stammering regrets for his behavior.

"What behavior?" Clare wanted to know, but Jack could not remember.

"It will all come to light," he said.

Then he began to believe they knew what he had done and were about to accuse him of it. He would not come near them. He would have abandoned the boat, but he was sure there were animals in the water, crocodiles and fish with large sharp teeth. He saw airplanes come down the river in formation, yellow Piper Cubs with men hanging their heads out pointing at him. He crawled into bed and pulled the covers up, but when he closed his eyes he saw the planes. There were bodies strapped to the wings, and bodies were being dragged behind the fuselages, bodies that spun hideously in cold sunlight and bounced off the surface of the river.

He fled the sight of this, but there was nowhere to go. He banged around the deck, threw himself down the cabin steps, rolled on the floor. He knew the pilots could hear his thoughts, and he could not stop himself from thinking of his terrible crimes. "They're coming to arrest me," he screamed. "Save me, oh Jesus, darling, save me."

He thrust himself under the lower bunk, screwed himself as tightly as he could into the narrow space. He pushed his face against the cold hull and cried out for Jesus to save him. "They can hear me," he shrieked. "They know everything."

Clare ignored him. Rubens, with a look on his face of horror and disgust, tried to coax him out from under the bunk. "Everything is okay out here," he said. "Whatever's not, we'll fix."

He talked steadily to Jack, talked to him as if he were of sound mind, spoke of the interesting life Jack had led, of his childhood on the lake in Minnesota. He told Jack he admired him, that he considered it a privilege to travel with him. "You'll probably make more money with this book than on ten bank robberies," he said. "Won't that be wonderful?"

Jack had been torn in two. He knew this was so because he could see the narrow red ditch that ran between the halves of himself. Then he saw children standing on the shore of Lake Superior and he understood there was a party and the children were fishing in celebration of his birthday. They pulled golden muskellunge from the lake and set them on the rocks. The fish gleamed brightly, but as Jack looked at them, they turned into severed heads that began to roll along the rocks toward him. The heads were Clare's and his mother's, and then he saw they were his own head, rolling across the lichen-streaked rocks. The heads spoke to him and they told him of his damnation, they told him they knew everything about him and told him he was to live forever in a torment of loss and bitterness, that young boys would spit in his face and old men revile him, that women would bitterly curse his name.

He could not draw his attention away from the wild imaginings. "Put a bullet in me," he cried. "Somebody shoot my head. Please shoot my head."

Rubens sat beside him on the floor, his big moon face peering out of the light at him, talking to him.

Clare crawled under the bunk, stuck her pistol under his chin, and ordered him to cease. "I'll kill you," she screamed, "if you don't shut the fuck up."

Jack could hear her voice, but she seemed to be in another room, talking to someone else. He did not know that he himself was talking. He was listening to voices, soft insinuating voices that begged him to relieve them of their suffering, that begged him to attend to them. These were the voices of children, Jack knew, voices of the retarded children in Anacondia. They had come to reproach him, they had come to beg him to save them, but Jack could not see how this was possible. "How can I do for you," he cried, "when I can't do anything for myself? Oh you boys, oh you little girls, I am so sorry."

He wept then, hot bitter tears that burned in his throat.

He could not say when the spell left him. He did not know how long he had been under a spell. Once, before it ended, he got up in the middle of the night and went out on deck. The boat was deserted. The moon was filling to half. It set a narrow tiled path on the water. Small flying shapes flickered in and out of the light above the path. They were bats. Their skinny bodies slid and capered in the light, appearing and disappearing. Night butterflies, he thought. They were very beautiful.

The next morning—or ten mornings later, he didn't know—he waked in a red and chilly dawn. He felt the cold in his bones. It was the first time he had felt weather in a long time. He crawled out from under the bunk, pulled a blanket off a chair, and wrapped himself in it. He was very hungry. He found a loaf of bread and ate slices of it. As he was eating Rubens waked and swung his legs over the side of the bunk. He asked Jack how he felt and Jack was able to answer him sensibly. It surprised them both. "I'm tired," Jack said, "and cold."

He looked around. The cabin was messy, and it smelled of urine and feces. "Where's Clare?"

"She left the boat three days ago."

"For good?"

"No."

Jack felt very weak, weak in his bones. "Do you mind if I sit down?"

"Let me help you."

Rubens set a chair for him. Jack dropped into it. "I'm dazed," he said. "I can't remember much."

"Not much happened."

Jack shuddered. The hand of darkness moved across his brain. He could hear tiny voices calling to him. He put his head in his hands and moaned.

"What is it?" Rubens asked.

"My mind's busted."

The words made a tinny sound in Jack's ears. He thought he was being taped, but this did not seem right. He strained to make himself stay in the present there in the cabin, where Rubens began to make coffee. He watched the writer's broad back as he bent over the sink, watched his hands work. He looked at the gray unwashed porthole, and he looked at the steps leading topside and at the rectangle of brightness the dawn was building there. In the rectangle, rising like a fish to the surface, he saw clouds and a ray of light that was glassy and clear as water, and he held this in the focus of his mind, straining hard to stay with this slim shaft of light, which seemed to waver and nearly collapse as he looked at it. It was sunlight and he knew it as sunlight.

Then he knew his body, he smelled himself and saw his legs in the gray jeans and saw his hands, which looked worn to him, and then in a moment he tasted coffee in his mouth and he knew this taste. There was the sound of birds. He took the coffee and went topside. They were tied up in a cove among some birches that still held on to their leaves. The leaves hung in the limp branches in bunches and tufts. The branches trailed onto the deck. Jack took one in his hand, stripped the leaves off, and brought them to his nose. They smelled dusty and faintly acidic. Rubens had followed him up.

"Where is Clare?" Jack said. He remembered he had already asked this, but he did not feel the need to apologize for asking again.

"She said she was going to do some work."

"Did she say when she was coming back?"

"No. But she said if we got rousted from here to meet her below the Carthage bridge north of Paducah."

"Kentucky," Jack said. "We're in Kentucky."

"Yes. We have been."

"How long?"

"Two weeks."

"And I have been crazy the whole time."

"Kentucky'll do that to you."

Jack didn't laugh. He was thinking of Clare. She had tried to kill him. He had a memory of this, of his wife looming over him accusing him. He flushed. He could sense her presence still, hear her voice.

He sat down on the rail. Behind the willows the bank rose sharply. It was matted with leaves, maple leaves, beech leaves, in yellow and red not yet faded. He could smell the woods. "Is this a random location?" he said.

"She made me stop here. She said she had to get off. She said she wanted to get some business started."

"That means she was going to rob something."

"I feel terribly uncomfortable about that."

"How'd you feel with me going crazy?"

"Pretty bad. I was scared to death. What was it?"

"Murk and dust."

"From what?"

"A head blizzard." Everything in the past, each moment until now, ground to fine powder and blown into storm.

"I'm glad you found your way through it. But I don't want to be part of another crime. I can't take it."

"Maybe we'll rest a moment. Maybe we'll seek an easement."

"That's good."

Out on the river sunlight caught the world in its arms. "Let's go up to Carthage," he said.

There was a creek beyond the bridge and he put the boat in it. Up the bank and downriver slightly was a shopping mall. The developers had kept a screen of woods between the mall and the creek. The sound of bridge traffic drifted down over the creek, but no one came back there. He and Clare had stopped on the creek before, on a houseboat they rented one summer, years ago, he remembered, before the mall was built. Then raccoons had come down to the water, and if you showed up on the right day and were still long enough, you might see deer, a doe and her fawn maybe, appear at the creek's edge to drink. He remembered an evening years ago when the tops of the maple trees had blazed gold with sunlight, some combination of light and yellow leaves that converted the woods into a fancy of celestial treasure. "It's these nights, when the gold explodes," Clare had said, "that make you think we're in the last days—and it's all right."

He'd agreed with her.

She did not come the first day, or the next, or the day after that. He was weak yet; the light hurt his eyes. He felt a sadness, a melancholy without rebuke or anger in it, like the sadness of a child who has begun to accept his grief. The creek surface had a coppery sheen and the trunks of alders standing in the water were stained orange. There were vines in the trees, thin ropes that hung down leafless. At night he could hear the humming of generators. Rubens said it was awful what the corporations had done to the country, how the government let them pollute the rivers, but to Jack their immediate environment was beautiful. He did not mind the copper stain on the water, and the denuded vines looked elegant to him, like lines of expectation, he thought, strung from past to future. He was lonely, though; he wanted to be among people.

"I have to leave this boat," he said.

"What about Clare?"

They sat on the aft deck eating apples Rubens had bought at the mall.

"I mean when Clare comes," Jack said. "I mean then."

"Do you mean you don't want me to go with you?"

"That's right."

"It's probably best."

Jack smiled at him. "You don't want to stay anyway, do you?"

"I'd like to take a break."

"What will you do?"

"I want to go rest awhile, visit my folks. Get away from the gangster life."

"Think you can?"

"Oh yes, I do. I think so."

"That month we lived in the woods in Pennsylvania—I used to think about all the animals out there who never got to go inside. Homeless people make you think of that now, in cities. You see them on the streets. A lot of them won't go to shelters, they just live on the street. They stay outside all the time, like raccoons, in the weather and the pressure. When you're young you think you want to live a life that never lets up. But then you get old and you find out you can't take it."

"Maybe your—attack—was a rest."

"I wish it was, but you can't really rest when you go crazy. It's more like everything you were up to accelerating. It's even more strenuous than life was before. It's right after the spell that you can rest a little. Like the exhaustion and quiet that comes after a fight. I feel easy about things right now."

"It seems a little pitiful."

"It does, doesn't it?"

"Like peace is what you feel when you stop whacking yourself with a stick."

"A lot of people, that's all they get."

Rubens scratched his wrists. "You sounded like Clare just then. I could hear her in your voice."

"I know. Sometimes there's a reversal. We become each other. It seems that way." It didn't now, in fact it seemed stupid to think this, but he didn't correct himself.

"You spend so much time together."

"It's more than that." It's nothing like that, he thought.

Everything he'd seen was still real to him. The planes, the children, and even the fish turned into heads rolling on the rocks. He was not frightened by this. It all seemed simply a part of his life. These sights joined the array of sights he remembered. The boy in the woods had not reappeared. Yet, everything—it was all there. It was impossible to lose anything.

*(At dawn I went out, he said, and found Father sleeping in a green Adirondack chair under a white birch tree. He sat with his head thrown back, his mouth open, snoring. His head was wet, glistening with dew. The dew was like a silver cap on his pale scalp. I wanted to touch it, not because, even, this was my father, a man who suffered—*I did not care about his suffering*—but because the damp, the sun just striking the fair dewy skin, was beautiful. Do you understand?)*

An urgency began to build through the next days, a pressure. It was different from the madness. He became restless. He became discontented with himself. Do nothing, he told himself, say nothing, stay still. The restlessness grew. He cleaned the boat, washed bulkheads and the deck, collected the trash and carried it up the bank, dug a hole and buried it among the alder bushes. He cooked meals, baked cookies in the small oven.

Then he began to go out at night, to walk along the mall perimeter. One night he crossed the parking lot and sat in the McDonald's reading a newspaper. The world was going to hell, so the paper said. In depleted, distant countries battles raged. Racial tension screeched. Mayors begged to be taken seriously, to be given another chance. He read the sports pages, the business and society sections. At a nearby table a mother forced her Cub Scout to eat his fish sandwich. "It's better than a hamburger," she said forlornly. She looked around at Jack with a humiliated and despairing eye. The Cub Scout stared straight ahead like an operative resisting torture. Jack read his horoscope. *Extend yourself,* the message said. *Open your arms. You have what it takes to tell friend from foe.* An old woman in a stained black beret slobbered over her fat burger. She swiveled her head every time the front door opened, glaring at whoever entered. There were teenagers off to one side berating one another, testing their wills against everything. He could hear fragments of a conversation behind him in which a man begged a woman for forgiveness. "I'm in agony," the man said. "I will be in agony for the rest of my life if you don't forgive me."

The woman answered, but Jack couldn't make out what she said.

"That's not enough," the man said. "I have to have a sign."

Shouts came from the kitchen, a bright, hell-colored place.

Then a black man in a small high-crowned gray fedora asked if he could sit down. "Mind?" The place was crowded. Jack said okay.

The man slid heavily into his seat and began to unwrap a large hamburger and french fries. Jack sipped his coffee. The man ate enthusiastically, almost desperately, Jack thought, as if he was starving. Jack watched him closely. He remembered watching his father eat, and how it disgusted him. His father ate in large bites, shoving the food clumsily into his small mouth. Bits always collected in the corners of his mouth and sometimes there were smears on his chin, even on his cheeks. As a child Jack had hated this, and as a teenager, too. His father never noticed the crumbs. Jack had told him to wipe his mouth and his father had good-naturedly done this. It embarrassed Jack in front of his friends.

"You got ketchup on your cheek," he said.

The man looked at him blankly. He didn't stop chewing.

"Right there," Jack said. "It's up near your ear."

"Don't you start in on me," the black man said.

He was heavyset; the narrow hat brim was turned up.

"My father used to drive me crazy with his eating habits," Jack said.

"Don't get us confused," the man said.

"You don't look a thing like him, but the way you eat brings him back to life for me."

"He's dead?"

"Yeah. He passed on eighteen years ago."

"Probably 'cause you wouldn't leave him alone about his eating."

"You don't have to say that."

"You're right. I'm sorry."

"It's okay," Jack said. "I'm a career criminal, so I'm used to abuse."

"Like that woman behind you," the man said, pointing with his half-eaten burger.

"I was listening to them."

"I hate that business," the black man said. "The way some men go on weaseling their way out of hurting a woman. Now, *that's* what makes *me* sick."

"Me, too. Can I have one of your fries?"

"Sure. Take the rest of them. I'm just eating anyway out of nervous tension. I don't need food."

"What's got you nervous?"

"I'm on my way to beat the hell out of my daughter's husband."

"Abuse?"

"That's it. He got caught beating her up. Can you believe it? He took a bullwhip to my child. A god-knows whip. It is a horror movie. I wake up in the night and I see it happening in my mind. I'm from Cleveland. I drove down here these last two days to confront this scoundrel. My wife said not to come. She is scared for me, but I had to come. Corine is my pride and my beauty."

He wiped his mouth. "Do you have children?"

Jack said he didn't.

"They are what makes life possible. Children. All the dishonesty and abuse and hatred clears up when your child smiles at you."

He set his hamburger down. His hands moved among the torn debris of his meal, arranging it, tapping it. Jack saw that he was crying.

"I'm sorry," he said. He patted the man's thick wrist.

"It's more than I can bear," the man said. "When my daughter told me, I got sick to my stomach. I had to put the phone down and go vomit. This animal," he said bitterly, pushing the words through his teeth. "It takes all my Christian charity not to go and kill him. I *want* to kill him. I want to wring his neck."

"You think you can keep from doing it?"

"I don't know now. I was wrestling with it in the car. Wrestling with the devil, you might say. I decided to come in here and get something to eat, to calm myself down. Then you started picking on me."

"I'm sorry about that."

Jack ate a french fry. "Why don't I go with you?" he said.

"Go where?"

"Over to your daughter's house. Is that where this is going on? Maybe it would be good to have somebody with you when you confront this guy."

"I don't really know you."

"I'm Jack Baker. I'm on my way upriver on my boat. I just stopped here, too, for something to eat. I understand abusive conduct. I have a righteous feeling about it, too."

"You want to keep me company?"

"I wouldn't mind at all. Actually, I'd be honored to keep you company."

In the distance, almost snubbed into silence, a lonely orchestra played. Jack could almost make out the tune. A wisp of cold air curled around his ankles and for an instant he thought of his father beating him in the snowbound car. For a second, as brief as the remembered and passing memory of the scent of crab apple blossoms in his mother's garden, he could forgive everything.

"What's that?" the man said.

"Nothing. I was just remembering something. You want to go?"

The man's name was David Williams. He introduced himself on the drive over to his daughter's house. "Everything about this has surprised me," he said. He leaned over the steering wheel, peering at traffic lights and street signs, never glancing at Jack as he drove. "I'm a research programmer for the Cleveland Museum of Science," he said. "I work with a team whose job it is to excavate old programs that have to do with studies of various ancient historical documents and artifacts. This is far from anything I'm used to dealing with."

"It always is," Jack said.

The streets were wet and glossy. He felt as if he had just arrived from a foreign country where he had been humiliated and disgraced.

"You say you have experience with this business," David Williams said.

"Yes. I used to work with the Nashville Human Resources Department, as a counselor. I took calls from troubled youths."

"My son-in-law is certainly a troubled youth. I do not understand how this happened at all. I understand frustration. I understand failure and regret and all that, and I certainly understand mistreatment, but I do not understand why someone would take up weapons against a loved one. It just doesn't follow. I have worshipped my wife since the day I met her thirty-five years ago. I am from the old school, I know, but that's how it is."

"I understand completely. My wife is a jewel, too."

"That's it, a jewel. I was an ignorant country boy when I met my wife. I was raised on a farm in Ohio. I met my wife at the state fair in Columbus. We were both showing fat steers. It was unusual to have two black children in the farm exhibition, and even more unusual to have a black girl. It wasn't the strangeness that made me fall for her, but it *was* love at first sight. She was wearing a blue 4-H jacket and an orange bondini hat and she was washing her steer, a big Hereford, with a water hose, and rubbing him down with a rag. Like you'd wash your car. She was an utter dazzlement to me."

"I can imagine. My wife was one to me, too."

"Is that so? It is startling when it is."

"Yes."

"I was terrified of her, but you know, she was as friendly as your neighbor. I'd never encountered such, not down in Haley, Ohio. Someone so beautiful and so obviously special, who was so nice."

"It's a kind of miracle, isn't it?"

"That's exactly what it was. I traipsed around after her the whole week. Her steer won honorable mention, beat out my little Angus. She seemed to enjoy my company. It was terribly exciting. We wrote after that and then I went up to Madrid, Ohio, to visit her, and then she came down to visit. It went on like that for six months, and then we got engaged and then we got married. June 12, 1961."

"That's a pretty story." But then the man's life rose before him, a hidden version, the version he would never tell, in which he was afflicted with a sorrow no one could distinguish from commitment, in which he was a man unable to understand the workings of modern life, in which children disappeared from city streets and were never heard from again, in which mothers sat alone in movie theaters crying at sentimental pictures depicting the sanitized adventures of conventional families, in which fathers, tossed out of jobs they had given everything to, walked the streets muttering to themselves, ashamed.

David Williams laughed—ruefully, Jack thought. "You know," he said, "I was so naive, even as a farm boy, so naive about women—I had them on such a pedestal—that I almost went back home to my parents on our wedding night."

"It's an intense experience."

"It certainly was for me. And I don't mean the sex. I mean the physical nature of women. That was what was so upsetting."

"What do you mean?"

"It embarrasses me to say it. You're a young man. Things have changed."

"Not that much."

"Maybe not. Maybe not."

They were entering a suburban neighborhood. Large naked trees stretched big limbs over the street. The houses were set back among smaller trees. Each house appeared to be a variation of the one next to it.

"I heard her in the bathroom," Williams said.

"What was she doing?"

"Urinating."

He put his hand over his mouth.

"She went in to change into her nightgown," he said. "The walls were thin in the motel. I could hear her. I heard her urinate. I had never heard a woman urinate before. It was shattering. I knew in theory they did that, but I had never thought of it in practice. It shocked me. In a way, I guess, it disgusted me. It was as if I thought of women as beings who did not make such lowly sounds. I was so taken aback, I can tell you, that I was unable to make love to her when she came out. It was a terrible time. It took me two weeks to face the truth and tell her. She understood. I think that moment—when I told her what had me all balled up, and she understood, and forgave me—was the keystone to all the love that's been with us ever since."

"Now this, huh?"

"Yes. Now this terrible business."

Williams parked on the street and they got out. They stood together on the patchy sidewalk in front of a small wooden house. The lights were on all through the house. Williams began to apologize.

"It's all right," Jack said.

"No," Williams said, "I mean I am not sure now that it's a good idea for you to go in."

"Can you handle it alone?"

"I don't know. I am scared to death. I work with computers and historical documents. I feel very comfortable working with such materials. This is confusing to me." He shook his head. "But, I swear . . ." His voice trailed off.

"You'd better let me come," Jack said.

"I swear," Williams went on as if Jack had not spoken, "this crazy son of a gun, hitting my daughter. Oh Lord, it makes me think the world is going to hell. It fills my heart with such sadness."

The man turned aside then, stepped away onto the scrubby lawn and bowed his head. Jack saw he was praying. He bowed his head, too, but he was thinking of how things could come to this, and how, if he let himself, he could just keep going in this manner. He was now in a suburb in Paducah, Kentucky. He could let one thing after another happen and there would be no telling where he would end up. In prison surely—eventually—always—but where until then?

"Okay," David Williams said, "you come with me."

There was music pouring from the house, old-fashioned dance music. They could hear it through the front door. Williams knocked and the door opened. His daughter stood there with one arm flung back. She was breathless and sweating. "We were dancing," she said. "Arthur was showing me the fox-trot." She kissed her father.

Arthur was a large light-skinned black man wearing gray suit pants and a white shirt with red suspenders. He was flushed and sweating, too. A tightness clamped itself onto his face when he saw Williams. He had the look, the controlled tense look, Jack thought, of someone who had been recently violent. Williams introduced him. "My friend," he called him.

"Come in, come in," Arthur effused. "You are welcome in our house."

Arthur rushed out to the kitchen and brought back several soft drinks. He didn't turn the music down.

"We were learning to dance to some of this good white music," he said to Jack, grinning a wide hysterical grin. "It is charming music."

"Let's show them," the daughter said. Williams sat on the edge of a flowered sofa staring at his daughter. He studied her as if he was looking for scars. "I have come a long way . . ." he began. "There are certain things I want—"

"Yes, Daddy, I *know,*" the woman said. "I know *all* about *that.* Mama called me. It's all straightened *out.* Come, *come on,* Daddy," she said, "watch us."

Arthur took her into his arms, swept her up. She fell back into his embrace, swooning, it seemed to Jack, her head falling back on her narrow shoulders, letting herself be taken and spun. Arthur twirled her lightly. He swept her through steps that carried them around the room. The music was orchestral music from the fifties, some post-swing business that Jack didn't recognize.

The dancing went on and on. One song ended and another began. Williams raised his hand in the brief silence between songs, but Arthur continued to twirl his wife around the room. The music started again and they rushed away again dancing feverishly. They continued for song after song. This went on for twenty minutes, then longer. Williams watched. He seemed to be in a dream.

The couple swept by, bucking and dipping. They revolved, the woman's thin arms lifting in arabesque shapes, fluttering, until, as if caught by a rope, they stopped in front of Williams. "Dance with me, Daddy," the woman pleaded. "Please come now and dance with me." Arthur stepped back, bowed and offered the woman's hand, lifted to his father-in-law flat on his palm, as if her hand—her whole life—were balanced there. Williams glanced at Jack. There was a doggish, embarrassed smile on his lips. His eyes were sunk in his head. He looked as if he had been ordered to enter solitary confinement.

"Thank you," he said, getting to his feet. He lifted his chin, gulped. "I think everything will be all right," he said to Jack.

"Everything what?" Jack said.

"Everything here. Everything in this house. I have faith."

"In what?"

"Who is this fellow?" Arthur said gaily.

"A man I met," Williams said, looking away from Jack.

"Perhaps he had better go," Corine said.

"We were glad you could come," Arthur said. "Friends of Father David are always welcome."

"Always," Corine said.

She pushed into her father's arms. "Swing me, Daddy," she said. "Go with the music." The father stumbled into a clumsy dance step. His daughter tugged him away across the carpet, toward the entrance to the dining nook. Arthur hovered near, dancing, lifting one foot, then the other, in a slow, light stomp. He glanced over his shoulder at Jack, smiling, offering a look of benevolence and dismissal. "Good-bye," they all said, almost in unison. "Good-bye, good-bye."

"Good-bye, Mr. Baxter," the daughter cried. "Good-bye, good-bye."

Jack found himself outside the house, standing on the front steps. He turned back to the door. As he did so, the porch light went off. He started to knock, but he let his hand drop. The sound of a car horn came from the street. There was a station wagon parked behind Williams's car. Clare was in it, smiling at him.

She got out and ran up the walk. They embraced. What's going on? she asked. He started to tell her and then stopped. "I don't exactly know," he said. "It's odd—this rattled daddy—"

"We have to go."

"Why?"

"They'll catch us if we don't."

"I'm beginning to think they'll catch us anyway."

"Are you still crazy?"

"Not the way I was."

"In a new way?"

"These people I was with—this man—sometimes—Jesus, I am bamboozled—you can't tell how deep the con goes."

She kissed him hard then, lurching into him, pushing herself like an insistence against his body, pulling herself onto him as if to climb up him—he caught her, held her, half dragged her—she panted, struggling as if trying to perform some maneuver she couldn't quite—and had to—remember, as they stumbled to the car.

She had seen him get into the black man's car and followed, she said. They drove away fast. There was nothing behind them.

• • •

When Donnie opened the trunk Suok was in there, dead. He'd suffocated, too, under black tape set over his mouth and nose. Tit for tat, *Donnie said. The goons beat Jack. They beat him and dragged him to the river and threw him in, and then Donnie made Boudreau go in after and get him, pull him out. Jack could see the sky, but it did no good. This was like the first time in prison when they beat him. There's no letup, he remembered, you have to give in to it. The goons beat him in the face. He lost consciousness and then he came back; he discovered they were kicking him. He didn't feel it, but then he did and he sensed the hole opening below his gut, sensed himself falling, and he knew he was going to die. Donnie looked down at him laughing.*

"There are long periods when I have no sense of things fitting together," he said.

"Are they supposed to?"

"I wish they would."

They were on a state road in Kentucky, traveling south and east, fifty miles below the river. They were on the way to their ex-partner Robert Joleen's house.

"I think it's a good idea to go see Robert," she had said. "We can get him to drive us." Robert was the only partner they had worked with besides Mamiel, who was dead.

They'd decided to let Rubens fend for himself.

"I couldn't take any more of him," Clare said. "He was like a bad day in geometry class. Like a theorem gone sour or something."

"You've thought about him."

"I had to."

"Where did you go?"

She went home, she said. She had looked in on the Manigault estate. "I thought I would solve this problem by myself. I thought I would be a help to you so when you came out of your fit you wouldn't have it hanging over you."

What happened, he wanted to know.

Nothing, she told him. "Exactly nothing."

The place was surrounded by goons. Donnie and his buddies were there, she said, big men in sports coats and hunting boots walking around the property. They had made it a fortress, some kind of outpost for meanness, she said. "I couldn't get through."

She drove hard, not wasting any time.

Why do you want to go to Robert's? he asked.

Because the car is stolen, she said. "I did a couple of robberies." She told him about one of them, the bust-up of a bank in a suburb outside Hartsville, across the river. "A man got shot," she said. "A hostage."

"Yours or theirs?" he said.

"Mine. The guard shot him. I took him, I had to—the whole thing didn't work without you—I grabbed this guy—a shield really, not exactly a hostage, but I grabbed him, this little guy with a black-dyed mustache—"

"How do you know it was dyed?"

"—it dripped on me—grabbed him and held him in front of me as I was trying to get out, but this guard, a big guy in uniform, pulled his pistol—no, he already had it out—and he shot the fucking hostage. I couldn't believe it."

"I wish I'd been there—no, I don't."

"You don't?"

"No. I'm glad I wasn't. I don't want to do it anymore."

"Is that what the craziness was about?"

"I don't know the answer to that."

"Are you lying to me?"

"No," he said, "I think I've reached the end of it."

When he said it he knew he had.

"Are we going to retire, or what?"

"I hadn't thought about that."

"We don't have enough money to retire."

"We could get jobs."

He searched the passing woods. They were black without gaps. Then the woods ended and they ran through fields that were like huge bays of emptiness pushing back under the starry sky, places where great pieces were missing. (*His father had come in, he said, wearing a suit made of dew.*) "I'm tired," he said.

"That craziness you went through wore you out."

"It isn't just that."

"We can't get jobs, Jack."

"We had them in Anacondia."

"Apple picking and substitute school teaching. That was the best we could do. Those were the jobs we would have been holding down when the FBI found us."

"Maybe they wouldn't find us. Maybe it would be like Rubens said—a cottage in some town in Florida or somewhere, two people living out their lives harmoniously, anonymously."

"That's a fantasy, Jack."

"So is this, Clare."

She unwrapped a stick of gum, bit half sharply off and offered the other half to him. "It's the last I got."

"Thanks."

"Honey," she said, "I love you, but if you make me live that kind of life, I will wind up a cranky old woman who menaces children and poisons neighborhood dogs. Or vice versa. I know it. These last weeks, these last years, my goodness, I have been thinking, too. We have to get this money up in Vandalia. Donnie has his claws in my family place, but we can get around Donnie. Daddy is sick—Will wasn't lying about that—"

"Did you see him?"

"Who—Will? No, but Daddy really is sick. We have to get the money before he passes."

"If there is money."

"If there is. There has to be. Then we'll be all right. We won't be all right, I know, but we can push not being all right back a few years. Maybe we can retrain ourselves. Maybe we can go to night school. You can finish your law degree. I can open a kennel or something. But we've got to have the money. There has to be something between us and the ground."

"There always has to be."

"And I'm more of a fugitive than you."

"That's right."

They turned off the highway and then turned off another time and one more. They found a clearing in the woods and parked there. She had blankets in the back. They wrapped in them and lay down. "I'm glad we could have this private time," she said.

"We haven't had much of that lately."

She pressed against him. His mind wobbled, lifted, his thoughts drifting among the peeled branches of oaks and maples, rising toward the clearing sky. He didn't know what was happening to him. Maybe he was already just following from one thing to the next. Maybe he had been doing this all along. Maybe planning was not planning at all. His thoughts were separated, insubstantial. They could have been the thoughts of another man, left in his head, like trinkets in a drawer in the house you rented; the place you found yourself in, he thought, after the job paid out and you carried your satchel of bullion into some stale room somewhere off the track of America; where you threw open the windows, he thought, and because that wasn't enough to make the place smell lively, you threw open the door, too, and you took the covers off the bed and you put the new sheets you'd bought onto the stained mattress, and you lay down on the bed with the lights off, he thought, and you watched the dark creep into the room, watched the star shine and listened to the crickets and you tried not to think of anything (*Father had gone upstairs to his study and closed the door. He was like a smell, he said, a bad odor, that drove everyone out of the house—like some cloudy fumigation, as if life were a roach infestation and his presence was the extermination of it: we scattered*), you tried to get your mind to go blank. . . .

She was talking. Her voice entered him quietly, took possession of him. He let it; he wanted it to.

She spoke of her ride, of her three days of adventuring. Was it three? He couldn't tell. She had robbed and fled, escaped. There were pictures for her, as always, tableaux and snapshots: a man washing a blue pickup truck, a woman slapping a little boy, three calico cats sitting side by side on a wall. She'd sat at a red light watching a man in a lot across the street split firewood. The man, who gripped the ax like someone unused to such work, had one of those chemotherapy shadow hairdos, she said, the kind you could see through. In Litchfield, Kentucky, cheerleaders in bright gold skirts had pranced down the sidewalk on their way to a cheering place. "I listened to a woman in a store explain the difference between coral snakes and king snakes," she said. "How does it go? 'Red and black, friend of Jack.' Yes. I liked that. 'Red and black, friend of Jack.' "

" 'Red and yellow, kill a fellow,' " he said.

"I didn't like that one so much."

Her hands made brief, startled figures.

She had not been able to speak to her father, she said, but she had gotten into the house. Like a phantom, like a burglar, she had entered, by way of the roof. There was an old treehouse in an oak beside the back porch, above the kitchen, she said. "I climbed it, there's a stick ladder nailed to the tree. The tree's grown," she said. "It's bigger. I could feel it."

She had entered the treehouse, where as a girl she and her dead brother James had played the game of lost adventurers. "Once," she said, "maybe it was the first time I saw him, Will sneaked into the yard. We saw him looking at us through the fence around the little yard. He was peering at us from behind the old horse trough. James went down and captured him and then we tied Will up. I helped James. I'm ashamed now I did it, but I did. We hauled him up by his hands into the tree and hung him that way, by his hands from a branch below the treehouse. We left him there. My father came home and found him. His arms were pulled out of the sockets. It was terrible. Daddy took him to the doctor and he dropped him there, called his mother I guess and made her come get him. Will was left out like a letter in the rain over and over—"

"Rural free delivery."

"Nothing free about it."

She had entered the treehouse again—for the first time, she said, in twenty years. It still stood, nailed on struts between two great branches. Their childhood artifacts were in place, she said. "Everything was there: the table and the cupboard and the little chairs we sat in. There were plates on the table and glasses with must in them. There were the little pots Mother gave me, and there was James's bow and arrow in the corner and his baseball glove, or one of them, in a chair by the window. I had to grope my way, but I could feel everything. It was like finding a vanished civilization. Like finding your own civilization vanished."

She had taken her customary seat at the table. Under her quick fingers the plates and cutlery had arranged themselves into their old settings. The child she had been took its place inside her body. She could see through its eyes, see the cups brim with Kool-Aid, and taste the stale jellied biscuits she had once served. Her brother sat in his place across from her teasing her and refusing to eat.

"I hate sentiment in other people," she said, "but I indulge it in myself. It's unseemly, I know. I sat there in that cramped ugly little house, for ten minutes I guess—I couldn't tell—mesmerized by the terrible story everyone's life had become. I'm not reflective, but I started thinking about what had happened. Each of us, we children, has turned out such a wayward creature. I'm the only one who has amounted to anything, and look at what I have amounted to. I don't despise what I have become—I love it, but it's a troubled life, to say the least. It made me angry. Suddenly, sitting there with my hands sunk into the past, I wanted to burn the goddamn place down. Not just the treehouse, but all of it. Daddy's house and the whole farm."

She rolled against him. Her hand rustled through the covers and grabbed his wrist. "I am amazed how I can hold all of it," she said. "The hatred and the love. Up in the treehouse my heart swelled up like a gourd. It filled with love for my brothers. And I wanted to burn everything down. Destroy it all, them included. I have spent my whole life trying to find some way to reconcile these opposites in me—I've thought it was what I was supposed to do, at least what I had to do, since I couldn't stand to be like some rocket ship blasting between them at the speed of light all the time. But the truth is I am simply both, a hater and a lover, a woman ready to embrace and forgive at the same time I am a woman ready to destroy. Don't you think everybody mixes that up? Don't you think everybody believes they have to be one or the other?"

"I don't know. Maybe regular people don't get the range set so wide."

"Maybe you're right." She chuckled. "I haven't really spent *my whole life* trying to get such notions straight. I have been busy robbing and killing. I have been pursuing the enterprise of existence. You and money and good times and the fast ramble."

"You certainly have a flair for it."

"I've got an enthusiasm, don't you think?"

He rolled away from her slightly. "Damn. I wish we had Rubens here."

"Why in the world?"

"Something came to me."

"Well, save it for him, then."

"We probably won't see that boy again."

She sighed. "Probably not." Her fingers tightened. "I did see Daddy, though."

"I thought you didn't."

"I didn't speak to him, not regular style anyway. I got in the house."

"With Donnie's pals around?"

"Yes. I crawled out the limb beyond the treehouse, swung down onto the roof, and went in through my mother's bedroom window. Everything was the same there, too, as best I could tell. My mother's things were on the dresser. Her brushes and her silver comb and her necklace with the garnet in it. She used to say the stone was a ruby pendant, but it was only a garnet. It was curled up in a silver box. And the rest of her stuff was there, too: her wheelchair and her cane and the little stand they used for dripping fluids into her body when she was dying. Her bedpan was there and her tin tub was leaned against the wall. The trench in the center of her bed was there. Where she lay for those years. You could see it, I could feel it, I mean, in the dark. I didn't turn on the lights. I pressed my hands down into it, this scooped-out place where she lay, and then I pressed my face into it, and then I lay down in it, like a woman laying herself down into a grave. It scared me how delicious it felt. I lay there and I could feel myself descending. Do you know what I mean?"

"Sure."

"I am some kind of irregular Lot's wife. The one who got away from Sodom and looked back. She was coming up out of hell, free at last as they say, and she looked back. It kills me. I know I am that woman. Where is the place in heaven for the ones who look back?"

"I ask myself that all the time."

"You do? My mother was a Lot's wife, too. She looked back. But she was a liar. She didn't die from loss of me. Her dumb, weary *philosophy of life* killed her. Sure—my father and James and me, too, the criminal cheerleader, killed her, and Will and the difficulty of living on such a farm and the winters and her genes—they all killed her; and she killed her—but it was her, her *way* of looking that really did it. She was the one who lived the life. And she lied about every bit of it. Don't you know? That's how it goes. These people lie. *People* lie. They get themselves crunched into some corner—they see it as a corner—and they lie about how they got there. They try to convince themselves and everyone else it was some*body* put them there. It was the *blame* that killed her. Jezooks. If she had cut that out. If she'd noticed she didn't care about getting out, that she knew the truth about who she was, rough wife of a rough husband, not a lady rider at all but a selfish woman who needed the roughness and the scuffle, who wanted to brag and bluster and sit in the kitchen late at night ordering the dark around. Looking back ought to save you. Hell—

I don't know—look back, look ahead, you still have to admit the truth. What was I saying . . . ?"

"That's the thief."

"Your thief. I don't want to hear about the thief."

"He was the same." *(That was the day, he said, Mother decided on divorce. That was the day, he said, Rita decided to seek her life elsewhere.)* "No," he said. "You're right. I don't want to hear about it, either. What did you do?"

"I put dreams into his head."

"Whose?"

"Daddy's."

Jack sighed. He was tired. The day swayed on its stem. "What dreams?"

"I couldn't get out of the room. Not into the house. I was afraid to go into the hall. I couldn't hear anyone, but maybe someone was sitting outside the door to Daddy's room. So I crawled back out onto the roof. I slipped along the roof to Daddy's room next door. He had the curtains drawn back. There was a man sitting beside his bed, one of the New Orleans goons. I'd seen him before, some pitiful guy with an answer for everything. He was sitting by the bed. He was reading something to Daddy. Out loud. At first I couldn't make out his voice, and then I could. It was *Peter Rabbit.*"

"What?"

"Yeah. Isn't that amazing? *Peter Rabbit*—the children's story. Daddy was paying close attention. You might have thought the guy was reading his will. Some rabbit was making tea, setting it out. I leaned my head against the edge of the window and listened. It soothed me. I felt calm. This strange little English story. And then my father, who was lying on his back under his white chenille bedspread, lying in this lamplight the color of orange marigolds, turned his head and looked at me. The expression on his face was rapturous. And it didn't change when he saw me. We looked at each other, one rapturous, one—murderous, I guess. And my heart went to him. It went straight out of my body. It was amazing. I hated him and yet I loved him. And this little dumb story, this tale, of a bunny rabbit, that I remembered as I listened, was the key, in some way. It all lasted about five seconds. Then, as if I was not there at all, my father turned back to the thug. He kept listening, my daddy did, to the story. I got out of there."

• • •

(What Clare almost never mentioned, he said, and he never understood why she didn't, was that the lion attack took place in the snow. It was snowing on the woods and fields of Pennsylvania, and the lions—he didn't know why—had been left out in it. She had gone to look for them, he guessed she had driven out to do that. She'd seen them, she said, by themselves on top of a low ridge—three lions, standing in the snow. Their breath was white in big puffs, she said, and the snow powdered their coats, turning them into ghost lions, white lions in the snow. She said she'd never seen anything so beautiful. . . .)

It was as if the madness was talking to him again. It was trying to piece something together for him. His father had been there, too, that next day, the day they'd fled the house, the day he saw the boy. *I was not alone, he said.* His father had been right there, out ahead of him in the water, swimming toward his death. Sunlight shone on his father's blunt bald head, shone in his black eyes, which stared wildly. His father had stepped off the rocks at twelve-fifteen, naked, and pushed his skinny white body out into the lake. The water was too cold for swimming, too cold by far in May. Jack had watched him swim in flat overhand strokes toward the emptiness of the lake. He had swung his skiff around and rowed toward him. As he leaned forward over his knees, experiencing in his chest the sharp serrated pain of desperation, even before the first stroke formed, he had looked back at the woods. It was then he saw the boy staring at him, smiling at him.

7

Even when he was alone he wasn't alone—that's what he thought on the road, running fast through farm country past cornfields caved in by fall, past bean rows and fields of cabbage in which tufts of fat leaves hung on bare stalks, Robert's place out ahead in the brown mist of woods back from the river north of Croswell Dam—Robert, a mechanic they met in a bar in Chicago, a fixer who insisted on the proper order for everything, a driver, a good one, but a man with a tender heart who'd had enough after two years and returned home to the farm—thinking as they sped along of how he was never alone, of how even in madness on the river, when the wooden hull peeled back and he saw men on horseback riding through fire, he was not exactly alone, some sense of consciousness, of a self distinct from what he saw still operating in him, a miracle of a kind, he thought, a kind of transubstantiation really, a miraculous uplift—like some casual aside, toss-off miracle Jesus might have performed as a bit of warm-up before dinner maybe, before he got down to business—more a revelation, actually, than a performance, a recognition, he thought, the way the personality goes on, continues through history (and its varieties of torment and experience) to build its little personal fiefdoms there by the side of the road, desperados and saints, ordinary Joes putting up their little fruit stands where passersby might step in for a sack of tomatoes and a cold soda.

Each house they passed looked empty. It was one of those stretches where you could imagine the world depopulated, stripped. Yes, he thought, but somewhere inside was a woman, maybe a small child or two. Maybe even a sick husband, some guy knocked down by a tractor recuperating in the big bed. Or maybe, around back, where he couldn't see, a butter and eggs man, a lover, loitered on the back steps peeling an apple with a silver knife. Everything each of them touched was connected by lines of steel to a thousand different articles, each lived in the center of a web.

It was what you were connected to, he thought, that drove you crazy.

They stopped at a filling station at a crossroads a few miles outside the town of Drewsburg for gas and a map.

"I'm going to wash up," she said.

"All right."

He went over to the snack machines. They were in an open hut beside the station. A small boy, maybe eight or nine, was trying to put coins in the soda machine. "Let me help you," Jack said.

"I want a Mountain Dew," the boy said. "And a Snickers." He had rat-colored rough-cut hair and wore a blue satin jacket.

"You only have enough money for a pop."

"Would you get a Snickers for me?"

"Sure," Jack said.

He got the drink and the candy bar. "Where're your parents?" There were no other cars at the station. There were two white farmhouses across the road, brown cornfields beyond them, no cars there, either.

"They left me," the boy said.

"What do you mean?"

"They forgot me. They drove off while I was in the bathroom."

"I'm sure they're coming back."

"Ralph hates me," the boy said. "He keeps telling Mama to get rid of me."

"Who's Ralph?" He sat down at a picnic table in front of the machines. "Sit up here."

The boy sat down beside him. "Ralph's my mama's boyfriend," he said. "They met in Kansas City, where we were living. Ralph hates me. He's got a big gold ring and a pistol."

"Big pistol?"

"It's a giant. He shoots at things when we're driving."

"Does he hit them?"

"Sometimes. He shot a cow yesterday."

"Where was the cow?"

"Out in a field."

"A real gunslinger."

"He hates me. He says I'm bad luck."

"You don't look like such bad luck to me."

The boy finished his drink. "Could I have another?" he said.

"Sure."

Jack got it for him. Beyond the hut another cornfield stretched away toward the woods. "What's your name?"

"Billy."

"Mine's Jack."

Everything was dangerous now, even a boy. He liked the child, but he had no pity for him. He was like a dog, lost and standing in the road. Maybe he would get hit, maybe he wouldn't. Maybe he would find other dogs, meat, life. Now there were a handful of dead men. Men who had waked, eaten breakfast, kissed or not kissed their wives, gone to work. Morty used to say, "I put my shoes on myself this morning, but I don't know who'll be taking them off tonight." They were all dogs in the road, hopeful dogs, or defeated dogs whining about their fleas, standing in the road looking around.

The boy drank his soda with the bottle in his mouth. "You drink it like that, you're going to get your teeth knocked out," Jack said.

He showed him how to drink it. "That's how a man does it," he said. "You keep your lip between the glass and your teeth."

"I like to get a lot in my mouth all at once."

"Just tip it up, it'll pour."

Clare came out of the filling station. Her hair was wet, combed back. "We're only about ten miles from Robert's," she said.

"This is Clare," Jack said to the boy. "Clare, this is Billy."

"How do, Billy."

"They left me here," the boy said.

"Just drove off without him," Jack said.

"Who did?"

Jack told her. As he was speaking a dirty white Chevrolet Impala drove into the lot. "That's them," the boy said.

The car pulled up to the hut. A thin woman with tangled red hair got out. The man driving, a lean man with short black hair combed stiffly forward, sat at the wheel. He didn't get out. "Where have you been?" the woman said.

"I been here," the boy said, "drinking a drink."

"Billy was wondering if you left him," Jack said.

"What are you doing telling a strange man your name?" the woman said. She punched the boy in the shoulder. The boy dropped his soda. "Mama," he said, "don't."

"He's been okay," Jack said. The woman smelled of alcohol. There was a wild, grieving look in her eyes.

"Come on," the woman said.

"I don't want to go," the boy said. "Ralph hates me."

"Ralph doesn't hate you." She turned to the man who sat staring straight ahead. "You don't hate Billy, do you, honey?"

"I'm about to start," Ralph said.

"Maybe you should be sweet to that child," Clare said.

"Maybe you should mind your own business," the woman said.

Clare took two steps forward and slapped her across the face. The woman fell backwards, bounced off the side of the car.

"Hey," Ralph said. He opened the door and started to get out. As he came up, Jack kicked the door, slamming it hard against his body.

The woman pulled herself upright, lurched at Clare. Clare met her with a fist, a hacking right in the face. The woman went down in a heap.

The man reached back along the seat. Jack grabbed his collar from behind, jerked him hard. He pulled him out of the car and dragged him along the ground. He let him go. The man gathered himself on one knee. "What's this?" he said. He smelled of alcohol, too.

"Get on your feet," Jack said. The boy was crying.

"I don't want to," the man said.

"Okay," Jack said. He kicked the man in the face. He went over backwards. His head hit the ground, bounced. He lay still.

"Mister," the boy said, "don't hit him again."

He knelt down next to his mother and began to rub her hands.

"Shit," Jack said. "There's no way to make this come out even."

"The guy in the station's watching us," Clare said.

"Call him out. Maybe he wants some, too."

"Better let it go, sweetie."

"Damn." He ruffled the boy's hair. The boy shrank from him. "This is what I mean about starting things," he said. "You start something and then everything's out of control." He squatted down in front of the boy. "Listen," he said. The boy turned his wet face away. "Listen. You tell Ralph and your mother that if they mistreat you any more, we're coming back to get them. You understand?"

The boy nodded.

"It won't help," Clare said. "They're drunk. And you can tell they're naturally mean."

"How can you tell that?"

"No toys—nothing in the car for a kid."

"Well," Jack said, standing up, "I don't know how to do any better than this right now, do you?"

She smiled. "No sir, I don't."

Jack reached into the car, took the keys out, and threw them into the cornfield. "Okay," he said, "let's go."

Clare patted the boy on the head. She had hardly looked at him. "You're pretty," she said.

"Just hang around here," Jack said. "By the time they find the keys, they might be sober."

"Are you going to leave?" the boy said.

"We're on our way now."

He gave the boy a dollar.

"That's not much," the boy said.

Jack laughed. "You're as bad as they are." The boy walked off toward the cornfield. "Where're you going?"

"To find them keys."

"His fate's sealed," Clare said.

"That's something we ought to know about."

Driving fast, pushing the car, Jack said, "Always some mess behind us now." The sky was clearing in the east.

"It's been this way all our lives," she said. "And they're not really messes."

"What would you call them?"

"Adventures?"

"Why were you in the bathroom so long?"

"I had to wash up." She looked at the wet fields. "I feel all the time as if I have to keep shedding myself. These last weeks make something grind in me, like a millstone grinding corn."

"Which is it?"

"Which is what?"

"A skin you're shedding, or grain you're grinding?"

"All of them. Everything. A skin, a grain, a coat I take off, a sea change, caterpillar to butterfly, child to woman, light to dark, life—"

"I get it."

"Don't get aggravated."

"I already am aggravated."

"At me?"

"No, sweetie, not at you."

"You really think we can't rob banks anymore?"

They crossed a short bridge over a creek. Algae had turned the concrete railings green. "I keep seeing the afterlife."

"How do you mean?"

"I keep seeing us all, sitting around looking at each other."

"If there's an afterlife," she said, "we'll be robbing banks there, too."

"You think it's like that?"

"Sure I do. Robbers rob, killers kill, thieves steal—each of us'll play his part."

"What about the ones who get robbed . . . or killed?"

"Them, too—the same. The money will reappear freshly in their pockets. The murdered will rise up whole and be murdered again."

"That's an ingratiating philosophy."

"How else could there be a perfect harmony?"

"I thought you didn't believe in heaven."

"It's not exactly what I believe in, but it's what I sometimes see."

"Cowboy heaven."

"Yes, like that."

He rubbed her shoulder. "I like the way you think."

She giggled. "In heaven you'll like it just as much."

He looked her in the face. It came to him that he didn't know, that he'd never known, what she was thinking.

Robert's house was a few miles outside the town of Danton, Kentucky, off the state road that ran north toward the river. There were wild plum bushes and sassafras shrubs by the road. The ditches were deep, like ravines, and filled with thick brown grass. Far out in a cutover field among a few bent cornstalks, a flock of gulls walked about. "Look at that," Jack said, pointing at them.

"Strange sights make you think you're going right off the edge of something," she said.

"Yes."

She began to cry. And then he began to cry. Both of them sobbed, hard. The sobs were thick, hot wads of grief in their chests and in their throats. They cried separately, without touching each other. He pulled the car over to the side of the road. The rain had stopped, but the car was wet and the bushes and the fields were wet. They sat upright, both of them looking straight ahead, crying. Then they moved toward each other, both at the same time, took each other in their arms. They held each other tightly.

They dragged him through the cornfield and threw him down at the base of a large oak tree. They began to beat him, each taking a turn, Donnie standing to one side urging them on, some other goon holding a gun on Clare as he made her watch. Each blow entered his consciousness as if it penetrated his body, each one knocked him farther away until he was on his back looking up into the swollen branches, which were wide enough for a child to stand on, to run along, he thought, which would lead him into the sky. . . . They beat him until the blood ran out of his face, out of his ears and nose, out of his mouth, until he could smell his own blood mingled with the smell of oak leaves, with the smell of the ancient dirt, which stank of death and decomposition, which stank of disasters, of failures, of losses flushed down drains in decrepit houses, of betrayal, of corpses in hasty graves, of animals curled around their own deaths, of rust, of abandoned civilizations, of encampments where murder took place, of the clothes rotted off a child's swollen body. . . .

After a while the sobs passed. The tears sank back into them, like water sinking into the ground.

He rolled the window down, breathed deep. "Well," he said, "it's a fine world, isn't it?"

She gave a small, croupy laugh.

"We'll have to pay Robert to help us," he said.

"I guess so."

"I'll give him some of the gold."

"All right."

He rubbed her shoulder. "We know so much about ourselves, and about each other, and about everything, that we've become a mystery," he said.

She bent her neck to kiss his hand. There was a soft look in her eyes, but under the look was the same fresh, hard will. "That's okay," she said. "I like everything to be familiar, and completely strange at the same time."

"I do, too," he said.

The house was up a lane that ran through a small orchard of aged apple trees. Fruit littered the ground. There were big oaks, almost leafless, around the house itself. The ground under the trees was bare, muddy. Behind a long open porch, the house rose three stories. It had been painted yellow a long time ago, but now the sides were gashed with gray boards and streaked with dark splashes of mud, as if the house had been tipped over into a puddle and then set back upright.

He took the vest from the backseat, shook one of the thin sheets of gold from the side panel, bent and folded it in his lap. It made a rectangle the size of an envelope.

"You're such a one for preparation," she said.

"It's lucky for you."

"I know. If it wasn't for you, I'd be blasting my way through everything."

"I like that quality in you. You're forthright."

She grinned. "We've always been so good for each other, haven't we."

"Give me a kiss."

She kissed him, climbing over onto him.

"What is this?"

"The eroticism of violence," she said, giggling.

"Violence is not erotic."

"Yes, it is. All the books say so."

"You don't read books."

"I know what they say."

She drew her legs up, leaned her chest against him. "What do they say?"

"After almost every crime and always after punching out local fools, criminals like to get laid."

"You're a coarse girl."

"Oh honey, I'm worse than that."

She unzipped him, snaked her hand in. "Ooh—see: you're prepared."

"Take your pants off."

"Yes sir."

She thrashed her jeans down her legs. She didn't wear panties.

"What a beauty you are," he said.

There were two green bruises on her thigh and her legs weren't shaved, but they were beautiful, long and slenderly muscled with scarred kneecaps where she had fallen as a child.

"Let me slide over," he said.

He pushed them out from under the wheel, lifted her so she sat on top of him. She squatted with her legs drawn up.

"Where's the socket?" she said, fumbling between them.

"I think you've got it."

"Sometimes even I don't know where it is. Oh, there, I have it."

"No better feeling in the world," he said, leaning back.

"Than what?"

"Entering you."

"I'm pleased with it myself."

She pressed her haunches down hard. "Whoa," he said, "go slow. You don't want to kink it."

She raised herself, sank. He leaned his head back. "Oh, Jesus," he said. "It's the heart of Africa."

"Kiss me."

"Yes."

He took her lips, at the same time driving hard up into her. She groaned.

He lifted her, brought her down, lifted her. It became a rhythm both of them gave in to. He felt strong, as if he could lift her all day. She leaned away from him, raised her knees, pushed away from him, drove back. "It's like building a cathedral," he said. "One of those anonymous workers, raising stones to the glory of God."

"Your face is shining."

He thrust into her. He felt her own quick rhythm start, like a motor inside her running fast. Her face reddened, then she tensed, her body became rigid, for a moment every inch of her became a fortress she was holding together by will alone, holding and raising it all. He felt the thick, collected heat inside him, and then a burning rope in his guts snapped taut, and they seemed to crash against each other, both at once, broke apart and scattered. For slowly ticking moments there was a clean, cleared space inside them and around them, like a patch of ground the wind had swept clean.

They sagged against each other. She sighed.

"Isn't this fortunate?" he said.

She laughed softly.

There was no anger in him, no rage at all. There had been none.

"You came inside me," she said, slightly surprised.

"I remember that."

"I don't mind."

"Why not?"

She looked at him then, looked into his eyes, which were a little sleepy and almost distracted, and he could see, as he might see something moving in twilight at the edge of a wood, what she was thinking.

"Maybe it will be like that," he said.

She didn't answer him. He drew her head to him and held her. Their lovemaking had never been sentimental, it never made them one creature, but it drew from each of them a plain and spare perception of the other. Each saw the other's separate and distinct human face, the remarkable flesh, each could hear the companionable heart beat.

The sky was clearing. A western breeze was breaking up the congested, slate-colored clouds. He could smell the sweet scent of the fallen apples.

"Let's go get Robert," he said.

(He was a strong swimmer, he said, it took me a while to reach him. I started slow, too. And then he wouldn't get in the boat. The boy . . . —he looked at me: me. *You understand I was flabbergasted, torn. I couldn't not go after Father, but the boy . . .)*

They ran lightly up the steps, adjusting their clothes. He gave the door a cluster of quick raps. After a minute it opened and Robert poked his face out. "I was watching you," he said. "You're a couple of shameless scoundrels."

"We're a tired pair, Robert," Jack said.

"Well, you can't rest here."

"Say hello, Robert," Clare said.

"Hello, Clare. What are you doing here?"

"We need your car."

"I haven't got any car to give you."

"Here, Robert," Jack said. He took the folded gold out of his coat pocket and handed it to him.

"What is this?"

"It's ten thousand dollars in one convenient slice."

"I still can't give you my car."

"Well, then, Robert, we'll just have to shoot you," Clare said.

"Ah, damn. Damn you two." He stepped back, held the door open.

Robert led them through a short hall into a living room that was cluttered and dark. An old woman sat in a torn plaid armchair watching television. Beside it was another chair just like it. Robert sat down there. The woman didn't look up. She had a pale, cachexic face and huge dark eyes. "Oh, come in," Robert said. "Mama's almost deaf, you can't disturb her."

They sat down on a sofa opposite. The cushions gave like feather pillows. The old woman glanced at them. She worked her mouth. "Who's this?" she said.

"The house is on fire, Mama," Robert said. "These are devils come to get us."

"Fine," she said. She grinned at them, a detached, mocking, self-conscious grin, like a monkey's. "We have soup," she said.

"We haven't got any soup, Mama."

"That's nice."

She stared at the television. On the screen two women in what looked like huge red wigs sat across a table from each other talking. "What are they saying?" the old woman said.

"It's time for old women to be cracked in the head and stuck in the grave," Robert said.

"It's politics, isn't it," the old woman said.

"How you been, Robert?" Jack said.

"Worse every day." Robert was a large man with bushy, black hair, but he looked shrunken. The skin under his jaw was slack.

"You don't look well, Robert," Clare said.

"I got cancer," Robert said. "I got it down in my bowels."

Jack leaned back. The room smelled of Lysol and, faintly, of food. "Can't they do anything for you?"

"Nothing that would cure me."

"What did you say?" the old woman asked.

"I said you're dying, Mama. You're going to be dead before morning."

"I can't go to town without a new dress," the old woman said.

"She's dying, too," Robert said to Clare. "We both got cancer. It's like it was contagious."

"That's too bad."

"You got a car, Robert?" Jack said.

"I got a pickup, but I don't want to give it to you."

"Then you can drive us."

"I think they're clowns," the old woman said. She was looking at the television. "I think they're from the circus."

"They're devils, Mama. They've come to drag us down to hell."

"I like clowns," his mother said. "But they scare me."

"I can't go off and leave Mama," Robert said.

"Robert," Clare said. "We have to have use of your truck. If we don't, worse things than two old friends coming to visit are going to happen."

"I expect so." He looked at Jack. "I thought you were in prison."

"I was, but I got out."

"Don't want to go back in right yet, eh?"

"I got a tumor," the old woman said. "It's killing me."

"Don't worry, Mama. I'm going to murder you in your sleep."

"We'd like to lay over tonight, and then tomorrow go across the river," Jack said.

"What you running from?"

"You don't want to know."

"You're right, I don't. I don't want to know a damn thing about it." He glanced toward a window that was grimy with dust, half-curtained against the clearing day. "They can get me for harboring for just letting you in the house."

"The farming going well, Robert?" Clare said.

"It's not going at all. We got some pigs, but the rain drowned the corn and the barley didn't make. It's a good thing we're dying."

"You always wanted to get back to your farming."

"I got back to it. I got back to it and down in it and now I'm going to be buried in the middle of it."

"At least you got to find out."

"I'm sleepy," the old woman said.

"You just got up, Mama." He looked at Jack. "It's the cancer makes her talk like that. It takes everything out of you. Like you worked all night instead of slept and you got a hard day ahead of you. It's harder than farming."

"I expect it is."

Robert shook his head, looked down at his hands. They were veiny and streaked with bruises. "You hadn't changed at all. You're the same way now as when I ran with you. You don't pay attention to anybody but each other. You figure you can get out of whatever you get into and the hell with everybody else. I hadn't seen you in six years—I guarantee you I hadn't missed you for a second—and you walk right in and take over. I got to jump up and drive you where you want to go, or lose my truck. It don't matter to you."

"I know we're disruptive, Robert," Jack said.

"Disruptive? Jesus, Jack, you and your words. Disruptive. You two ruined me. I been here all this six years. Come back here to live quiet and farm, but it was impossible. I been running all the time I was here. It's what gave me the cancer, I know it. It's what gave Mama the cancer, sitting in this house worrying about me so agitated. Disruptive? I look out the window every morning expecting to see my past coming up the drive after me, some deputy or somebody creeping up on me."

He began to cough. His mother looked alarmed. Her eyes snapped back and forth from the television to her son. "I knew you were coming," Robert said through the coughing. His voice was wet, murky.

"How'd you know that, Robert?" Jack said.

"Donnie Bee. He told me."

Jack tensed. "Where'd you see Donnie?"

"He came out here to the house. He wanted to know if I'd seen you. I told him I hadn't."

"Did he have anyone with him?"

"He had a couple of guys in the car."

"Do you know Clare's brother Will? Was he with them?"

"I couldn't tell."

"Traded one gang for another," Clare said.

"He's after you," Robert said.

"I'm surprised," Jack said.

"There's money in it somewhere, you can see it. And anger, that pure anger."

"I think it's mostly anger," Jack said.

"What'd you do to him? No, don't tell me. I know. You ran over his ass, too. Just like you're doing to me."

"You don't have to run over Donnie for him to come after you."

The old woman began to jiggle her legs. "I want to go to bed," she said.

"All right, Mama," Robert said. "You were in the paper, too." He got up; the gold slid off his lap.

"What paper?"

"Just a minute, I'll show you." He raised the old woman to her feet. A look passed between them, between son and mother; it was a look, Jack thought, of infinite, emptied-out, and broken-down futility. Robert stared at his mother as a man hit in the face might stare dumbly at a wall, at an empty patch of light on a bare floor. "I'll take you to bed," he said.

"Will you take me to bed?" the old woman said.

"I'm going to take you to heaven, Mama."

He hoisted her in his arms like a desiccated bride. Jack and Clare got up. They followed mother and son across the hall to another living room, which had been set up with two beds. Between the beds was a low table with a lamp and medicine bottles on it. The furniture had been pushed back against the walls.

Robert took the old woman's dressing gown off and tucked her in. She stroked his wrist. "I'm too old to be wandering around," she said.

"You're just a dead woman who needs to be in her grave, Mama," Robert said.

"I can feel every one of my bones. They're clanking."

"Time to sleep, Mama." He closed her eyes with thumb and forefinger. "Rub my head, Robbie," the old woman said without opening her eyes.

Robert massaged the top of her head. Her hair was iron gray, springy, and looked very clean.

"I'm going out to move the car," Clare said.

Robert didn't look at her. "Put it in the barn."

"That feels nice, Robbie," his mother said.

"Enjoy it while it lasts, darling." He stretched his neck, rolled his head. "You don't have to stand over me, Jack. I'm not going to run off."

"Sorry, Robert. I'm just curious."

Robert switched off the lamp. "Sleep tight, Mama."

He led Jack out into the hallway. From a long bench against the wall he took a newspaper. "It's the *Courier*—Louisville," he said. "There's a big article on you. It came out last week. Mama used to cut things out of the paper and now that I'm dying I've started."

It was a feature article distributed on the Washington Post News Service.

"Rubens," Jack said.

"Who's that?"

"The guy who wrote it. He interviewed me in prison. He was traveling with us until a few days ago."

"Well, he thinks you're king of the bandits."

Rubens, too, had a secret life. Like everyone else, a life that went on in the middle of action and regulation, elsewhere. He must have left the boat while Jack was under his spell and filed the story.

Robert followed him out to the front porch. They sat down on the steps. The afternoon was running on toward sunset.

"This is a pretty place, Robert," Jack said.

"Funny like that," Robert said. "It's a disaster. Everything's broken down—most of it never did work—it's like the fields are poisoned. But it's pretty just the same."

Jack began to read. His skin tingled. The article was a newspaper version of his biography, and Clare's, a summary of stories from prison—so long ago now—a speculation about his escape, and then a version of their lives in Anaconda, and of the botched bank robbery. Rubens was the confidant of desperadoes, the observer, the cool head given access to the highest levels of hoodlum planning.

He was an informer.

"Who's Donald Bernardnick?" Robert said. "Is that Donnie Bee?"

"Shut up, Robert."

His life, late and early, lay spread out before him. It was a life different from what he knew. Rubens quoted Donnie Bee, Donnie saying "in his high-pitched voice" that the bank robbery had been masterminded by Jack himself, the Midwestern Robin Hood, Jack, who had spent a year living undercover in Anacondia, Tennessee, planning and preparing with his accomplice James Acajou, the gambler. Donnie had intervened to save his own interests and in repayment of old scores, but the intervention had been botched by the unfortunate imposition of Jack's fellow desperado Clare Manigault, his wife, and an even more ruthless operator than Jack Baker himself. Rubens had insinuated himself into the affair through personal contacts with Baker during Baker's incarceration in federal prison. He had become a confidant and a kind of secretarial service for the bandit, his factotum really, so Rubens said, running errands, attending to local needs, all while gathering information for the government and for a book he was writing. He had planned to refrain from revealing his intentions, but Mr. Baker had suffered a mental collapse on a boat on the Ohio River and was unable to continue his escapades.

"The sight of the once-ferocious bandit writhing on the deck of his tiny cabin cruiser, crying out for help and begging his demented wife to shoot him, was more than a man could bear to see," Rubens wrote. "His crimes spoke through his madness, in voices of guilt and shame. Mr. Baker confessed to save his soul, but it was too late for a soul so besmirched. He hid under a bunk, spitting and mewling like a tortured kitten, soiling his clothes, weeping.

"The man who boasted of his fearlessness, who was famous for his cool recklessness under fire, who had tricked his good friend Donald Bernardnick, who had masterminded one of the most daring escapes from federal prison in recent memory, had become a terrified wraith, a creature of the shadow world, hijacked by shadows.

"To this observer, it was clear that Mr. Baker had never been anything but a shell, a man with no core, no sense of moral values or love to hold him together. He himself knew this, as was clear when he begged his wife to put an end to his pain and by his incessant prattle about the Christian Savior, an entity Mr. Baker blasphemed against regularly while at the same time imploring him to come and save his skin.

"Slowly, as I watched this criminal descend into his madness, I began to piece together a line of cause and effect. It became clear how his early crimes led to his late downfall. He was a man in whose face guilt was written in huge, bloody letters. Mr. Baker had sown the wind and reaped the whirlwind. As has been the case so often in modern times, a man of power and accomplishment had, through his own hubris, through his own deception of himself, come to believe himself invulnerable, and suddenly, horribly, had discovered the terrible error of such a belief."

Jack put his hand on the page. Blood hummed in his ears.

"He lays it on, doesn't he?" Robert said.

"I never saw it put quite like this."

"What was that happened to you?"

"I cracked up."

"Was it as bad as he said it was?"

"It was worse."

"What about the rest of it?"

"What he says I did's nothing to what I really did."

"Reporters—they never get it right, do they?"

He hadn't anticipated this. Or if he had—if he had—he hadn't cared. This was what happened when you let go. "I let go," he said. "I relaxed my grip."

"What?"

It didn't matter what your story was. It just mattered how deep it went.

He looked down the lane. The low sun had turned the branches of the apple trees black. Beyond the road that ran in front of the farmstead a field of brushy, withered corn stretched away toward the woods. The broken stalks looked like something retracted, something being pulled back into the earth.

"This rascal's got you in all kinds of trouble, Jack," Robert said. "He's stitched you into one federal crime after another. I don't see how a truck ride's going to set you loose."

"It looks pretty weighty when you add it up like this, doesn't it?"

"Looks like it hadn't got but one way to go."

"Would you rather have this or the cancer?"

"Doesn't make any difference, I don't guess—but I reckon I'd rather get killed moving than sitting."

"Yeah. You don't get any miracles with cancer."

"Nor with this either, I don't suppose."

"No."

"It was the way you were always going, Jack. You didn't expect anything different, did you?"

"I don't think about it like that, Robert. Don't you wear shoes?"

Robert massaged his socked feet. "Not in the house. Not since Vietnam."

"You weren't in Vietnam."

"It was my time, though. It changed me." He pulled at his long toes. "Isn't there anything you care about, Jack?"

Jack laughed. "It looks like I care about being a big shot and taking advantage of my friends."

"Fidelity," Clare said, coming up. She was carrying two shotguns. A raincoat was slung over her shoulder. "Your truck looks well kept, Robert."

"It does run."

"You were always dependable that way."

There was a picture of them with the article. Taken years ago down in the Keys, back at the beginning. Their faces shone. They were—Jack was sure of it—the brightest blossoms on the tree. Even in the grainy gray tones he could see it. He remembered it all, remembered the day when the wind blew the mingled scent of flowers and dead fish across the bay. He remembered the boat ride and the moment at the dock in Islamorada when she turned to him with a smile so beautiful he thought he would die from looking at it. It was a smile that promised everything. The world itself seemed available to such a promise. All he had to do was reach for it.

That was it, he thought. There was always something we would reach for. What that was gave us away like a snitch.

(I bent toward the boy with each stroke, he said. It was like a hesitation, my chest surging back toward shore as I bent into the oars, reaching with my body, it seemed, toward what I had suddenly found, and now, just as suddenly, was losing. I felt—yes—a pure anguish. Do you understand? I could see the boy the whole time. As I drew closer to my father the distance between us lengthened. The boy made no sign to me. My father didn't call for me. It was his eleventh suicide. . . .)

A wind blew up and cleared the sky out, bringing cold and a frost that lay down on the grass by midnight. They drank still-run apple brandy in the kitchen, the three of them sitting among their guns under the yellow ceiling light eating homemade pickles and fat peeled tomatoes they dug out of a jar. From time to time hard pains crossed Robert's face, like the after-shocks of blows administered deep inside. He gathered them in, as a man would stop a ball with his chest, grimacing but saying nothing about them. They spoke of the old times, but only briefly, without nostalgia. Crimes always carried; they had staying power, the menace of their future was always in the present moment.

Robert remembered fleeing a robbery past a high-school baseball game and how there were a number of children—orphans probably, he said—pressed against the chain-link fence beyond the outfield looking in, and how, he said before Jack hushed him, the children looked so forlorn and gleeful at the same time, how they yearned to get into the park and were excited by the game. It was how, he said before Jack told him to be quiet—it was how I always felt, he said—

"I could hold down the corner of a bank," he said, "but my mind wouldn't stick."

"You used to shout and cry out in your sleep," Jack said.

"Sometimes now I do it when I am awake, too."

"You'd scare a whole house of hard men," Clare said.

"Now there's only Mama, and she can't hear."

"That's lucky," Clare said.

She got up and began to pace. She loaded and unloaded a .38 revolver as she moved about, shaking the brass shells into her palm and clicking them into the chamber. The light brought out the streaks of gold in her cropped hair.

"How far am I going to have to take you?" Robert said.

"How far is it, Clare?"

"About a hundred miles. We can cross the river up above Vandalia. There's a railroad bridge about a mile from my daddy's house. We can cross there."

"What is it you're going to do with your daddy?"

"Save him from himself."

"And from his money," Jack said.

"What's he got into?"

"He's become the tool of his own greed and resentment."

"He supposedly put a price on my head," Jack said. "That his psycho son has been trying to collect. It's hard to tell actually if this is true, or if it's only a figment of everyone's imagination. But we are going up there to straighten everything out. As best it can be straightened."

"I know how that business can fixate your mind."

"He's caught in it," Jack said.

Robert slopped a little brandy in his glass. It was the pale gold of ginger ale. He scratched the rim of the glass with his fingernail. "You, too, looks like," he said.

"More than you can imagine."

"We're drawn to it," Clare said. "Something is pulling us."

"Maybe you ought to resist that. Like I done."

"We're just passing through," Jack said. "I think we have to go through this part, like you'd go through a storm."

(No matter how bad it looks, he said, sometimes you go. No matter how you're torn, no matter how beautiful the boy. . . .)

"That's what I thought about cancer. At first. I was just passing through this element. But it's come to stay." He took a sip of brandy, winced. "Oh, that hurts. See," he said brightly, "there it is like a cat scratching at the door."

"Where we're headed is easy to see all right," Jack said. "You pointed that out this afternoon. You were always like that, Robert. You have a gift for confirming the obvious. Do you remember that time, Clare, when Robert recited the directions for robbing the bank in Snellville—that bank in Illinois—as we were trying to get away? We'd already done the robbery and Robert was laying out the plan for us."

"I like to have something to refer back to. It makes me feel secure."

"There's not really anything behind us on this one."

"Doesn't it scare you?" he said.

"It's not real," Clare said.

"Donnie's going to make you think it's real—this is, I mean, this is real. When he came out here he had a look on his face like a man who would do whatever he had to to get his payback. He and his two palookas went through the house looking for you like they were looking for rats."

"When was he here?"

"Last week."

"It was a good thing for you you hadn't seen us."

"He made me wish I had *never* seen you."

He was thinking of the river, of the first afternoon, late, when they came up on the island, of how the tree shadows laid out on the water looked like the foreground of darkness. He thought of Jimmy, of Coodge lying in his green shroud. Jimmy would keep making plays in a rooster fight after the third or fourth pass, he would press the bet even after the cock's breast was torn open and its eyes poked out. Jimmy had an instinct for it; the bets often played through. Maybe that was all it was, he thought, and all you had to hope for: instinct that would kick you through to the other side. And maybe it was desire, and maybe it was love, and maybe it was undeflected concentration. And maybe it was just a list of maybes he was checking off to pass the time.

He took a bite of pickle. It was vinegary and hot. "We buried Jimmy Acajou ourselves," he said.

"I liked Jimmy. He was a funny man. Where'd you bury him?"

"On an island. Back down the Mississippi."

"Did you kill him?"

"Hell no."

"Donnie smothered him," Clare said.

"How could he do that?"

Jack told him about the flight upriver, about Jimmy's stroke, about hauling him to Anacondia. He told him about their stay in the town, about Jimmy in the nursing home, about Donnie Bee and Rubens.

"That's where you got that gold square," Robert said.

"Buster put it together for him."

"It's like a pirate story."

Clare laughed. "All this is."

"I know about home burials myself," Robert said.

"Who do you have buried?" Jack said.

"My daddy's out there, and my brother, too. We put them in the ground ourselves. Mama and me and the neighbors. We're going out there in a few minutes."

"Is it a special occasion?" Clare said.

"We do it almost every night, Mama and I do. We got a little house out there. Sometimes we stay all night. You want to come?"

They agreed to. It was something else they hadn't seen. Everything seemed to fit now. Robert got his mother, bundled her up in a plaid wool jacket, set a knit cap on her head. He got lanterns and he brought the bottle of brandy with him. He carried a satchel.

It was cold outside, almost raw. Jack hugged Clare. She grabbed him back, hard. "Have you been thinking about how we are going to come up on the farm?" she said.

"Pretty quietly, I guess. I thought you were thinking about it."

"I would as soon bust in."

"I suppose that's why I'm here."

"The curb on my gallop."

Robert led them down a path that ran through pine trees. The wind made a sound like the sea in the tops of the pines. In a clearing among the trees there was a small cemetery surrounded on three sides by an iron picket fence. The fence had been let down on one side and in the opening there was a square wooden shack, or three quarters of one. The side facing the graves was open, too. Robert directed them through a small gate. There were half a dozen stones and two fresh open graves. There were bouquets of flowers on the occupied graves and, strung on slim poles, cutout figures made of tin and aluminum foil; above one of the graves, trinkets, rings, and small charms were strung on a wire between two branches stuck in the ground.

"These graves look new," Jack said.

"Refreshed," Robert said. "They're for Mama and me. I dig a little on them every week, to keep the soil clean."

"Do you have a timetable?" Clare said.

"No date, but we're both close."

They went into the shack, which was equipped with table and chairs and a small woodstove. There were cabinets along one wall. Robert set the lantern on the table. From one of the cabinets he took a fiddle case. He opened it, took out a scarred gray fiddle, and began to tune it.

"Did you bring my ring?" his mother said.

"I have it in my pocket."

Jack started a fire, using wood from a pile in the corner. Clare walked about among the graves. After a while Robert began to play the fiddle. He played a rich old tune that Jack had heard before but couldn't place. The lanterns threw their shadows onto the ground. The old woman stepped out into the cemetery and began to dance. She moved slowly, her arms raised, crooning to herself. Every few moments she would make small barks and stamp her feet. There was a rinsed ecstatic look on her face.

Robert moved out among the graves, playing and dancing. "You dance, too, if you want," he said. The music soared up among the pines and blended with the sighing of the wind.

Jack took Clare in his arms. They swayed together, moved, their feet shuffling, then finding the steps; they glided lightly among the graves. She seemed very delicate to him and it came to him again how he loved the light small bones of her body, loved her grace and the counterposition of it, if it was that, to the toughness of her will. That first time years ago, in Lauderdale, when she struck the charter boat captain, and later, when she robbed the store, and then later, when she kissed him—her will fierce, demanding—she had never changed.

The four of them danced, Robert playing the fiddle in long sweeps of the bow, crouching and rising as the music soared. The old woman began to sing. She sang about love and about the loss of love, about riders coming through the night, about love rising in the moonlight to face death coming like riders through the dark. Her voice was low and clear, the words only slightly blurred by her deafness. She swayed above her husband's grave singing, holding herself in her arms. There was sweat on her face. Then she sank down at the foot of the grave, slowly lowered her face until it touched the grass. Robert stopped playing. He took a ring from his pocket, knelt beside her. He gave the ring to her, then unfastened the wire string fifty or sixty other rings had been slipped along and held the end of it to her. She kissed the ring and slipped it onto the wire. The rings made a soft jingling sound. She said something, murmuring words. The words sounded like wedding vows.

Clare sank to her knees behind the old woman. She pressed her hands flat against her chest and raised her face. Her eyes were closed. Jack stepped back, startled, as if she had splashed something on him. The wind soughed in the pines, it made a high whistling sound. Robert began to speak the words of a prayer, quiet words about death and the promise of paradise. The old woman swayed on her knees beside him, her lips moving.

Jack felt an immense agitation, a pressure that seemed to come from behind him, from the dark woods and from the sky, and from the earth itself. A weight began to lean against his back, like a large open hand pushing him gently. He felt it; the weight was huge, but it did not move him, he did not even have to strain against it. He saw himself toppling slowly forward into the grave, into a shaft that dropped into darkness. He didn't move, but he could feel himself falling, slowly tumbling, flesh falling through earth.

And then his mind let go and he seemed to be lifted, high up so that he could see the country around them. He could see the rolling hills cut by ravines that ran toward the faraway river, see houses and lights in the windows and families sitting around kitchen tables, men and women and children talking to one another at the bottom of a huge darkness that went on forever above them. He could see faces and he could hear their voices, which were faint and confidential, hear the steady earnest speech each was making to some family member who sat listening. He could see the eyes of the listeners looking intently into the faces of the speakers, and it seemed to him that all of them, the speakers and the listeners, were rapt and lost to everything but the words, and then it seemed to him that all of them, the people in their houses and the houses themselves and the farms and the woods around them and the dark empty rivers rolling to the sea, were oblivious to the immensity, to the great dark above them and around them, to the endless unrolling of space. This frightened him, his insides shrank, but then even as he seemed to wither inside himself, he realized that it was this obliviousness, this ignorance, that saved them. Knowledge of the dark was not in their faces, in no face was there awareness of the heavy crashing sea that rolled above them, and he saw that they were not only unconscious of the dark, but protected from it by their unconsciousness, that they were not abandoned and lost to a knowledge that would save them, but protected from a force that could destroy them. And he remembered that in the old story it was not only pride and fear that had ignited the lust for knowledge, but a kind of pure dumb trust, and it seemed to him that this myth he had lived by, the myth of the Fall, of the error that separated him, and everyone, from simple union with everything around him, was only a myth, a story that had no meaning, because he could see in the faces the ignorance, the obliviousness to the dark swallowing sea roaring above all their heads, and they were protected, held back from knowledge of this, and always had been, all but a few of them who had somehow tumbled out into it. And it seemed to him, standing, swaying now above an old woman and her son, above his wife, whose face was afire with a fierce beatitude, that this was a movement and design of love, like the love of a father, or of the universe itself, of a force shielding the frail business of bodies and minds from the crash and raving outside, shielding them from the harm of it, from the sight of it, even from the sound it made.

He dropped to his knees beside his wife. Even this, he thought, this strange ritual out here in the pine woods, is accomplished in ignorance, without knowledge of what swarms above us. It made no difference what these Joleen people did. Betrothed to death, they celebrated death and the life it gave them, but they could not see what massed and howled above their heads. This was good, Jack saw. It was as it should be.

Robert picked up his fiddle and began to play from his knees. The music rasped, moved briskly, the notes lifting a tune into the air that rose quickly as if it had to get up high without delay, as if the tune needed a platform like a house in the trees to sing from. Robert played hard; the notes banged against one another, coupling and uncoupling, jerking at one another as if the stronger were pulling the weaker from a fire, rushing back in to pull out others, tirelessly. Then there came a slow fall, a softening moan sliding downward into a calm place where the tune rested, licking itself, murmuring endearments. The music filled the clearing. It fluttered along the edges, brushing the trees, flowing along just under the lowest branches. Then it moved faster, groping for a way through the woods, for a way up. There was a hesitancy, a faltering in the discrete notes, a tremor; the music sensed its restraints, but then just as it poised to cry out in frustration, it found a way, and the sleek notes rose through the encirclement and soared free.

Clare leapt to her feet and began to dance. Jack pushed up behind her and danced with her, neither of them touching. They whirled and glided, jumping among the graves, sideslipping and leaping. Robert got up and began to dance with them. The old woman continued to sway on her knees. Jack lifted her to her feet and began to dance with her in his arms. She moved with him, seemed to ride in his dance like a child he was carrying home. Above them in the east, above the tall pines, the glow of the rising moon was yellow like the color water would be if wedding rings were washed in it and the gold soaked off.

They danced until they were exhausted. Until the old woman fell asleep in his arms. Until Clare sank down into the grass.

Robert stopped playing. He walked to the shed and put away the fiddle. Then he came out and took his mother from Jack's arms. They gathered up the blanket and the brandy and the guns they had laid on the table, and started back. The path was dark, but in the dark it was not hard to find their way. . . . *Just follow along,* Robert said when he stumbled.

The singing and the music went on inside Jack. It was like a drunkenness he couldn't shake off. It tingled in his body as Robert laid out blankets for them in the living room, as he unfolded a cot and brought pillows. Clare didn't want to sleep upstairs, so they made do on the sofa and on the cot. Her face was flushed, she was excited and she didn't want to close her eyes. They decided to take turns sitting up, watching out the front windows for whoever might come sneaking up the drive. In Anaconda, for weeks after they arrived, they had sat up at night, one of them nodding at the living room window, a pistol cradled in blankets, watching the yard as the moonlight seeped across it, wondering who might be coming, what official search might reach its conclusion that evening on their front porch. They didn't have to explain anything to one another.

Clare took the first watch, but neither slept. They listened to Robert talking to his mother in the room across the hall. The old woman thanked him for bringing his friends to the ceremony. "I'm glad you have people who love you," she said.

"They don't love me, Mama, or anybody else," Robert said.

"The stars were close tonight," the old woman said.

"They were almost on top of us, Mama."

"They don't get no hotter, but they get closer. Soon I'll be able to touch them."

"Sometimes I can almost smell heaven," Robert said.

"I can see heaven all around me," his mother said. "I can see it like I used to see the morning dew shining on the fields, like my garden on a spring morning touched and shining with the dew. I had no idea it would be like this. Did you think it would be like this, son?"

"It's not like that for me, Mama. It's scary for me."

"I can't hear what you say, but I can see what your face says. You don't have nothing to worry about, son. I thought we would be lifted up, like in the song, but instead heaven's being drawn down to us. There's not a thing we have to do."

"That doesn't make it easy, Mama."

"You got to hug up to your troubles, son. You got to meet them like they're your long-lost love." She cackled softy. "I thought I'd be dead long before I ever started talking like this."

"Me, too, Mama."

"I don't think I'm fooling anybody."

"Me either."

"Good night, Robert," Jack called.

Clare got down from her lookout on the back of the sofa, knelt beside his cot, and kissed him on the mouth. Her lips were soft and warm. "We weave in and out of trouble," she said, "but we've never called it trouble."

"We don't really address it at all."

"Do you think that's wrong of us?"

"No. I think it's one of our endearing traits."

"If it didn't drive us crazy." She stroked his hair. "Everyone says we look alike. People say we look like brother and sister."

"We're the same height, we're coarsely blond, we're the same build. . . ."

"Not quite."

"Bone structure, I mean. My hands and feet are bigger. I got a cowlick and you don't. Our eyes are different colors."

"We must have ancient ancestors who were kin."

"It's more than that."

"Sometimes I know exactly what you are going to say, and sometimes you surprise me."

"When it's like that it's almost perfect."

The room was dark. Moonlight lay in long white patches on the floor. "I think something is shifting in me," she said.

"Between us?"

"No. Just in me. I think I know what makes me get so angry."

"What?"

(I turned around . . .

"Misunderstanding."

"Between you and me?"

. . . to look at him swimming.

"No! Between all of us."

"I still feel the music inside me—that tune."

His shoulders gleamed . . .

"I do, too, a little, an echo of it." She tapped his face lightly. "Misunderstanding is not exactly the word. It's more like lying. We won't own up to what is going on."

"What is going on?"

He was completely alone—but that wasn't it . . .

"The way it is between you and me is the way it really is . . . between all of us. I think it's possible to accommodate anything."

"Probably."

There was work to do. Suicide is work to the end . . .

"I was thinking about Daddy. I could see myself singing over his grave. It was like I sat beside his grave holding his heart in my hands, and it was my heart, too—"

His blunt bald head. He was still determined . . .

"No," she said, leaning across him to get the apple she'd brought from the kitchen. "No. Not that. Not my heart, too. I'm such a touchy woman. Daddy looked right at me and I didn't scare him. I have been scaring him all my life. He must be dying. I know he is. And some ruffian from New Orleans was sitting beside his bed reading him a children's story. And he was calmed. It knocks me out. The dancing in the woods, these idiot lovers Robert and his mother dancing all night on the back of their disease, and you, honey, with your little boy peering at you from the hemlock grove. I don't know. It is clear we can go too far. The lash simply cuts too deep. We don't get over the humiliation and horror of what has happened to us. This drives me crazy. Up to a point there's plenty of sustenance, plenty of stuff that'll soothe us, but there's a place we can cross over into where nothing can calm you down. I was so shocked to see my daddy listening to a children's book, but he was and he was quiet in himself. I could see it. I could feel it. But there are those who aren't, no matter what. It's too late. The whole world I think is divided between those who can be reached and those who can't."

"Which are we?"

He didn't look back . . .

"We've run very close to the line. I think I have mostly crossed over. You nearly, too, but not quite so much. Will is already gone. James was gone. Donnie, he's long gone. It's hard to speak about because I think until the moment it happens, until the last second when you can still see a way back, still hear Mozart or the voice of your loved one, when you can still make out beauty hanging like red holly berries in the trees, you think it won't happen. We can't really conceive it, I mean. And then when it happens, nothing helps. Mozart's pretty maybe, but he really can't touch you anymore."

"You're turning into a conjure woman, like those women you used to go to in New Orleans."

"You don't have to be a witch to think like this."

But then he was thinking—in amplification—*still swimming*—of his high-school football field, of the August dark coming on as they stayed late for summer practice, of the smell of the lake just beyond the trees, of how the light, clean scent of the water swelled in the trees and drifted over them as they toiled at their game. The twilight would come on slowly like a long argument winding down and he would look up into the gathering dark, into the clear and fading blue above the trees, and he would think of the open waters, of how they stretched away from that abraded place *where Father had attempted to accomplish what he would later accomplish with his pistol, an historic spot in the water, which, so Jack imagined, probably still smelled of his body, the way the lake smelled of tankers and ore barges, smelled of the fight and the descent into the crystal water, which grew blacker, from which light faded, as they sank, so that even now, alive in the arms of a woman he would do anything for, it seemed to him the father had not been pulled from the water, that tonight,* as every night, *he could still hear him, the submarine father, traveling in the dark and the silence beneath the surface, tracking death, sending forth every minute the soft pings of his sonar like unanswerable questions pressed dissolving into the dark: Where am I, where are you, where am I . . . ?*

He had watched Billy Compton get his knee smashed on a running play and laughed. He had seen the clouds gathering in the west, behind the sun, stockpiled like armaments. From the gymnasium came the shouts of girls playing volleyball. There was a rash of burglaries. A boy, someone he knew, a sweet success, was assaulted on his way home in the dark by someone wielding a hemlock branch. Men chipped out of snowdrifts. The rocky beach. *There was his father swimming . . .*

. . . disappearing.)

"I can't shake the idea," he said, "that every thought I have is meant for every other thought. There's no inconsistency at all, no matter what I come up with."

"So we need each other to break the pattern."

"Maybe to add to it, too."

"No matter what?"

"I don't know. It's got me stumped."

"My daddy never sang to me, but there was a long time when I told myself he did. It was so important to me. That was where my need for him settled. On songs he sang. I gave him a repertoire. Show tunes and ballads. Sweet songs. I sang them to myself. In the end that was all I had. But I liked it. I liked singing to myself. After a while I forgot about Daddy singing. I just liked hearing the songs. I liked hearing myself singing them. You add to that—usually."

"I'm so glad." His mind idled, lay back a moment, he pushed into a tiny den where he could smell the grass, the leftover seeds and flower heads. *A children's story,* she'd said.

"Yeah. The truth is I could kill him. I know it. I could kill you. I almost did on the boat, like a tide in me I got swept along and there I was firing a gun. I have to live with this. You do, too, for the time we're together. We put up with each other. It goes on and on. I wake up and you're squatting on a deck looking out over the river, where the day is lying in a mist on the water. We snuggle up listening to the sounds coming from some little goofball village on the other side, and then the sun comes up and the water starts to sparkle and you fix me breakfast and we eat together sitting on the stern with our feet trailed in the water. Across the river we can see the hills of Missouri or someplace shining in the morning sunlight, and it is so beautiful it begins to affect our minds, so we think we have already forgiven everyone who ever harmed us, and no one will ever harm us again—"

—everyone harms everyone—

"—I'm flabbergasted that I can think like this. That I can come up with this string of thoughts. It is so wild to be a human being. I can't get over it. Oh God, Jack. Doesn't it amaze you? We live right on the edge of a cliff. Do you remember the time we robbed that hospital, that clinic, and this patient came out in the hall as you were dragging that administrator by the collar and began to call you Daddy? Do you remember that?"

"Yes."

"And how he wanted you to come with him? He kept saying 'Daddy, please come now, please come now'—and how wild his eyes were? And how his voice was like a child's voice, like a man, I mean, making a child's voice, squeaky and false like you'd make for a child, and how he was unshaven, with black whiskers and mad torn hair, this man crying in this fake little boy's voice for Father to come? How desperate he was?"

"Yes."

"Aren't we all like that all the time—somewhere? What is it we have seen?"

(My father, he said, pulled me down into the water. When I reached for him, he grabbed my arms and pulled me in. He tried to take me with him. He grabbed me, wrapped his arms around me, and turned for the bottom. I fought him, as I had not fought him in the car, fought for my life. I bit my

father's mouth. The pain made him release me. The pain—something—brought him back—I rose with him to the surface. There was blood in his mouth, his lip was torn; it hung by a flap against his chin. I helped him into the boat and rowed him to shore. The boy was gone.)

"I don't know," he said.

"I wish there was somebody here to eavesdrop on us. Rubens or somebody. That's what we needed—somebody to listen in. We should have taped this. Mailed the tapes to bankers and schoolteachers and little kids taking their first baths by themselves. 'Here, honeys, here is life in America, down in the valley where they keep the loot and the pain.' How many places have we robbed? A thousand? One million? I wish we had robbed every one. Every little bank and grocery store and lemonade stand in America. Every one. I want to wipe the smirks off their faces. I want to make them admit they are in pain. I want them to shout."

She stopped. Sighed. Laughed.

"Sometimes," she said, "I wish I didn't rant so. I make myself into a mockery."

"Of what?"

"Of an incorrigible bank robberess. Though I don't know a lot of bank robberesses."

"Hazel Willis—I remember her. And Francy Kramer."

"Jane Burke."

"That's right."

"Who was that woman who used to travel around with that bunch down in Texas?"

"Arlete Sims. I'd forgotten her. She got shot at a gas station in Amarillo."

"She did? How do you know that?"

"Somebody in prison told me. Willie Concheverra, the guy she used to run with. He was the one shot her."

She laughed. "I hate when that happens."

"Me, too. It ruins the split."

"I always keep my eye on you, just in case."

"I know you do, sweetie. I never forget it."

They went on talking, but he began to lose track. The room had a fatty, leathery smell, a smell of old age and sickness, but the smell didn't bother him. It was a little like the smell of his father's office, which stank of deer hides and face powder and of an unwashed body. He could hear her voice talking in the room and then it was talking inside his head and then it was in his sleep, a low melodious voice, faintly rasping, as if one side of each word were not quite as smooth as the others, each tugging slightly as it came loose from its moorage in her throat. He heard the words and then there was nothing but the rhythm of the words and he seemed to ride on the rhythm, which began to merge with the rhythm of the tune Robert had played until both were the same, until both became part of the rhythm of sleep itself and of the larger world sleep rode on. Inside him there was something tender and aching, a softened, bruised spot, and in his sleep he returned to this place and knelt down to it and took it in his hands as he might take up a small animal, an animal that was somehow part of him, and he began to stroke it, to murmur the song to it in a soft voice that was his own voice, but was also the mixed voice of everyone sleeping. What he held was soft and warm, but it had sharp claws that pricked his skin, lightly, not trying to hurt him, but as if it wanted something from him; he began to suffer over this because he could not think what it was he could do to ease the creature's need and it seemed to him as he swung in his hammock inside sleep that this was a terrible problem, something terrible and unsolvable that would not disappear until he could bring ease and comfort. He moved in his sleep, turning so that it felt as if he turned downward; he began to fall or slide down a long slope that was dusty and dark, and he could feel himself falling, tumbling, skittering downward; he tried to save himself and as he tried he realized he had forgotten the soft place, the animal of himself that he wanted to comfort, and this hurt him more deeply, he thought in his dream, than anything ever had, and he began to moan and to cry out, his voice harsh and broken like the cry of a hurt creature out in the dark woods, some solitary running animal who was caught in a trap, and then he saw himself as what he had become, saw himself held in his own hands, the animal he had tried to soothe, and he did not understand this even as his hands began to squeeze the life out of the creature, which was only his own self or his heart or his soul at the center of him, which seemed to be singing as it gave in to the pressure of hard hands killing it.

And then he dreamed in a different way, dreaming fact so that it didn't seem he was dreaming, only remembering, recollecting how they'd walked around the docks at Indian Harbor, day after day, each eyeing the other, come there for that purpose, already crazy about one another before they'd spoken a word, both too shy to speak, walking around the docks, peering into boats, standing in the crowd around the weighing stations. She was blond, her face was so burned by the sun there were white streaks on her cheeks and the bridge of her nose was torn, the skin crusted. She was lean, she moved quickly, abruptly, she walked on the balls of her feet. He watched her argue with a fishing captain, saw her strike the man in the chest, saw the surprise in the man's face, the glee in hers, saw her step back as if to walk away, then turn, come back, and shove the captain over the side of his own boat. He'd come up to her then and grinned at her, stuck out his hand. She took it, shook his hand hard. They didn't speak. He'd followed her off the docks, gotten in her car. She drove to a beach above Lauderdale, got out, they walked the strand through the bushes and the sea grapes. They walked for an hour, or walked and sat on the sand looking out to sea. Four blue oil tankers crept along in a line; he remembered this in the dream that was not a dream. After a while she got up and he followed her back to the car. She drove him to the docks, let him out; they hadn't said a word to each other.

In the dream he stood looking down a sunlit street at her. Everything he saw had happened.

They met at the docks, took drives, walked on the beach, never talked. They held hands once, both sweating, red-faced, not looking at one another. Then she stopped at a grocery store. Walked in—he watched through the windshield—pulled a pistol and robbed the place. She strode out stuffing bills into her jeans. The next day they stopped at a gas station. He went in and robbed it. He brought the money out in a plastic sack, gave it to her. She grinned. "You're perfect," she said.

He was. So was she. They both knew it.

They moved into a cottage motel off U.S. 1 between Lauderdale and Boca, a peach stucco place with a large interior court where the owners had planted coconut palms and rubber trees. The cottage had a bedroom, kitchen, and a screened porch, and they lived there happily, robbing various small places miles away, returning late to cook steaks, to sit out on the screen porch in the twilight listening to the redbirds in the rubber trees calling to each other.

He dreamed that he took her in his arms and this was true, it was a memory of taking her in his arms, the fierce drive of it, the way it was all right to go as far as possible, no one could understand them, they were alone with each other, there was no other world. They would wake early in the morning and make love. There was no one in the world like them. They rarely talked.

He turned in his sleep, dreaming.

He could see her at the end of the street, in white clothes, sunburned.

They lived apart, in a happiness of apartness.

There was no one like them, they were like no one else. They were attached to nothing, to no one. Banks were like monuments to their love, going to a bank was like going to the Acropolis to see the Parthenon, to visit the great edifices, the big theme parks of their civilization. Here was the heart of things, the symbol of their love and their separateness. They walked in with guns and took money. Then they drove fast and disappeared into the blank summer afternoon. Later they discovered themselves naked in a river. Or walking by the ocean. Or frying ham sandwiches in a peach-colored cottage. They came to themselves and there were only the two of them in the world and no one could say anything to them or stop them or even approach them with confidence.

It was like having all your bills consolidated in one easy payment, he told her.

This life together, she said, is that what you mean?

Yes, he said, that's what I mean.

Robbing banks?

Yes.

And so it was. There were no taxes, they made no reports, they asked no one's permission. There was no cleanup. They never saw the place again.

There was no past.

There was no future.

In the dream that was life as he remembered it she took a swig of strawberry soda, leaned over and spit it into his mouth. The soda was cold. He could taste it as they entered the bank.

She was laughing.

There's no one like us, she said.

He agreed. There never had been. There never would be again.

She stuck out her slim red tongue at him.

Everything they ever did—in each other's eyes—was forgivable. It was impossible to make a mistake.

So he dreamed. Yet as he dreamed, the knot, the trapped animal in his side, hurt.

• • •

He waked. Clare slept at the window. The moon had turned the room into a museum for soft gray shapes. He got up without disturbing her. What was out in the yard might have drawn closer, but what was outside didn't scare him.

We are all going to be killed, he thought, every one of us. Yes, yes, it was true, as his father believed, death was the key to everything.

The animal ached in his side. Maybe I have cancer, too. But even that would pass, as he would pass. It all goes away, he thought. Nothing in the past helps for long. What matters is what continues. But memory is continuance. This changes, though. One time the trees were saffron, another they were yellow. She left you: you left her. Even betrayal faded. There was only the tendency. The willingness to continue. Repetition. Rhythm. The discount momentum of a botched life. As all were botched—just as Clare said—distorted, freak contrivances slung like coyote pelts over a fence. But whose trophies? What disorder was corrected in the mind of heaven by their feckless, crippled strivings? Whose father was it got pissed off? There should be something in every household that could be looked at every day. Like a painting you loved, but better, or a loved face. Something that would last. That would hold.

The ache wouldn't go away. That convict on the cross, the thief. He'd rebuked his buddy who'd taunted Jesus. That was the hard part. Shutting your buddy up who was exactly your double, at least your partner, surefire example of everything you understood and believed in, for—for this fool, this scrawny nutcase in his rented body, some jerk, some asshole everybody saw through, who had come to the terrible end he deserved, whose clothes, even, had been stripped off him and dispersed in a lottery. This guy who was mumbling to himself about his father forgiving everybody. First you had to say no to everything you held dear. And then say yes to the nut. It was just too hard, even for a thief.

He went out into the hall. A white tear bulb lit the area from a socket near the floor. Large shadows draped the eaves. There was more light under the bathroom door, like an empty page spilled onto the parquet. For a moment his confusion stopped him. He could not place himself in his life, in this hallway that smelled of dusty fabric and muddy feet. The shadows were nets.

None of this is a theory I am working out, he thought. I am the jailhouse lawyer in my own life. There is no proper adjudication. Every trial is a mistrial. Every witness has perjured himself. The judge is on the take. The prosecutor is a psychopath, and you, with no training or courage, are left to defend yourself. Each door leads to the electric chair.

There is no penalty that fits the crime.

Do you understand, Your Honor, how much I love crime? It is pure beauty. True fission. Each act of crime creates more crime. There is always more. Thus, in crime, we never die, Your Honor. All writs are served. Do you understand? If there is always more, then we never run out. Betrayal is the key, Your Honor. Rubens understood this. He betrayed me, betrayed Clare. It is the most beautiful crime, betrayal. That is why I love Clare so much, Your Honor. She would kill me in a second. Betray me absolutely. There is no feeling like betrayal, Your Honor. It is like a sponge inside your heart filling with love. Love pumps through you, it drips from your fingertips. This is my blood, Your Honor.

But no, he thought, no. The thief hated the other guy. It was like jail, the snitch down the row, the guy you'd stab if you got a chance. There were no hatreds like the hatreds in prison. Of course he would betray the other thief. Fuck you, Mac, go die, I'm taking my chance.

There it is, Your Honor: Betrayal.

As if at that moment his name had been called from a long list a voice muttered its way down, he went to the bathroom door and pushed it open.

The old woman sat on a stool at the sink washing herself. She was stripped to the waist, her white nightgown puddled around her belly. Her large speckled breasts hung down like exhausted conspiracies. Her arms were creased above the elbow and looked as if they had been tenderized with a mallet. He stared at her, searched her body. The washcloth glided along, *like an ore boat lifting through canal locks, banging the sides,* touching her in the creases, dipping into hollows where a lifetime's shadows had collected. Without surprise she looked at him. She smiled with eyes some drug or god had turned golden like the eyes of a blessed child looking fondly from a dream of happiness. There was no place on her time and disease hadn't worked over.

She didn't speak. She nodded her head like one who had been waiting for the others to join her. The prosecutor, acting on the People's behalf, gripped him hard. *She's as good as you,* his big, low voice said.

The words caught him like a blow and the blow caught him napping.

There were bottles—medicine bottles, perfume bottles, lotion, an empty birch beer bottle, *jars containing fingerprints and tears*—crowded on every surface. Old clothes lay paralyzed in agony on the floor amid the greasy residue of unhappy baths, washups, and nights staring into the mirror looking for one moment's release from despair. The shower curtain, colored like a rainbow and half torn from its hooks, bunched like a portable promise, was streaked with mold. The sink was stained by copper tears.

(The bathroom could have been in Chicago, he said, in a transient hotel converted to apartments for poor people, or in some river town, out behind the grain elevators, or in Duluth, down Skiddy Street, where the white trash lived, where the men who had busted out of mining jobs or jobs on the ore boats, or no jobs at all, had come home to turn their faces against the wall, where women washed clothes for a living and dreamed of becoming queen for a day, a bathroom in a battered row house on Skiddy, he said, some ex-farmer's bathroom the ex-farmer was too drunk even to notice anymore, where his wife knelt on the floor washing from her spindly child grime and specks of saliva some tough boy had spit onto him. . . .)

Her eyes did not beckon, they only looked out at him. She did not need him. She did not wait for him to complete her life in any way.

You see what you have done? the prosecutor said.

There was the smell of ammonia. Of gases seeped up from deep inside the earth—*the ruin and the loss, he said, the dumb avid washing, the hopeless tenderness, the gunfire, the flight, the silence, the way night came down around itself like a flock of starlings settling into pine trees, the way even after the worst job, the job where they'd killed three men and a woman holding a boy in her arms, the job in Oklahoma where the Indian deputy got cut in half by a threshing machine, any of these, or any other, how any, he thought, came down at last to the long day's end, to the silence of sunset and the quiet under the trees where she sat with her hands cupping a container of coffee, sipping it, looking at him with her cool gray eyes*—this was what was here when she lifted her eyes—*Not* as good as, *he said, speaking to the jury. Not even no different from.*

He's a liar, the prosecutor shouted.

. . . the vows broken, he thought, the absolute failure of everything loved to endure—*they are all me.*

The futility. The rancid breath. The sweet dreams of love in the cornfield. The time in Venezuela we walked eleven miles through the mountains and the way we touched each other as we walked and the moment we stopped where the road turned beyond a date grove and we could see the bay like a pale blue floor laid down at our feet and you waved a ten-bolivar bill in my face and swore you would give me one every time I brought you to such a beautiful place. The pistols. The murderous rages going on all night until you called the cops and we had to leave the god-damn motel fleeing for our lives.

She's you.

I object, Your Honor. The prosecution is leading the witness.

But I thought . . .

The woman looked at him. She stepped forth from her eyes and entered him. He was grazed, jostled—*by molecules, he said, by flesh, by bone and thought, by last-minute objections and by lies told forty-five years ago, by a tone, by simple reasonableness converted to scorn, by hope and hopelessness, by desire the deceiver, by fingernails drawn down bare skin, by lust, by aversion, by carefully plotted but misleading intentions, by a child in the womb, by the daze of inestimable adolescent delight, by blood, by grace, by careless lingering affinity, by several days in a home-less shelter outside Dallas, by dry snowless winters on a farm in Kentucky, by deceit, by facts, by daylight and dark, by the fruits of sin, by God, by Jesus standing on his toes on the cross, by Allah, by Moses and David, by Abraham, who was ready at God's bidding to murder his child, by hood-lums and hoodlum children, by church, by community, by government placed like a boulder on top of the people's heads, by the collected works of Shelton Davis the farm-boy poet, by Gene Autry's Radio Ranch, by sleeping Presidents, by consanguinity and heraldry, by one look over your shoulder at life disappearing like a fast car, by cancer, by an old woman's odors and fetishes*—he was entered by everything. . . .

You know what this means, Your Honor. . . .

He did not notice himself stumble backwards out of the room. He did not mark himself as he closed the door.

He was outside in the hall, among the shadows that were looped and knotted in the eaves. There was silence, a pause without reversion. *The boy who looked at me was . . .* He could still see her raising her spotted hand, digging under her arm with the washcloth.

"Mister," she said, "I don't mind you looking at me." It was the woman's voice, Mrs. Joleen's voice coming through the door. She said, "I am lonely enough to enjoy that. I have seen you before. You came here to this farm years ago, with my son. You were a mischievous, vivid man. There was something familiar about you."

"What was it?" he whispered.

"You were full of yourself, Mister. Like a little cock rooster. I wanted to stroke you. After my husband died I wanted to touch men. There was a time when I let myself. They came to me. My son never knew. They came to me in the night like animals charmed from the woods. It was exciting, my body filled with desire for these men, but the desire was like a sand house—it washed away. You brought that back to me. I remembered. I saw my husband in you, which is what I was looking for in the other men. And then I saw it wasn't my husband. It was love itself."

"I'm not your husband."

"I would go up into the attic of this house and sing to myself. I would dress in the old work clothes that belonged to my husband and I would lie on the floor singing and crying. Sometimes I dressed in these clothes when the men came to see me. I told one man that he was making love to Hansford and it made him sick to his stomach. He never came back."

"Not me."

"You brought—not my husband back, but that day when I realized it was love I was after. Love drives us crazy, Mister. We will kill to get it and we will kill to get away from it. We have to have it, Mister. I realized this. You reminded me then, and you remind me now."

I plead nolo contendere, Your Honor.

"You are mocking me," he whispered.

There was silence behind the door. He pressed his face against the cool wood. The wood smelled of incense. "Are you there?" Had she spoken at all?

Do you confess?

"Mister," she said. "Life is long enough. No matter how short it is, it is long enough to get everything done."

Are you ready?

Like you ask me if I want a hot dog? Like you ask me as if we were getting into the car at a mall outside Muncie, the two of us tired and hungry, lost in this town where the office buildings are painted pale blue like birds' eggs? Like an aside, you ask me, like something you remembered just before sleep jimmied the locks?

Are you ready?

No, I'm not ready.

Are you ready?

Then he saw himself get to his feet—had he fallen?—saw himself step into the bathroom, watched as he sat down on a stool before a dirty sink under a mirror with a familiar coppery crack in it and began to wash his disintegrating body with a gray rag. He felt the soft, spotted weight of his body. The flesh drained downward. He saw the corroded face, the eager, avid eyes alive in the puddles of flesh, saw the light inside the eyes like a ferret leaping at movement, fierce, carnivorous, familiar. . . .

He touched his own wild, woman's face.

(Even my own suicide attempt, he said, afterward, was a ruse. I sat upstairs with my .22 rifle in my hands looking out at the ore boats docked under the conveyers, and I clicked one bullet into the chamber and then I clicked a second bullet in and then I sat there wondering why I wanted a second bullet, but I didn't know, it was as if—maybe I thought this—someone might come and finish the job—who?—and I sat by the window waiting for the right moment, but it wouldn't come—I didn't tell him this—until he entered the room and found me and stood looking at me in horror without speaking while we listened to a hermit thrush cry its sweet okla oklee *from the birches at the bottom of the yard—until, very slowly, he went down on his knees and begged me not to do this, and I waited patiently for him to finish his speech and then said, All right, I won't, if you won't. He waited ten years. It was ten years later, on my wedding day, when, at last out of sight, he thought, okay, he was free to put the pistol in his mouth, a man sitting at his desk wearing my mother's face powder to cover the nail heads of cancer, free to put the gun in his mouth and pull the trigger.)*

He touched the ruined, beautiful face.

Are you ready?

Yes.

It's only the facts that haven't worked out, he said.

The morning was cold, bright shined; there was frost the color of spittle on the grass, on the limbs of the apple trees, in the dirt under the gardenia bushes off the back steps. Fluffed birds chittered in the lower branches of the oaks near the house.

He watched Clare dress. The scars gleamed under her ribs.

You are beautiful, he told her, you're more beautiful than it's legal to be.

Outlaw body, she said and came down to him on the cot. They made love silently, as if they were holding their breath.

Sometimes, she said as she wiped between her legs, I can feel you all the way through me, as if your cock has little threads and feelers on it and they are snaking into the corners of me. I like that so much.

I enjoy visiting exotic places, he said.

You pick up the customs quick.

They ate breakfast in the kitchen, eggs and salt ham the old woman fried. Jack helped Robert haul one of the living room armchairs outside and put it in the back of the truck, under the canopy they lifted off sawhorses in the barn. Robert attached a small tank of butane to the side of the truck and ran a line to a heater he placed in the bed. "We use this for deer hunting at night," he said.

"Isn't that illegal?"

"Us criminals don't mind that."

"You've come around pretty smartly to the idea of helping out."

"I liked it before, when I drove to the banks. It wasn't you folks that made me stop doing it."

"What was it?"

"I got scared. It made me crazy."

"We used to hear you thrashing around at night, calling out."

"Sometimes I would hear *you.*"

"That's what Clare tells me. I don't remember it."

"I could remember it—my own, I mean. It started to seem like everything was looking at me. Not just the people, but the animals, too, cows in the fields and the birds and shit."

"Good thing you came back here."

Robert lifted the heater into the truck. "It didn't help," he said. "I was just as scared out here among the corn as I was pulling a pistol in a bank."

"You don't seem scared now."

"It's the cancer that's straightened me out. It spooked me so bad I got over being scared."

"Kind of hair of the dog."

"Maybe. When they first told me I had it, I was so frightened I used to feel like at night I was being smothered. I would feel death like it was lying down on top of me. It was all this heavy blackness and emptiness. I used to wake up with this grinding inside me, like my insides were being slowly rubbed to dust against a stone."

"What changed?"

Robert snapped a match, stuck it to the burner. The burner made a soft *whump* and a short line of blue flame ran along the lower edge. "I don't know," he said. "Angels come, I guess."

"What angels?"

"The regular kind."

"Wings and white suits?"

"Not exactly, no. Nothing really to see—but yeah, kind of, in a way. Right in the middle of the suffering, right when I was being dragged down so low, a pleasant feeling would start up. It was like standing on the sidewalk in Chicago, looking at the Christmas windows in Marshall Fields. . . ."

"A sweet dumb happiness—I know."

"It was a surprise. A little touch of glee. I was flabbergasted. I spent my whole life fighting my way through to what I thought I wanted—I never thought there was any other way to go about it. Then in the worst time, the time when I had to fight harder than any other time, I just couldn't make it . . . I tried but I couldn't make it . . . and all of a sudden the whole business just let up. I was being ground to powder, and then I was free."

"The angels did that?"

"What else could it be?"

"You didn't really see them, though."

"Not them, not exactly. But I could see something. The night it happened, after it happened, I could see through the walls."

"The house walls?"

"Yeah. Like they were invisible. I could see my cornfields and I didn't hate them anymore. They were beautiful. And I could see the little yellow flowers on the pea vines, and I could see the midges hanging in a cloud over the field, and I could see the dust on the leaves—it was all beautiful. Like I had never seen it before, or I'd never seen how beautiful it was. I saw the corn leaves all touching each other, needing each other so they could pollinate and go on living, and it was like some voice, some angel, was pointing it out to me, like I didn't have a care in the world, nothing to do but look at corn rustling in a breeze, soak it all up with my eyes."

"We saw the corn on the way in—it's a mess."

"Yeah, it is."

"Seeing all that didn't make you want to work it?"

He clapped his hands softly in front of the blue fire. "Hell, no. I didn't want to do a thing to it. It didn't matter. It was beautiful however it was, flourishing or broke down, it didn't matter."

"Shit, Robert, I don't know if we want *you* driving getaway."

Robert coughed up a laugh. "Heh. It's true. I might get so busy admiring the view I forget to move the car."

Jack put his hand on the pistol in his waistband. The metal was warm from his body. "I got a touch of all that last night," he said. "More than a touch. But I don't like it at all."

"I don't expect you would, Jack. I don't think you ever liked things to work out."

"What I want to work out has already worked out."

"I don't see how you can say that. You're going on forty years old and you're on the run from just about every normal setup in American life. With Donnie Bee you even got the crooks after you."

"Doesn't look that good, does it?"

"It doesn't look good for you at all. Hell, man, if I was you, I'd take the rest of that money you say you got from Jimmy and go to some real quiet place."

"I don't want a quiet place. We just came from a quiet place."

Now as he talked his mind seemed to move along on a level, without penetrating anything. He was moving past, maybe through, but he couldn't get inside anything. It was like riding in a car, all day, every day, counties, states, everything disappearing behind him. "I've never been on the run," he said, "not really."

"I don't see how you can say that."

Jack looked sharply at him. Anger flared. "There's never been anything after me," he said coldly. He turned his head, spat on the ground. From the back porch Clare looked out at him. "It's what gets me about your kind of talk, Robert," he said. "It's the same with you and all these guys. The good guys and the bad guys, it's all the same. You think you have someplace to get to. You grind up your lives worrying until you wear yourself out, and then when you're exhausted and beat totally to shit, you sit there and call it peace. It's not peace, Robert. It's exhaustion. There is no quiet place. You think you see glory because you notice the sun shining on the fucking cornfields. Well, it's not glory, Robert. The corn is what it is. It's fine like it is. Now you're dying, now you understand that the churning in your guts is Mister Death, and you're ready to see jewels in every bush. You guys wear me out. You think life is this precious gift, this delicate wonder, this fucking Christmas window. It's not, Robert. It's not *anything* you can call it. It doesn't need a fucking description. It doesn't need to be understood. It doesn't need to be appreciated or treated right. It's not a goddamn woman, Robert. It's not a car that you have to keep running right. There's nothing you can do to it that'll hurt it. There's nothing you can leave out of it, or take from it, or put in it that'll ruin it at all."

He banged the bottom of his hand against the truck. "You greasy little narcissists all think like this. You think life depends on you. You think you got to do something, or get something, or sell something, or say something that'll set things right. All you see is a reflection of your puny self in everything around you. 'I am dying—my, don't the world look good.' Fuck that." He stepped back. "I ought to shoot you right here. I ought to shoot you and stick my hand in the hole and pull your guts out."

Robert lurched onto his hands and knees. "Jesus, Jack," he said. "I'm sorry."

"Shit on it, Robert. You're a gas mouth." He whirled away from him. "Clare!" he yelled. "Clare, get that old woman and let's go." Clare nodded once and disappeared into the house. He turned to Robert. "Get out of that truck bed, pal. Pull up to the back porch, let's load your mama and go."

"Okay, Jack, I will." He scurried out. The pain in his guts must have made a grab at him because he groaned and stumbled. He caught himself, rubbed his thighs. "I appreciate you letting me bring Mama," he said. "She likes to get out."

"Don't say anything about it," Jack said.

There was an abandoned house on the other side of the oak tree. It was filled with hay. He could see the yellow bales stacked in the windows, even up on the second floor, and stacked on the porch and filling the doorway, which stood wide open. A house of hay. They beat him to his knees and they beat him to his belly and then they turned him over and beat him. When he shifted his head he could see the house, see the yellow hay where the sun struck it, shining in the windows, and for a few minutes he could see how beautiful this was, gold and distinct in the ragged woods, but then the blows knocked him past this and he couldn't tell what was beautiful from what was not.

Robert drove the truck around in a wide circle to the back porch. Jack followed, scuffing chilly dust up as he walked, angry now for sure, thinking, as if this was what such mornings brought him to, of children clumped together watching cartoons on television, of probing with his fingers into the spring behind the house for the wedding ring his mother had flung there, of his father pointing out the spot on the lake where the first French voyageurs came ashore. "From that moment," his father had said, "the West belonged to us. That one scuff mark on a rock was the mark of Cain on all this land. We continue under that mark," he said. But these words seemed to be spoken quietly now, with a great tenderness, and his mother, hovering above him as he probed the spring, seemed to be smiling.

He came up on the back steps as Robert got out. The driver was imperfectly shaped, bent over as if the cancer had become arthritis.

"You look rusted," Jack said.

"Sort of," Robert said. He steadied himself on the porch post as he climbed the steps. "You don't have to think of this as something you got to do," he said. "We can put a stop to it any time; it's not destiny or anything."

"I have already been humbled by my destiny," Jack said.

"You mean that reporter writing about you?"

"I wasn't thinking about that. I wasn't thinking about destiny, either. I don't even want to hear about destiny, or any of that prophetic bullets-around-the-corner bullshit, is that okay?"

"It's okay with me, Jack." He went inside.

Then Clare was coming down the steps carrying guns and a thermos of hot coffee. She came straight up to him and kissed him on the lips. "You look perked up," she said.

"Do I?" He stroked her hair. "I think I have gotten out of my depth."

"You've always been out of your depth. We all are."

"Death has brought Robert to the notion that everything is beautiful."

"Like the song?"

"No. Like the life."

"Who cares what Robert thinks?"

"Is that the way it goes?"

"For us, dear. We wouldn't be in this line of work if we cared too much about what other people thought."

He laughed. "Where was my head?"

"Back there under that bunk on Jimmy's cabin cruiser, I guess, honey. Help me with all these supplies, will you?"

They were all still in him, all the roughhouse notions; and the action and the movement were in him, the jumps and the turnarounds like some kid spinning off tackle in a football game, all the quick thought and the speed of flight, the car waiting with its engine running, the trees brushed glossy black by rain, the cops shooting, all the sweet escape techniques and the danger like the taste of hot peppers in his mouth, and Clare screaming into his ear to floor it, to load the pistols, to *go on go on go on*. . . .

He knew the coffee he stowed in the cab was hot, sugared just right, and the guns were oiled—disassembled, cleaned out, oiled, and put back together. She had taken a bath and there was not a spot on her body the soapy cloth had missed. You could sniff behind her ears or between her toes and smell the fresh scent of cloves. She knew exactly how many miles, plus tenths, they were from her father's back porch, how much gas it would take to get there. She could tell you what the farm fields of Indiana looked like in the first frosty week of November when the broken cornstalks bent under rain and the winds blew the last of the red oak leaves out over the collapsed furrows. She knew the family names of the birds flying overhead and what the blue circle around the moon portended, what that scurrying noise was in the grass, there at the edge of your hearing. There were nights when she stood just outside his dreams calling his name, and like a small boy set free in wonder into the summer fields, he would come out to her, out of the dream into the world she inhabited, into the wild, open savanna where all the animals were familiar, where the sky reflected the color of her eyes back to her and the smell on the breeze was the smell of her body. . . .

It came back to him like a promise he had made that he already knew what it was to lose this . . .

• • •

. . . to take the gun in his mouth, to look straight up through blood into Donnie's face, to watch the hammer click back and hear the laughter around him, to see through the blood beyond Donnie's head the flock of crows flying to nowhere, to see himself on his knees under the big oak, a man with rips in his scalp, rips in his body now, Donnie grasping the gun, forcing his mouth open, talking to him, telling him secrets about what would happen to him, confiding in him like a robbery, going confidential, Jack, this is for you, buddy, eat you every bit of it. . . .

"I think I am going to get a makeover," she said.

"I thought that was what this trip was about."

"Nothing we're doing here will change us. I mean hairstyle and face."

"That's unsettling."

"I want a complete redo: hair, lips, eyes, everything. I want to look like Doris Day in *Pillow Talk.*"

"You're too sexy for Doris Day."

"I'm going to stand in the shadows with pale skin and pale hair and startle little boys."

"You already do that."

She kissed him again. "Take that worried look off your face. Under my new face I will still be me."

"That's what I am worried about."

"I like your vest."

"Thank you, dear. It gives me such a rich, golden feeling."

They helped Robert put his mother in the back of the truck, in the armchair under a blanket. She made slow, queenlike gestures as Robert adjusted the earphones of a Walkman over her head. "My hair's got static in it," she said. "This thing won't electrocute me, will it?"

"I thought she was deaf," Jack said.

"She can hear a little bit if I turn it up real loud," Robert said. He had on a red-and-black-checked coat and a bright red deer cap. "She likes to listen to church music. You'll be fine, Mama," he said, "just settle back."

The old woman had said nothing about last night; she didn't seem to recognize him at all, not even at breakfast when, sitting across from her, he had tried to stare a hole in her skull. He reached into the truck to touch her, but she was too far away, except for her slippered foot; he patted her toe. She grinned at him. "I've been going on trips all my life," she said. "I always have a good time."

"Me, too," Jack said.

In the truck, behind the wheel, as they headed down the drive, Robert said, "I didn't feel so good about this last night, Clare, but I feel okay this morning."

"You've got your hands on real things now," Clare said.

"Yeah, that's it. I'm holding a blue steering wheel in a red Ford truck behind a 218-horsepower motor that's washing five quarts of number thirty weight oil through its innards. I'm on my way across the big river to Vandalia, Indiana, where I'm going to drop two nutcases off at their relatives' front gate. By the way," he said, "thank you for the gold. You'll have to tell me the whole story of it sometime."

"Look at those deer," Clare said.

Three does and a buck browsed in the cornfield beyond the apple trees. One of the does, slender flanked with a wide white blaze, looked at them. Her flag went up. All four bolted. "They come right up to the house sometimes," Robert said. "Deer, coons, rabbits—all of them come out of the woods these days."

"Overpopulation," Jack said.

"Yeah, sure, but sometimes it seems like they've just had too much of the woods life—just too damp and dirty and exhausting to go on with."

"Like us," Clare said.

Robert glanced at her. "You'll never get enough." His dark eyes were tired, worn.

They came to the end of the drive. Straight ahead there was another cornfield and off to the right across the road a stand of young sycamores beside a shack with a broken-through roof. Robert turned that way, onto the dirt road that ran toward the highway a mile up. As they approached the shack, passing the last apple trees on the right, Robert looked toward the sycamores. "What is that?" he said. He rubbed at a smeared place on the windshield. As he did so the glass beside his palm splintered. For a second Jack thought he had somehow driven his finger through it. Then the glass under his palm popped and his hand snapped back and caught him in the face. His head hit the back windshield and jerked forward. There was a rosy hole above his left eye. He slumped against Clare. Then they could hear the rifle popping and the truck veered right and bumped down into the ditch.

Jack threw the door open and they crawled out. Robert fell over along the seat. His eyes were wide open. He looked as if he was choking, but he wasn't. "Leave him," Clare said as Jack reached into the truck, "he's gone." In the back of the truck the old woman was hollering for Jesus. They crouched by the hood.

"Do you see him?" Jack said.

"He's over there by that shack. Under the porch, I think."

Jack fired three quick shots at the shack. "This pistol won't do much from here," he said.

The rifle cracked again. There was a pause and then four shots in succession. The last two hit the truck with a clapping metal sound. The old woman stopped screaming.

Jack sat down beside the wheel. He stretched his legs out. Clare bent low to the ground just in front of the truck. She shot twice with the pistol, jerked back. "I am so tired," Jack said, "I could just go to sleep right here."

"That's just scarediness, sugar. I feel exactly the same way."

"If we don't watch it, our lives are going to be played out entirely before an audience of killers and the dead."

"What an unpleasant thought," she said, "but why don't we tend to this before you start philosophizing?"

He leaned over onto his hands and came up onto one knee. "Oh man, goddamn." He rubbed the pistol against his pants leg. "I liked those deer," he said, "didn't you?"

"I liked them fine."

"I want to live someday in a place where deer come into the backyard. Or someplace again. They used to do that up in Minnesota."

She snapped off a shot. "I like Minnesota."

"You do? I thought you didn't."

"It probably would be better than this."

"I guess we ought to circle on around here."

"Okay. Which way do you want to go?"

"I'll go across the road and cut through the cornfield. You go along the ditch."

"You want a signal?"

"No. Just don't shoot me if I get close."

"Okay."

Jack kissed her and moved along the truck to the rear. The old woman sat straight up in her chair. She wore blood like a new coat of paint. Her cheeks and throat were red, there was blood on her chest, and blood was beginning to pool in her lap. Her eyes were open and she was breathing with a small rasping sound. Her left hand stood up off the chair arm, the fingers twitching. Jack could hear the music from the Walkman. It was a hymn, "Love Lifted Me." The hand jerked lightly as if she was keeping time to it.

"We have a little delay here, Mrs. Joleen," Jack said. "An obstacle. I'm going over now to clear it out."

She didn't answer him.

He'd known every day of his life what it was to go too far, to rush on past the stopping place until he was out there, hung in the air, falling. Whoever knew him knew about this. I wish I could tell you, he said to the woman. I wish I knew *what* to tell you.

The rifle cracked again, twice, three times. Clare returned fire. She had two pistols and she used both of them, firing one, then the other. The revolver made a thicker sound than the automatic's flat metal clap. Jack sprinted across the road, dived into the ditch, and scrambled up the other side. The weeds were slippery with frost. His heart beat hard, he could feel the strength of it. He didn't know whose work this was, but it was probably Donnie's.

I am loose in the freshly stupendous world, he thought, in the absolutely revulcanized and renovated creation, but I act just like always in it.

Here he was, shooting off guns.

He crawled under the fence and made his way into the cornfield. The stalks were broken, gray, streaked with mold, and the dirt under them was black and sticky. Where the shucks had been torn back, the ears were bright with yellow toothy kernels. He could see all this clearly, and he could see the four clouds hung up in the west like fixtures and the big naked oaks at the end of the field and the place where the corn was battered down and the black frost-burned strips of bean vine tangled with the stalks, and if he went down on his knees, he could see the fine friable dirt and the crystals of frost like tiny beads embedded among the grains and the mealy organisms suspended between life and death. There was a radiance in everything. Sometimes the world couldn't help it. He could see this. You jump for that, he thought. When the time comes, like a thief you grab it.

He felt a sudden exhilaration. As he looked through the cornstalks at the battered house, which was filled to the rafters with hay bales, somewhere close by which shots were being fired at him, some assassin who thought the time had come, drawing a bead . . . he felt free.

It was just an idea I had, he thought. . . .

He could hear Clare firing. She let go with the shotgun once; just for emphasis, he guessed. The shooter fired back and then the rifle went silent. Jack ran up the row until he was even with the house, then he turned in toward it. He crawled across the furrows. Stickle burrs and beggar lice caught in his jacket. The rifle had stopped. He could see the shack down to the windows. A breeze snagged in the tops of the big oaks and pulled them back and forth. It looked as if the trees were waving.

Then a car engine started. There was the crunch of tires on gravel. Jack jumped up and ran toward the house. He could feel his whole body; it felt as if he were flying. From the far side of the shack a blue sedan headed fast toward the road. There was one man in it, jammed down low in the seat.

Clare stood up in the ditch and began to shoot at the car as it came toward her. She fired one pistol, lowered it, raised the other and fired. The car ran straight at her. The man reached out the window and began to pop at her with a pistol.

It was Will.

A shot hit the road surface with a fat, sizzling sound, kicking up dust. Clare stood straight up, holding one pistol propped on the other, firing. The car hit the road, bumped high, continued across, and slammed into the ditch. Clare jumped to the side as it went by her. She fired two shots after the car stopped. Then she walked to it and leaned in the window.

"Wait," Jack yelled as he ran toward her.

She fired once and stepped back. Flicking the chamber open, she shucked the shells into her palm and hurled them at the car.

"Goddamn it, Clare."

He crossed the road. Clare turned toward him, slowly, as if she stood on a pivot. Her face was white and her eyes looked as if they had been set on fire.

"Fucker," she said. "I got the fucker."

"Did he hit you?"

"I shot the fucker straight through his head, Jack."

He took her in his arms, but she pulled away from him. She lurched down the ditch and fell to her knees. Weaving, she began to retch, hacking and spitting, making a noise like a sick animal, shaking her head. "Agh, agh," she said, stroking the ground with the gun. She bent down with her arms out in front of her and pressed her face into the grass. Then she let her body turn and sink until she lay on her side. She drew her legs up.

He knelt beside her and stroked her head. The sky was clear except for a few clouds up near the white remote disc of the sun. The edges of the clouds nearest the sun were bright.

After a while he helped her to her feet and held her tightly as he sometimes had to after a difficult encounter. He could feel her pulse throbbing in her arms and even in her waist as he steadied her. She did not seem to know where she was. She stared out over the big field, or maybe, he thought, she was looking at the bare sumac stalks in the ditch or at the sassafras bushes against the wire fence, or maybe she was counting the blackbirds in the distant flock wheeling south under ragged clouds, or maybe she didn't notice any of this, but only watched the ongoing incredible mystery playing inside her, some aspect of this.

He let her be and went over to the car and looked in at Will. His brother-in-law slumped against the door in a mess of bloody glass and brain matter. The brain bits were pink and white with orange highlights. His eyes were almost closed; the lashes were long and there were squint tears at the corners; Will looked as if, even in death, he was drawing a bead on something. His hands lay cupped in his lap, palms up, fingers slightly curled; bits of brain, like specks of oatmeal, speckled the skin of his wrists. "Poor idiot boy," Jack said. "You look more lost than ever."

The thought came to him that he didn't even have to desire peace, or God, or any of it, he didn't have to come up with a vision or a motive or a tendency, no rush was necessary toward love or crime, or toward a quiet day beside the lake before the worst happened. It would come, whatever it was, of its own accord.

Clare came up behind him, leaned against his back. "I would rather look at him through you," she said. "Like you were my window."

"Fine."

"Oh, Will," she said. "Oh my."

"He was a killer to the end, sweetheart."

"Not every minute."

"Good."

He walked back to the truck. Robert lay sprawled along the seat, a look of confused disappointment in his face. Mrs. Joleen had stopped breathing. She sat upright, but her arm had fallen into the blood in her lap. Jack shivered. He didn't mind that she was dead, but now he couldn't tell her, he couldn't find out from her what part was dream and what part was real. This part he was looking at, the bloody face, the gray coat and the blue dress, the blood staining everything, the earphones still full of music, looked like a dream, but it couldn't be. And last night, and last week, and the ride up the river, and Anacondia, Tennessee, and on back, to prison, to banks, to—it all looked like a dream. He could feel the cold now, and it was sharp and particular, but it, too, could become a dream soon enough, a tug into sleep. There were beads of blood on her yellow slippers. He reached in, touched one, and brought it to his mouth. The blood tasted of iron and made him think of the well water he had drunk from a bucket at his mother's cabin in the north woods. He thought of a spring day, of the sun glittering on the grassy reeds in a tamarack bog. Thought of whitetail deer crashing through the undergrowth, of a river, yellow as brass, shining in the sun. There was a meadow scattered with flowers, with cinquefoil and alpine daisies. He had never seen a place quite like that, almost but not quite. He could see it now. It was in his head, but he nearly could touch it, he nearly could walk out into it, it was so real.

Bless her, he said. Here, he said, not moving, let me buy her a ticket that will carry her all the way. I know the difference, he said, between what's dream and what's real. Now I do, he said. Bless this dead woman, he said. He meant it, even though there was no taste to the words.

She got down on her knees and begged Donnie to stop, but Donnie wouldn't stop. Jack could hear her voice, and it scared him because there was nothing in her voice but the plea. He bucked when Boudreau struck him. The pain sizzled, he spun into shock, emptiness; pain blew him back.

"Give him your fist," Donnie said. "Make him eat every fucking inch of it."

• • •

They couldn't leave this time without more, so they loaded the bodies into the back of the truck, drove them to the house, carried them one after the other inside to the kitchen, stripped them and washed each for burial. They didn't have to talk about it. They brought another table in from the living room and they set the bodies on the two tables faceup. The bodies were completely white except for Robert's, which was red on the face and hands, a farmer's body. They washed each one carefully, working together on each, turning the hands in their hands, washing under the arms and between the legs, lifting Will's small, tough genitals, pressing the folded washcloth against Mrs. Joleen's scuffed, hairless sex. Robert's fingernails were dirty and he had a maroon birthmark the size of an orange in the small of his back. Mrs. Joleen had a spray of fawn-colored freckles across her shoulders, like a redhead's freckles, which Jack had not noticed last night. This made him think that possibly the woman he saw in the bathroom was not Mrs. Joleen, or if it was, the experience was a dream entirely, and not partially, as he already thought. But she was familiar to him otherwise, her breasts and the belly sagged onto the hips were, and the feet like burst hulls of feet curled onto themselves. Will's head was in pieces like an eggshell, but the pieces were still attached to one another by the undersetting membrane. They patched him with tape and strips of cloth they wound around the skull. His eyes wouldn't stay closed and so Jack took tiny pieces of tape and set them in the sockets. Will's body was hairless and bony and had a crunched-up look as if a long time ago something had been subtracted from it and never put back. Jack felt a rush of hunger for his brother-in-law, as if he wanted to engage him in serious conversation, ask forgiveness or something, but this passed like a rebel government giving up power and he was able to look Will in what was left of his face and mildly think of him as a man who had come to no good end and come to the only end possible for him. This did not seem to have anything to do with the body.

Then they stood back and looked at what they had done; after they had clothed the bodies in fresh laundry and crossed their hands on their chests, they looked at them and tears filled Clare's eyes as they sometimes did when she looked at something become suddenly fixed for good, but neither of them said anything. Jack jiggled the bullets he had gouged with his long fingers out of Robert and Mrs. Joleen. Then Clare took a book from her coat pocket and read a page. The book was *Peter Rabbit*, which she had bought at a bookstore in Litchfield before she committed the bank robbery. It was a page about one of the rabbits setting out to market. To Jack the words sounded powerful and were filled with elaborate signals about life and destiny. Good for us, he thought, and thank you, Beatrix Potter, which was the name of the woman who wrote the book.

"Read that last part again," Jack said.

Clare read it again slowly.

"It's beautiful, isn't it," Jack said. The words were like the flowers they didn't have, they were like wee sprigs of violet or foxglove you could set on the bodies so the dead would go down into the earth carrying beauty in their fists, so you could have a place to rest yourself inside so much death, a place of peace at the center of it.

"It's not so terrible," Jack said, thinking the thought, letting the thought of impossibility and disaster fade out for a second as he listened to Clare read the passage again.

She looked up. "Yes, it is. We wouldn't be doing this if it wasn't."

"That's a fine book," he said.

He went into the living room and rummaged among the books he had seen there on a shelf beside the fireplace. He found a copy of Shakespeare's plays, brought it back, and read a random passage, from *Coriolanus*, the spot where the king sees everyone turn against him.

"That's stirring, too," Clare said.

"If we could keep this up, we'd probably be completely reconciled," Jack said.

"To what?"

"You name it."

They got more books and read passages from each, brief paragraphs. The readings were of diminishing impact. They grew tired.

"It's typical of us," Jack said. "Good once—ought to be good many times."

"We'll never be satisfied," Clare said, "not for long."

She took her brother's cold hand in hers and stroked it. In her face Jack saw the old woman she would become. It was like the new moon holding the old moon in its arms. She kissed her brother's fingertips.

His body seemed to rattle and quiver. It should be better than this, he thought, but he knew it wasn't going to be. It was terrible, all right. These poor people. They lay faceup on the tables, Robert and his mother pushed together on one, Will by himself on the other. The bandages around Will's head looked like a silly party hat. Headed into eternity as a fool, Jack thought. Yes. Clearing ground for us in a fool's paradise.

Donnie stared into his eyes. Jack could see himself, tiny, like a baby mashed into the womb of the eyeball, like a fetal space traveler, hurtling through the empty, incarnate miles.

They stopped at a convenience store to use the outside pay phone. Jack dialed the number to the sheriff's office.

"This is Donald Bernardnick," he said to the deputy who came on. "I have lost my mind out here at the Joleen place—you know where that is?—and I have killed everybody."

"What's that?" the deputy said. "Who are you and where are you?"

Jack gave Donnie's name again. "I'm out here at the Robert Joleen place"—he gave the address—"and I have called you now to confess these terrible murders. The Joleens are dead and my friend Frenchy Parteet"—he spelled the name—"is dead, too. I was visiting, there was a big argument—they confronted me with crimes I committed down in Tennessee, where I murdered James Acajou and masterminded the attempted robbery of the First Steamboat Bank of Anacondia—and, God forgive me, I came out blasting. I shot them all."

"They're dead?" the deputy said.

"That's what I'm trying to tell you, you idiot. Excuse me. I shot every one of them. It's too much for me. I had to call. Please come on out here. I can't stay myself, but I wanted to let you know. Not one of them, not even Frenchy, who was a weasel, deserved to die."

"Stay right where you are. We'll get somebody to you in just a minute."

"Thank you, Officer," Jack said and hung up the phone.

The first time he got shot he had been sitting beside a river in Kansas talking with Johnnie Bestfield about the indecipherable nature of women. Lester Wheeler, a tortured and erratic soul, had come up to him and shot him in the chest. Lester was mad about something someone else had said about him—that he couldn't think his way to the end of his sleeves on a clear night—which he concluded erroneously Jack had said. It was the kind of misunderstanding that came up among thieves. Jack had just leaned back to gather himself for what he imagined as an eloquent disquisition on the subtle and delightful tendency of a woman to aggrandize the man she loved when Lester came up. He had waved his pistol up and shot Jack in one oddly dismissive motion. "There, take that, you goddamn bastard," he'd said. Johnnie had pulled his own pistol and shot Lester in the back as he was walking away.

The group had scattered. This was during the time he and Clare had split up, during the time she had taken up with Donnie Bee. The men left Jack on the riverbank. Kansas was wild country to them and it was useless to try to find a doctor. Jack had lain on the bank watching the river go by until he passed out. The sheriff's deputies found him. They'd been called by Johnnie as the only means for saving Jack's life. The deputies didn't know what they had. They hauled Jack to town and handcuffed him to a bed in the hospital.

That night he had wakened to the sound of someone in the room. It was the deputy assigned to guard him. The man was kneeling beside his bed. Jack didn't know what he was doing, and then he did. The man was wildly praying. He clenched his hands at his chest and he implored God to care for him and his loved ones and to bless this poor wounded man here and bless the sheriff and all those in trouble on the roads. He prayed for a long time and his requests included many people specifically and generally. Finally he stopped. He raised his head and looked at Jack. His eyes were furious and lonely and seared by space winds. He seemed to be returning from some shore where he'd been looking out at the area where everything he loved had been torn away. He might have been speaking directly into the ear of God, but the look in his eyes said it was no use. It was a look Jack had seen in prison. Some loser, some brother to a thief, beaten to the concrete who looked up at you with terrible, vandalized eyes. There was nothing you could do about it. There was no Jesus for such desolation.

The three dead people now—as he put down the phone (and how did this happen?)—felt like plugs inserted into his chest. Like permanent stopped-up places he would have to return to and fiddle with from now on. No, he thought: like knobs on a radio—*yes*—he could spend the rest of his life spinning, trying to tune in some lost station he longed to listen to. The twenty-four-hour news station of paradise. How did this happen?

He turned from the phone to meet Donnie Bee himself standing in the parking lot with a pistol in his fist, smiling at him.

This seemed right in line with everything else.

"Donnie," he said, thinking that he could walk out of this situation into someone's house and tell them everything, "it's disturbing how suddenly I look at the world differently, without being able to do one single thing in a different way. Is it ever like that for you?"

"How you doing, Jack?" Donnie said.

"I'm pitched up a little high right now—how about you?"

"I'm rageful and just about delirious with frustration."

"Let's talk about it, DB."

Across the road a field of moth-eaten soybean bushes shined. The golden wings of the sun, he thought.

"Fuck," Donnie said, and then someone Jack didn't see cracked him across the back of the skull and he went out.

8

And that whole ten years of the suicides, he said, you could add it up, we lived on pins. We kept an eye on him. I did. I looked for giveaways. Mother left. She gave her heart to righteousness, to resisting the authority of an oppressive government, and she slipped away, like a freed slave slipping away downriver. I went with her. But I would come back to Father. For a long time there was nothing at all we could do. We couldn't talk, we couldn't take trips together, we could hardly eat a meal. It was like a joke. Maybe he would drive the car off the road, maybe he would stab himself with a fork. He wore dark glasses all the time, even in the house. When he got cancer he used face powder to cover the spots. I would come to his office and visit with him, this snowbound man, sit with him in the long yellow sunlight up in his office that overlooked the docks, and we would watch the ore boats leave the harbor. They moved so slowly, like thoughts moving in a mind resisting everything, and we would lean back in our chairs like two old conspirators, never saying a word, as the shadows grew longer. Sometimes we would be sitting there still at dark. Eventually I would get up and turn on the light. He would be there, in his shades, as quiet as a man patiently waiting for a bus. The last afternoon nothing changed. He came to the wedding, but he didn't participate, left before the reception. We drove by on our way out of town and I went up by myself to see him. He was peeling an apple, sitting in his orange leather chair by the window. I sat with him awhile.

There was no breakthrough. After a few minutes I got up and we shook hands and I left. That night Mother called and told me he had shot himself.

When you're young you think you can fix things. You think there's a clue you're missing. If you can find it you can hunt your way back to the place things went wrong and fix them. But there's no clue. Nothing is missing.

"Yeah—my old man," Donnie said, "who I'm not supposed even to remember, was the stopper in the bottle of my life. Do you know what I mean? I was like a lightning bug trapped in a clear glass bottle, and my daddy was the stopper. They say I was found wandering on a country road in Lafayette Parish, out near the New Bethel Baptist Church, a boy ten or twelve years old who was so bamboozled and out of his head he didn't know his name or where he came from or who his folks were. It was a ruse. I had all that information, but I didn't want to tell a soul. I had just killed my old man. I had pulled the stopper out of the bottle I can assure you.

"Do you know how it is when you can't get your breath? He wouldn't let me have a life of any kind. He made me his slave. He made me wash the dishes and tidy the house—when we had a house—and he made me plant the garden and change the dirty sheets on his bed and clean up after him and his whores. He stayed up all night playing cards. He wouldn't let me go out of the house on those nights. I'd have to wait on him and his foul cronies like a fucking ten-year-old butler. Open beers and pour drinks and wipe the snot off their noses. I'm not going to tell you what happened to me some nights when one of those drunken louts tried to take advantage of me. It's my daddy I want you to know about. He wasn't the first man to come up behind me in the dark, but he was the last. One night he told me to go out and pull him some radishes to eat with his beer and I did that. I was standing out in the garden smelling all those fancy spring smells, all that fucking dirt and the flowers, the plum flowers and the pear flowers and all that, when my daddy came up behind me and put his hand over my face. I couldn't breathe. He threw me down in the dirt and he tried to come up my ass like they do in prison, but he didn't realize I was still holding the knife I'd been digging out radishes with. I twisted under him and came up with the knife and caught him right under the breastbone. I felt the knife go into his heart. I felt the heart give and then burst like a plum. His blood spewed all over me. It drenched me like he was nothing but a bag of blood. It got in my hair and in my eyes and even in my mouth. It made me sick to my stomach.

"He rolled over on his back and he reached a hand up to me, like he was drowning. I thought even then he had a word of love for me, some kindness, but he only wanted to pull me down with him. He grabbed me by the neck and he began to squeeze. I stabbed him again. And then I stabbed him some more, hard, banging the knife against his side. It left my hand bruised. I was crying, all that. And my daddy, he was grinning at me. This big wide grin like it was all a joke. He held that grin until he died. Until he sank under me.

"I rolled his body down the bank to the river and I dragged him and rolled him into the water. I was only ten years old, ten or twelve, I don't know. I was strong, but I thought I would die getting his body into the river. There was a tugboat passing and it swept its light over the bank, but it didn't catch me because we were under the beam. The gold light shot across the trees and where it caught behind me I saw the eyes of a possum up in a big sweet gum. Red eyes like the devil. I knew then what my place was. Where I was going. I pushed my daddy out into the stream and let him sink. Then I got out of there. I was seeing visions, sparks and curlicues, terrible riders that haunted me for a long time. Later, authorities found me wandering on the road talking to myself. They said I didn't remember anything. But they were wrong. I remember everything.

"Did this set me free, Jack—what do you think? Am I a free man? Or am I a man captured by his past? They say you can't change the past, Jack. But memory is not the past. Memory changes all the time. Look around. Nobody wants to remember, not really. Oh, that couple that lost their baby, they don't want to remember. And that man who everybody said was a genius, who is now clerking at Motel Six—he doesn't want to remember. But me, Jack—I want to remember. I want to remember what it felt like to push that knife into my daddy's breast. To feel his puny heart give. He had a heart like a sparrow, Jack. A little, hot, pierced heart.

"Look at the Rube there. He thought he wanted to remember, but he didn't really. He wanted to escape consequences. Save his soul, et cetera. Now he just sits there moaning like a sick dog. A writer. He put this story into the paper, but what good did it do him? He corrupted our stories, he told lies and made them sound like the truth. He didn't watch what he was doing. Now he's at the end. I found him on Coodge's boat. He was typing into a little computer. He was writing a story about us. He had all the details. He was there when you went crazy and he was there when I smothered poor Jimmy. He put this down in his computer. I made him show me how to work it. I made him unroll it for me so I could read it. I got a copy made. He thinks you and me have a lack of attachment—is that how he put it? Wait, I have the thing here. Yes. Here it is. Hand it to me, Boudreau. Look, right here . . ."

Their silence is impenetrable. It is a country without custom or policy. They themselves are the ones most in awe of the power they have unleashed. Destruction, dehabilitation, erasure are all they want to think about. They sit for hours in a room without speaking, attached to nothing but their crimes . . .

"Yeah, Rube. I'm so attached to my crimes I can't go home to New Orleans. I can't enter my own house. I am a fugitive in my own city. In my own state and in my own country. Can you believe it? Look at what I have built. I own a catering company. I own a trucking line and a storage facility for vehicle parts and waste products. I underwrite a float at Mardi Gras. I am known, throughout the Quarter, throughout the Garden fucking District, and the rest of the city too, as a soft touch. This man has snaked into my life, he has weaseled in here and misrepresented me. I beat him to pieces, Jack. I, as they say, abused the little fuck. Look at him, writhing around in that chair. He thinks the ropes won't hold him, but they will. The ropes always hold, Jack. He thinks somehow this will all blow over. Isn't that remarkable? He's been pounded to sausage and still he's hoping there's some way out of this.

"Hey, Rube, hey, fathead, big mouth: how about you now? You want to ride around with hoodlums now? What was that you said? Yeah, here: *They are like monks in the desert, driven to the extreme edges of the world by their unendurable, irresistible knowledge of the equivalence of their and the world's disorder.*

"Disorder? What the fuck disorder? I have been putting the world in order since I was a little boy. You don't know the half of it, Rube. Let me tell you, it is not disorder, it is fucking ruin. We are in pieces, Rube. Nothing works. That's why we want simple lives, you shithead. Gold, murder, oblivion—these are simple, Rube. They work. Erase the rest. You're right, erase the goddamn rest.

"Ah, Jack. Here, *fuck*—Boudreau, hit Jack again. Yeah, in the face. How you feel, Jack? Did that hurt? Your nose is broken and I think the bone bridge under your eyes is broken, too. Boudreau is very good at hitting. That towel he wraps around his knuckles works well, don't you think? Hit him again, Boudreau. Crack him.

"The truth is I despise you, Jack. You superior bastard. You're hurting, but I don't want you dead on me yet, Jack. You've got a ways to go yet. It took me too much work to capture you. You were a clever fuck, Jack. You could always get out from under. Don't worry, Clare, he isn't going to die just yet. I'm going to cut off his head. That's right, Jack. Actually, I'm going to totally dismember you. What trouble you have caused me. Chasing all over the Mississippi River region after you. Like I'm some kind of Tennessee Valley Authority operative chasing a flood. That fucking Will. He promised there was money at the end of this rainbow. That's why I let him stay at the club in New Orleans, Jack. I knew Clare would bring you down there and Will said if we got you we could get this money. I knew old Will wasn't long for this world. You could see it in that ferrety face. You know how a man's neck gets thin when the death mark is on him. Some are like that, eh, Jack? *Will* would cut you. I had him drive with old dead Mikey out to the country, carrying Mooger to his grave, and he didn't mind at all being the one who sliced Mooger up. Mikey said Will cut slivers off a magnolia tree and shoved them into Mooger's eyes. He shoved them into his face, too. That was strange. These stickers shoved into his face. Will had some odd plan. But he was telling the truth about the money. You know how I know? I talked to the old man. He said he wanted you dead. That's what he said. He would pay for it, he said. He put a big down payment in my bank account. He was a terrible old fellow. But you know what? I think it didn't have to do with you at all. *I* have to do with you, but all this didn't, Jack. That old man didn't really care about you. He didn't even care about getting his daughter back next to him. He *certainly* didn't care about Will. He's dying. He's upstairs right now dying. *That's* what it's about. He just fucking wants to take somebody with him. He's so scared and lonely and enraged about dying he wants to lay waste around him. He wants fucking company. And this is the way he lived his life."

They remember nothing. Their own lives are mysteries to them, obscure half-remembered fantasies and dreams. They recall incidents, but without relation to other incidents. There is no plan, no direction beyond the conniptions of impulse. They are without beliefs of any kind, they have been washed clean, brought forth by indifferent parents into a world in which there is nothing they can understand. They know no one, no one knows them. They are the solitary men who, in the restaurant or the bus station, or in the back rooms of your life, turn their faces to stare at you with looks of contempt in their eyes. They live without reason, aware in the heart of themselves of their wretchedness. They know they are unredeemable. They know there is no government, no law, no way of life can shape or change them.

"How are you, Jack? Slipping away? That's your own death you see before you. I originally had slightly other plans, but this will do. Do you know the story of King Louis XI and the Duke of Burgundy? You don't? Do you know, Clare? Of course you don't. Don't look at me like that. I mean you have always been too busy using up energy to study history. Loving animals, all that. Shoot, I don't mean to offend you, darling. But the king. The duke rebelled against the king, it was in the eleven hundreds. I used to know the exact date. The king crushed the rebellion like a tomato in his hand, captured the duke and transported him back to the palace. He had a cage built in the yard, an iron box with bars, put the duke in it and raised the whole thing up onto a pole set just outside his bedroom window. I wonder if the king made this up as he went along or if he had it worked out in his mind beforehand. It was diabolical. Every morning the king would get up and look out at the duke in his cage. He wouldn't say a word to him. What was there to say? Isn't that elegant? What he'd do—he'd nod, once, very solemnly, and then he'd close the curtains. He did this every morning—once a day—for twelve years, until the duke died. He never let him out, not one day, and he never spoke to the duke. *He was his own brother.*

"More water, Boudreau. I think of that duke out there. This noble man, pampered maybe, but feisty enough to go to war against his brother. Caught in a cage. What was the first night like? Did it snow? Did it rain? Was it cold? Did he hunker there shivering, still anticipating some fresh maneuver in the drama? That must have been the horror of it for him. Waking finally to the knowledge that everything that would happen had already happened. That's what drove your papa, Clare, to send Will and me after you. *Everything had already happened.* There just wasn't any more. Not worth doing anyway. The duke had to sit in that drafty cage twelve years and listen to his heart beat. I wonder if it made a saint of him or a madman. Every day with a lock on it."

There is no life without forgiveness. And for these men there is no for-

giveness. This is central. Life is expressed through action and contemplation. What is is joined to what was and what will be by our ability to forgive and let go. We remember, but we don't dwell in remembrance. These men are without this faculty. They have forgotten nothing. Thus, they have been converted from a means and example of energy exercised to pure engines of despair.

"Oh God. You remember Joliet, Jack? I swore I'd never go back to jail and I haven't. I don't get you, my friend. I would have chosen some other line of work after Joliet. You must have known they would catch you and lock you up again. That's where I won't forgive you. I won't forgive him, Clare, for doing this to you. I know you got a mind of your own and all that, but shit, you're married to Jack, and he wouldn't stop with the fucking banks. Look at me. I have spent maybe a total of one day and a half in this house, and I have got old man Manigault's signature on a notarized document giving me title to all his property. I get cash outright. The will holds no surprises for Donnie Bee. There is nothing left to distribute. Who knows how I got this to work out so neatly? The nurse knows, but I am going to shoot her. Boudreau and Parteet know, but they are in my employ and will profit by keeping their mouths shut. Who else is there? Oh yeah, little Crawford, my faithful driver. He stays out front there with the car and knows nothing. Jack, you're a dead man. That leaves only Clare. Only Clare.

"Let me pause here and catch my breath. I raise my hand to you, Clare, in tenderness. I am filled with love. All this you see before you will pass away. You are like me. Nothing here in this world has staying power. You forget, like me. Each day we get up and the world we look out on is brand-new. The duke has died and we look out on glorious morning. Bethink yourself—is that the word?—bethink yourself, girl. I will bring you to my palace. The whole of Lake Ponchartrain is spread out below my windows. I have a yellow gazebo with red geraniums growing around it in white china pots. You will love the speed boat. Don't hold this against me. Please don't. It was necessary. You can see that. I am the one who understands you. And I am the one who needs you. For me and you life is just a spree. See. I know. Just a spree.

"Ah, what am I saying, right? Words of a clown. Would you dare love me again? What a fool I am. Jesus, Clare, I would cook for you, clean for you—turn your face away, Boudreau—I would get down on my knees and worship you. But this is not important to you, is it? You see me for the bad weasel I am. A lowlife—yes? Ah, Clare, how do you change a woman's mind? What is it happens in your brain that sets you against me? Don't you know how it is with the lions? You're an animal tamer, you should know. You know how when the new big lion runs the old lion off the lionesses get over their grief and come along. It's nature, Clare. You know this is what will happen. Rube missed it. It's not about forgiveness, Clare. That doesn't matter. It's about got to get it. It's about I can't go one inch further unless I get it. Jesus.

She is afraid of the river. She is afraid of solitude. She is afraid of the daily run of human life. There is however an extraordinary—commonness about her. An ordinariness.

"Oh, man, this Rubens. If you'd quit all that moaning, buddy, you'd get to enjoy some of the work you've done. Boudreau! Stick a rag in that man's mouth. Go get one. You got one? Good, a bandanna. Stick it in that fuck's mouth. I can't stand any more of his moaning. Look here, Writer Boy. You got it down on paper. I thank you for it. You said, what, you said she was like a mysterious thought that appeared inside your head, like some *unnatural natural thought* you had never conceived of before. I know what you are talking about. Exactly. What is it? Yes, right here you say *She would go out and lie down in the garden at night, lie under a shower of white stars. She told me she talked to her imaginary children then, as she lay out among the bean plants . . .*

"Imaginary fucking children. Yes, yes. I remember—what do I remember? I remember how you'd go out on the dock in the early morning. Clare. How you'd stand there leaning over the rail looking at the mist on the bayou. You'd lift one foot behind you. The bottom of your foot was golden, like while I was sleeping you'd been walking around in bullion. How mysterious you were to me. I couldn't get enough of watching you. I'd sit up in the bed in the middle of the night, as excited as a boy who'd just been told it was Christmas. I'd look at you. I'd run my finger down your body, tracing the shape of you. I wanted to force you so deep into my mind I'd never forget. You think I didn't know you were leaving? I did.

"Imaginary children. You fooled him, too, Clare. You made us all think what you wanted us to think . . .

Yet she too is without hope. There is no rehabilitation for any of these people. She is beautiful, but her beauty will not save her. She is smart, but her brains will not save her. In the end she is only another selfish sufferer.

She moans in her sleep, I have heard her. Like a frightened animal she runs through the woods, hunted by her crimes.

"He breaks off there. Can you believe this, Jack? In one place she is his goddess, in another she is his devil. Jack. Is this you, Clare? I want to break into sobs. Some nights I drive around town alone in my Jag. I look into shop windows, I look into apartment windows, I wonder what is going on in these worlds I can't enter. Over there you see a man arguing with his wife. Over there you see a boy correcting a dog, an old woman sucking the ball of her thumb. What is going on? I can't make it out. They are a mystery to me, all of them. The world is a strange, elusive enterprise, Jack. Some of us have to use a few more nails to get it to stay in place. I need Clare. We are cut from the same bunch. What do you say? Let's go upstairs and say good-bye to the old man. Get this thing over with. Go on to the next phase of glory. What do you think?"

Jack said nothing.

When they jerked him up he thought he was inside a new religion, one constructed from wobbly light and drapery, but it was only the disordered room, only the ruffians, the Cajuns with guns, pulling him to his feet, dragging him up the stairs to the father's bedroom, where Donnie, wild again, slapped the old man dying on the bed, cuffed him and rolled his slack body like the corpse he would soon be.

"I don't know what the fuck I am looking for," Donnie said, "but I know I am looking for something. What is it, Jack? My timing is off, I can see that, but you can help me."

Clare flew at Donnie, or flew past him. As he shrank from a blow, she sprawled on top of her father. Her arms went out and pinned the old man to the bed. There was a nurse somewhere, cringing. There were big dark paintings on the walls, of gruesome biblical scenes and of scenes from the hunt, one over the bed in which a bear was being torn apart by dogs. Jack's mind did not seem to belong to him anymore, but belonged instead to sorrow and to panic and to an idea like a monstrous obsession that if he could find the tunnel out of here, the Underground Railroad train that came up somewhere nearby in a green field, he would be all right. But there was no tunnel. There was no train. Gradually he knew this. Propped upright, he knew this. He screamed. Donnie swung around and hit him in the face.

Jack could see his fist bounce *(lying on his back under the oak, he watched the fist come at him: he could see the short, snappy punches and then he couldn't. When he was a boy his father built big radio sets that he trained at the stars. He wanted to pick up messages from space. Maybe there was something out there that could help him.* A rock struck him. *There were still a few leaves in the oak, maroon leaves smudged with black, white oak the last tree to turn in fall, no oaks, though, in northern Minnesota, only birches and tamarack and the firs, though in his mother's backyard in Brandis there was a peach tree she bundled in burlap each winter—the peach never set fruit—and his sister, another tree without issue, had never gotten over any of it, Rita talked yet of the rainbow opposite the moon, he would be eating dinner with her in some fancy restaurant in Minneapolis and she would go off into her depressed reverie, staring, coming out of it to clumsily proposition the waiter . . . and he was the same*—honoring this under the oak tree—*because, at the oddest times, in the middle of a job, or riding in the car with the cops trailing, he, too, would crank up the past, and it would frighten him, the whole business about his father and the boy at the edge of the woods*—don't you realize I knew I would be all right—*and his father swimming straight down into Lake Superior—he remembered the smell of grapes on his father's breath, and how he hated the blotchy skin on the back of his father's neck—his father was a blond with papery blond skin that smoking ruined—remembered Father sitting on the porch in summer cutting pictures of castles and estate grounds out of magazines, pasting them in a book, a real-estate agent for the dispossessed, hanging these pictures, or Xeroxed reproductions of them, on his office walls so the poor ex-farmers and salesgirls hoping against hope that they could come up with the loot for one of the dilapidated VA homes Father handled could see them and get some clear idea of what they, like him, would go their whole lives without—these* children, *hoping, every one of them, for a treasure to reveal itself, for some new version to appear, a version in which things worked out, and they were loved—which was what he would discuss with Father if he had a chance now, say, Father, would you like a cup of tea, say, Father, I love you despite everything*—Please understand this—*instead of which his attention was drawn to the sky, which stood in pieces among the branches, like different versions of sky, or several skies cut into pieces and hung in the oak tree, under which he could see the hand working him and he could hear Donnie grunting as he bent over him; and then, it was so odd, he wanted to stroke Donnie's hair, wanted to smooth the cowlick of gray hair standing straight up, to touch the small hyacinthine froth of curls at his neck . . .)*, but he didn't feel the blows.

"I'm not going anywhere," he said.

Then Clare rose behind him, dragging up the Colt pistol her father kept under his pillow in case of bandit attack. She thrust the pistol awkwardly—like an amateur, Jack thought—poking it at Donnie's chest, and fired. The shot kicked Donnie off his feet. The Cajuns came up with their guns, but they were no match for Clare. She put bullets into them like stitches. They went down—one, Boudreau, crying out a name Jack couldn't catch, the other gasping in surprise. Boudreau twitched, his leg quivering as if he'd run too far; he pushed himself up and then fell back dead. The other lay on his back looking up from the brassy carpet with eyes the life scurried out of like terrified mice.

Donnie pulled himself to his knees. He reached into his coat, but Clare brushed his hand away. She put the pistol against his forehead just above the brows. Donnie's eyes jerked up, madly, foolishly, as if he thought he could snatch the barrel with them. She pulled the trigger and for an instant Donnie's eyes went completely white. He jerked to the side, lunging as if there was something final and necessary over there he was going for. He sprawled onto his side, and lay still—everything on earth rushing on without him—as blood gathered, seeping, beginning to fill in the edges around his body.

"There you go," Clare said.

As if called—now, as his daughter turned to him, as she wheeled with a look of disgust on her face—the old man groaned and made blind scratching motions at his chest. He didn't see anyone, he didn't know what was going on, didn't care—Jack could tell this, even nearly unconscious, not caring much now himself—Manigault couldn't take the world anymore, had no place in it, and then Clare could see this, too—Jack could tell—realized this as she whirled on her father, raising her fist to strike, and then stopped, with the fist raised, understanding—Jack could tell—there was nothing to destroy anymore. Jack could see this knowledge enter her and shake her, deftly wring her. She shuddered, she seemed about to fall, but didn't, she glanced at the nurse, a question the nurse answered with her eyes; and then—Jack could tell—they all, even the nurse, explicit in her terror, sensed the room clearing, as if they were in an auditorium where some amateur theatrical was taking place, a tragicomedy maybe—they sensed this—in which the production had gone wrong, the actors become disabled, the props broken, the curtain snagged on wires, tearing, pulling down lights—and the play itself, like a country they'd given their hearts to, collapsed, and they, the audience, deceived, befouled, left with the shattered pieces of an art, must, as they could only—nothing else left—begin the journey home. Her hand dropped. She ordered the nurse to help her; they lifted Jack between them, grasping him by the shoulders and under his knees, and carried him down the long dark stairs.

"You're lighter than you used to be," she said.

"You are, too," he said.

Again, for a moment, her face was his face. They were eating breakfast in a small café, some county seat. It was one of those brief, inexact towns—the West is full of them—so small they hardly get started before they begin to break up. A few dozen houses with their unswept approachable streets, church like a white schooner, a courthouse square open on two sides to wheat fields. Someone's painted the trunks of the maple trees white. There's a school and an auction barn and a bank. Houses in such a town, stores that went out of business, stranded hearts, sometimes stand abandoned for years. There's a listlessness in certain faces, as if they are sanctified. You can smell the wheat fields in your sleep.

They set him against the doorpost and the nurse held him with her strong right arm like the bar of a gate set across his chest and then Clare went into the living room, where Rubens was stalled in a pool of blood, and Jack watched her tip the writer's chin back and look into the sooty holes his eyes had been gouged from, and he heard her speak to the man, whisper to him as she had whispered when she crawled under the bunk of Coodge's boat—What do you want now?—and he could see her slender thumb trace the shape of Rubens's mouth as the writer, tongueless, tried to respond, and he saw her hesitate, saw the cleverness and the momentum empty from her face as she looked down at this man who swung off the edge of life like some monkey hanging from a terminal branch, and Jack could see that she did not want to go on with what was coming—he knew this was so—and then it was as if he entered her body, as if he put her on like a coat and bent down with her to kiss Rubens on the lips. He thought he was looking at her, but he must not have been because he did not see her shoot him. He only heard the gun go off.

Then she came out and she and the nurse got her father's wheelchair from the corner of the hall, snapped it open and put Jack into it. She looked down at him blankly. Then they jimmied him through the front door, tipping him, Clare's arm around his shoulders to keep him from falling. They had him out onto the porch before either Clare or the nurse—or Jack—noticed (remembered) Crawford, the boy driver, a scornful and disputatious youth, who stood abruptly up from behind the car, raised his pistol, and shot Jack in the chest. The shot knocked him out of the chair.

Clare's gun was in her pocket. She couldn't get it out quickly. The boy fired again. The shot caught her in the neck. She jerked sideways, grabbing at her weapon, got purchase, came up with it, and fired two shots into the boy's face. He went down on the other side of the car. The nurse screamed steadily. She ran screaming back into the house.

Sitting across from her in the café, bright sun streaming, he thought, If I blink, she will blink. Sometimes she tipped her head, sometimes she scratched meditatively under her chin just like he did. People would look at them funny, sometimes. It was October, month of harvest, month when the stray, wild wheat turned yellow in the road ditches, and combines sailed the fields like frigates. The town had set a permanent flame burning at the corner of the square to memorialize the generalized war dead. They'd stopped to look at it. She'd dipped her hand in the flame, passed her fingers through the light blue snap of it. "To remind us where all those little dead soldiers went to," she said, licking her fingers.

He liked to look at her big, lean hands, at her long fingers, and at the scars across the knuckles where she'd skidded from a gunfight onto her fists. He watched her pour milk into her coffee from a pitcher with a spout shaped like a blue cow's head. The cow's mouth was a narrow slot.

"To be realistic," he said, "the milk ought to come out of the bottom."

She shook the final drops from the pitcher. The milk made pale circles in her coffee.

"That might be too much realism."

"For whom?"

• • •

There was nothing left after that but the two of them lying faceup on the porch. They lay in their blood.

"I hate this," Clare said after a while. "Fuck."

She couldn't get up. Jack crawled to her.

She moaned. "Don't let me stop," she cried.

There was the sound of sirens in the distance. He touched her face. For years no one had touched her body but him, no one had touched his body but her. It was amazing how when you loved someone you just kept going with it. You were tied to the saddle, you didn't even have to stay awake. It was like a journey—a story—he'd read, two friends traveling a road that went around the world. The path met itself and the journey never ended. Yeah, he thought, and sometimes you had to call it love when you just couldn't get your hands on the one you wanted to kill. Luck, or love, life gone wild in a corner, taking all your attention, some boy doing a trick with a smile, the worst happening and everything going on anyway.

He didn't have to figure it out.

Jack caressed her cheek with the tip of his finger. He lightly touched her here and there.

Then he thought he was going crazy, he thought this was some other universe's holding cell, he thought he was in a terrible drunk tank world where lunatics played loud radios and the noise, which kept up like rat screams all night long—as men with horribly charged expressions beat their fists bloody against concrete—was concentrated into one aperture through which every human being on earth was forced to draw his conclusions about life—thought this was his destiny unfolding on the porch there, where the furniture was covered with pale green painters' cloths and curls and blisters of gray paint stippled the house walls; and then he realized, shuddering, that he was not even there anymore, he was somewhere far down inside his own body, so far down he couldn't be sure what was taking place topside, couldn't be sure she had even been shot, or if either of them had; he tried, as a man might try to rise from deep below the surface of a lake, to reach her; couldn't; and then, groaning, if that was him, he did finally, he touched her face and knew he was touching her face. She looked up at him and he could tell she didn't know him—and then she did.

“There are five thousand minute details,” she said. “I am dying.”

“Yes.”

“Don’t tell me. There was a field of flowers, of Queen Anne’s lace—no, of some white stagecoach flower, some prairie flower—we walked out there. Do you remember?”

“Yes—”

“No, you don’t—you never remember—but there was a white boat in the harbor, with a blue stripe at the waterline—where was it, Jack, that house on the ridge we hid in, and coming up the hill the windows were gold in the sunlight so you said gold went all the way through to the other side—”

“I don’t know, Clare—”

“No, you don’t know—”

“Yes—”

“You were angry at me, that time we camped—in the snow—because I forgot socks—”

“Yes,” he said.

“Some people save all their money, they save everything, hold it back.” She caught his eyes. “Why don’t you tell me to stop talking so much?”

“Do you want me to?”

“No. Oh, Jack, I am sinking down.”

He drifted away, rode loosely atop a ball of pain that seemed to dissolve in the ocean around him, then in his own mouth—he tasted a sweetness.

She grabbed at him, caught a piece of his coat, pulled at it. Her eyes jumped. “I see it,” she said. “Oh, shit.”

She closed her eyes. As he held her—he wasn’t even touching her, he realized—she swallowed hard twice, and then there was a brief period in which she breathed lightly and raggedly, more and more faintly.

Then he leaned down and tried to blow his breath into her mouth, but he was short-winded himself; he gasped, coughed. Their teeth clicked, he jerked, a front tooth caught her lip, opened a tiny cut, but she didn’t respond.

He looked into her face. While he was—*what*—while he was talking, to some prison guard, to some panicked bank teller, to some wrenched representative of crime—to some father, some brother, some god—she had vanished . . . and left this pale excrescence, a figure he'd never seen before.

He watched the blood gradually stop flowing.

She said, "Did you read the story in the paper about the girl who shot her parents and then went back and shot all the chickens in the chicken yard?"

He laughed. "No."

"She said she couldn't stand having to feed the chickens anymore, or collecting the eggs. She said it was humiliating to be a slave to such dumb creatures."

"So she shot her parents?"

"They were the ones who made her feed them."

"It's a little extreme."

"I keep picturing her standing out in the chicken yard shooting all those birds. Forty-eight chickens, so the paper said. I wonder who counted them. She used a shotgun, double-barreled, the same gun she shot her parents with. She had to reload two dozen times."

"Or more, if she wasn't that good a shot."

"Well, they were penned up. But still, you're right. Forty-eight chickens. What was she thinking about when she shot them?"

"Probably about the bead she had to draw on the next one."

"I'll bet she wished there were a thousand of them. I'll bet she wished the shooting would never end."

Then he lay on his back, like a man resting up for something, listening to the sirens coming closer. The sound was like birds flocking into the trees, singly at first, then in larger numbers, birds lighting in the threadbare trees. He tried to hold himself steady, get his mind straight. He didn't want to go into what was wrong or right about the situation. It wasn't that kind of experience, that wasn't the point. He wished he had a little more time. Then, for a while, maybe he could think about the afternoon the two of them sat by a river in eastern Kansas, after one of those jobs when nobody got killed and there was ample loot, and the partners, if there were partners, and the cops, if there were cops, had passed on to other considerations. They'd sat by the river in sunlight not doing anything, almost satisfied. In the shallows near the bank there were schools of minnows. He'd scooped some in his cap and brought them to her. She'd held her cupped hands up and he'd poured the glittery fish into them. For a moment they'd looked down into her hands as if they were peering into a wishing well. Fleet, gasping, quick and dying, life flashed. There was time enough.

They crossed the street to the courthouse square. Some birds, grimy-looking starlings, had left the trees and were walking around on the lawn. The store fronts made an L around the square. On the open sides, to the east and north, the sun shone on the fields of Nebraska wheat. The wheat had been harvested in places: long raw swathes glittered where the combines had rolled through. Beyond the fields low hills rose in shades of brown and tan. There were trees in the low places, white distant silos, maybe a river. Out where the hills began there was a long curl of smoke from a brush fire. That was the way they would go after they took the bank, toward the fire.